RECKLESS RIDE

The wind sang in her ears and hair as she leaned over the neck of the horse, demanding even more speed from him. He gave it to her with glorious abandon, as if he were desperate for freedom himself. Marissa's heart sang with the speed, with the feel of the horse beneath her, and with the confidence that her riding skill would save her once and for all from the brute who had carried her off.

And then she heard hoofbeats pounding behind her.

She glanced back and stared through the loose tendrils of hair that blew across her face. She couldn't believe it. The ultimate warrior was practically breathing down her neck. He looked like something out of a Viking movie, with his whitish mane of hair, his huge shoulders, and his strange blue trousers.

Marissa faced forward again, her heart pounding in fear. He could catch her. The damned man was riding like a maniac to overtake her. She would have to take chances to outride him—chances she wouldn't normally try with an unfamiliar mount. But she would rather court danger than allow Alek to capture her again.

THE NIGHT ORCHID

Patricia Simpson

HarperPaperbacks
A Division of HarperCollinsPublishers

This is a work of fiction. The characters, incidents, and dialogues are products of the author's imagination and are not to be construed as real. Any resemblance to actual events or persons, living or dead, is entirely coincidental.

HarperPaperbacks   *A Division of* HarperCollins*Publishers*
10 East 53rd Street, New York, N.Y. 10022

Cover illustration by John Ennis

First printing: July 1994

Printed in the United States of America

HarperPaperbacks, HarperMonogram, and colophon are trademarks of HarperCollins*Publishers*

❖ 10 9 8 7 6 5 4 3 2 1

*Dedicated with love to
mon homme d'air—
the stuff of which
heroes are made*

I am a free man and the son of a free people!

—Celtic saying

THE NIGHT ORCHID

Prologue

Northern Italy, 285 B.C.

"Alek, don't forget to ask about a love potion!" Alek's friend, Rowan, slapped him good-naturedly on the back. "See you at sunrise—if you're still alive!"

"I'll be alive," Alek replied, shifting his weight. "You can count on that."

"I wish it were me they'd asked." Rowan glanced at the sacred grove of oaks which stood sentinel on a hill in the dusk of spring. "It's a great honor, being asked to share in a ceremony."

"The question is, what kind of ceremony is it? You never know what magic the Druids will practice."

"Maybe it's the sex magic—if you're lucky."

Alek was grateful for the waning light that hid his blush. Though twenty years old and a veteran of countless battles, he was still a virgin—just another facet of his life that he took pains to conceal.

"You're not afraid of the Druids, are you, Alek?"

"What—me?" Alek snorted in contempt.

"They'd never harm the finest warrior in Gaul."

"Some claim my father is the finest warrior in Gaul."

"No, he isn't," Rowan retorted. "He's just the meanest. The Druids want the finest man they can get. And that's you, my friend."

"You could be wrong, Rowan." Alek crossed his arms over his chest. "This ceremony could be a plot of my father's, a way to get rid of me."

"Even your father wouldn't want you dead now, Alek, not with that Roman dog Caius breathing down our necks. We need every able-bodied warrior and he knows it."

Alek considered the words of his friend as he directed his gaze up the grassy slope to the oaks. He had visited the sacred grove on only a few occasions, and each time the visit had made the hair on the back of his neck stand up, as if a mysterious invisible presence resided there. Usually he didn't believe in anything he couldn't see or fight, but the grove and the Druids shook his convictions, which is why he steered clear of the strange priests of his people and the centers of their power. Unlike most of his fellow warriors, he avoided the grove, especially during Beltane, when men took women in celebration of life and fertility and simply the joy of being human. Marriages and pregnancies resulted from Beltane, neither of which was a luxury Alek could afford to indulge in, though many a maid had dropped hints that it was he they desired to join with during the festival.

Rowan pulled his tartan cloak around his shoulders in an effort to ward off the evening chill. "Well, are you going to stand here all night, Alek?"

"No. I'm going."

Rowan held up his hand. "I salute you as a free man."

Alek returned the salute and noticed that Rowan's face was suddenly much graver than during the last few moments of lighthearted jesting. "And I you, my brother." They clasped forearms and for an instant looked into each other's eyes, joined by a camaraderie built over years of serving as partners in battle. He and Rowan had grown up together, had become men together, and now Rowan served as his rider when they went up against the Romans.

Alek released his grip and stepped away. "It is time."

Rowan nodded silently and left Alek on the trail leading to the sacred grove and his duty as a Senone warrior.

Setting his jaw, Alek strode up the trail, oblivious to the cold breeze that wafted through the forest. Years spent as a warrior had made him impervious to physical discomfort. He could sleep in the snow with nothing but a wolf pelt to shield him from the elements. He could withstand a bone-shattering blow without so much as a blink. He could cut a man in half and never think twice. He was a warrior through and through, an instrument of destruction, a shining example of a Gallic man. Whatever the Druids required of him, he'd accept with calmness and courage, his usual way of facing anything that was thrown in his path. Years of living with an abusive father had tempered him well, hammering strength and endurance into the child's body that had grown into a man capable of meeting the toughest challenge. Yet his childhood had also annealed his heart with a hardness more unyielding than stone and a determination that never wavered.

Alek gained the top of the hill and walked on until he saw the oak grove rise up in front of him. For a moment he stood on the edge of the clearing, weighing the heaviness of the night as the pungent smell of mud and new grass assailed his senses. There was a reason why the

Druids measured time by the moon instead of the sun. The night had a soul full of mystery which forced a man to look inward, a much more potent span of time than the daylight hours. In the night, a man was often alone with his thoughts, a time some men dreaded, a time others cherished. Alek frowned, knowing how the hours of twilight could eat away at the very heart of him.

He strode forward, wondering why no priests were in evidence other than a single female figure who stood near the altar. As with the other times, the hair on the back of his neck raised. He resisted the impulse to shudder.

"Alek," the female Druid called out. "Welcome. Enter."

He walked across the clearing, wishing he had brought his battle axe, for he trusted no one, not even the priests. He considered the melodious voice and tried to figure out what woman stood concealed in the white hooded robe of the Druids, but couldn't identify the speaker from her brief commands.

"I have come. What do you require of me?" he demanded, trying to peer into the shadows of the cloak.

"I require your honest heart, Alek," she answered. "To defeat the Romans, we must perform a most sacred ceremony. We must fuse the spirit of man and woman and send that energy to the Roman encampment. In that way, we can defeat the enemy who tries to drive us from our homeland."

Alek clenched his jaw. Was she proposing the sex magic, as Rowan had mentioned? He would do most anything for his people, but even he had limits. He also knew through firsthand observation of the incidents in his mother's life that a woman suffered when a man slaked his lust upon her. The act of coupling was a cruel and bestial activity, and the last thing he would ever inflict upon a defenseless woman.

He also refused to allow a woman to take his seed, adamantly opposed to fathering a child who might possess the dark attributes of a changeling, the same attributes he possessed. What if a child resulted from the ceremony—a child whose dark hair and brown eyes marked him as an outsider, as Alek had been marked? He would rather die than sentence a child to the life of concealment and dishonesty that had been forced upon him. Though he had reaped every honor a warrior could garner, he was never able to fully accept the accolades, for a lie dishonored his soul and robbed him of glory, though no one would ever suspect his inner torment. He often wondered if a world could exist where he could be himself, without the deceit, a place where he could lead a full and natural life.

"Where are the others?" he asked, checking the clearing again for signs of her companions. Druidic rituals were rarely performed by just one priest.

"There is no need of the others." She stepped forward. "All that is required is a woman and a man. You are the champion of the Senones, Alek, the strongest man among us. Your spirit and mine can defeat the Roman Caius."

"And you?" He scanned the shadowed cowl, fairly certain now of the Druid's identity. "Is it Linna who stands before me?"

"Yes." She pushed back the hood of her cloak to reveal her flaxen hair, plaited in two thick braids that rested on her chest and disappeared in the folds of her robe. Her face, raw-boned and fair, was too angular to be beautiful, yet Linna's bearing and grace were all the eye truly beheld, and she was seen as beautiful. A bit older than Alek, she had spent nearly two decades learning the knowledge that the priests passed down, committing all things to memory, for the Druids kept no written records.

"How can you perform a ceremony, Linna? You have not yet taken your vows."

"I shall do so soon. Regardless, I have the knowledge and the skill that is required."

But did she have the stomach for it? Alek doubted it. He glanced over her shoulder at the altar, which Linna had draped with a covering made of the white fur of winter rabbits. If he didn't extricate himself soon, he'd wager a flagon of wine that he'd be lying on that rabbit fur with her on top of him. How could he get out of this situation without offending her?

"There is nothing to fear, Alek."

"I am not afraid."

"Good." She smiled and turned, chanting a low-voiced incantation as she circled the altar. Then she lit candles, placing one to mark the east, one to mark the west, and two more at north and south. They sputtered in the breeze, but did not go out. Alek watched her perform her preparatory rites, trying to think of a plan of escape. If he walked away, he would shame her, something he wouldn't do to a Druid, or any woman for that matter. Yet if he confided in her the reasons for his vow to avoid women, his secret might be spread through the whole of Gaul and he would be made a laughingstock. Even Rowan, who knew him better than anyone, was not aware of Alek's innermost secrets. He shared them with no one, as his mother and father had taught him to do by concealing theirs from him. And sometimes he wondered if his phenomenal strength could be attributed to his virginity.

"Alek, come to the stone."

He squared his shoulders and walked to the altar. For a moment he looked down at Linna's ruddy face, made harsher by the candlelight, and tried to see into her heart. Linna was putting on a convincing display of the priesthood, but he wondered if this were simply a way of bedding him at last. He had not failed to notice the sidelong glances Linna often sent his way, glances that spoke of her desire for him. But did she realize what coupling would entail? Yet if this were truly a Druidic ritual and he refused to participate, there was no telling what misfortune might befall him.

"Divest yourself of your weapons," she began, glancing at the short sword and dagger he wore slung at his hip.

Alek unfastened the belt of the scabbards and lay them upon the grass, all the while keeping a guarded eye on the dark trunks of the oaks. He rarely went unarmed, and felt naked and vulnerable without his sword. For his own protection, he retained the dagger that hung from his belt.

She reached down to the base of the altar stone and picked up a small clay flask and a bronze chalice. Into the cup she poured a brown liquid whose perfume wafted upward to Alek. He had never smelled anything of such cloying sweetness.

Linna mumbled a prayer over the chalice and then lifted it in both hands to offer it to Alek. She wanted him to drink from the cup? Would she drink from it as well? This ceremony too closely resembled the Gallic marriage rite for his peace of mind. He would only go so far with this ceremony, just until he found a way to get out of it.

"Drink."

"What is it?"

"Night orchid nectar. The finest wine you will ever taste."

Alek looked askance at the chalice. The Druids used

hundreds of plants for healing and for their rituals. Not that he was an expert in plant lore, but his mother was a healer, and as far as he knew she never mentioned night orchid.

"Night orchid? I've never heard of it."

"Oh, it is a rare plant, Alek, very rare. A highly prized member of the orchid family."

"What effect does it have?"

Linna smiled a bewitching, extraordinary smile. "Night orchid, my dear Alek, can be a poison or—in just the right proportions—the stuff of which miracles are made! Drink, and soon all your questions will be answered."

She put the rim of the chalice to his mouth, gazing at him the entire time, hypnotizing him with her light blue eyes.

Against his better judgment he swallowed a draught of the syrupy wine. The night orchid nectar oozed down his throat, spreading an odd sensation of wanton well-being in its wake.

Her bewitching smile grew provocative. Without breaking eye contact, she tipped the chalice to her own mouth and sipped the nectar.

"Take one more drink, warrior," she murmured.

He obeyed, trying to fight down a silly grin that threatened to dance on his lips.

"Good, yes?" she asked. Linna drained the chalice and set it upon the ground. When she straightened, she pulled open the front of her gown and let it fall from her shoulders, revealing a strong stocky body as white as the moon above. Her breasts were huge, with dark brown areolas in sharp contrast to her pale skin.

At the sight of her naked flesh, Alek felt a rush of heat pass over him. Instantly his loins betrayed him with a sudden sharp arousal that he could not conceal.

Linna padded up to him and placed her hands on his wide shoulders. Wasn't she afraid of what he might do to her? She was only a woman, while he was a strong man whom no one had ever toppled. "Are there still questions you want to ask, Alek?" she purred.

Alek was surprised to discover his hands had settled on her waist. He hadn't recalled reaching out to her.

She stood on tiptoe and pressed against him, drawing his head down to kiss him.

"You and I will make magic together," she breathed. "The best kind of the magic, the strongest."

He didn't reply. He couldn't. His body was on fire for her. All he could do was pull her against him and crush his mouth upon hers. Was the night orchid an aphrodisiac? Surely it must be, for he never would have reacted to Linna's body so strongly otherwise. Yet what should have been outrage at having been manipulated passed through him as casually as if he had been thinking of what he had eaten for supper. Had Linna put a spell on him?

She embraced him and kissed his chin and then the skin above his mouth.

Alek yanked away, thinking she mocked him for his lack of mustache, the badge of a true Senone warrior.

"No, Alek." She clutched his limed hair and pulled him back. "Don't pull away. I have longed to kiss you there, my clean-shaven warrior." She ran her fingertips over the bare skin above his upper lip and smiled. "To kiss a clean-shaven man is a pleasure for a woman. Didn't you know?"

"No."

"All those great warriors with their huge thatches of hair hanging down are like wild beasts compared to you. The women often speak of you and want to be kissed by you."

"You flatter me, Linna," he murmured, running his hands down her back to her ample rump. He could barely keep himself from pinning her against the altar stone and coupling with her. And yet, in the back of his mind burned the vow he had made to himself, a vow that even the night orchid couldn't erode, a vow that had been hammered out of years of doubt and shame. He would not, could not do this to a woman. With an unbelievable burst of willpower, he tore his hands off her and backed away.

"This is no ceremony," he cried, hampered by a tongue that had grown thick in his mouth and slurred his words. "You have brought me here to shame me!"

"I have brought you here to save your people!"

He backed up a step, staring down at her, trying to marshall his sluggish thoughts.

"Alek!" She fell to her knees in front of him and clutched his thighs in her strong hands. "You can't deny your people, Alek. You must do this for them. The time is right. The portents are all there."

"Linna!"

She put her mouth to his breeches, pressing her lips against the swelling there. He could feel the moist warmth of her breath through the light woolen fabric, and the sensation drove him over the edge.

Alek groaned and closed his eyes, trying to control himself and master the urge that most men his age had joyfully pursued for years, the most natural of urges that he had denied himself.

"No!" he gasped, even as her fingers unfastened his breeches.

"Yes," she replied, pulling them down.

What was she going to do to him? Then, as Linna surrounded him with her warm lips, he flushed with a strange sensation totally unconnected to the sex magic she was weaving. Alek felt an odd tingling sensation envelop him, beginning with his hair and shimmering down his body until it thrummed in his toes.

"Wait!" Linna cried. "Something is wrong! Someone is—"

He heard Linna calling his name, as if she were far away and growing more distant. Her words held both alarm and fear, and then the sound of her voice disappeared altogether, replaced by a loud buzzing noise humming in his ears. He heard someone speaking in the tongue of the Senones, then in the monotone language of the Romans, and finally in some abrupt dialect he couldn't identify. He fumbled with his breeches, trying to cover himself in readiness to meet the presence that had descended upon the sacred grove. Who was speaking to him—a god or a devil? And why had he surrendered his sword?

Plunged into utter darkness, he listened to the urgent voices around him and saw a pale figure coming toward him, a figure of a man so insubstantial, he looked as if he were fashioned of mist. What spirit approached? Was it a being from the Otherworld or the spirit of a Roman? How could he fight a creature of mist?

Then, to his horror, the figure passed through him, right through his chest. Alek felt his heart stop beating, his blood stop flowing, as the figure seemed to snag on something deep inside him. For a moment Alek hung in astounded disbelief, worrying that he was about to become possessed by a demon. Then, as if the figure unhitched itself from his body, it passed on, leaving him while someone grabbed his arms from the back. Immediately, Alek struggled, sure that the priests had appeared to trap him for more of their magic. Vainly, he tried to see his captors, but he was a prisoner of a darkness more opaque than any he had ever experienced.

He pulled at the hands that held him, suddenly aware that he could understand the abrupt dialect which had seemed foreign to him just minutes before.

"Hold him still, dammit!" a clipped voice shouted. "So I can inject the sedative!"

"I can't! He's too strong!"

"David! Watch out!" a female voice cried.

Suddenly the darkness lifted and Alek found himself in a grove of trees that he didn't recognize. On an altar stone nearby, he saw a golden-haired woman lying in a daze, her body partially draped in a white cloth. He flung off the person who held him from behind and whirled to face a second who stood to one side. He snatched his dagger out of its sheath and faced his opponent. A gray-haired man reached up, holding a weapon in his hand the likes of which Alek had never seen. The weapon was fashioned of a small bottle with a needle on the end, a weapon whose delicate lines held no threat to a seasoned warrior like himself. Before he could lash out and knock the odd instrument away, however, the balding man nimbly stepped to one side and jabbed the needle into his shoulder. To Alek's astonishment, the puny weapon completely devastated him without drawing a drop of blood. Before he could take a single step, he lost all control of his limbs and everything went black.

1

Rosebud County, Montana, 1993

During roundup and branding, Marissa Quinn had almost forgotten her visitor of the week before. But as she bent over the bull calf, she saw in her mind the face of the man who had come to make an offer on the ranch. Marissa squinted her eyes and shut out the vision.

"Now!"

Marissa knew better than to glance at the young bull's face as she raised the branding iron, but she did anyway. For an instant, she looked into his white-rimmed eyes, full of fear and distrust, and knew a moment's hesitation at what they were about to do to him. No matter how many seasons passed, no matter now many young bulls they altered, she could never reconcile herself to the practice of cutting. Though it was a venerated way of ensuring the best genes for the herd and guaranteeing a number of docile, weight-gaining

– 13 –

steers, she had a hard time accepting the manner in which cattle ranching insured a strong herd. They altered nature. They cut off the glory of the males of the species, relegating most of them to the ranks of plodding beef producers. Only the biggest and the best were allowed the full spectrum of life as nature intended.

Then she remembered the words of her father, how he had trained her to be hard-nosed and practical, raised her to accept and follow the intractable laws of the range for the glory of a strong herd. Cutting was a way of life, a natural law of the rancher, and it had to be done.

Breaking eye contact with the young bull, Marissa pressed the white-hot iron against his russet flank as Jeb Vincent cut his testes off with one swipe of his razor-sharp knife. The scent of blood mixed with the acrid odor of man sweat and burning hair and flesh filled her nostrils with a smell she both loved and hated. The calf bawled in protest and pain, wrenching at the hands that held his legs and head, struggling to escape.

"Hold him down!" Marissa ordered. She backed off and watched her hired hand inject the new steer with a vaccination for black leg. Shorty, a neighbor and friend of her father's, burned the calf's horn buds with a straight hot iron to keep the horns from growing. Then, in a flurry of nylon rope and flailing hooves, the new steer was set free to return to the herd. He shuddered, shaking off the violence and pain, and then bounded toward the sea of white-faced cattle, the pride of the Crazy Q.

Marissa pulled off her dun-colored cowboy hat and wiped the sweat from her forehead with the sleeve of her plaid shirt as she surveyed the corraled animals. This was the last bunch of calves to be branded, the end of some of the hardest work on the ranch. When it was done, they would have wressled over five hundred calves to the ground. She couldn't have managed without the assistance of her neighbors, Shorty McRell and Jeb Vincent, and a handful of high school boys from the nearby town of Coleton. But the arrangement wasn't one-sided, and certainly wasn't because she was a woman rancher. All the ranchers helped each other during spring roundup and branding. Only the really big spreads could afford year-round hired hands, and the Crazy Q, at thirty thousand acres of rolling prairie and ponderosa pine, was just an average ranch. The only permanent employee at the Crazy Q besides herself was her hired hand, Corky Stevens, a leather-faced, ex-rodeo champion who would have looked naked without the ever-present hand-rolled cigarette hanging from his lip. His breath smelled like a manure pile at close range, but she had learned to live with it.

Marissa pushed back a stray wisp of black hair from her temple. At eleven-thirty, the sun was already baking the prairie, rippling its surface with shimmering heat waves and shrouding the grassland with an oppressive midday stillness. Even the hawks had forsaken the Big Sky for the shade of the pine groves. Sweat trickled down her back. Sometimes she wondered why she labored so hard. But all it took was a visit from a city slicker like the one last week, and she knew she would never do anything else but work the ranch.

"Last one, Jeb," she stated. "Time for lunch."

"Good. I'm hungrier than a two-headed sheep dog," Jeb replied, plunging his hands and knife into a bucket of disinfectant.

"I hope your ma's cooked some of them chicken pies," Shorty put in, winding his rope in a coil between thumb and elbow. "Those pies of hers are just about the finest damn eatin' this side of the Mississippi."

"I think she did make pies." Marissa slapped her hat against the side of her leg, shaking off the dust. She recalled seeing her mother rolling pie crusts when she left the house at four-thirty that morning. Most women on the ranches spent their days cooking huge meals and washing the grime out of their menfolk's duds. Marissa was a rare exception to the rule, since she spent her time among the men, forced by birth and temperament to ride the range. Her father, Wilbur Quinn, had been blessed with two daughters and no sons. But over the years Marissa had done her best to become the son her father never had, and she had fought and scratched her way into the sacred ranks of the cattle ranchers. Now, at twenty-three, she was an accepted member in that male-dominated club, and was known for her masterful hand with horses and her expertise with a lariat. To get there, however, she had given up a few things—like learning how to bake a blue ribbon chicken pie, feeling at home in a dress and heels, or simply knowing how to communicate with other members of the fairer sex. She couldn't relate to womantalk, to the endless complaining about husbands and concerns for children, and the constant prattle about household cleaning products. She was best on the back of a horse, where she didn't have to speak at all, at least not in the tongue of a human being.

She plopped her hat back on her head, covering the black hair that many mistakenly attributed to Indian blood instead of the Irish heritage that branded her with distinctively white skin and raven brows. "What I'm looking forward to, Shorty, is a nice cold lemonade."

"Now you're talking, Half-pint!"

"Who are you calling Half-pint, you old buzzard!" She cuffed Shorty on his arm as she walked by, a head taller than the old cowboy whom she had known since she was a child. He seemed to be getting more stooped and bow-legged with every year. Pretty soon he'd be wider than he was tall. He smiled his gap-toothed grin and slung the rope over the saddle horn of his horse.

"Where's the chow?"

As if on cue, an old blue pickup rolled toward them, churning up a cloud of dust behind it as it bumped along the dirt lane to the branding corral.

"Come on boys," Marissa called, pulling off her leather gloves. "Let's eat."

Her mother, plump, tiny, and florid, served them from an assortment of coolers on the tailgate of the truck. Marissa piled her plate high with food, taking nearly as much as the men. She had ridden hard, worked hard, and could put the food away without gaining an ounce of weight. She sank down on the bank near the road and lifted her lemonade to her lips.

For a long glorious moment, she let the cold drink slide down her parched throat. She closed her eyes and, though she tried to keep her mind blank, she couldn't help seeing the face of the stranger that had burned into her thoughts since the moment he had crossed the threshold of her office.

He had been one of those city boys, wearing a charcoal-gray thousand-dollar suit and impeccably polished cowboy boots with toe and heel rands of engraved nickel—sissy-boots, as her father used to call them. He had sauntered across her office floor, rolling his lean, city-slicker hips, and holding out his fine, manicured hand.

"Hi, Miss Quinn. Bob Hales," he said, grasping her fingers. He had a lean, handsome face, sharp dark eyes, and black hair, the kind of clean, distinct features that came from Sioux blood clashing with that of a Highlander or a Swede, and then gently sculptured over the years to form a new and better breed. Marissa shook hands and sat back in her chair, thinking to herself that if Bob Hales were a bull, they wouldn't cut his balls off. They'd save whatever DNA spiraled inside him to form such a tall, good-looking man, and try to spread those genes around.

"What can I do for you, Mr. Hales?" she questioned cooly, keeping her private musings to herself. No man would want to find out she was weighing the pros and cons of castrating him. She studied him, leaning back in her chair, and didn't offer him a seat so she could take his measure for a few minutes and put him on the defensive.

"I've come all the way from Billings to see you, Miss Quinn." His glance darted around the knotty pine office as if trying to locate something. "I've heard you're the best horsewoman in these parts."

She ignored the compliment. "Want a drink?" she drawled.

He glanced at her and grinned. "Why, sure. That's some drive from the highway. Thought my car would break an axle."

"Should have come in a four-wheel drive." She rose from the chair with an easy grace born of her active lifestyle and walked over to the bookcase at the side of the desk. She could feel his perusal of her jeans, down vest, and shining dark braid, but she was accustomed to long looks from men and had learned to return the stares with unabashed surveys of her own. Marissa opened a cabinet door and reached for a shot glass.

"Spring breakup must have torn up that road pretty good," Hales said behind her.

"It's always like that, Mr. Hales. We don't cater to visitors much here at the Crazy Q. Friends know enough to come in a truck or on horseback."

"I see." His smile froze on his lips but dropped from

his eyes, and in that instant Marissa took a dislike to him. She'd learned many things from working with animals, but the most important tool she'd gained was the ability to read eyes. And this pretty man's eyes were cold and calculating. He was here for something. He didn't have the flashy teeth and glib tongue of a salesman, though, and was too darned good-looking to be an insurance agent. Why had he come to the Crazy Q? And what did he want with her?

"What'll it be, Mr. Hales?"

"Call me Bob." He stepped closer, and she caught a whiff of his expensive but overdone cologne. "How about a scotch and soda?"

A sissy drink if there ever was one.

Marissa expertly mixed his drink and then poured herself a shot of Canadian Club, her father's favorite whiskey. She handed the scotch and soda to Hales and noticed with amusement that he was surprised by her choice of liquor. She closed the cabinet and strolled toward her desk. Not many women downed whiskey straight up—only those with a tough gizzard and raw determination. Since she was seventeen, she had practiced drinking whiskey in the privacy of this office until she could do it without allowing a single tear to well up after the liquid fire had slid down her throat. She had attacked drinking as she attacked everything else in her life, with guts, intelligence, and heart, and had chosen the toughest road to make her strong. Now she could drink a shot without batting an eyelash or chasing it with water.

Marissa leaned against the edge of her large pine desk, smiled, and raised the small, heavy-bottomed glass. Then, with one clean gulp, she showed him what she was made of and what he had come to face, giving him a message as plain as day. She was one tough cookie, and he'd better not cross her. She winked at him and motioned him to a chair while she remained leaning against the desk, retaining her dominance by making him look up at her from his seat.

"All right, Bob," she began, drawing out the single syllable of his name. "What kind of bee's in your bonnet?"

He flushed slightly and she knew she had him on the run.

He crossed his legs as if he intuitively sensed her thoughts of castrating him and held his drink above his crotch, the tall, bulky glass serving as a blatant phallic symbol. Marissa crossed her arms, wondering if he were trying a bit of his own psychological warfare on her.

Though she had been crawling the walls lately, seized by the wildfire of estrus that was sweeping across the spring prairie, she had never been the type of woman who acted on impulse. She couldn't take the chance of someone starting a rumor about her. It would ruin her business, her dealings with the other ranchers, and her hard-won reputation. Besides that, there wasn't a man in Rosebud County, or in the entire state of Montana for that matter, who could hold a candle to her late father, Wilbur Quinn. And she wasn't about to let a lesser man near her. So, she kept herself clear of even the barest hint of trouble, which caused other rumors to circulate about her—that she didn't like men in the way a woman should, that she was a tomboy, a female maverick. She let the rumors fly. Anyone who knew her, those she counted as friends anyway, knew she was a woman through and through. And though she felt near to bursting on these spring nights when her breasts and loins ached for a man, she never once had given in to her feminine nature. At twenty-three she was still a virgin, a fallow field waiting for the right season to bloom, and wondering if she would remain barren forever.

In a way, she had been castrated herself—if that term could be applied to females—and perhaps that was why she found it so difficult to alter the young bulls. She knew what their lives would be like afterward, because she lived such a life herself, a life of asexual servitude. If things went on as they had for the last few years, she would never know how it was to be a woman, she would never escape this ranch and her duty to it and her family. In another ten years, she would be past her prime, hardened even more by life on the ranch and her own strict code of behavior. It was tough to be a woman in a man's world. Perhaps she had become too tough, too hard. The whiskey burned in her gut. She looked down at Bob Hales and watched him take a drink.

"Well now, Miss Quinn, I don't have bees in my bonnet. What I do have is a blank check."

Marissa clutched her elbows. Money only meant one thing: he wanted the ranch. She made no response and waited for him to continue.

"You're a no-nonsense woman, Miss Quinn. I can see that. And I don't want to waste your time. There are a lot better ways of spending the day with a beautiful woman."

She surveyed him steadily, without betraying the rage that began to build deep inside. "Such as?"

"Dinner. Candlelight. Dancing. I bet you'd look like a million bucks in a slinky red dress with your hair up."

"I wouldn't waste a dime on a slinky red dress, Mr. Hales."

"A woman like you would have a town like Billings at her feet."

"Why would I want that?"

"Because you deserve it. I look at you and ask myself why such a beautiful woman would want to kill herself for a dirt ranch."

Marissa straightened, her arms stiff at her sides. "Are you calling the Crazy Q a dirt ranch?"

"I'm calling it a dinosaur, Miss Quinn, a relic from the past that most of these hard-boiled old-timers can't let go of. But you're young. You're smart. You can see the future of cattle ranching."

"And?"

Hales took another drink and looked up at her. "You know how much work it takes to run a ranch. Is it worth it, Miss Quinn? You got land payments, tractor payments, taxes, salaries—and for what? How much can you put in the bank these days? A smart woman like you knows that profits aren't what they used to be."

Marissa glared at him. His words were too close to the truth, too close to home. There hadn't even been enough money for two college educations, so her older sister, Leslie, had been sent to school instead of her. Leslie had gotten off the ranch and was just beginning her career as a research biologist in Seattle, Washington, leaving Marissa to run the family business.

"Know what I'm saying, Miss Quinn?"

"I hear you, cowboy."

Obviously feeling he was getting the upper hand, Hales got to his feet and pointed his glass at her. "There's no future in cattle, Miss Quinn, not unless you got a big enough spread to make it worthwhile, not unless you got the latest equipment, know the newest technology for raising prime beef."

"The Crazy Q raises the finest beef in Montana, mister."

"So I've heard. But at what price?" He put his glass on the desk. "Are you going to give up the best years of your life beating yourself to death like your daddy did? Sure, I've heard that Wilbur Quinn was a saint in these parts. But he died young, didn't he? Burned out with heartache and beaten down by the sun."

"You don't know beans about my father, Mr. Hales."

"Don't I?" He arched an eyebrow. "My father did the very same thing, Miss Quinn. He scraped a living off the earth out near Choteau. Died of a heart attack at the age of forty-five. You think I don't know ranching?"

"You're a goddamned dude!" she retorted.

"Yeah? Well, I've gotten out. I've wised up. I'm not pissing my life away on some cowboy dream—pardon my French."

She turned her shoulder and stared out the window, trying to regain her composure. He was giving voice to the doubts that had plagued her for the last few years. What kind of life was she living here on the ranch? What kind of future did it hold for her? And when she got too old and crippled to ride the range, who would do it for her? She had no children. And the way things were going, she never would.

"You don't have to kill yourself, Miss Quinn. That's what I'm here to tell you." His voice grew softer, more intimate. "I'm tasting the good life now. I live off the interest of my land, Miss Quinn. I've made some smart investments. I'm putting money away, much more than I ever did as a rancher."

She was silent, unwilling and unable to turn around and face him.

"You could have enough money to buy a nice house in town, take some vacations, get your mom set up in a nice condo for retired folks in Billings. How long is she going to keep slaving away on the ranch? She doesn't deserve a life like the one she's got. And neither do you."

"It's the only life we know."

"I'm telling you, Miss Quinn, that it's not the life for a woman like you. It's a doggone crying shame for you to be holed up out in the middle of nowhere like this."

"I love the land."

"But you hate it, too, don't you?"

He reached for her shoulder and she shuddered involuntarily, not because of his touch, but because of the roiling emotions that threatened to shatter her tough facade. She did hate the land. She was hobbled with it, a prisoner of her father's dream, and his father's dream before him.

"I've got a check in my pocket, Miss Quinn. You just say the word and you can have a brand new life."

She breathed in and looked toward the rolling hills in the distance that marked the eastern boundary of the Crazy Q. She loved that view, the sight of the new spring grass bursting up from the prairie and of the ever-changing, unbelievably blue sky of southeastern Montana. This ranch was in her soul, in her blood, and in her heart. To give it up would be like taking a dump on her father's grave and her grandfather's as well. She wouldn't do it. She'd never do it.

"Who's buying?" she asked, pretty sure of the answer without being told.

"The power company."

Bingo. She whirled around and her braid slapped her shoulder. "You want me to sell my land so they can turn it into a goddamn strip mine?"

"Hey, money's money, Miss Quinn. What will it matter to you, once you've moved to the city and have started enjoying life for a change?"

She was so angry she thought the blood vessel in her right temple would burst. "You want me to let them rape my land?"

"Who said anything about rape?" He took her shoulders in his manicured hands. "The power company's real good about restoring the overburden."

"You bastard!" She jerked away.

Hales stared at her and took a step backward.

"You gave up your land to the power company. And now you're pimping for them!" She stomped to the door and flung it open. "Get out, Hales!"

He pulled himself up straight, refusing to take orders from a woman.

Marissa jabbed at the open doorway. "I said get out!"

"You're making a big mistake, Miss Quinn."

He sauntered across the room, his sissy boots thumping an uneven staccato on the wood floor.

"I'll be back in a month or so, when you change your mind."

"I'm not going to change my mind, Hales," she said as he walked past her. "And if you ever set foot on the Crazy Q again, I'll shoot your balls off—if you have any, that is."

"Think you're something, don't you?" he sneered, snatching his hat off the hall table. "Just wait 'til the big boys come calling."

She glowered at him.

He saluted her by flicking the front brim of his perfectly brushed hat. "Nice talking to you, Miss Quinn."

She slammed the door and strode back to her office, crossing the floor to her desk and then back again, trying to walk off the waves of rage that coursed through her. She would never sell the ranch. She could turn a profit. She was as good a cattleman as they came, as good as her father had been. If he could take it, so help her God, she could, too.

Marissa drained her lemonade and gazed out over the herd to the dusty blue hills in the distance. The sun beat on her shoulders. Her feet ached. Her arms ached. Her butt ached. But she'd get up tomorrow and do it all over again.

She watched her mother approach and let the hardness in her eyes ease. Margaret Quinn understood the ways of women and nothing of men. She required soft handling and gentle words, something Marissa sometimes forgot to remember.

"Mom, this potato salad is great."

"Thanks, dear. I put olives in it this time." She placed her hand in the pocket of her apron.

"The olives are good."

Margaret drew out an envelope and held it out for Marissa. "This came in the mail, dear."

Marissa set her empty glass in the grass and reached for the envelope.

"It's from Leslie. I don't know why she addressed it only to you."

Marissa scanned the familiar flowery script of her older sister and noticed a strange, uneven slant to some of the letters. It was unusual for Leslie to write only to her and not to her mother as well. Though her curiosity was immediately piqued, Marissa felt a sudden pall of disquiet that warned her not to open the letter in the presence of her mother. Over the years she had learned to trust her twinges of intuition, which had saved her life and that of their hired hand Corky more than once. She folded the envelope in half.

"Thanks, Mom."

"Aren't you going to open it?"

"No time. We've got to drive the herd to the summer pasture before Shorty and Jeb go home."

Marissa stood up and stuffed the letter into the back pocket of her jeans. She'd read it later in the privacy of her evening bath. Whatever pressing subject Leslie had written about would have to wait.

o   o   o

That night, Marissa bent over the bathtub and tested the water with her index finger. She didn't want to get her bath too hot and drain what small amount of energy she had left. Satisfied with the temperature, she straightened and pulled back her waist-length hair, fastening the wavy tresses on the top of her head with a couple of silver combs. Then she peeled off her dusty, sweaty clothes and let them drop in a pile in the middle of the bathroom floor. For a moment she glanced at her figure in the mirror. She took after her father's side of the family, a clan of tall, rangy men and women, with long bones and spare flesh. Yet Marissa often wondered if her desire to be as tough as a man had stunted her development, leaving her flat-chested. Compared to her sister and mother, she had insignificant breasts and too-slender hips—a woman not made for breeding, as Jeb Vincent had commented once.

Marissa frowned at the profile of her lean body and then picked up the letter from the counter near the sink. She padded to the bathtub, turned off the water, and stepped in, sighing as she sat down.

The water was heavenly after her rigorous day. For a moment she lay back, slipping under the surface until her chin touched the water. Then she opened the envelope and pulled out a single folded page. The lines made her sit up in alarm.

2

Dear Sis,

I know you're busy this time of year, but I have to ask a favor of you. And please don't tell Mom. You know how scared she is of the big city, and how she hates to have me living so far away. I don't want to worry her, so keep this to yourself, okay? That's why I wrote instead of called, because Mom would be able to tell by the sound of my voice that something was wrong. I don't exactly know how to tell you this, but I think something is going on. I'm not sure what's happening or who's doing it, and I don't know anybody well enough to ask for a second opinion.

It may sound crazy, but I think I have been drugged and sexually assaulted. I don't know who would do this to me. I'm losing chunks of time that I can't remember, especially at night. I'm afraid to talk to my boss, Dr. Woodward, about it. He's so conservative and brusque, so devoted to his research, that if I mention memory loss, he'd probably let me go for good. He resents anything that takes him off track or wastes his time, and I don't want to jeopardize the chance I have of working with him. The man's a genius, Sis, I can't tell you how much of a genius. I don't want him to think I'm some kind of an hysterical female.

But I know there's something different about me. The physical signs of assault are there. And I've even been feeling odd in my head, kind of woozy and anxious, which is definitely not me at all.

Could you possibly come to Seattle for a short visit? I know spring is one of the busiest times at the Crazy Q, but you're the only one I can trust, Sis. You're not as gullible as I am—you could always spot a phony or a cheat a mile away. I need help, and I don't know who else to ask. If you can't come, I'll understand. But this is one time I could really use my little sister.

Call me as soon as you can.

Love,
Les

Jolted by the fear and helplessness Marissa read in her sister's letter, she launched out of the tub and grabbed her cotton robe. Leslie should have called her days ago, instead of sending a letter. What if something had happened to Leslie between the time she mailed the note and the time Marissa received it? Sexual assault and memory loss weren't just everyday problems. Marissa wrapped the belt of the robe around her waist while she strode down the hall to her bedroom and the nearest phone. Heart pounding, she dialed Leslie's number and waited for the long-distance connection.

The phone rang and rang until the answering machine kicked in.

Marissa left a short message and then hung up. Now what? She glanced at the clock on her night stand. Six o'clock. That meant it was five o'clock in Seattle. Leslie was probably on her way home from work. She'd wait a while and call her again.

What had her sister gotten herself into this time? Leslie was her opposite in just about everything, including her flair for the dramatic and her penchant for torrid affairs with the wrong kinds of men. In the three years Leslie had lived in Seattle, she had found at least half a dozen less-than-grounded men with whom to get involved. Marissa had heard all her tales of romance, from each breathless beginning to every tearful end. So far, however, Leslie had come through with nothing more battered than her heart. Had her luck changed? Had a man sexually abused her? If that were the case, Marissa would track the bastard down and make him pay for hurting her sister and rue the day he ever crossed paths with a Quinn.

Fortunately the branding was done, which left her free to go to Seattle for a few days. She'd make a plane reservation and then quickly finish her bath. Of course, she would have to think of something to tell her mother to explain why she had to go to Seattle. She'd simply tell her that Leslie was having man trouble again and wanted some company for a few days. She knew her mother wouldn't leave the ranch, much less the state of Montana, so it was safe to assume that Margaret wouldn't even consider accompanying her to Seattle.

Only for Leslie's sake would Marissa go there. As far as she was concerned, Seattle was a glittering city of overdressed yuppies, uptight, over-caffeinated people who lived in condominiums, bloodthirsty criminals, and insufferable traffic. The prospect of visiting Seattle made her nearly as nervous as it did her mother, but she'd never let anyone know it. She'd stared into the face of a rattlesnake, been caught in a stampede, and been dragged by a horse. If she couldn't handle the big city, she had no right calling herself a Quinn.

Leslie didn't answer her phone all night. Tired and worried, Marissa woke Corky up before dawn to drive her to the airport in Billings.

Seattle, Thursday

Marissa was plenty nervous when she arrived at Leslie's apartment in the Woodland Park area of Seattle. Not being able to reach Leslie on the telephone worried her. She didn't like it one bit. But she had been reluctant to call Dr. Woodward, for fear that he would suspect something funny was going on, and she didn't know any of the names of Leslie's coworkers or acquaintances. So she had flown to Sea-Tac Airport and taken a cab to the north end of town, hoping to find Leslie at home by now.

Leslie's apartment was in a renovated mansion located near the Seattle zoo. The house was two stories tall, with a huge porch in front and a turret on the side. Marissa surveyed it as she hurried up the walk. She'd seen similar houses in Billings, but had never actually been in such a fancy one. Trust Leslie and her artistic streak to have chosen a place like this to live. Marissa walked up the stone stairs and found the directory at the side of the front door. She located Leslie's number and pressed the buzzer. There was no response. She pressed it two more times, waiting until she was certain no one was going to answer. Then she dropped her leather bag at her feet near her boots and rang the bell of Mrs. Pitts, the apartment manager, at a separate door off the main foyer. Since she had no key to get into Leslie's apartment, she was counting on the manager to let her in.

The porch light blinked on, and for a long stretch of time Marissa stood waiting, listening for the slightest noise in hopes that the manager would open the door. In Montana, folks didn't make a practice of locking their doors, and they certainly didn't make visitors wait forever on their stoops.

"Who is it?" A female voice called out.

"Marissa Quinn. Leslie Quinn's sister."

She heard a dead bolt turn over and the door opened slightly, still barricaded by a lattice of chains. An elderly woman's face appeared in the crack.

"Take off the hat."

Marissa swept off her Bailey's Black Velvet, worn only on special occasions, and smiled a big Montana smile, full of open goodwill, even though she was being treated with outright rudeness. But she had expected rudeness in the big city.

The old woman surveyed her. "You're Leslie Quinn's sister?"

"Yes, m'am."

"You don't look a thing like her."

"So I've been told."

"She's a blond. Just a tiny thing."

Marissa shrugged off the comparison, accustomed to such insensitive comments when it came to sizing up the differences between Leslie and her.

Mrs. Pitts stuck her nose close to the chains. "So what is it you want, anyway?"

"I'd like to be let into her apartment, if you don't mind."

"Don't have a key?"

"No. I've come all the way from Montana, m'am. Leslie wrote me a letter, saying that something was wrong."

"Dear me!"

"I've been trying to get a hold of her, and she doesn't answer her phone. I think there's something going on and I need to find out what."

"I've noticed she hasn't been home for the last few days myself. She always stops and chats, you see. I thought maybe she'd found herself a nice young man."

"I don't think so." Marissa fingered the rim of her hat, and the small silver buckle on the band glinted in the porch light. "I think Leslie may need our help."

"Oh, my."

"Yes, m'am, that's why I need to check her apartment."

"She did tell me you might be coming. She's a nice girl, that Leslie."

"Yes, m'am."

Mrs. Pitts squinted and gave Marissa a final once-over, from the tips of her black deerskin boots to her French-braided hair.

"Well, I don't usually do this sort of thing, Miss Quinn—"

"I realize that, m'am, and I appreciate it."

"But for Leslie, I guess I can bend the rules." Her voice lost its hard edge.

She closed the door, and for an instant Marissa thought her request had been refused. Then she heard Mrs. Pitts sliding the chains to one side. Soon the door was opened wide and a stooped seventy-year-old woman hobbled out, fumbling with a big ring of keys.

"Wait a minute." She shuffled back into the open door of her apartment and returned with a brown grocery bag. "Leslie's papers have been piling up all over the porch. I put them in a bag so nobody would trip on them and get hurt. Here." Mrs. Pitts handed the bag to her.

Leslie's papers had piled up? That meant she had been gone for a while. Had she disappeared just after writing the letter? Marissa picked up her suitcase, as if to block out the cold shaft of anxiety that coursed through her. "I'm sure she'll appreciate your concern, m'am."

"Oh, I'm not doing it for Leslie," Mrs. Pitts retorted. "I've got insurance liability to worry about."

"Ah." Marissa smiled. She already liked the old woman, whose crusty personality and scrawny body reminded her of Shorty McRell.

"If she was going somewhere," Mrs. Pitts continued, locating the key to the door, "why didn't she notify the paper boy?"

"She might not have known she was going to be gone."

"Sounds suspicious, if you ask me." Mrs. Pitts unlocked the front door and motioned Marissa inside.

Marissa passed into the foyer, dimly lit by an ornate chandelier. Behind the tiny, gray-haired manager was a wide staircase that curved up in a graceful wooden arc to the second story.

"We can't be too careful these days, Miss Quinn," the manager explained, turning to lock the door behind her. "There's all kinds of nut cases wandering around."

"I understand, m'am."

"Leslie's mail is overflowing, too." She nodded toward the old metal mailboxes near the door, where magazines and oversized mail littered the floor. "Why don't you toss her mail in the bag with the papers."

"All right." Marissa bent at the knee and scooped up the periodicals and envelopes, checking to make sure they all belonged to her sister. With each envelope that dropped into the grocery bag she felt more uneasy, as if the pieces of mail were minutes of Leslie's life ticking away.

She stood up, worry gnawing at her.

Mrs. Pitts glanced down at the bag. "That's better. Leslie's apartment's on the second floor. Follow me."

Marissa took stock of the house as she ascended the stairs behind the elderly manager. The place smelled old, with the deep mellow scent of well-circulated dollar bills, and the bannister was polished, both with furniture oil and years of human hands sliding along the smooth wood. The fir millwork had never been painted and was still a rich red-brown, and the doors still sported turn-of-the-century hardware. The stairwell was decorated in green-and-gold wallpaper, and a well-worn black-and-green oriental carpet marched up the steps. Marissa wondered how many people had lived in the house, how many families had inhabited these rooms before they were apportioned into separate apartments. Just like renovated old mansions, families weren't what they used to be, splitting up, moving apart from each other, losing touch. Leslie was the first Quinn to move out of the state of Montana, and it still hurt to think she was so far away, almost too far away to call for help, and too far away to prevent someone from hurting her.

Leslie was probably all right. Most likely there was a reasonable explanation for her absence, which they'd laugh about after this was all over. But Marissa didn't feel like laughing now. She was getting more worried with each passing minute. Frowning, she watched Mrs. Pitts open Leslie's door and flip on the lights. Marissa was taken aback by the sight. Plants were everywhere— on windowsills, in pots along the walls, and on most of the the the furniture.

"Leslie just loves plants," the manager said, strolling into the center of the main room, which was dominated by a huge prayer plant on the coffee table next to a bust of Emily Dickinson. "She gives me cuttings all the time."

"Plants are her specialty."

"She gave me some of these black night orchids a few months ago." Mrs. Pitts pointed to a shelf filled with plants whose broad leaves bore an intricate black lace design at their centers. "Never seen anything like them. Probably as poisonous as anything you'd ever want to grow. She told me they were very rare plants, to treat them like babies and maybe they would bloom."

"Have they?"

"Not yet. Looks like they're getting buds, though. My secret is boiling the water I put on my plants. Do you boil your water, Miss Quinn, to get the impurities out?"

"I'm afraid I don't have much of a green thumb, m'am."

"You don't?"

"That's my sister's specialty. I'm more into horseflesh and cattle."

"Oh." The manager looked at her askance, as if she had just admitted to an interest in something more boring than carburetor repair.

Marissa deposited the grocery bag on an ottoman near the couch. "Well," she said, "thank you for letting me in. I appreciate it." She held out her hand, accustomed to meeting and dismissing men with a strong handshake. Mrs. Pitts seemed taken aback by the gesture, but shook hands anyway.

"I hope Leslie's all right," the old woman remarked as she walked into the hall.

"I hope she is, too, Mrs. Pitts. Goodnight."

"Goodnight."

As soon as Marissa closed the door behind the manager, she turned and carefully placed her hat on a side table and then surveyed the apartment with a more discerning eye. The living room was a jumble of emerald green and ruby-colored pillows, Victorian furniture, and hand-knitted afghans—a departure in both style and color from the knotty pine and blue-and-white gingham motif of their childhood home. But Marissa was more interested in signs of a struggle than decor as she crossed the carpet, searching every corner and pulling back each curtain to inspect windows for evidence of break-in.

She moved down the hall and passed through Leslie's bedroom, done in red and white with gold accents and myriad framed pictures of the family, the ranch, and Seattle. The closet was full of clothes and more shoes than a woman could possibly need. Marissa glanced in disdainful good humor at the dozens of pairs of shoes, from high-heeled pumps to thongs, seeing in the shoes another way in which she differed from Leslie. She owned exactly four pairs—her dress boots, plain black with tooling up the sides, her work boots, a pair of running shoes, and a set of black flats that she'd had for five years and wore only to dressy functions and church, on the few occasions she attended such affairs. Marissa closed the closet. No signs of struggle ruffled the serenity of the bedroom.

The bathroom, with its massive claw-foot tub and collection of ferns, was as neat and tidy as the bedroom, with Leslie's toothbrush hanging from a rack above the sink. Wherever she was, she hadn't taken her toothbrush, and Leslie just wasn't the type to take a romantic trip without her toothbrush. Dry towels and washcloths hung near the tub, evidence that Leslie hadn't used them for a few days. Even the soap in the holder was dry.

The last room Marissa inspected was the kitchen. It was the only modern room in the apartment, with new oak cabinets and ivory-colored appliances. In keeping with Leslie's lack of culinary skills, the only thing the two girls had in common, the refrigerator was practically bare. The dishwasher was full of clean dishes. But the sink was stacked with the remains of breakfast—a plate with dried egg yolk and crumbs, a coffee cup, and a tumbler still partially filled with orange juice. The last meal Leslie had eaten in the apartment was breakfast. But when? Suddenly she thought of the bag of papers collected by the manager. After sorting through them, she came to the conclusion that Leslie hadn't been home since Saturday night or Sunday morning, a span of four or five days.

Had Leslie been missing since Sunday? Marissa leaned against the edge of the counter and ran a hand over her black, wavy hair. Where could she have gone? Could she be lying on the ground out in the middle of nowhere, dead? The thought made Marissa lurch away from the counter and pace the floor. What should she do? The only other person who might have a clue to Leslie's whereabouts was her employer. No matter what trouble it caused for Leslie, Marissa decided to track down Dr. Woodward in the morning and find out what was going on.

Marissa fixed a cup of coffee and called her mother to tell her she had arrived in Seattle without any trouble. She assured Margaret that everything was all right, asked if the power company had been in contact with her, which they hadn't, and then hung up. Taking her coffee cup into the living room, Marissa turned off the lights, pulled back the velvet drapes, and looked out across a small lake which was surrounded by a running path and park. She remembered Leslie telling her about the place—Greenlake, if she recalled correctly—and how people used it for exercise and socializing.

Sighing, Marissa leaned against the fir woodwork, sipping her coffee and wondering how in the world she would ever find her missing sister in such a huge city. There must be a million buildings and at least two million cars. Even at ten o'clock there were people jogging around the lake and cars rolling through the park. And so many lights! Marissa sighed again and looked up, trying to find the constellation of Orion, the giant hunter, in the diluted Seattle heavens, aching for the dark solitude of the ranch and the brilliant stars of the huge Montana sky.

At eight-thirty the next morning, Marissa was champing at the bit, waiting for Dr. Woodward to arrive at his office at the University of Washington. Accustomed to rising early and still tuned to the earlier time zone of Montana, she had been up since four and had spent hours waiting impatiently for the rest of the city to get up. Now she sat in a reception area, drinking a cloyingly sweet concoction called a mocha espresso given to her by Woodward's secretary. Marissa sipped it and flipped through the pages of *Time* magazine, convinced that her father would have termed mocha espresso a sissy drink for owners of sissy shoes. She liked the taste of good strong coffee and thought people were fools for covering up the taste of an honest brew with cream and chocolate.

Suddenly a man pushed open the door and hurried by.

The secretary raised her index finger, trying to catch his attention. "Oh, Dr. Woodward, there's someone to see you."

He paused and then turned slightly, his hands hovering at the placket of his trenchcoat, as he glanced down at Marissa.

She returned his stare. Woodward was probably in his fifties, balding on top with steel-gray hair and a moustache and beard that were immaculately trimmed around his ears and mouth. He was imperially thin and exuded the confident air of a physically fit, well-disciplined man. His compelling blue eyes, ridged by dark lashes, were direct and full of intelligence, evidence that his intellect was as well-exercised as his figure.

"Yes?" he asked, briskly unbuttoning his coat.

She rose and held out her hand. "Howdy. I'm Marissa Quinn, Leslie's sister."

"Leslie's sister?" He ignored her hand as his stare sharpened into a weapon, probing her face. "To what do I owe the pleasure, Miss Quinn?"

"I'd like to talk to you about Leslie for a minute."

"I'm sorry, Miss Quinn, but I haven't the time. I've got a class to teach in exactly ten minutes."

"I'll be quicker than a jackrabbit in a prairie fire, Mr. Woodward."

He stared at her as if trying to interpret the unfamiliar idiom and then apparently remembered himself. "That's *Doctor* Woodward."

"Fine. *Doctor.*"

"Very well, but I can spare only a moment."

She followed him into a sterile room lined with bookshelves and computer equipment, bereft of plants or artwork that might soften the harshness of his stark metal and oak furniture, which was scrupulously neat—a far cry from her own littered desk. His office commanded a magnificent view of a wide canal, but she suspected that he was the kind of man so obsessed with his work that never took notice of the world outside. Near his phone was a photograph of a strikingly beautiful young blond woman, which she assumed was his daughter.

"How can I help you?" he asked, pulling off his trenchcoat and hanging it in a closet behind the door. He took off his suit jacket as well, and reached for a white lab coat.

"I believe my sister is missing, Dr. Woodward. And I'm wondering if you know where she might be."

"I haven't the faintest idea." He yanked on the lab coat and buttoned it with quick, deft fingers. "She hasn't bothered to show up for work for the past few days either."

"Oh? Since when?"

"Monday, as I recall." He adjusted the knot of his tie and then walked to his desk, pulled out a pen, and hung it inside the pocket on his chest. He gave the pocket a quick pat and reached for a pile of books and a tray of slides.

"Well, now," Marissa mused. "It isn't like her to go off without telling anyone."

"Perhaps she's having relationship trouble."

"I don't think so. Leslie would have told me about a beau."

Woodward shot her a derisive look, as if disdaining her provincial language and views. "She hasn't mentioned Steven to you?"

Marissa glanced at him in surprise. "Who?"

"Steven. She talks about him all the time. Maybe he convinced her to drop everything and fly to the Mexican riviera or some other god-awful place."

"Without telling anyone?"

Woodward glanced at his watch. "Look, Miss Quinn, I have work to do."

"Is there anyone else who might know something about her?"

Woodward walked into the hall without answering her.

Marissa squeezed the coffee cup in her hand, doing her best to squelch the anger at being put off by this man. She went after him. "This Steven character. What's his last name?"

"I haven't the faintest idea, Miss Quinn."

"What does he look like? Do you know where he works?"

"No, I don't." Woodward turned, exasperated. "Listen, Miss Quinn, I'll tell you what. I'll ask around today, make some inquiries about Leslie. Come to the house tonight and perhaps I'll have some information for you. All right?"

"Fine."

"My wife and I are having a few people over this evening, but you won't be interrupting anything if you come by at seven."

"I'd appreciate it."

He reached into his lab coat and pulled out a tablet, scribbled an address on a sheet, and tore it off.

"Seven o'clock precisely, Miss Quinn. Do be prompt."

"Thanks." Marissa took the paper. "You've been real helpful, Doc."

For a moment he glared at her as if he were considering reprimanding her for the sarcasm or for the use of a nickname. He didn't look like the type of man who countenanced nicknames, which is all the more reason she gave him one. Dr. Woodward definitely had a burr under his saddle, but that didn't give him the right to treat her like dirt.

"Good day, Miss Quinn."

"So long, Doc." She shook his hand, put on her hat, and strolled past the secretary, who stared at her as she walked by. Hadn't she ever seen a woman wearing a cowboy hat? Or hadn't anyone ever called Woodward "Doc" before? These Seattle types were the rudest, most uptight bunch she'd ever met.

Marissa accurately retraced her steps through the labyrinth of the health sciences building and went out to the front to catch a cab. She'd buy a city map so she could locate Woodward's address, get some lunch, and look for clues in relation to this Steven character when she got back to the apartment.

As she stared out the taxi window, she thought of Woodward. Leslie had called him a genius, a veritable saint of biological research. True to form, Leslie had misjudged him. Woodward wasn't a genius; he was nothing but a pompous ass. And the only reason she'd ever talk to the man again was to get information on Leslie's coworkers and acquaintances. She'd put up with his arrogance for a few more hours, and after that the good doctor could take a hike. If she didn't get any leads from Woodward, then she'd go to the police first thing in the morning.

3

That evening, Marissa rang the bell of the Woodward house, a huge century-old home that commanded a beautiful western view of Greenlake. It was built on a bluff above a quiet street, and rose up three stories from the porch on which she stood. She glanced at her watch. It was precisely seven o'clock.

The door opened to reveal Dr. Woodward, who was dressed in gray slacks, light blue shirt, and a deep charcoal cardigan that set off the blue of his eyes. Woodward seemed surprised to see her, in his repressed fashion, as if he had expected her to arrive late. "Ah, Miss Quinn."

"Good evening," she greeted.

"Why don't you step in for a moment?"

He motioned her into the house, and she passed into the main hall, where an even grander staircase than the one at Leslie's apartment house dominated the room. Dark, formal furniture, probably all antiques, and restrained jewel-toned fabrics spoke of wealth and stability in the kind of house that defied relaxation and stamped out the slightest hint of spontaneity with its oppressive conservatism. She'd take a good old ranch-style house with a lived-in look over this showplace any-time.

Marissa turned to face Dr. Woodward and smiled. She could smell a wonderful aroma of roast beef and herbs and wished she had been invited to dinner.

"We can talk in private in my office," he said, nodding toward the living room, "Come this way."

Before they could leave the main hall, however, Marissa heard the sound of high heels clicking on the oak floor behind her.

"Is that Ruth and Bill?" a woman's voice called out.

"No, Diana," Woodward replied, his tone terse with vexation. He would have continued walking, but Marissa, not wanting to be rude, hung back and prevented him from leaving the hall.

The footsteps ceased and Marissa heard a soft, "Oh!"

She turned around and found herself looking down at a small woman not much older than herself, who stood framed in the doorway of the hall, the same woman she had seen in the photograph on Woodward's desk. Marissa was immediately struck by the woman's delicate bone structure, draped in a navy cotton dress of understated elegance. Diana had the same dainty figure as Leslie, with slender wrists and ankles and a frail neck. If Marissa were born to a pair of jeans and cowboy boots, this woman was born to silk suits and fine leather pumps. Only upon a second glance did Marissa take notice of Diana's silver-blue eyes and shoulder-length pale blond hair, the color of which could never have been obtained from a bottle.

Behind her appeared a tall, brown-haired man with wire-framed glasses, standing close enough to suggest natural familiarity, perhaps more. Was he husband, boyfriend, or lover?

"Diana, this is Leslie's sister, Marissa." Woodward's introductions were made in the same terse tone, as if he were impatient to get down to business and usher Marissa out of the house as quickly as possible. "Miss Quinn, my wife, Diana."

Wife? Marissa was truly surprised, for the difference in ages between Dr. Kyle Woodward and Diana had led her to assume they were father and daughter.

"Nice to meet you," she said, masking her shock and extending her hand.

"Will you be joining us for dinner?" Diana shook her hand with a cool and rather enervated handclasp.

"Actually I came by to see your husband about Leslie."

"She's only stopped by for a minute," Woodward put in.

"Well, you must stay for dinner," Diana touched her forearm. "You're a stranger in town. The least Kyle could do was ask you to dinner."

"Miss Quinn may have other plans, dear."

Marissa couldn't resist plaguing Woodward with her presence. Either the man didn't like her or he had something to hide, and she decided to stay and find out which one it was. Besides, whatever was on the menu smelled better than anything she'd had since she got to Seattle. "Actually, I have nothing planned, Doc. I'd be happy to have dinner with you."

"Good!" Diana beamed. "If you like, I'll take your hat and bag."

"Thanks." Marissa swept off her hat and gave it to Diana, along with her leather purse.

Marissa heard Woodward sigh resignedly behind her. "In that case, may I present our good friend, David

Hodge." He motioned toward the tall man standing behind Diana.

How good a friend was he to Diana, Marissa wondered, ever attuned to the body language of both man and beast. His shoulders hovered above Diana's in a picture of protectiveness and dominance, as a stallion often stood by his mare. Diana stepped aside to allow Marissa to shake David's hand.

"Hi, Marissa." His hand was also chilled and his brown eyes flitted across her face and then away. Why was he nervous?

"Howdy. Nice to meet you."

"David is at the university, too," Woodward explained. "He's a botanist."

"And do you know Leslie?" Marissa asked.

"Yes," David replied. "She's a fascinating woman, with all those stories of growing up on a ranch."

"I'll bet you have some tales to tell, too," Diana said. "Why don't you come into the family room? We were just sitting around having a chat."

"Thanks."

Diana guided her into the large kitchen decorated in creams and peach, a room somewhat less formal than the front of the house. But the counters were so spotless, the rack of copper-bottomed pans hanging from the ceiling so gloriously pink, and the sink so scrubbed and clean that Marissa seriously doubted anyone really used the kitchen. Only the wafting aroma of meat cooking made her eliminate the possibility of a caterer. She followed David and Diana into a small sitting room at the end of the kitchen, where a cheerful fire crackled on a hearth that separated the cooking area from an intimate cluster of couch and chairs.

"Would you like an appetizer?" Diana offered her a

plate of stuffed mushrooms and cubes of honeydew melon.

Marissa caught the quaver in Diana's voice and glanced at her delicate features. For a moment she stared deeply into Diana's eyes. Diana was as nervous as David, but hid it well with a direct gaze and perfect posture, probably falling back on years of training and a birthright of good breeding to camouflage her disquiet.

"Thank you." Marissa selected a cube of melon while Diana set the tray upon the table in front of the couch and sat down at one end. David joined her.

Woodward trailed in and stood near the counter. "There will be just the four of us, by the way, Diana. Ruth and Bill had to beg off, due to illness."

"Oh, that's too bad," Diana replied.

"Bill came down with the flu." Woodward motioned toward a chair, "Do have a seat, Miss Quinn."

Just as Marissa approached a chair near the fire, she heard a strange noise below her—probably in the cellar—the sound of a muffled yell and something crashing around.

"What was that?" she exclaimed.

"That?" Woodward's smile froze in place—the warning sign of a phony or a liar—and in an instant Marissa lost all trust in him. "Oh that. That's my nephew lifting weights downstairs." He forced a chuckle. "He gets carried away sometimes, doesn't he, Diana?"

"Yes," she replied, reaching for an hors d'oeuvre.

"He's a brute." David pushed up his glasses, stretched his arm along the back of the couch, and crossed his legs at the ankles as if to give an impression of casual repose, but he appeared anything but relaxed to Marissa.

"Won't he be joining you for dinner?" Marissa asked, trying to pry more information out of them.

"Oh, no." Woodward slipped a hand in the pocket of his perfectly creased slacks. "He follows a strict diet—macrobiotic, I believe. Besides that, I'm afraid the boy is rather a dull conversationalist."

"He's a brute," David repeated, chewing rapidly on another mushroom.

Unnerved, Marissa sat down in the upholstered chair near the hearth. The popping sound of the fire seemed twice as loud as usual because of the tense silence that filled the room. Marissa kept her attention trained on the background, anxious to hear the sound again, for she was unconvinced by Woodward's story. He seemed to be listening as well.

"Can I get anyone a cocktail?" he suddenly inquired. "Miss Quinn?"

"Do you have a beer?"

"I have some dark ale."

"Ale would be fine."

"Ale for me, too," David replied, reaching for a mushroom.

"White wine, Kyle." Diana leaned back and gracefully crossed her legs.

"I'll have to go to the wine cellar for the ale, if you'll excuse me."

Marissa watched him go, wondering if the ale was simply a reason to go down to the basement and squelch the source of the strange noises. Were the Woodwards hiding something? Were they connected with Leslie's disappearance? She planned to sip her ale slowly, intending to nurse a single drink all evening so she could keep her wits about her.

She took a moment to study Diana. There was something tentative about Diana, something hidden from the casual observer but easily marked by a trained eye. Marissa had seen similar nuances of character in the herd. Cattle with the same tentative natures were the ones picked off by cougars, wolves, and bears. Predators could spot a sick cow, an orphaned calf, or an animal that wasn't quite right, and would cut that animal from the rest of the herd, ensuring the process of natural selection and survival of the fittest. With the instincts of a wolf, Marissa knew that something very wrong haunted Diana.

As if feeling the effects of Marissa's scrutiny, Diana broke the awkward silence. "So you're from Montana, too?"

"Yes. I'm the brawn of the family. My sister's the brains."

David grinned, relieved by her sense of humor. "I can't recall whether Leslie said you raised beef or sheep."

"Beef. The best in the state."

"I've always wanted to live in the country," Diana commented in a wistful voice as she raked her fingers through the back of her hair. "I love the countryside. I think in the country I could discover a place where my inner spirit would find peace. A place where I fit in."

David looked over at her. "Inner peace?"

"Yes." She smiled tremulously and sank back against the length of his arm. "A place where I would feel truly at home. I've never felt at home here."

"I can understand that," Marissa interjected. "Seattle would take some getting used to."

"It's not just Seattle. I have never fit in. Never. Kyle attributes it to my childhood neuroses." Diana's pale eyes clouded to indigo. "But I don't. I believe it's something deeper, Marissa, something far more elemental than that."

"Such as?"

"Don't think I'm crazy, but have you ever felt as if you were born in the wrong century?"

Marissa had never questioned the era in which she was born, just the body in which she had been trapped. Had she been born a man, her life would have been much different and infinitely easier. But before she could relay her sentiments to Diana, she saw Woodward coming back with their drinks. His cardigan was hitched up on one side, perhaps from reaching for a bottle or perhaps from struggling with someone.

"There you go," he said, handing her a tall glass full of brown, frothy brew.

"Thank you."

For a moment everyone fell silent again as Woodward served the drinks. It was as if the topic of conversation had died the instant Woodward returned. She wondered if Woodward's rigid correctness stifled freedom of expression just as the house stifled all sense of hominess. Marissa shifted in her chair.

"Did you find anything out about Leslie?" she asked, hoping to catch him off guard.

At her question, she noticed a quick exchange of glances between David and Diana. What was going on? Did they know something about her sister? She switched her attention to Woodward and found his gaze and demeanor calm, almost unnaturally impassive.

"No one knew anything, Miss Quinn, I'm sorry to say."

"I don't like this. I'm going to the police first thing tomorrow. I don't care if she's run off with this Steven character and might get embarrassed by an investigation. I'm just plain worried."

"You've every right to be." He took a drink of his wine. "Do keep me posted on what you find. I'm anxious to get Leslie back in the lab, as you may well imagine."

Marissa nodded.

"Well," Diana declared as she looked at her watch. "Shall we eat? The roast should be done."

"Marvelous," Woodward replied.

Dinner was just as stilted as the cocktail hour. It seemed to Marissa that everyone at the table was preoccupied, forced to keep the conversation going, when all they really wanted to do was attend to their own agendas. Marissa wanted to slip downstairs and have a look around. Kyle Woodward wanted to pretend that everything was completely normal by discussing national politics. And it appeared that Diana and David wished to bow out to worry over a secret that linked them together.

Diana had just risen to clear the table for dessert when they were startled by a loud crash at the back of the house. Woodward jumped to his feet while Diana dropped an expensive piece of china, which shattered on the wood floor.

"It's him!" she shrieked. "I told you not to bring him here! I told you!"

"Quiet!" Woodward snapped. "I can handle this. David, come with me."

Woodward strode out of the dining room to the kitchen while Marissa watched in shock and curiosity. She heard Woodward banging around the cupboards and then his quick footsteps fading in the distance. David followed him.

"What's going on?" she demanded, putting down her napkin.

Diana had turned as white as the damask table cloth, and was backing through the shards of china, oblivious to the ruined porcelain at her feet.

"Diana, what's going on?"

"It's—it's—" she clutched her throat. Her eyes were huge, the pupils dilated with fear. "It's Kyle's nephew!"

Marissa had never heard anything so preposterous. What was this nephew anyway—a murderous lunatic? Why would Diana be terrified of him? Then she heard a roar of rage so intense, so bestial, that the hackles rose on the back of her neck.

"Dear God!" she gasped. "What is it?"

"Run!" Diana screamed, backing into the china cabinet. "Run!"

But it wasn't in Marissa's nature to run. Long ago she had learned to face danger head on and nip it in the bud before it paralyzed her. Picking up the carving knife from the table, she dashed to the swinging door that led to a hall and then to the kitchen. She heard David shout and the sounds of struggle somewhere at the rear of the house. Then David's limp body came sailing through the air and landed at her feet with a thud. Marissa glanced down, saw that he was still breathing, and loped down the hall toward the source of all the noise. Glass was breaking, furniture was cracking, and Dr. Woodward yelled in pain. Marissa raised the knife and skidded around the corner, damning her slick cowboy boots, and came upon a scene she wouldn't have believed if she hadn't seen it with her own two eyes.

Dr. Woodward was pinned against the wall, his feet dangling, his features contorted in fright and his face beet red from the pressure of a man's hand clamped beneath his jaw. Marissa gaped at the man—if he was a man. He didn't look like any man she had ever seen. He was tall—at least six-foot-three—with a strange ridge of whitish hair shaped like the mane of a horse. He was tremendously built, with shoulders like a bull and massive biceps ringed with golden bands. He wore no shirt and had on a pair of crudely cut pants of an outlandish blue color, which were cinched at the waist with a wide belt and wrapped in leather thongs up to his thighs. He roared again, shoving Dr. Woodward further up the wall until Marissa was certain he would break Kyle's neck. She had heard that steroid use could turn men into violent beasts, but there was more going on here than simple hormone abuse. If this man was Kyle's nephew, then she was Miss Missoula, Rodeo Princess.

"Hey!" she shouted to divert his attention away from Dr. Woodward. "You! Big boy!"

The creature turned in surprise and glared at her. His features were much more finely wrought than she had would have imagined, judging from the rest of his muscular body. For an instant she did nothing but gape at him. Then she regained her wits.

"Let him go!" Marissa demanded, brandishing the knife.

Was that amusement she saw in his eyes? Rage flared inside her. No matter how big a man was, if he laughed at her, he would soon find there was nothing funny to laugh about. She lunged at him, planning to jump on his back and hold the knife to his throat. He was a big brute, probably incapable of quick responses. Marissa vaulted toward him and was horrified to learn she had misjudged him. He not only turned to face her, he grabbed the wrist that held the knife with one big hand and caught her against his bare chest with the other, all in a single sinuous movement. For one chest-heaving instant he held her to his body and stared into her eyes. Marissa glared right back, amazed at his agile reflexes and the hardness of his chest, and shaken to her very core by the gleam of admiration that flashed in his dark brown eyes. Then he smiled and squeezed her wrist until she was forced to drop her weapon. The knife clattered to the floor.

Woodward slid down the wall, choking and gasping for breath.

"Don't hurt her!" he croaked. "For God's sake!"

Marissa twisted in the brute's embrace, trying to extricate herself from his grip, but now that he had two hands free to clutch her, he held her fast.

"Let me go!" she demanded, pounding his chest. His muscles were like plates of bronze and her blows had no effect on him.

His smile broadened at her useless display, pulling at one corner of his mouth to reveal strong white teeth. At his grin, she flailed him all the harder, but to no avail. He hauled her off her feet, slung her over his shoulder, and flung open the back door.

"Miss Quinn!" Woodward called after her, his voice cracking.

"Let me down, you—you—you monster!" she shouted, kicking her feet and battering his back with her fists.

"Still!" The word rolled off his tongue in a strange cadence, as if he were unaccustomed to speaking English, but she couldn't quite place his accent. "Be still, woman!"

"I will not!" She kicked even harder as he loped across the dark back yard.

"Be still!" he ordered.

"You big bully! Put me down!" She lashed out with all her strength and yanked his long, crispy mane of hair.

The creature growled in protest and ground to a halt. "Enough!" he bellowed and raised his hand as if to slap her across the fanny. No man had ever laid a hand on her in violence, and she was stunned into silence by his potential mistreatment of her.

"Good!" he declared, pleased with her sudden change. He ran down the walk toward the back of the property, looking for a gate in the fence. Finding none in the darkness, he kicked the planks with such force that the cedar splintered with a cracking noise that Marissa was sure would alert the neighbors. She hoped someone would look out and see she was being kidnapped. While her captor threw aside the boards, he looked over his shoulder at the sound of voices shouting at him to come back.

"Don't use the pistol!" Diana cried from the back porch. "You might hit Marissa!"

Marissa was grateful for Diana's good sense, but as she was carried off into the night by the violent brute, she wished someone would have tried a shot after all. How would they ever catch up with him? What would he do to her? And where was he taking her? Her helplessness only served to infuriate her.

"You're messing with the wrong chiquita, big boy!" she declared in his ear.

"Be still!" he replied.

Her pride stung at the thought of having been bullied into silence, but she decided it might behoove her to humor him for the time being. Soon he would have to stop and put her down, and then she would make her escape.

4

Alek loped down a grassy slope and leaped over some flowering bushes, his pace barely slowed by the woman he carried over his shoulder. She was light of weight and had little if any spare flesh on her frame, but her hipbones banged against him with every step he took. By Teutates, the woman was thin. Had she been decently filled out, her bones wouldn't be hammering an agony into his shoulder. He ignored the pain and kept running. The farther he got from his prison of the last few days, the better. At least the woman had ceased her struggling.

What he would do with her, he hadn't the vaguest idea, except perhaps use her as a hostage to get what he wanted from Doctor-Wood-Ward. She could also serve as a source of information, perhaps an interpreter, if he found he couldn't fully understand the language here. Alek turned and ran down a road which was covered with a black substance much smoother than any Roman road made of stone, and lined with strange wagons of painted metal and even stranger black wheels. Where in the name of Aveta was he? Had he been whisked off to another world by the Druid magic? He had heard that Rome, the capital of the sworn enemy of his people, was a grand and fantastic city, but the tales he had heard of Rome had never mentioned huge painted wagons or lighted globes that hung overhead and showed no trace of flame. Some of the houses he passed by were so large, they appeared to be fortresses unto themselves. Could he possibly have landed in the Otherworld?

Suddenly, out of nowhere, one of the painted wagons veered around a corner and blinded him with light. For an instant he hesitated, and in that instant, the wagon screeched and slid sideways toward him, while a loud blast of a horn and the sound of the woman screaming nearly deafened him, confounding him all the more. With his senses bludgeoned by light, noise, and movement, he careened to the right and stumbled on a shallow ledge at the edge of the road. Alek tripped, falling to his hands and knees in the wet grass between the road and a footpath, and flung the woman to the ground beneath him. She sprawled on her back, slightly in front of him, with her head just missing the hard surface of the footpath.

"Watch where you're going, buddy!" The driver cursed behind him.

Alek hardly took notice. His entire concentration was captured by the sight of the woman he straddled.

In the muted cloak of twilight, her dark hair blended with the cropped grass on which she lay, serving as a shadowed backdrop. Against the dark frame, her pale face floated like a pool of light—a perfect oval with strong cheekbones and a wide, full-lipped mouth. But what caught his attention most were her eyes, so different from the blue eyes of the Senones and so like his own brown ones. But her eyes were much darker than his, nearly black, and they were on fire—blazing cauldrons of outrage, indignation, and wariness. He had never seen such eyes before, especially eyes set beneath such dark swooping brows.

"Idiot!" she exclaimed. "You nearly got us killed!" She squirmed, as if to wiggle out from under him.

Alek clamped a hand over her wrist and pinned her to the ground.

"My name is Alek. Not Idiot."

In answer, she twisted her features as if she heartily disagreed. Her futile efforts to pull away from his grip only made her angrier, her expression more distorted. Alek let her struggle until she realized she wasn't going anywhere unless he permitted it.

He stared down at her, catching his breath and his wits while he surveyed her female attributes, most of which were hidden by her mannish clothes. He had to admit that she had a strikingly exotic face and was one of the most beautiful women he had ever seen. But what kind of female wore breeches and a thick leather shirt?

"You are injured?" he asked.

"What do you care?" Her nostrils flared and her breasts heaved as she stared back at him. "Just let me up, you big oaf!" She spoke out of one side of her mouth in such a way that her bottom lip pursed slightly outward. Alek found himself wanting to kiss that full ripe curve.

"And don't get any ideas!" she added, glaring at him.

"Ideas?" Her speech mystified him. If there was one thing he needed right now, it was a plan. Any and all ideas were welcome, as far as he was concerned.

"Listen, Alek, or whatever your name is. Let me go, and I won't press charges."

"Press charges?"

"I'll just walk away. No hard feelings."

"No. I want you here."

"You'll never have me. I'll scratch your eyes out first!"

She reached up with her free hand and almost clawed his cheek before he grabbed her wrist and pinned it to the ground near her head. Now she was completely at his mercy and she knew it. Her breath came hard and fast, but still no fear dampened the fire in her eyes. He could easily kiss her now or do anything he liked with her. Most warriors would take advantage of such an opportunity to couple with a beautiful woman and assert their dominance. But Alek wasn't just any warrior. And this woman beneath him was not just any woman. He could tell by her spirit and courage that she was no ordinary female. Courage such as hers was to be applauded, not plundered.

"Come, she-devil," he said, rising to his feet and pulling her up with him. "We will go."

"Where?" she asked, trying to yank her wrist from his grasp.

"There." He pointed to a large wooded area across a footbridge which spanned a wide avenue. Beyond the woods gleamed the outline of a lake. Alek felt more sure of himself at the sight of the forest and lake. Trees and water were part of his world, things he could understand. He could hide in the undergrowth until he devised a plan, while at the same time be close enough to water for survival purposes. All he had to do was get to the woods without being run down by a wagon.

Painted wagons seemed to be everywhere. Another one went down the road behind him, filling the air with noxious fumes and a loud, unusual humming sound, far different than the familiar creaking and bumping sounds of the wooden wagons of his world. More paint-

ed wagons rolled in both directions beneath the footbridge, and Alek was amazed to see that no horses were
required to pull the vehicles. This had to be a magical
place. Surely he couldn't be in Rome. The Romans had
no such vehicles. If they had possessed wagons like
these, they would have used them in the campaigns
against the Gauls, and easily captured all territory from
Iberia to Hibernia. He turned, heading for the bridge.

"Wait," the woman hung back. "Why don't we go
back to your uncle's? I'm sure we can talk this over."

"My uncle's?"

"Dr. Woodward."

"Doctor-Wood-Ward is not my uncle."

"Oh? He said you were his nephew."

"He lies." Alek clutched her wrist more tightly.
"Come."

He practically had to drag her to the footbridge and
grew impatient with her lagging pace, especially when a
running woman in very tight clothing stopped and
stared at them. Alek had no wish to draw attention to
himself and he couldn't permit his captive to cry for
help, so he took the first idea that came to mind. As the
runner approached, Alek turned his hostage around
until her back was pressed against the railing of the
bridge and she was shielded from view by his broad
back. Then, he did the only thing he could think of to
keep her quiet without arousing the suspicions of the
passing stranger. He kissed her.

Her lips were soft and supple, even though she
clamped them tightly together to deny him entrance to
her mouth. She choked in protest and tried to pound his
chest, but he caught each wrist in his hands and trapped
them between their bodies. She arched backward in an
attempt to break from his mouth, but he leaned forward
until she could bend no more. He knew the kiss was

supposed to be merely a ploy for silence and was well aware that the woman was not enjoying the experience, but he couldn't help physically responding to the bow of her body, which thrust her hips against his and presented her breasts to him. Even in this strange world, surrounded by foreign people and objects he could not identify, he was overwhelmed by the urge to caress this woman, to turn her rigid refusal to clinging softness, and to take her down onto the wet dark grass and make her his own. Raw need for her flared inside him like the flames that leaped when Druids tossed magic powder on a fire. A flush drenched him, from his leather boots to the tips of his limed hair, and he realized if he didn't break away, he would be tempted to take her by force. That he would never allow himself to do.

Alek pulled back from her mouth, unwilling and nearly unable to fully release her and step away from her body.

"How dare you!" she sputtered.

He wanted to say something nice to her, explain how her fearless eyes spoke to his warrior soul and how her body made his self-control crack. But he knew that nothing he could say would please her at this point.

Instead of soft words, he threw a gruff warning at her. "Be still, or I will kiss you again."

"You animal!"

She raised her chin and glared at him, her full lips darkened and slightly swollen from the hard lingering kiss he had pressed upon them.

He wished she *would* try to yell. He wanted more than anything to kiss those lips once more. Unfortunately, she remained silent.

"Come." He grabbed her wrist and hurried across the bridge, hoping they wouldn't meet anyone else. Once they reached the other side, he pulled her off the path and into the shadows when anyone approached. Each time he had to pin her against him and clamp his hand over her mouth to prevent her from crying out for help. She was hard and tense in his vice-like embrace and once even bit his palm, but he held fast, relishing the moments she stood pressed against him.

She was slender where the Senone women were wide and ample, inflexible where they were soft, and her hair smelled fresh and sweet where the Senone women smelled of smoke and wool. He was nearly overcome by the notion of pushing his nose into her hair and drawing in a great draught of her scent. More than any other time in his life, he wanted a woman—this woman. Perhaps his episode in the sacred grove with Linna had primed him for these wild imaginings. Whatever it was, he had to get his mind off kissing her and smelling her and find a place to hide for the rest of the night.

Alek pulled her off the path and across a clearing to a stand of closely growing willows near the water's edge. If they could find a fairly dry spot upon which to pass the night, he was certain that no one would notice them among the twisted trunks of the trees. He picked his way over gnarled roots and standing water choked with iris blades until he found a knoll surrounded by foliage and the drooping veils of the willow branches.

"This is good," he commented, gazing around in satisfaction.

"For what?" she answered.

"We will pass the night here."

"Like hell! I'm not staying here with you!"

"You are my hostage."

"I'm your nothing! Nothing! Do you get that, big boy?"

He glared at her. No one, not even his friend Rowan, called him names.

"Do not call me boy."

"What will you do—kiss me?"

He grabbed her upper arm and yanked her to his chest so that he could look directly into her eyes and impress upon her the seriousness of the situation. "If you need a stronger threat, woman, I will make one."

He glowered at her. She blinked and glowered back, her chest heaving. Though he admired her brave talk, he would not countenance disrespect from anyone, not even from a beautiful woman of this Otherworld.

"You will obey me, woman. In all ways. We stay here." He stepped away from her.

She frowned, obviously annoyed by his commands. "Aren't you carrying this ultimate warrior stuff a bit far?"

"What are you saying?"

"Well, look at you—speaking in that fake accent, dressed in that ridiculous costume. Who does your hair, for crying out loud?"

Alek crossed his arms. "My hair?"

"Yes, your hair. You look like a wild man. Who's going to take you seriously when you go around looking like that?"

Alek swallowed back his outrage. Didn't she know to whom she was speaking? He was the champion of the Senones, the strongest man in his tribe. No one had ever called him ridiculous. Everyone took him seriously, for he was not a man to ridicule or cross. Why, he could snap her in two with his bare hands. One cuff and he could knock her senseless and put an end to her misplaced contempt.

Alek caught himself. The thought of raising a hand against a woman made him flush with shame. In his mind he saw a vision of his father, Brennan, striking his mother again and again until she surrendered in silent weeping and allowed the hulking warrior to slake his lust on her. Alek shut off the memory and turned away. He would never ever strike a woman, no matter how angry she made him, no matter how disrespectfully she acted, no matter how much he wanted to take her against her will. And he would never, on any account, slake his lust on a woman and make her cry. To even think of it made bile rise in his throat.

He bent over to untie the thong at his ankle so he could use it to bind the woman's wrists to his, all the while keeping a wary eye on her to make sure she didn't try to escape. He heard her step up behind him.

"Why are you doing this?" she asked, her voice more level than it had been moments before, as if she realized she could not deter him from the path he had chosen.

"So Doctor-Wood-Ward cannot find me."

"Why don't you want him to find you?"

Alek straightened, unwrapping the thong from around his left leg. He was uncertain of how much to tell the woman. Complete silence might be the best tactic with her, so he said nothing.

"Why were you trying to hurt Dr. Woodward?" she continued.

"Because"—Alek slipped the thong free—"he puts something in my arm that makes me sleep." Alek bristled at the thought of his helplessness and the reminder of his childhood, when he was powerless and could not fight back. Now that he was a man, he wasn't accustomed to defeat, especially the ignominious defeat brought on by Doctor-Wood-Ward's tiny weapon. "I am through with sleeping."

"Perhaps he thinks you're too dangerous and imbalanced to be let out in society. The use of steroids is known to alter a man's personality."

"Steroids?" Alek narrowed his eyes. "I do not know this word."

She glanced at his chest and arms. "You could have fooled me."

Her quick perusal made him flush anew. Did his figure impress her? Or did she actually find him ridiculous? Other women seemed to think he was pleasing to look at. Why didn't she?

He shut off such thoughts. "Turn around and put your hands in back of you," he demanded.

"Why?"

"I am going to tie them together so you cannot run away in the night."

"How long do you think you can hide here?" she countered.

"Your hands, woman!"

Reluctantly she put her hands together over the back of her thick leather tunic and then glanced over her shoulder at him. "Once it gets light, someone is bound to find you. It's useless, you know."

"Be still!"

He gave an extra hard tug on the thong and she fell silent. Then he tied the leather strap to his own wrist, linking the two of them together. He pulled the thong, forcing her to follow him to the base of a towering willow. Alek sank to the ground, his back to the ridged trunk of the tree. For a moment she stood facing away from him as if refusing to join him.

He pulled on the thong, knowing that if she didn't comply the pressure would hurt her shoulder joints until she was forced to her knees.

"Sit down, woman," he ordered and pulled the thong taut.

Finally she dropped to one knee and pivoted to face him. "Coyotes will gnaw off their own foot to get free of a trap," she said. "Don't be surprised if I'm gone in the morning."

"Oh?" Alek smiled slightly and pulled the tether just enough to knock her off balance. She toppled over, her shoulder slamming into his chest. Before she could struggle away, he grabbed the thick black braid of her hair and forced her to look up at him. "I sleep like a cat," he warned her.

She glared at him. He had another, even stronger urge to kiss her, the result of her half-sitting in his lap. Her lean rump braced on his thigh made him want her all the more. He ached to run his hands under her shirt and search for the womanly secrets he knew lay beneath the heavy leather. He longed to stroke her slender flank, which was covered by a close-fitting black material that hugged her flesh like a second skin. To force his mind off her and occupy his hungry hands, he released her braid and reached for the scarf tied around her throat.

"What are you doing?" she demanded.

He pulled the scarf free. "I have told you to be silent, yet you chatter like a bird."

"Wait a minute, don't—"

He cut off her protests by gagging her with the scarf and tying it around the back of her head. She struggled and continued to make muffled noises of outrage.

"Go to sleep, woman."

She jerked away from him, moving away on her knees until the tether stretched too far for comfort.

Alek gazed at her. *She-devil.* With her as his prisoner, he would probably not get a single hour of sleep.

Alek was aroused from a fitful slumber sometime later by a shoe prodding his calf. He jerked awake, surprised to find that he had actually fallen asleep. He shook off the cold cramp in his shoulders and glanced at his hostage.

She stared at him and made an insistent sound behind the gag. Didn't the woman ever give up?

"Go to sleep." He waved her off and tried to find a more comfortable position. He wished he had a cloak to warm his bare shoulders, for the night was damp and chilly.

He felt her prod him again.

This time he was annoyed. "Be still!" he barked.

"Bphh-mphh." She kicked him and then hobbled up to him on her knees, inclining her head toward him as if asking to have the gag removed.

Sighing, Alek reached up and loosened the knot.

"Bathroom!" she exclaimed. "You big bully!"

"Bathroom?" he repeated, unfamiliar with the word.

"I have to relieve myself."

He frowned. "I do not understand you."

She screwed up her features, in what he deduced was a common expression for her. "Come on, Alek. Enough of this play-acting."

"I am not playing."

"You can't be serious! You don't know what going to the bathroom means?"

"No."

She made a squatting motion.

"Ah." He nodded. "I will take you to the bushes there." He pointed to a copse of trees and underbrush at the edge of the small knoll.

"Oh, no you don't!"

"You are not going alone, woman."

"Oh, yes I am. And I'm not going to do it in the middle of a city park, either. I want a bathroom!"

"What is this bathroom you speak of?"

"It's a place where *civilized* people go to relieve themselves." She scrambled to her feet. "I saw one just up the path before you dragged me to this four-star willow retreat of yours."

"There is a bathroom nearby?"

"Yes. Just up the path."

He held up his hand. "If I untie you, you must promise not to run away."

"I promise."

Even though she gave her word, he kept a watchful eye on her as he unfastened the thong from his wrist and then from her hands. He couldn't depend upon the she-devil to keep true to her vow.

She shook the stiffness from her shoulders and elbows and sighed in relief. Then she tramped through the dead grass and swept through the willow branches, obviously certain of her direction. Alek kept close behind her, confident that, should she try to bolt, he could easily catch her.

When they gained the trail that bordered the lake, she pointed to a small structure twenty feet away.

"That's the rest room," she said.

"You go there." Alek instructed, checking the trail for approaching people. He saw nothing, only painted wagons rolling by on the street at the top of the slope. "I will stay in the shadows and watch the door." Before she could leave his side, he took her upper right arm in his hand and squeezed her flesh. "If you run, I will catch you. And then I will punish you."

Her eyes widened for an instant as she stared at him.

"Understand, woman?"

"I understand, Conan."

Still glaring at him, she pulled her arm away and then proudly stomped across the grass to the bathroom. Alek watched her go, gazing in appreciation at the slender lines of her legs and wishing he could see the outline of her behind. Unfortunately, her thick leather tunic concealed her backside as well as her upper torso.

If she ran, he'd have to go after her and bring her to

the ground. He smiled at the prospect. The thought of wrestling her to the earth appealed to him, and the mere idea of her beneath him made his blood race. He knew he was in danger of becoming obsessed with the she-devil, which was the worst thing that could happen to him in this strange land. What if she was trying to cast a spell on him to make him remain in her world? She could be a demon in disguise, just waiting to take advantage of his attraction for her, waiting to make a prisoner of him. He wanted no connections to this Otherworld. It was imperative that he find a way to return to his homeland as soon as possible. That meant not wasting time mooning over some sharp-tongued female who happened to have caught his eye, demon or not.

He crossed his arms over his chest and watched her disappear into the small building, and realized he had a need to relieve himself as well. He turned, still keeping sight of the bathroom, and vented his bladder.

Just as he was finishing, he heard the she-devil scream.

5

For the second time that night, Marissa was grabbed by her long black braid and dragged against a man's chest. This time, however, she slammed into the figure of a man who reeked of cheap cologne and cigarettes instead of the honest smell of leather and sweat. He wasn't as tall as she was, and she would have tried jabbing her elbow into his gut, except for the fact that a dozen or so of his buddies swaggered up, forming a ring around her in the dim light of the bathroom. They were all dressed in a similar fashion, from their tattered black jeans with red hankies tied above their knees, to their white T-shirts and leather jackets. Marissa had read enough in national magazines to suspect that she had run into a gang. And most likely they had been hanging around the women's rest room, waiting for an initiation victim.

"Hey, Ray," one of them taunted with a wicked smile. "Nice babe you got there."

"My new girlfriend," the man in back of her replied.

His breath smelled of beer. Marissa nearly choked from the odor wafting up around her. "Say, what's your name, baby?" He nuzzled the small of her neck with a grizzled chin and then reached in front of her and pinched her left breast. Was he the one to be initiated, and would he earn membership by raping her? His hand shook and she realized he was nervous.

Marissa wrenched away, but only managed to yank her own hair. As long as the man held her braid, she was trapped, unless she wished to pull her hair out by the roots. Her scalp stung painfully and she retreated in frustrated surrender. Ray clutched her more tightly.

"I said, what's your name?"

"Annie Oakley," she replied through gritted teeth.

The rest of the gang laughed in a tight unpleasant sound.

"Smart-ass!" the guy standing in front of her exclaimed. He took a drag on his cigarette. "I don't like smart-ass women."

Marissa stared at him, her neck bent at an awkward angle because of the other man's grip on her braid. She had learned long ago that the moment you broke eye contact with a rattler was the moment the snake would strike. She didn't plan to take her eyes off the man in front of her for a instant.

"I don't know," Ray put in. "Her smart ass feels mighty fine to me!"

More guffaws echoed in the dark rest room. He forced her rump to press against his crotch. Marissa stiffened. She wasn't going to let any man take her without a fight, no matter how many of his cohorts were there to back him up. Loathing every second of his fumbling caress, Marissa waited for Ray's attention to center on his goal at the base of the zipper of her jeans. Then she raised her foot and brought the heel of her cowboy boot down hard on his instep.

He howled in pain and released her hair as he staggered backward, hopping on one foot. Marissa took advantage of the moment to break away, ramming the man in front of her with her shoulder and knocking him aside. Then she heard a blood-curdling yell—the same yell she had heard at Dr. Woodward's house—and all hell broke loose.

Bodies flew everywhere—against stall doors, into the walls, over the trash can, out the door, and at her feet as Alek routed the entire gang with his bare hands. He used surprise as a factor, certainly, but his most powerful weapon was the sheer size of the man and his incredible roar. Marissa watched in amazement, reminded of the voices of lions or the trumpeting of bull elephants, as he roared and picked a man up bodily and threw him out of the rest room. The others scrambled around him, looking as ineffectual and small as toys. Within moments the rest room floor was littered with broken and moaning gang members, their noses bleeding and their arms cradling their abdomens as they doubled up in pain. One guy hung over the trash can and puked.

Marissa stared at Alek, who stood above Ray with his booted foot to the man's neck, and realized that the huge warrior had probably saved her life. The dim light outlined the rippling magnificence of his chest and abdomen and gleamed off his armbands and the thick gold necklace he wore at the base of his throat.

For an instant their glances locked and held—his flashing, golden-brown eyes and her black ones—as she struggled with the concept that Alek had come to her rescue and in doing so had fought off more than ten men. What kind of man possessed such strength—such *balls*? She had never seen a man take on so many opponents and come out the victor. What chemical or weight-lifting program could enable a man to vanquish ten others? Was this guy for real?

Before she could react, she heard the distinct sound of hoofbeats pounding in the distance.

"The cops!" somebody yelled.

Immediately, the gang members scrambled to life, as if alarm overrode the pain of their injuries. Alek released his prisoner and let him run off, turning slightly to watch the man race out of the rest room.

In moments, the gang members vanished into the night. Marissa stumbled forward, her legs rubbery as the sudden flood of adrenaline left her system. She wobbled up to Alek, trying hard not to display the slightest hint of her weak-kneed relief, or the fact that she just now realized how frightened she'd been.

"Are you injured?" he asked.

"No."

She hobbled past him, more confused than ever. She owed her life to this man, and yet she was still his prisoner. She had never been more relieved in her entire life than the moment she had looked up to see Alek in the doorway of the rest room. And yet she wondered if he had fought off the gang only to save her for himself. Other than kissing her, he hadn't threatened her in that way, but then he might simply be biding his time. He still controlled her fate. He still held her captive. And that made him an enemy.

She stumbled out to the wet grass and spied two mounted policemen galloping across the lawn toward the rest room. She waved them down, running to meet them before Alek could grab her and drag her back into the shadows.

The horses thundered to a stop near the rest room and one of the policemen swung down from the saddle.

"What's going on here, Miss?" he asked, stepping up to her in his crisp navy uniform with his tall black riding boots.

"I've been kidnapped!" she replied.

"By who?"

"Him!" she pointed to Alek, who stood near the door of the rest room about thirty feet away, warily watching them.

"Jesus," his partner exclaimed. "Where'd he come from—a cable TV wrestling show?"

"I don't know where he's from or who he is. But be careful. He's quite strong."

"C'mon, Ed," the officer on the ground said, slipping his billy club out of his utility belt. "You stay right here, Miss."

"Gladly." As the officers walked toward Alek, Marissa stepped closer to the horses, close enough to feel their warm sweet breath and smell the familiar scent of oiled leather and horseflesh. For the first time that day she felt a sense of ease as part of the trappings of home surrounded her. One of the horses lowered his head to sniff her coat and snorted near her ear. She reached up and patted his nose as she watched the policemen approach Alek.

She hoped they wouldn't hurt him. After all, he had just saved her life, and he hadn't done her any real harm. But there was no denying Alek was a dangerous man who shouldn't be running free in the streets of Seattle. She wouldn't be suprised if he were suffering delusions and hallucinations because of the steroids he had taken for bodybuilding. He might really believe that he was a warrior from some forgotten era. Could he have slipped so far from reality that he had become the man of his hallucinations? Heck, in the last few minutes, she herself had totally forgotten that he was just acting the part of the ultimate warrior. For those few minutes when he had come to her rescue, he had *been* the ultimate warrior.

And she was repaying his courage and strength by turning him over to the police.

Marissa pulled her suede jacket together in the front and gave her shoulders a shake, as if to slough off the notion that she was betraying him in some way. She looked down at the ground near her feet and chided herself for even entertaining such a ridiculous thought. For crying out loud, the man had kidnapped her. He had tied her up with a leather thong and ordered her around like a dog. He might have done much worse to her during the night. She had every right to turn him over to the authorities.

Suddenly Marissa heard a strange *oooph* noise, the sound someone makes when the wind is knocked out of him. She glanced up in alarm to see one of the policemen doubled over in the grass. Alek couldn't possibly have resisted billy sticks and handguns, could he? She backed up a step, fearing the worst and realizing her assumption that she was safe might be woefully unfounded.

Then the second officer was hurled through the air and landed in a rhododendron bush. Marissa blanched, knowing all traces of her safety net had just collapsed. Alek had dealt with the two men as if they were so much kindling. What would he do to her? As if he heard her thoughts, Alek glanced her way and lunged forward. She was next.

For an instant Marissa froze in place in utter disbelief. He had overwhelmed the policemen with shocking ease. And now he was coming for her. In moments he would be upon her, and this time he'd be angry. She had flagged down the officers. She had betrayed him. He would punish her for certain.

More frantic than she had ever been in her life, Marissa whirled around, caught up the reins of the nearest horse and leaped on his back. He whinnied and pranced smartly in protest at the unfamiliar rider, but Marissa's master hands and knees brought him under control in a matter of moments. Then she swung him around, urged him forward with a smart jab of her heels, and they galloped off in the direction of Leslie's apartment at the south end of the park.

She heard someone fire a shot and then another, but she didn't look back.

Marissa had never stolen a thing in her entire life, and never in her wildest dreams would she have believed she would steal someone's horse, especially a horse belonging to an officer of the law. She knew she might be getting herself in deep trouble. But she was in a frenzy, too desperate to get away from Alek to worry about the legal ramifications of her actions. She'd deal with them later, once she'd left the Incredible Hulk in the dust.

The wind sang in her ears and hair as she leaned over the neck of the horse, demanding even more speed from him. He gave it to her with glorious abandon, as if he were desperate for freedom himself. Marissa's heart sang with the speed, with the feel of a horse beneath her, and with the confidence that her riding skill would save her once and for all from the brute who had carried her off. She swore under her breath at the thought that a man had actually slung her over his shoulder and threatened to spank her. She rode all the harder, as if to outdistance the humiliating memory.

And then she heard hoofbeats pounding behind her.

She glanced back and stared through the loose tendrils of hair that blew across her face. She couldn't believe it. The ultimate warrior was practically breathing down her neck. He looked like something out of a Viking movie, with his whitish mane of hair, his huge shoulders, and his strange blue trousers. The only thing lacking was a horned helmet.

Marissa faced forward again, her heart pounding in fear. He could catch her. The damned man was riding like a maniac to overtake her. She would have to take chances to outride him, chances she wouldn't normally try with an unfamiliar mount. But she would rather court danger than allow Alek to capture her again.

In the dim glow of the streetlights, she saw a rock wall up ahead. She gauged the distance and her speed, and hoped the warrior didn't know the fine points of taking a jump. In preparation of the real jump, she visualized her horse carrying her over the three-foot wall and then, in a graceful arc, she brought the gelding up, spanned the fence, and hit the ground on the other side without breaking stride. Marissa dared not look back and lose precious moments to see whether Alek made the jump or not. She just kept riding, pounding down a slope toward the end of the lake.

To her dismay, she heard the pause and then the impact of the mount behind her as the horse jumped the wall and galloped onward. Alek had taken the first jump successfully. Damnation! She muttered a few choice names for him under her breath and raced toward a parking lot. There she took the railing that bordered the lot and rode for the other side, took another railing, and urged her horse up a steep muddy hill. If Alek made the jumps in the parking lot, he might not make the hill, simply because he was a much heavier rider.

The muscles of the horse's haunches bunched and strained as they struggled up the hill. Marissa urged him onward with words of encouragement and praise. Flecks of foam spattered the sleeves of her coat and her fingers were frozen with the cold, but she rode on, desperately aware that Alek was close behind. Who was this guy? The man rode as if glued to the saddle.

With a great heave, her mount gained the top of the hill and lumbered forward, winded and blowing. Marissa knew she couldn't ask him to keep up the breakneck pace. Yet if she slowed down, Alek would catch her for certain. She nudged the horse onward, desperately trying to find a recognizable landmark that would tell her she was near Leslie's apartment. But in the dark, everything looked foreign. She glanced around, fighting off panic when nothing appeared familiar. She'd simply have to skirt the perimeter of the park until she spotted the old mansion where Leslie lived. But would her horse last that long?

Between the edge of the park and her was a grove of elm trees and a long drive. If she could just make it down the drive and spot the apartment, she could possibly outrun Alek and get into the house before he caught up with her. Once inside, she could call the police and have them reclaim all the animals—the two horses and the wild man.

She weaved through the trees, trying to throw him off. But he continued to dog her heels, and was so close that she could hear his horse blowing. Marissa pounded along the turf toward the gravel drive, hoping her mount wouldn't hit a hole in the dark and break a leg.

The last stretch would be an all-out sprint to the finish, with the winner dependent on the heart of the horse beneath him. Marissa leaned forward, lifting slightly out of the saddle. She charged down the lane, calling for more speed. But, to her horror, she saw a dark shape out of the corner of her eye. The other horse was gaining on her. Though she begged for more, her mount had given all he could give. Alek continued to gain, as if in slow motion, and soon she saw the knee of his breeches and his big hand.

Then, she realized he was standing up in the stirrups. She shot a glance over her shoulder and saw him swing his left leg over the back of his mount. What in the hell was he going to do? Jump off? Was he crazy? He was grinning like a fiend. She jerked forward, jabbing her heels into the sides of her horse in one last effort to pull away.

The horses pounded neck to neck, like chestnut locomotives, while Alek moved to one side. Marissa kicked out with her left foot, trying to hit him in the knee, but he managed to move aside and avoid being struck. Frantically, Marissa rode on, frustrated and shocked by the fact that he could outride her, so furious that she felt hot tears pull out of the corners of her eyes. This was unbelievable. What was happening to her? She never cried. And she was damned if she would let this man see her cry. She'd get away from him somehow.

As if to deny her even that small victory, Alek suddenly vaulted from his horse and leaped onto the back of her own mount. The impact nearly knocked her out of the saddle, but she had tucked her boots firmly into the stirrups, which saved her from falling. His arms came around her as he grabbed the reins, and his chest thrust up against her back. But, worst of all, his thighs slapped against hers, and his thighs were the hardest flesh she had ever felt, as if the man were made of marble.

"She-devil!" he panted in her ear. His hot breath sent a chill down her neck and back. "You cannot get away from me that easily."

Marissa refused to acknowledge his boast.

His arms tightened around her as if to show her that she was his prisoner and would not get away this time. "You ride like a demon!"

"You ride like an idiot!" she retorted. "You could have gotten both our necks broken, jumping off a horse like that, taking—"

"Enough!" he snapped. "Where is your lodging?"

His voice had an odd breathlessness to it, as if he were not merely winded, but tired. She turned, trying to peer into his face, and caught sight of a crimson smear on his shoulder. Blood? Had he been shot? She turned to face forward again. So what if he were shot? Why should she care? Maybe if he grew weak enough, she could get away from him.

"What's the matter," she flung back at him. "Don't you want to stay at the 'Willow Inn' back there at the lake?"

"I am injured," he replied. "You will take me to your lodging. Now!"

By that time they had reached the edge of the park, where a busy street served as a border between the wooded area and a residential section. Alek pulled the horse to a sudden halt at the curb. Marissa felt him stiffen behind her as the traffic whizzed by them. She remembered their last experience with a car and had no wish to repeat it.

"Give me the reins," she demanded, "before you get us killed."

He relinquished them and dropped his hands, splaying his long fingers across her thighs and hooking his thumbs around her hips. No man had ever ridden behind her since she was seven years old, and no man had ever held her like this, with such blatant possessiveness and familiarity. She was so taken aback by his insolent hands that she almost missed the light.

Marissa nudged the horse foward and clomped across the street, hoofs ringing on the asphalt. She could just imagine the sight they must make to the drivers on either side of the road, and only hoped someone would call the police to report them.

They gained the far curb, and she guided the horse down the sidewalk. Behind her she could hear Alek's heavy breathing and felt the slump of his body against hers. How seriously was he hurt? Would he remain conscious long enough to get him to the apartment? Marissa hoped so. She had decided the best recourse would be for her to comply with his wishes, take him to the apartment, and call Dr. Woodward on the sly so the good doctor could come by and pick up his out-of-control acquaintance.

"You are a most maddening woman," he muttered in her ear.

Marissa blinked in confusion, surprised by the admiration and the unmistakable sound of a smile in his voice. She hadn't expected humor or regard from this man, and she certainly hadn't expected to flush with pleasure at his compliment. But flush she did—to the roots of her hair. Marissa stared forward, mortified by her own reaction and grateful for the darkness that hid the red badge of her embarrassment.

Within minutes, she had found Leslie's apartment house. She took the horse to the end of the sidewalk and stopped.

"This is where I'm staying," she remarked.

Alek slid off the horse and stood waiting for her to dismount. When she looked down at him she saw a dark hole the size of a penny in his left shoulder. The policemen must have found their mark. How could the warrior have performed such feats of horsemanship with a wounded arm?

He followed her line of sight. "The weapons of this world are strange to me," he motioned toward his shoulder. "So small, but so powerful. A man does not have to come close to strike."

"Yes." She had to agree with him on that point. "We've become impersonal in a lot of ways."

She heard the echo of her words and frowned. There she went again, slipping into Alek's fantasy, thinking he was from another time and place. It wasn't like her to escape reality or even want to escape reality. She was a no-nonsense kind of woman with a lot of responsibilities, none of which included wandering around with an ultimate warrior in the middle of the night.

"He is a fine horse," Alek commented, stroking the lather from the gelding's neck. "I will keep him."

"No you won't. We're in the middle of a city."

"I may have need of him."

"No way. The police will be looking all over for him." She gave the horse's rump a quick slap and sent him trotting away, confident that someone would see him and report his unusual presence before he could get into trouble in traffic.

"Come on, Alek," she nodded toward the house. "I'll help you with that wound. And then you're on your own."

"No. You stay with me, woman. You are my hostage."

"Right." Tiredly, she walked toward the porch. "I'd almost forgotten that little detail."

They strode up the walk and into the foyer without speaking. Marissa was thankful that Mrs. Pitts wasn't peeking out her window at them, because she wasn't sure how she would explain Alek's presence.

She led him up the stairs, aware that he surveyed the house in awe and fascination. Marissa pulled the keys out of the pocket of her jeans. Luckily, she hadn't put them in her purse, which had been left behind at the Woodward house. Otherwise they wouldn't have been able to get back into the apartment. She slipped the key into Leslie's door and turned it as Alek came up behind her.

"This is a large house. You must be a powerful woman," he commented. "Rich."

"No." She shook her head and motioned him into the room. "I don't even live here. This is my sister's apartment. Lots of people live here."

"Your family?" he asked, padding to the center of the living room.

"No. Complete strangers."

His dark brows came together in confusion but he apparently decided not to pursue the subject.

Marissa flipped on the lights and startled him. He whipped around, hands up to defend himself, as if remembering the incident with the car headlights. When nothing else happened, he straightened and looked up at the fixture overhead.

"Lights," she said, walking past him.

"Lights," he repeated staring at the ceiling while he followed her into the kitchen.

She hung her keys on the key rack by the coffee maker and turned to face him. "Sit down and I'll get a bandage for your shoulder."

He pulled out a chair so that it faced away from the table and then lowered himself to the seat. For a moment she stared at the incongruent sight of the half-naked warrior sprawled on the dainty piece of furniture. He leaned back against the table, one arm stretched across the walnut surface behind him. When he breathed, the tight muscles of his abdomen rose and fell, reminding her of the tight flesh of a race horse. He was flat and supple. Not an ounce of extra flesh hung over his belt. She gazed at him in awe, for she had never seen a man in real life who was so well built.

"You go?" he said, obviously wondering what was keeping her.

She realized she had been standing there gaping at him like a novice barrel racer mooning over a dashing rodeo champion, succumbing to the same weakness of idol worship she had disdained in other females. Why would she even look twice at this guy? He was nothing but a domineering brute. Before another blush could brand her face, she turned on her heel and stormed down the hall to the bathroom, hoping she hadn't appeared as foolish as she felt.

Marissa banged around in the bathroom, searching for tweezers, bandages, and antiseptic, and finally located the items she needed to doctor the warrior in her kitchen. Then she took off her jacket and hung it on the back of the bathroom door. She washed her hands thoroughly and carried the supplies in a clean towel to the kichen table.

Alek watched her line up the items.

"This might hurt," Marissa warned.

He shrugged, as if pain were of no consequence to a real man.

She explained how she was going to try to find the slug and pull it out with the tweezers. "Sure you don't want something to ease the pain?" she asked. "I think my sister has some whiskey."

"Whiskey?" he questioned, glancing at the bottle of hydrogen peroxide. Was he pretending he didn't know how to read? Why did he insist on playing this warrior charade? Didn't he realize yet that she wasn't buying into his act? She sighed in exasperation and bent over his shoulder.

"Well, Mr. Big, here goes nothing."

6

Diana Woodward waited up for Kyle and David, hoping to learn they had found Marissa Quinn unharmed and had recaptured the warrior. But at ten o'clock, when the two men trudged into the house empty-handed, she knew her worst fears were confirmed. The brute was still on the loose. And most likely the Montana woman was still his prisoner.

"No luck?" she asked anyway, taking Kyle's coat.

"None." Kyle smoothed back his hair. "David's staying over, in case the warrior comes back and tries to make trouble. I trust the guest room is prepared?"

"Yes." Diana glanced at David, trying to ignore the way her heartbeat quickened at the news. "Then let me take your coat, David."

"Thanks."

"Would you two like anything? A snack?"

"No. I'm going to retire. And I suggest you do the same, David. The night may prove to be a long one."

"Right," David replied. "See you in the morning. Goodnight, Diana."

"Goodnight." She smiled at him, hoping the disappointment she felt at not having a chance to talk with him didn't show in her eyes. "There are fresh towels in the guest bath. If you need anything, just call."

David walked up the stairs as Kyle watched him, his sharp features hard with fatigue. Did Kyle suspect anything had gone on between them? If he did, surely he would have said something by now. Perhaps her indiscretion had gone unnoticed. She prayed her husband would never find out, for it would ruin all of them. Diana crossed her arms together over her chest and decided to turn Kyle's thoughts to something other than David.

"Kyle," she began, clutching the sleeves of her robe. "What are you going to do about the warrior?"

"David shall continue the search tomorrow when it's light. If he doesn't find anything, I will go to the police and tell them the warrior is my mentally deranged nephew, and have them find him for me."

"What happens if he hurts Miss Quinn?"

"We'll deal with that if and when it occurs, Diana." He put his hand on the newel post. "Now, however, I plan to get some sleep."

"Promise me you won't continue with this research."

"Definitely not!" He walked up a few steps. "I have every intention of continuing!"

"But you're dealing with human lives, here, Kyle. It's not as if you're using laboratory rats."

"I haven't hurt anyone, Diana." He paused at the landing.

"Oh? What about Steven? You don't even know what's become of him."

"I believe that Alek and Steven have exchanged physical realities. He is most likely as fit and chipper as our brutish friend."

"And what about Leslie Quinn?"

"Leslie?" he pressed his lips together. "She'll be fine."

"How do you know? You don't know what effects the night orchid has on a person."

He stared down at her, tapping his fingertips on the bannister.

Diana hesitated. Was she pressing too hard? Would he fly into one of his rages? She didn't know anymore. She felt as if she had lost touch with her husband over the years as they'd drifted further and further apart. What had happened to the idealistic man she had married? Had the idealist lost himself to fanaticism?

"The night orchid potion must have some powers which you aren't aware of," she continued, talking to his back as he turned to go up the rest of the stairs. "How else can that brutish warrior know English?"

"The roots of his language must be similar to ours," Kyle replied. "Enough to permit him to recognize the basic structure of our language."

"I don't think so."

He turned and gave her a withering glance. "Since when did you become a linguistic expert?"

She refused to buckle beneath his stare. "I'm just using common sense."

"Common sense, Diana? Is this something new?"

She ignored his sarcastic slur. "I was only thinking of Leslie Quinn's welfare."

"Leslie's welfare is none of your concern. I suggest you return to dabbling and leave the serious work to the scientists." As if dismissing her, he turned and marched upward to the second floor.

Supercilious bastard. Diana stood at the bottom of

the stairs, seething with rage. Dabbling. He called her mythology series dabbling! No matter how many prizes in literature she won, no matter what critical acclaim she achieved, her work would always be dabbling to him because it concerned the glory and tragedy of the human race and the way people related to the unknown and the Higher Powers, and was not based on hard facts and computer analysis. *Supercilious bastard.* That's what he was—a self-satisfied, supercilious bastard. She wanted to pummel his back, call him terrible names, pull his hair, and tell him what she really thought of him and his computer output. Instead, she turned on her heel and stumbled to the kitchen before she resorted to violence.

She couldn't believe she had considered striking another human being. It wasn't like her to think such thoughts. Yet ten years of marriage to Kyle Woodward had eaten away at her character as surely as her disease had devoured her body. Over the years she had stuffed her troubles into a box with the assurance that she would deal with the problems later. Now she was realizing that the box was full and there was nowhere else to ditch her resentment and anger—nowhere but out in the open. And the prospect of dealing with Kyle openly was a very frightening one.

What would she do if he threw her out, or if she couldn't take it any more and simply fled? What would she do for medical coverage? How could she get a job? And in her last days, who would take care of her? She had no family. She had only Kyle. And perhaps David. But she would never ask David to accept her baggage, not in her condition. How could she tell Kyle what she really thought of him and their marriage when she knew her future, however stunted, depended upon him?

She'd simply have to hang on, just as she always did.

She'd hang on for better times, perhaps a better life the next go 'round. If she died pure of heart and truly contrite for that one night with David, perhaps she would be granted forgiveness and a happier existence in her next life. She could only pray that if she were good enough and lucky enough, David might share that new life with her where they would be free to know complete and honorable love.

At Leslie's apartment, Marissa stood at Alek's side, too close for her own comfort, but forced there by the task of removing the slug. She could feel a sheen of sweat beneath her clothes, a product of her unswerving concentration as she carefully probed the wound so she wouldn't cause him undue pain. She shouldn't have cared one way or the other if her ministrations hurt him. He deserved it. The only reason he'd gotten shot was that he had abducted her and resisted arrest. Yet, she could never countenance hurting a living creature unnecessarily—even if the pain involved a half-crazed kidnapper. So she had been gentle and careful, and found herself holding her breath as she worked. She had watched her father take a slug out of the family dog once, but hadn't realized what demanding work it was until now. Finally, she pulled out the metal blob and held it up.

"There it is," she stated, glancing at the slug which had been stopped by the top of his left arm.

Alek reached up for the slug and grasped it between his fingers while Marissa released it from the tweezers. "This is what went into my body?"

"Yes. If that slug had hit an internal organ—your lung or heart or something—you would have been one dead honcho."

He rolled it around in his palm. "What makes this fly?"

"Something called gunpowder."

"Powder. Magic powder?"

"Hardly." Marissa reached for the gauze and peroxide. "There's nothing magic about guns and gunpowder. This might sting for a minute."

She cleaned the hole with the bubbling peroxide and wiped it gently with the gauze. Alek withstood everything she did without flinching, as if his wound was nothing but an inconvenience. Most men would have been weak from shock and loss of blood. She marvelled at his sturdy constitution.

Trying not to grant any more heroic attributes to the brute, she turned her attention to making a bandage, which she taped to his smooth golden skin.

"Done." She took a step back. "I hope I got it cleaned out enough."

Alek touched the bandage when she was finished. "You have kind hands for a she-devil," he commented.

She ignored the compliment. "You're lucky they didn't shoot any lower." She wiped her hands on the towel. "But they wouldn't have shot you at all if you had given yourself up."

"I did not want to give up."

"Why? One way or another, you're going to get caught. You can't go around abducting people and throwing policemen into bushes."

"Policemen?"

"The men with the horses. They guard our cities. Keep us safe."

"They did not keep you safe in that room—that bathroom."

She paused. He had a point there. Not sure how to answer him, she reached for the medicinal supplies, highly aware of his uninjured and perfectly formed right shoulder at her elbow. When she stepped away from his side, her stomach growled loudly.

"Sorry," she said. "I'm hungry."

He nodded.

"I'm going to make a sandwich. Do you want one?"

"What is a sandwich?" He rose and she was once again reminded of his great height as he towered a good head higher than she. Not many men were taller than she was, and his stiffened hair made him appear much wilder than any man she had ever encountered.

Though he might be a foot taller and maybe a better rider, Marissa was tired of the way he was playing dumb, as if he thought she was stupid enough to believe any of his nonsense. She didn't play games with men and she didn't appreciate it when they tried playing games with her. The time had come to put her foot down and make him tell her the truth. She crossed her arms and glared up at him. "Listen, buster. You can go on all night with your little game, but I'm sick of it."

"What game?"

"The game of I-don't-understand-what-you're-saying-because-I-don't-know-the-language. Your accent is so awful, I don't even recognize it. What are you trying to mimic—French? Spanish? German?"

"German?" He spat out the word as if it left a foul taste in his mouth. "German? I am a Senone."

"A what?"

"A Senone."

"Never heard of them. Where do the Senones come from?"

"The Romans call the area Venetia."

Marissa tried to recall the lessons of her high school geography class. She didn't remember a place called Venetia or a people called the Senones. She kept up with international news through magazines, but didn't recall reading anything about Venetia. Was he trying to pull a fast one by fabricating a name and place?

"You're saying that you live in a suburb of Rome?"

"A suburb? What is that?"

"An outlying area of a larger city. Do you come from Rome?"

He surprised her by laughing outright, which turned his fierce brown eyes to sparkling topaz.

"What's so funny?" she demanded, not seeing the joke and not willing to be the brunt of his amusement.

"Do I look like a Roman to you?"

He held out his arms, inviting her to survey him. She did look for a brief moment, marvelling that a man could be so thoroughly muscled and still be attractive to her. She had never liked the looks of bodybuilders, with their poses, their bulging veins, their over-developed chests, and their oiled flesh. Something about them seemed fake to her, as if their figures had distorted the original design—like the parlors of houses kept pristine for visitors and never trespassed by the family.

Alek, on the other hand, was purposely and finely fashioned, gracefully slender in the hips and powerfully taut in the shoulders. His muscles looked as if they had been chiseled by a force of nature and kept in tone by hunting, fighting, and heavy labor. He was as different from a body builder as a manicured poodle was from a hardworking stock dog. Alek appeared wild and perfectly honed for survival, like a cougar she had seen last autumn on a bluff behind the ranch. He was definitely not a civilized weight lifter who exercised in his uncle's basement. But if he wasn't Dr. Woodward's nephew, who was he? And where did a man get a body like that these days?

"Well?" he asked. "Do I look like a Roman?"

"I wouldn't know," she replied tartly, "I've never seen one."

"You are fortunate, woman, in your ignorance." He sobered suddenly and clamped her chin between his thumb and forefinger. "The Romans are a greedy people—greedy for gold, greedy for land, greedy for women. They are never satisfied. They always want more. And they will kill to get it. You are lucky that I am not a Roman, she-devil, that I am a Senone."

Something in the way his eyes glittered down at her induced her to believe him. Yet something in his words made her stop and wonder just which Romans he meant—present day or ancient.

How easily she fell under his spell! Was this how Leslie succumbed to the men she had known? Marissa pulled away and hurried down the hall to return the tweezers and hydrogen peroxide to the bathroom, chiding her foolishness with every step. What was it about this man that put a kink in her good sense?

When she came back to the kitchen, she found Alek looking in the oven.

"What is this?" he asked, holding open the door.

She sighed, realizing he had chosen to persist in his game of words. "That's an oven. People cook things in there—roasts, cakes, things like that."

"How is it heated?"

She glanced over his shoulder to see whether the oven was electric or gas fired. "See that metal piece in the bottom?" she said. "That's the heating element. It gets really hot when you turn on the oven and it heats up whatever you want to cook."

"How?"

"With electricity." She straightened before he could ask her any more questions. "Listen, do you want a lesson in chemistry or something to eat?"

"I will eat."

"Good choice." She reached up to a cupboard to check the extent of Leslie's larder. It was two o'clock in the morning. She was hungry and tired. All she wanted to do was to eat, get rid of the Incredible Hulk, and hit the hay.

Alek inspected the apartment while she struggled to make a decent sandwich. She was practically a stranger in the kitchen and had a low tolerance level when it came to preparing food, especially for a stranger who looked as if he'd prefer gnawing a hank of wild boar to the tunafish salad she had slapped together.

She found an apple in the bottom of the refrigerator, sliced it up, and poured two glasses of milk, and then carried everything to the small table where Alek had sat while she tended his wound.

"Chow time," she called, feeling more than awkward waiting on a man like this. She had never waited on a man. Her mother had handled all meals and social gatherings for as long as she could remember. Marissa glanced at the slices of bread, which seemed in danger of sliding off the lettuce beneath them. How did her mother make sandwiches hang together? Was it some kind of feminine secret? Hell if she knew. Her sandwiches might not be architecturally sound, but she was pretty sure they would taste all right.

She pulled out a chair and sat down just as Alek strode to the table. He stood looking down at her until she glanced up in exasperation.

"What's the matter?" she asked.

"Warriors do not eat with women."

Warriors didn't eat with women? She couldn't believe he had actually said that. She remained looking at him and felt her stare turn glacial and her body flush with heat when she realized he was serious. Women weren't good enough to eat with—was that it? She'd never been a second-rate citizen and she wouldn't start now.

She grabbed his plate and yanked it in front of her. He could burn in hell before she'd make him a single morsel of food again.

"Fine, Mr. Big. Starve."

He stared at her as if he couldn't believe what she had just said and done.

Marissa chomped on her sandwich and glared at the wall ahead of her, making a big deal of enjoying the midnight snack and refusing to acknowledge his presence.

Suddenly Alek slammed his fist on the table beside her so hard that the dishes rattled and Marissa started in alarm with the sandwich posed in midair, while the top slice of the uneaten sandwich bounced up and flipped onto the table.

"Woman!" he thundered. "You try my patience!"

She forced her pulse rate down. "You try mine." She shot a glance at him and took a bite of her sandwich, just to prove that she wasn't afraid of his anger. The lump of bread and fish stuck in her throat as he grabbed a handful of her braid and forced her to look at him.

"Where I come from, warriors do not eat with women."

"Haven't you ever heard the saying, 'When in Rome, do as the Romans do?'"

"I will never do as the Romans do." He forced her head back even farther.

"It's just a saying. Observe the customs of the country in which you travel, and you won't insult your host."

"I insult you?"

"Every time you lay a hand on me."

He stared at her for a long moment, his eyes burning into hers, and then released her hair. He turned away.

His back was an expanse of powerful ridges and sheaths of muscle on either side of a straight, proud spine. His hips were trim beneath the blue breeches, and she could tell from the way the leather thongs spiralled around his legs that his thighs were strong and trim as well. She could almost imagine his hips slung with weapons—a glorious barbarian, half wild and thirsting for blood—and the thought unnerved her. Marissa blinked and tore her gaze off him.

"So do you want your sandwich?" she asked, upset at her crazy flight of imagination and tired of his stony silence. Alek didn't answer her, but strode to the living room instead. When she finished her meal, she found him asleep on the couch with an afghan pulled across his magnificent chest. The picture presented of the huge man draped over the plush Victorian furniture, with his long legs and feet hanging over the end of the couch, almost made her smile. It was a marvel that the furniture didn't buckle beneath his bulk.

Yet there was really nothing to smile about. This man had threatened her life. He might even be connected to Leslie's disappearance, for all she knew. He could be a murderous psychopath waiting for the chance to kill her. The sooner she got rid of him, the better. And now that he was sleeping, she would call Dr. Woodward.

Marissa waited in Leslie's locked bedroom until she heard a car pull up outside the apartment. Then she slipped down the hall to buzz Woodward into the foyer. She tiptoed through the living room to the front door and pushed the button, just as she looked over her shoulder to make sure that Alek was still sleeping.

The warrior was gone. All that was left was the afghan bunched on the seat of the couch.

Marissa swore under her breath, yanked open the door, and stepped into the hall. Dr. Woodward and David Hodge, looking disheveled and sleepy, ascended the stairs below.

"He's gone," she called down to them.

"What?" Woodward replied.

"He must have heard me talking to you. He must have run off."

"Good God." Woodward gained the top of the stairs and pulled off his black gloves. "Have you checked the apartment?"

"No, not yet."

"He might be hiding." Woodward swept past her into the living room without being asked. Hodge followed him, rubbing a hand over his rumpled brown hair. David was fairly tall himself, nearly as tall as Alek, but much leaner, and the kind of man who exuded thoughtful gentleness instead of repressed violence.

Marissa returned to the apartment and shut the door, sure that a search of the rooms would turn up nothing. Where could a big man like Alek possibly conceal himself in Leslie's apartment? Marissa doubted he had stayed to play hide and seek with Dr. Woodward.

Woodward and Hodge checked every room with brusque thoroughness while Marissa stood in the doorways, feeling more violated by their determined search than she had felt by the warrior who had stood in the kitchen looking at the oven. A strange disquiet wafted through her, like a chill wind in the middle of summer, as she felt a subtle shift in her convictions. Whom did she trust? Efficient Dr. Woodward and nervous David Hodge? Or Alek, with his blunt macho attitude? No matter how Alek had ruffled her feathers, at least she had sensed a brutal honesty in his words and actions.

She couldn't say the same for the two men rummaging through Leslie's things.

"He isn't here!" Woodward said, slapping his gloves on his palm. "Where the devil could he have gone?"

"Greenlake?" Marissa ventured. "He took me there at first."

"That would be a logical place," Hodge put in, pushing up his glasses. "He would feel more at home in a wooded area."

"Yes." Woodward narrowed his eyes and breathed in a sigh of frustration. "This isn't what I need to spend my time on, looking for that brute."

"Why not let the police handle it?" Marissa asked.

"The police?" Woodward shot a hard glance at her. "I don't want the police in on my family problems. My nephew is a disgrace and we do all we can to keep him out of the public eye."

"What has he done?"

"He has fits of violence, uncontrollable rages. One of these days he may kill someone."

"Why isn't he in an institution of some kind?"

Woodward stared at her. David Hodge pushed up his glasses again and looked away.

"No Woodward has ever been placed in an institution," the doctor replied stiffly. "We take care of our own."

"At the expense of others." Marissa brushed a hand over her unruly hair. "He could have killed me tonight, Doc. And I don't appreciate it one bit. If he shows up again and threatens me, I'm calling the police, public eye or not."

"The best thing for you to do, Miss Quinn, is to get on your pony and ride back to Montana where you belong. You aren't doing anyone any good here, and you just might get hurt."

"Are you threatening me?" Marissa seethed.

"No. Simply offering you some friendly advice."

Marissa had seen more friendly eyes on a wolverine, and his words burned through her like a hot poker in snow. *Get on her pony and ride.* In his condescending, mannered way, Woodward was infinitely more chauvinistic than Alek. *Get on her pony and ride.* The more she thought about it, the angrier she became. She glared at him as the anger mounted to white-hot rage, and she would have slapped his face, but Woodward chose that moment to break for the door. He walked swiftly across the living room.

"Do call me if you see any trace of my nephew," he drawled, turning on the threshold. "And I'll keep you apprised regarding your sister."

"I won't be holding my breath."

He pulled on his gloves without breaking eye contact and, in that moment, Marissa knew she had made an enemy. She didn't play by the same rules of ettiquette that the doctor followed and made no pretense of cloaking her true intentions in polite but deeply chilled phrases. It was obvious he disapproved of her way of talking and her personality. The realization didn't exactly break her heart, however, because Dr. Woodward was the last person she would have wanted for a friend or ally. He passed into the hall without saying good-bye.

David put his hand on the door knob. "Be careful," he said, quietly, giving her a nervous smile. "Woodward's nephew is a brute."

"I know."

"You don't know everything, though. It's very important that we get him back. Be careful."

Without waiting for her to question him further, David hurried to catch up with Dr. Woodward. Marissa watched him go, wondering at his strange words, spoken in a voice not meant for Woodward to hear. What was going on? What was the big secret?

More uneasy than ever, Marissa checked every door and window, making sure all were locked tight. Then she took a long hot shower, trying to force herself to relax and forget about Woodward and his warrior and her ever increasing concern for Leslie. Tomorrow she'd go to the police. Tomorrow she'd get to the bottom of the mystery.

She stepped out of the tub and rubbed herself dry, wrapping her hair with a fluffy green towel. Then she pulled on her robe and walked to the bedroom. It was now three o'clock in the morning. She was so tired she doubted she could sleep. For a few minutes she took care of her dirty clothes and hung up her suede jacket. Then she climbed between the sheets while the events of the day whirled in her thoughts. Most of the visions included the towering form of the ultimate warrior, a man who was quickly emblazoning his personality in her mind. Her horse sense told her to distrust all three men, but her heart insisted upon replaying Alek's laugh and the sparkling topaz of his eyes over and over again until she fell asleep with his voice ringing in her thoughts.

Near dawn Alek slipped the key into the lock of Leslie's apartment, copying the movements he had watched Marissa make hours before when she had led him up the stairs and tended his wound. He had taken the keys from the rack in the kitchen where he had watched her hang them, knowing she was unaware that he observed her every move. His friend Rowan insisted that Alek must have eyes in the back of his head. But he had no demonic eyesight. What he did possess was a highly trained sensory system, the result of years spent avoiding the heavy and violent hand of his father. When a person had to fear for his life every moment of the day and night, that person developed extraordinary skills, or he simply perished. Such had been his life for years.

Silently, Alek closed the door and waited, listening intently to see if the she-devil had heard him enter her dwelling. He wasn't certain why he had returned, only that this was the last place Woodward would look for him now. Besides, he might still be able to use the woman as his hostage when he stormed Woodward's house and demanded to be sent back to his own world. He also needed a dry, warm place to sleep, for he could barely keep his eyes open, he was so tired. And for the last few minutes a strange, tight feeling in the center of his chest caught at his breath and made him gasp for air. What was wrong with him? Did the strange feeling have something to do with the chunk of metal that had been removed from his body? He had never experienced such tightness before.

Satisfied that the she-devil had not heard him, Alek slipped the keys into a leather pouch that hung from his belt. Then he padded down the hall, searching for the room with the red-and-white sleeping box, sure that he would find the woman there. The door was half-closed. He urged it open, hoping the hinges wouldn't squeak. Then he looked across the room to the long, slender form in the bed. The woman had unfastened her hair and it spread in wild profusion on the pillow beneath her head. He had never seen such a cloud of dark hair and wondered what it would feel like to have that hair slipping across his callused fingers. She faced the wall, with her back to him, and he was disappointed not to be able to see the expression on her face while she slumbered. He was certain that the she-devil's expression would soften in sleep, that her full lips would be parted slightly as she breathed low and steady.

A slow smile spread over his face as he recalled her fury and pride in her efforts to fight every step he had taken that night. And in his twenty years on earth, he had never seen a woman ride a horse the way she had. The she-devil had more guts than some of the men he fought alongside. But she had also insulted him and called him names. If a woman had behaved in that way to a warrior of his homeland, he would have had every right to punish her. Yet he couldn't imagine striking this woman. In her ignorance, she imagined that she was his equal, and she was so convinced of it that she made him stop and think about his own perception of women. Was this world a place where women were not meant to serve men, bear children, and tend the hearth? If so, what did women do here? If he expected food at her table, did that mean he would have to sit with her?

He remembered the phrase she had quoted. *When in Rome, do as the Romans do.* Did she expect him to throw over his customs and beliefs to embrace hers? When in the Otherworld, do as the Otherworlders? He frowned. If the she-devil thought he would bend to her will, she had a lesson to learn about his own sense of pride. There were some things a man just didn't do. And one of them was taking orders from a woman.

She turned in the bed, as if aware of his surveillance, and eased her arm above her head, which brought part of her torso out of the covers. Alek gazed at her, wondering what it would be like to change the cold fire of her black eyes to the hot flames of desire. There was no denying that this woman touched him in a way that no other woman had, with something that flared inside his chest as well as his loins.

He turned away abruptly, before his thoughts took him farther than he allowed himself to go. Silently, he closed the bedroom door and sank to the floor in front of it. The she-devil would not be able to leave the room without falling over him first.

Alek leaned back against the wood door and closed his eyes. Where was he? How would he get back to his home? And would he get back in time to prevent his enemy, Caius, from overrunning his land?

He sighed and recalled the first time he ever laid eyes on that Roman dog, the day he had stumbled on a scene near the river—a day that had burned into him to become a scar on his soul as surely as a wound became a scar on the skin.

7

Ballachulix, 293 B.C.

Alek and Rowan had been out hunting along the river. By the time they had both passed through twelve Samains, they had already spent years stalking rabbits and birds and had once even chased down a deer. The heat of the summer day had finally got to Rowan, who flopped down in a clearing and announced he was going to take a nap. Alek looked down at his friend as he stretched out his gangling limbs in the cool grass beneath an oak tree. Rowan was the sort of youth whose feet and hands grew much too large for the rest of his body, making him clumsy and uncoordinated, and often the brunt of jokes made by the older boys.

"Rowan, you lazy dog," Alek taunted, throwing the sack of rabbits to his friend. Rowan gathered his wits just in time to catch the bag, which he plopped beside him in the shade.

"The day is too hot for hunting, Alek. Our luck is bad because the animals have run for shade."

"Then come for a swim."

"I am tired, Alek. I just want to close my eyes and sleep." Rowan draped his arm over his eyes, as if dismissing his friend.

"All right. I will swim alone."

He waited for a minute for Rowan to change his mind, and then, realizing his friend was determined to lay there in the grass, he turned and loped down to the water's edge. Actually, he was glad to swim alone. He rarely had the luxury of spending time apart from the other boys and valued his private moments, when he felt at ease in the world. Though his fierce pride and natural athletic ability had earned him the respect of his peers, he always felt removed from them in a subtle way. They felt it. He felt it. No one spoke of it, but the feeling was always there.

Changeling blood ran in his veins. Because of his golden brown eyes, he had been marked by the chief Druid, who had come for him to take him for training when he was five years old. But his father, Brennan, had insisted that his only son carry on the warrior tradition of his family and take up the battle axe instead of the sacred sickle. The priesthood was no place for the son of Brennan. A year later, Alek's pale blond hair had started to darken, and the lies had begun.

Alek stood on the river's edge and removed his ankle-length leather boots. He glanced at the wide expanse of the Po River, which separated the Senone land from that of the Romans. All he could see on the other side was the wide bank of trees that bordered the river. But beyond the trees lay a patchwork of fields and vineyards tilled by the Roman farmers, who paid heavy taxes to support the legions that patrolled the borders and pushed farther and farther north and west, occupying and then ruling land once belonging to the brothers of the Senones. Alek unfastened the ornate brass buckle of his belt and frowned at the thought of the Romans, knowing he would fight them, as his father had fought them and his father before him. Yet the Romans kept coming, hungry for the resources of the north—gold, tin, iron, copper, and the land, always the land, for the soil around Rome was notoriously poor and could not feed the growing population of the south.

Alek slipped out of his breeches and dropped them on the sandy bank. He looked down at his chest, inspecting the surface of his skin as he had begun to check himself for the past few months. Already he was growing body hair far darker than the rest of the boys, more damning evidence of the curse of his changeling blood which his father had tried for so long to conceal. Every dark hair was plucked from beneath his arms. He would have to do the same when he began to grow hair on his chest—a chest that was more golden than the ruddy, sunburned color of the rest of his people, whose fair skin took the summer sun in a far different manner than his own.

Alek could do nothing about his skin, but his hair was another matter. In fact, he would take care not to get his head wet in the river, so the lime would remain to whiten the natural color of his hair. He sighed, knowing he would be a prisoner of his father's lies for the rest of his life. He would never know the feeling of true pride in his appearance, even though he was one of the strongest, most finely made boys his age, because he knew he would never attain the ideal of the Gaul male like his father—a towering, fair-haired, white-skinned, blue-eyed man with a huge drooping mustache and wild hair.

He waded out until the water lapped at his waist, tugging at him with cool, refreshing fingers. Alek leaned forward onto his stomach and let the current take him as he slowly stroked his arms. The water felt heavenly. He drifted nearly a half a mile before he headed for shore and swam across a wide, still pool that was deep and green.

Just as he neared the shore, he was startled to hear a man call his mother's name. Alek didn't recognize the voice. Curious, he swam to the shallows and rose out of the water, unconcerned with his nakedness. He waded to the sand and listened, and a sudden flush coursed through him. Off to the left, he heard the unmistakable sounds of coupling—the heavy breathing of a man and the muffled moans of a woman. His mother?

What was going on? And who was with his mother? Helin often walked great distances to offer her healing skills to the sick and injured, and served both her own people and the Roman farmers, even though Brennan tried to keep her close to the hearth. When it came to the infirm, Helin seemed to be blind to tribal loyalty and politics, which Alek found difficult to understand. He often asked her why she would go to such great lengths to heal a boy who might someday grow up to carry the Roman standard. His mother always replied in her gentle but assured way that had the sick boy been Alek, she would hope a Roman healer would give him similar aid. People were people, and the sooner the men learned that fact and ceased their wars, the sooner the world could turn its attention to more important affairs. In her own small way Helin tried to do her part to heal the scars between people, not inflict them, and she would continue to do so until she ceased to live.

Alek, immersed in stories of battle and the ways of men since the day he had left his mother's hearth, could not understand her world view. Neither could his father, and Brennan had punished her several times when she had defied him by answering a Roman plea for help. In this single aspect Alek sided with his father in wishing she would stay close to home and tend only the Senones. Though Helin refused to listen to Brennan or him, Alek would never have considered her actions worthy of punishment. But Brennan punished her often, vowing to beat some sense into her.

As soon as Helin recovered from the blows, she could once again be found working among her people or walking the road from Ballachulix to the river, where a boat would be waiting to take her to the other side. Usually she travelled in the company of a family member of the afflicted. But often she returned alone, sometimes late in the evening, after a child had been delivered or a fever had broken. So far her reputation and undaunted soul seemed to have protected her from harm on her journeys, both from men and the evil spirits that lurked in the darkness. But had her safe passage been blocked this time? Had she been set upon by a man and dragged into the bushes?

Alek bolted forward, hoping he wasn't too late to save her from being raped. But by the sounds he heard coming from the nearby glade, he was afraid she was already being assaulted.

He stopped for an instant to peer through the curtain of shrubs to survey the activity beyond. To his horror, he could see a man lying over the half-dressed body of his mother, his hips between her legs and his hands imprisoning her wrists near her head. One glance at his cropped hair and his short tunic told Alek the man was a Roman. *A Roman dog.* His mother's gown was hiked up around her waist and her braid had come unbound. She wasn't struggling, but then she probably wouldn't, because Helin had learned long ago that to struggle against the overwhelming strength of a man was a useless endeavor that would only beget more violence should she try to lash out. The man had ceased rutting and sank down on Helin, and Alek surmised his lust had just been slaked.

Bile rose in his throat, which gurgled up to a battle cry. Alek burst from the bushes, unarmed, naked and furious, yelling at the top of his lungs as all warriors roared when they rushed into battle.

The Roman turned in surprise and scrambled to his hands and knees just as Alek launched himself onto the man's back. Weak from having spent himself on Helin, the man crumbled beneath the impact of Alek's body, and rolled with him on the ground, each struggling for a death grip.

Alek was strong and an accomplished wrestler, but he was no match for the older man. He should have thought of a weapon—a rock, a branch, anything—but his rage had clouded his sense, and all he could think about was killing the Roman dog who had raped his mother.

He struggled, but the older man flipped him onto his back, pinning his legs with his lower body and his arms with large tan hands. For an instant Alek glared into the face of the man who had taken his mother and saw a strong long face, dark eyes, brown hair, and a sharply ridged nose much different from the blunt noses of the men of his tribe.

Alek spit in his face.

"Why you—" the Roman exclaimed, digging his fingers into the flesh of Alek's forearms.

"Son of a pig!" Alek retorted, refusing to acknowledge the agony in his arms.

"Spare him!" his mother cried, rising to her feet. "Please spare him!"

Alek didn't know to whom she was talking—to him or to the Roman. If she was entreating the Roman, she spoke as if the man had already vanquished Alek, which was far from the truth. He wouldn't go down so easily. As far as fighting went, he was his father's son, through and through.

He raised up and bit the man's forearm as hard as he could. In the instant the man flinched from the pain, Alek twisted, pulling up one leg, which he kneed into the Roman's groin. The older man gasped and let go of Alek's wrists. Although the Roman had the heavy power of a mature adult, Alek possessed the slender quickness of youth. He wiggled free and rolled away, jumping to his feet in a single movement. His heel banged against something that sent a metallic noise ringing through the clearing. Alek glanced down and spied a sheathed sword.

He swooped up the scabbard and pulled out the short pointed blade of Roman design, heavy in his hand, made for a full-grown man. It was no mere ornamental weapon, but the sword of a soldier, with a deadly tip and sturdy hilt. He raised the sword and felt a tightening in his loins. A sharp and sudden erection raised his shaft, just as he had seen happen to the Senone warriors as they plunged naked into battle. The jutting proof of his manhood fired his blood.

"You die, Roman dog!" Alek swore, lunging for the man.

"Alek!" Helin screamed.

To Alek's astonishment, he saw his mother take a stand between him and the Roman. She threw out her arms as if to shield the older man and keep her son from locking in mortal combat at the same time. Her action flabbergasted Alek.

"Out of my way, Mother!" he yelled, almost desperate now for a fight.

"No, Alek! Don't!"

Blood burned in his eyes, darkening his vision. Why was she doing this? Was this another way to heal the wounds between people? How much violence could she take from men and still allow them to live? He could never understand the way she stayed his hand and calmed him after his father had beaten her or him. And now this. Why would she forever keep him from defending her?

"I don't want you to fight!" she shouted. "Alek!"

The Roman stepped from behind his mother. Alek got his first good view of the man's tall, broad-shouldered physique and long, strong legs, and realized he would lose at hand-to-hand combat with him. Yet he stood his ground, not about to listen to his mother this time. He gripped his fingers more tightly around the hilt of the sword.

To his astonishment, the Roman lifted both hands from his sides, as if in supplication.

"Alek," he said, "I, Caius Sellenius, surrender to you."

Alek blinked in disbelief. Caius Sellenius? Every Senone youth had heard of Caius Sellenius, governor of Umbria. What was the governor doing on the wrong side of the Po?

The Roman dropped to one knee. Was this some kind of trick?

"Alek, accept his surrender. His men are about and will soon be back. They will find us."

"I am not afraid of the Roman pigs!" Alek exclaimed, feeling brave. He stepped closer. "I will take this dog to Ballachulix and hang his head above your door."

"No, Alek. You must let him go. And in return, one day he will grant you a similar favor."

"I want no favors from the likes of him."

Caius rose. "Your mother speaks wisely, Alek. I surrender to you privately, but I will not be taken to your father's place. The pride of a Roman soldier equals that of a Gaul, and I will kill you to defend it, though you are but a boy."

"He is not jesting, Alek."

"But this man—"

"Alek, I beg you. Leave him be."

Confused and angry, Alek glared at his mother and then at the tanned face of Caius Sellenius. He knew he didn't possess the strength to kill the Roman—though he certainly had the heart to try—but he was smart enough to predict the outcome. So what should he do? Alek stared at Caius, directly into the man's eyes, which were baffling in their unwavering intensity—not the type of gaze he expected in a man who had just raped a woman. Even his father had a hooded, guarded look in his eyes after inflicting himself upon Helin. Alek's resolve faltered.

"I will let you go this time, Roman cur," he spat. "But when I am a man, I will come for you. And you will pay for doing this to my mother."

Caius shot a brief glance at his mother—a look that bore nothing of the derisive cruelty he had seen in the eyes of his father—and for a brief moment Alek felt a twinge of unease, as if some instinct told him he might have stumbled onto something here in the glade that was other than it appeared.

The instant the thought entered his head, he dismissed it.

"Go, Caius Sellenius," he ordered. He reached down and threw the man's scarlet cloak at the Roman's feet. "Before I change my mind."

Caius did not reach down for the cloak.

"Give him the sword, Alek," Helin said.

"No, Mother. The sword is mine."

Helin stepped closer and touched his arm. "My son, you have no need of a Roman weapon."

"This weapon will kill that man one day." He looked back up at Caius. "I said go, Roman pig!"

Caius paused a moment at the edge of the clearing, glanced again at Helin, and then turned and loped away. Alek felt his mother wilt beside him. He draped an arm around her shoulders.

"Mother, are you all right? Did he hurt you?"

"No, Alek. He didn't hurt me."

"Why didn't you let me kill him?"

She turned in his arm and put her soft hand on his cheek. "Dear Alek, don't you know why?"

"No."

"You are too young. But when you are older, you will know. And you will be ready to act upon your age and your knowledge."

"I am old enough now."

"No, my son. You are yet too young. But soon you will be a man. And then"—she stroked the side of his face—"then you will be my champion."

He gazed down at her as her words warmed him. She embraced him, her womanly scent laced with the herbs of her profession and the smell of the man who had taken her to the ground. Though the male scent repulsed him, the woman scent did not, and he hugged her fiercely, wishing he were five years older and strong enough to slaughter the bastards who dishonored her.

Five years. Five years and he would raise his hand to any and all who dared touch his mother in violence.

"We must bury the sword," she whispered in his ear.

"Why?"

"Brennan must not learn of this incident. He will seek revenge before our people have recovered from the last war. We will only fall under the hand of the Romans if we move against them now."

Helin was right. If Brennan heard the tale of what had transpired in this glade with his sworn enemy, he would fly into a rage, whip his comrades into a frenzy of blood lust, and go on a rampage. The Senones could not bear to lose more men than they had already, not until the younger men rose up to fill the ranks. Five years and their numbers would swell. Five years and Alek would be old enough to thunder into battle with the rest of them.

"Bury the sword, Alek," she repeated. "And when you are a man, you can return to this place and take it up."

He nodded. Her plan had merit.

She pulled out of his arms and stepped back, wrapping the braid upon her head and repinning it. "I will leave you to your task," she said. "Brennan will want his evening meal soon."

"Yes, Mother."

She hesitated and then touched his cheek again. "You were very brave today, Alek. But most of all, you were very wise. Remember to be wise, my son, when the blood lust comes upon you. There are times when wisdom is far more powerful than the sword."

Once again her philosophy ran in complete opposition to that of his father's instruction, which was, in essence, strike first and to the brave belongs everything. But he was enough of his mother's son to listen to her blasphemy and actually consider it.

He still had trouble figuring out his mother's role in what had just transpired. For a woman who had just been raped, she seemed amazingly contained. And yet his mother had vast reserves of patience and forbearance, and a rather accepting fatalistic view of the world.

"Farewell, Alek," she called.

"I will catch up with you soon," he answered. Then he turned to the task of burying the sword and scabbard, which he wrapped in the discarded red cloak, his thoughts flying as he searched for a suitable place to hide the blade. Soon he would be old enough. And then he would avenge his mother against Caius Sellenius.

8

Diana waited until she saw the shadowplay of leaves and branches from the car headlights on the living room wall, signaling the approach of Kyle's car in the drive. Wearily, she rose from the sofa and retied her robe belt, wishing Kyle wouldn't bring the brute back to the house. She hadn't felt safe since the warrior had been imprisoned in the cellar three days ago.

Softly she walked through the house toward the cellar door, hoping to catch a glimpse of David before he retired for the night, or perhaps even exchange a few words with him. She heard two car doors slam at the side of the house and then was surprised to hear the front door open. Though it was well past midnight and most of the neighborhood was asleep, Diana was shocked that Kyle would bring the brute through the front entry.

Hurriedly, Diana retraced her steps and met the two men just as they were taking off their coats in the foyer.

"Where is he?" Diana asked, surprised to find them empty-handed once again.

"He ran off." Kyle whipped off his gloves and unbuttoned his coat with short angry movements. "Just my luck."

Diana glanced at David, who nodded slightly and regarded Diana with a gaze that seemed to wash over her, from her blond hair to her delicate satin mules. Kyle never looked at her the way David did. Kyle's glance was direct and hard, which made her feel as if she were a placeholder in his beautiful home—simply a part of the furnishings like the grand piano or the Louis XIV etagere in the corner—or a social asset to display at public functions. Once she had mistaken his hardness for discerning intelligence, but now she knew him for what he was—a cold, emotionless man who was driven by the lust to succeed. He was intelligent, no doubt about it, but his calculating mind was a poor substitute for a warm heart. He funneled all his energy and time into his research and rarely spoke more than two sentences to her when he came home late at night. Once Diana had yearned for a soothing touch or one word of love from him, but now she shrank from his slightest sexual overture.

Diana suddenly realized that she had lapsed into silence and was standing there gazing up at David's face.

"Good God," Kyle remarked, looking at his watch. "It's three o'clock in the morning. And I have to lecture at that seminar tomorrow morning."

"You'd better get to bed," David ventured, breaking eye contact. "I'll make sure the house is secure and then turn in."

"How about a nightcap," Diana put in. "Or a cup of tea?"

"None for me," Kyle replied, walking past her.

"How about you, David?" she asked, longing for a few moments alone with him. "I have some chamomile tea. It's very calming."

"All right."

"Good."

David unzipped his parka and shrugged it off, placing it in Diana's outstretched hand. The coat still held the warmth of his body. Diana hugged it to her chest as she turned to carry it to the coat closet under the stairs, and closed her eyes as David's musky male scent drifted up to her face.

Kyle hung up his coat and then turned. "Don't stay up too long, Diana," he warned. "You know how tired you'll be tomorrow."

"I won't."

"Goodnight, David."

"Goodnight, Kyle."

Kyle shot Diana a dark look full of meaning. She never should have offered tea to David and she had better not do anything even remotely suspicious with another man. Diana broke eye contact and was thankful for David's tall form standing behind her as she watched Kyle march up the stairs. She liked the way David stood beside her, almost as if he were guarding her. Kyle was not a demonstrative person and rarely invaded her personal space, as if he were put off by her in some way, or as if she had failed to live up to his exacting standards. She had spent so long aching for a simple human touch that now her skin felt as if it were crying out to be caressed by David's hands.

She drew in a long, resolute breath in an effort to dispel her dangerous thoughts. To allow David to touch her again would be far too hazardous. Yet she could hardly think of anything but being touched by him when he was in the house with her. For the past few months she had spent a great deal of time fantasizing about him, an occupation she knew was futile and destructive.

Their one brief night together a year ago had

destroyed her equanimity and peace of mind. She had not only violated the most sacred of vows, she had placed David in jeopardy. If Kyle ever found out about their brief affair, he would kill David, Diana was sure of it. Though Kyle wouldn't be caught with blood on his hands, he would arrange for tragedy to befall David, just as something had happened to the graduate student who had fallen in love with his professor's wife a few years before. Though nothing had come of the infatuation, for Diana had not been interested, Kyle was convinced the student had compromised her. The young man was found dead one morning from an overdose of drugs. Murder had never been suspected in the case, and no one ever questioned Kyle Woodward's part in the death—no one but Diana. The incident was her first inkling of her husband's dark side, which he cleverly hid from the rest of the world. Diana alone knew that Kyle was capable of deep-seated, unfounded jealousy, single-minded obsession, and cold-blooded murder.

Not only was infidelity out of the question, she was not in a position to invite the advances of any man because of her ailing health. It would be unfair to start a relationship knowing the affair would be short-lived and full of grief. There was too much at stake to flee to the comfort of David's arms, no matter how glorious their time together had been.

"Did you say you wanted tea or a nightcap?"

"Tea would be fine, Diana."

She nodded and walked down the hall to the kitchen, marvelling that she was alone with David. Though Kyle was an absent and unaffectionate husband, he was jealous of his young wife and rarely left her alone with men, especially David, who at thirty-one was much closer to her age.

David sat on a stool at the counter while Diana

filled the tea kettle and put it on the stove to boil. Then she turned and slipped her hands in the pockets of her luxurious terry robe, conscious of her casual appearance in his presence. She wore only a filmy nightgown beneath the robe, a flimsy barrier between her body and the nubby fabric of the robe, which was having an unusual effect on her breasts as she breathed. With each breath the fabric advanced and retreated over her nipples, making her more and more aroused.

"Do you think—do you think Marissa's call was just a false alarm?" she asked, in an effort to break the silence.

"No." David took off his glasses and massaged the bridge of his nose. Though he appeared at first as gentle and slight, he had wide shoulders, which were accentuated by the dark green sweater he wore, and long capable hands that she could almost imagine cupping her elbows or stroking her back. "I think the brute must have run off between the time Marissa called and the time we got there. She was pretty upset."

"I wouldn't blame her, having been carried off by him. Did he hurt her?"

"I don't think so. She would have said something, I'm sure."

"Thank God he didn't harm her. But how long before he does hurt someone?" Diana sighed and reached for a cannister of tea, in which she dipped two tea diffusers. "Kyle never should have performed that ritual. Look what's come of it."

"I know. And I got him interested in the Druids in the first place. I feel responsible."

"Don't be." Diana handed him a cup and saucer of tea while she sat down across the counter from him. "You couldn't have predicted his obsession with the subject. You couldn't have known."

"Still—" David broke off and scooped three spoons of sugar into his tea as Diana watched in alarm.

"David, you shouldn't eat that much sugar," she commented, worried about his health.

"I like sweetened tea. It takes the edge off."

"But it isn't good for you."

"I know." David lifted his cup and let the steam rise up between them. "But sometimes I do things that aren't good for me, simply because I want to." He took a sip and smiled at her. "And I'd do it again."

Her hand trembled slightly as she drank her tea and considered the underlying meaning of his words. "Doesn't your conscience bother you?"

"Not when something is right. And I know when it's right."

She blinked and glanced at his face, a fluttering glance that became entangled in the warmth of his eyes. She rarely saw him without his glasses and was surprised at the kindness and color she found there. Flecks of green and gold were sprinkled across his light brown irises, sparkling with the echo of his soft smile. In the diffused light of the kitchen, the planes beneath his eyes and on his forehead were highlighted in gold and bronze, which heightened the whiteness of his teeth.

"David, you don't know everything about the situation," she replied, overwhelmed by the sudden intimacy of his face and his words. "I've tried to tell you that, but you just won't listen."

"Why should I? I can see how he treats you. And it tears me up."

She stared at him, quite at a loss and almost feverishly distracted, and then looked down. "It isn't just Kyle."

She gazed at her hands, draped around the edges of the delicate saucer like the hands of a ballerina offering up the moon, and in the periphery of her vision she saw the curl of his fingers so close to hers. If she could only reach out and touch him. If he would only open his hand and slide it the few inches to hers and touch her, she wouldn't move away. She would just sit there and savor the moment and be grateful for that small gesture of friendship. She was starving. Couldn't he tell? She dared not look up at him, afraid that her hunger would flare in her eyes and he would see what strong dishonorable thoughts she harbored.

"Diana," he said lowly. "I know there's something wrong with you, something deep and sad. Why can't you tell me about it?"

She swallowed back a huge lump of sorrow and didn't reply or look at him.

"I'm your friend, Diana."

"I know." She traced the edge of the saucer with her pale fingernail. "I'm just not ready to talk about it yet."

"Then tell me why you won't leave Kyle. I know you don't love him."

She looked up at his face and found him gazing at her with an open expression of concern and interest, both of which were strangers to her. This time he didn't glance away as he usually did when she met his gaze. This time his warm eyes bore into hers as if he, too, suffered from an intense hunger and was trying to communicate his need through his eyes alone.

"Diana, what we had together that night—"

She jumped to her feet to interrupt him, afraid of what he might say and what she might blurt out in return.

"Would you like more tea? I've got raspberry." She tried to smile at him, but her mouth dragged down at the corners. "Cinnamon Spice?"

"No, thanks." With a sigh, David rose from his stool. He picked up his glasses and placed them on the bridge of his nose in a careful, calm gesture that would have been foreign to Kyle.

Diana watched him, wishing he would stay, wishing she could ask him to drink another cup and keep her company. But to ask would involve more questions that she couldn't answer right now.

David slowly walked around the end of the counter and came to a stop at the entrance of the U-shaped kitchen, where he leaned his right shoulder on the wall and crossed his arms. Though his stance was casual, there was no way to leave the kitchen without passing very close to him. He had, for all intents and purposes, trapped her there.

"Diana, try to look at the situation without giving it mythological significance."

"What do you mean?" She raised her chin slightly.

"I've read your books. I know your world view. People are tested and then damned or exalted, according to their honor or feats of strength." He sighed. "But this isn't mythology we're living here. This is real life. We're two human beings, Diana, who are caught in a situation that could be altered to benefit all those concerned."

"But what we did was wrong, David."

"No it wasn't, dammit!" He glared at her. "It was the best thing that ever happened to either of us. And if you'd quit flailing yourself over it and choose to use it as a catharsis for change instead of reproach, we might fashion a life for ourselves."

"Please, David, try to understand—"

"I understand," he retorted. "Diana, I love you. I would run away with you at a moment's notice. I would give up everything for you. What has grown between us isn't wrong. It's the most precious thing on earth."

She looked down, unable to say anything more because of the lump lodged in her throat. The urge to throw herself into his arms was so strong, she felt as if she might scream. She had to get away from him. She couldn't keep up this pretense of conversation much longer. Yet there he stood, blocking her exit. Much to her dismay, she felt a hot tear slide out of her eye and down her cheek.

"That we acted upon our feelings for each other doesn't make us criminals. It makes us human." He sighed again. "We're meant for each other, Diana."

"But the timing is all wrong. Maybe in another life, we—"

"I don't want you in another life," he replied, reaching out for her. "I want you now. In this life, Diana, this world."

"David," she cried. "It just isn't possible!"

"Anything's possible, love." He gathered her into his arms and pulled her to his chest. Diana let herself be surrounded by his height and warmth, surrendering her frailty to his strength. She couldn't believe how David's arms made her feel, and the instant he embraced her, she lost control. From the inside out, she fractured into a weeping, trembling wraith who clung to his sweater as if it were a lifeline. She pressed her cheek against his heart while tears rolled down her face and she shuddered at the release of years of need and denial. The mere touch of him crumbled the walls she had so carefully built up around her, and as she felt each falling stone she worried that once the ramparts lay in ruins, there would be nothing left of her. Yet she could still feel David. He was there, holding her, listening to her grief.

"Ah, sweet," he whispered into her hair. "Diana—"

The warm words upon her skin made her heart break in anguish. She slid her hands up around his neck and hugged him with every ounce of her strength, trying to show him how she felt without having to enclose her heart's desire in the trappings of inadequate words.

"Why can't we spend the rest of our lives together, Diana?" he asked, stroking her hair. "Why?"

"It's not that I don't want to." She squeezed him tightly and tucked her nose in the warm space just below his ear. "You don't know how much you mean to me—"

She broke off and squeezed her eyelids shut, damning herself for letting the words slip out. How could she be foolish enough to reveal her feelings, when the outcome would be damaging for her, Kyle, and David. She had to get control of herself.

"How much?" David inquired, cocking his head to try to see her face.

"Too much." Diana shook her head. "I'm sorry." She drew away, swallowing back her desire for this man, and stepped out of his arms. She glanced up at him, her eyes burning. "But I shouldn't be here like this with you. If Kyle should catch us, he'd kill you."

"Kyle doesn't scare me."

"He should."

"I want to know why you stay with him, why you put me off." He lay his right hand along her jaw and tilted up her face. "Be frank with me, Diana."

"I can't. If I told you what I was thinking, then you would know how I feel. And I couldn't pretend anymore that my life is all it should be, that I am all I should be."

"Aren't you?"

"No."

"And do you like pretending that your life is what you prefer?"

"No, but it's something I have to do."

"Why?"

"Because I'm a married woman. I gave a vow. I—"

"I'm not asking you to break your vows. I'm just asking you to be honest. For God's sake, Diana, anyone can see that something is eating away at you."

Eating away at her. Diana blanched. What did he mean? Was he talking about her emotional well-being or her physical health? Could he see that far into her? Could he see that something was eating away at her soul while it wove its cobweb of corruption throughout her body?

"I want to help you, Diana. But I won't force you to level with me, not if you don't want to." He released her chin and sighed as he gazed down at her.

"I can't, David."

"Why?"

"Because there are things about me that I don't want you to know."

"Why?"

"They're not good things. And I"—she took a deep shuddering breath—"I simply have to endure my life the way it is, for just a bit longer."

"And then what?"

"Then I will be free."

"How long will this hiatus of yours be?"

"Four months," Diana replied lowly. "Maybe six."

"That isn't such a long time." His tone was full of encouragement.

She looked at the wall behind him while the familiar but frightening black pall rose up from the shadows and came forward to consume even this brief bittersweet happiness with David. "No, it isn't a long time." Her voice was flat.

"After this hiatus, will you be able to tell me what's going on?"

"I'm not certain."

David reached out and grasped her left hand, which

he slowly raised. Diana watched in fascinated alarm as he turned over her hand, bent his head, and kissed her palm.

Starbursts of pleasure exploded in her arm and chest.

David lifted his head but didn't release her. "When you are ready to talk, I hope you will come to me."

She nodded, pressing her lips together to keep from breaking into tears again.

"Diana, there is something about you that I recognize and understand, as if we were old friends." He squeezed her fingers. "It's something I've felt with very few people, something that is precious and fine. And I believe you feel it too, don't you?"

She nodded again.

"It would be a shame to deny that rare knowledge. It's something beyond love, something that shouldn't be wasted." He lowered her hand and gently released it. "So when you arrive at a decision about your life, please let me know, will you?"

"Yes."

"I will always be here for you, Diana."

"I know," she finally replied. "And it means the world to me."

He kissed her on the lips, pulling her into his arms before she could protest, and then broke off before the kiss became too torturous.

"I'll let myself out," he murmured.

"All right. Goodnight, David."

"Goodnight."

She remained standing near the counter, staring at the empty tea cups, unable to watch him leave. A thousand conflicting emotions tore through her—bliss that he confessed his feelings for her, ecstasy that she had known the pleasure of his arms and the touch of his mouth again, and devastation that she must never allow herself or David to go any farther. After sharing these stolen moments with him, her task of denial would be much more difficult, almost impossible. But she would be strong. She would simply avoid him from now on and purge him from her thoughts. She could do it.

But even as she reached for the tea cups, she remembered the look of concern in his eyes and the way he had said he understood her. She had never felt understood, not until this man had stepped into her life. He was correct in his theory about knowing her already. She felt exactly the same way—that she had known David before and loved him deeply.

If she loved him as much as she claimed, she would protect his life by never again being alone with him.

Alek awoke much later than usual—long after dawn—with the vision of Caius Sellenius still fresh in his mind. He felt the familiar burn in his gut along with a sharp twisting of hunger. He was starving. It had been hours since he had last eaten. Frowning, Alek rose and glanced at the woman in the bed, whose blankets twisted around her long slender body, adding to his hunger.

Alek's frown sank deeper. How long would the she-devil sleep? And when she awoke and fixed her morning meal, would she demand that he eat with her? He would rather find his own food than sit down with a woman. But in this strange world, none of the plants bore any recognizable fruit, and most were only just flowering. Neither had he seen any small animals which he could kill with a well-thrown rock. Perhaps the woman kept grains or bread somewhere in the room with the cooking box. What had she called it—an oven? He'd go there and see what he could find before the she-devil woke up.

Alek stretched and idly scratched his chest as he ambled into the kitchen. After three days locked in the bottom of Doctor-Wood-Ward's house, he felt dirty and itchy and wished he could get his hands on a jug of water and some clean clothes. Perhaps he'd have to return to the nearby lake to bathe. No wonder the woman called him a brute. He probably smelled like a bear.

Alek plundered the shelves with doors on them, pulling out strange paper boxes and cylindrical bottles fashioned of a smooth gray metal that he didn't recognize. The most curious thing about the bottles was their lack of lids. How did one put items into the bottles or take them out when they were so tightly sealed?

In a drawer, Alek found a loaf of bread, sliced in thin wobbly pieces. Though the bread hardly looked substantial, he stuffed half a piece into his mouth, marvelling that bread could taste so bland. Then he searched through the other drawers while he chewed the rest of the slice. What he found was either hard or dry or in the strange lidless cylinders. Where was the meat?

Just as he was turning to check the other side of the kitchen, he heard a step in the hall behind him.

9

"*What are* you *doing here?*" Marissa demanded from the kitchen doorway. "How did you get in?"

Alek fished for the set of keys in his pouch and held
them up.

Marissa couldn't believe it. The man had stolen her
keys and let himself back into the apartment after Dr.
Woodward had left. How long had he been in the house
without her knowing?

"Give those to me!" She lunged for the key ring, but
Alek snatched it away in another display of his unusual
agility. He gazed down at her, while his chin remained
slightly raised in a pose both savage and haughty, which
accentuated the sharp ridge of his nose.

"Make me food, she-devil. Then I will give you the
keys."

"I'm not going to bargain with you, you—"

"Make some food!" He took a threatening step forward and just about raised his hand. She saw the movement and the quick snap of restraint as his arm tensed

and then relaxed. He had thought of striking her but had brought himself under control. What did it mean? Was he a threat? Or was she relatively safe in his presence? Marissa hesitated, not about to underestimate his propensity for violence. Though it irked her to concede to his demands, she thought it prudent not to test him further until she came up with a plan of escape.

"Okay, all right!" She scowled at him. "What do you want?"

"You choose."

"An omelet."

"Omelet?" he questioned sharply.

"Eggs, cheese, that sort of thing."

He nodded curtly, still as haughty as hell with his head thrown back and his proud, full mouth surrounded by the dark stubble of his beard. He stood there watching her as she banged around the kitchen, swearing under her breath at the unfamiliar surrounds and situation and the fact that a man was observing her every fumbling move. She had never made an omelet in her life and found the task more difficult than she expected. What she finally put on the table in front of the ultimate warrior was more scrambled eggs than omelet.

The toast was cold before she had time to butter it, and she forgot to make juice until the eggs were done. She frowned as she poured a tardy glass of orange juice and set it on the table. Not that she wanted to please Alek with her culinary skills, she simply didn't like doing a job unless she performed it with efficiency and competence. Much to her surprise, she had discovered there was just as much timing involved in breakfast preparation as there was in roping calves.

Alek didn't seem to mind the cold toast and the jumble of crusty eggs and scorched cheese. He shoveled the food into his mouth using the edge of a slice of toast and the tip of his dagger, barely taking the time to chew. Marissa stood to one side, watching him as she sipped her coffee and wondering where he had learned his manners, or lack thereof. But what did she care how quickly or crudely he ate? The sooner he finished, the sooner she could get him out of her life and begin her search for Leslie.

He reached for the glass of orange juice and held it up, while his eyebrows came together over the high bridge of his nose.

"What is this?" he asked.

"Orange juice."

He rotated the glass in his big hand as he inspected it closely.

"It isn't poison. It's good for you. Try it."

He flashed a sharp glance at her and then took a cautious sip of the orange liquid. His head jerked back slightly, probably from the unusual sensation of acidity. Then he tried another sip. In the next moment, he drained the glass.

"You like it?" she asked.

"Yes. It is good. Is it wine?"

"No," she replied, half smiling. "It's a drink made from oranges, a citrus fruit."

"Ah." He set down the glass. "The omelet was good."

She decided not to mention that she had destroyed any semblance to an omelet and had practically ruined the eggs.

"You make more?" he handed his plate to her. "I am still hungry."

He had just eaten five eggs and two pieces of toast with butter and jam. And he wanted more?

She took the plate. "All right. I'll make you more of the same."

"Good."

This time she used more margarine in the pan and managed to fold the egg into a pocket over the cheese. She was very proud of her efforts as she slid the omelet onto his plate and put it in front of him. Just as she finished with the egg, the toast popped up. She buttered it and placed it beside the egg. She might get the hang of this cooking business after all, once she did it a few more times.

Alek ate his second helping more slowly, with much more restraint, and she wondered how long it had been since he had eaten a meal.

"Why don't you use the fork?" she asked. "It's a lot easier to eat egg with a fork."

"This?" he replied, pointing at the fork near his plate.

"Yes."

"We don't have these in my land."

"And just where exactly is your land?"

"I told you. In Venetia, north of the Po River." He picked up the fork and weighed it in his hand, obviously unsure of how to hold it.

"Here," she snatched it out of his grip and curled her fingers around the handle. "Like this." She sliced off a wedge of the egg with the edge of the fork, stabbed it, and raised it up to her mouth. "See?"

"Ah."

She glanced at him and flushed when she noticed the amused look in his eyes and realized she had moved far too close to him for comfort.

"You eat it," he said.

"No. No thanks."

Before she could back away, however, he caught her wrist and raised her hand to his lips. His long tan fingers easily enveloped her fist, making her feel more defenseless than ever. He drew the egg off the tines of the fork with his strong white teeth and grinned a self-satisfied smirk at her, as though he were well aware of her disquiet in his presence.

"You speak of the Romans." She slipped her hand out of his grip. "Do they live near your land?"

"Rome is to the south and west. But the Roman dogs are everywhere, trying to drive us out." He raised his glass. "Do you have more of the orange juice?"

"Yes." She took the glass and refilled it.

"Thank you."

She was momentarily taken aback by his words of gratitude. For some reason she hadn't expected the brute to exhibit a shred of civilized behavior. Puzzled, she reached for her coffee cup and took a big gulp, wondering if she was underestimating him in other ways as well. She put her cup on the table and sat down across from him, unconcerned that he might object.

"Since you've come back here, he-man, you must have a plan."

"Yes. Today I will go to Doctor-Wood-Ward and get answers from him."

"Answers to what?"

"Where I am. What he did to me. How I can go back."

"Back to where?"

"To my people, the Senones." He tore off a piece of toast. "I must return to them as soon as possible."

"What does Dr. Woodward have to do with it?"

"He is a magician, a sorcerer. He has brought me here."

"What are you talking about?"

"Doctor-Wood-Ward has put a spell on me. He took me from the sacred grove of my people and brought me into this Otherworld."

"This isn't an Otherworld. This is Seattle, part of the good old U.S. of A."

"U.S. Ovay?" He put down the juice. "I have not heard of such a place."

"Then Dr. Woodward isn't your uncle?"

"I have told you that before, woman."

She inspected him over the rim of her cup, still uncertain what to make of the creature across from her. He was so outlandishly different that she almost believed him.

He finished his egg and sat back with a sigh. "That has satisfied me," he stated, planting both hands on his thighs. Then, as if in afterthought, he pulled the keys from his leather pouch and tossed them on the table. His willingness to remain true to his bargain surprised her.

Startled by his show of honor, Marissa lapsed into her usual sarcasm. "One thing I can say for you, Mr. Universe, you sure can put away the chow."

He raised his head and glared at her. "Why do you call me everything but my name?"

"Why? Habit, I guess." She shrugged. "I give everyone nicknames."

"I do not like these nicknames."

"Well, I don't particularly like being called she-devil either." She stared at him, flushing again at the realization that she *did* like the name. No one had ever called her she-devil before, and she felt as if the name suited her in a way that wasn't derogatory or degrading, especially when Alek said the phrase, as if in admiration.

"I call you she-devil because I do not know your name."

"Maybe I don't want you to know my name." She rose to her feet. "Maybe I don't even want you here. Can that concept get through your thick skull, Conan?"

"Conan? Mr. Universe?" He jumped to his feet, knocking over the chair behind him, and thumped his chest. "I am Alek, a free man, champion of the Senones! Alek!" He slammed his fist down upon the table again, rattling the dishes. "You will call me that and nothing else!"

She set her jaw. Violence was not the way to persuade her to do anything. In fact, he had just rung the death knell on his own request. If he had asked her politely to call him by his first name, she might have complied. But after this display of force, she would sooner eat barbed wire with a chaser of battery acid than call him by his real name.

"Like hell I will," she countered. "No one orders me around! Not even you! You got that?" Before he could answer, she whirled around and stomped out of the kitchen. Of all the obnoxious macho men, he had to be the one to land in her backyard. Well, he wouldn't be there for long. Dr. Woodward's family be damned. She was calling the police, and she was calling them now.

She stormed to Leslie's bedroom and snatched up the telephone receiver. She dialed 911 and waited for the connection to be made as Alek burst into the room. Marissa looked over her shoulder at him as she held the phone to her ear.

"What are you doing?" he shouted.

"Ordering a pizza—what does it look like?"

The moment the words were out of her mouth, she saw Alek streak across the floor. He grabbed her and spun her around, which yanked the cord of the phone right out of the wall.

"Hey!" she yelled.

"What are you doing?" he demanded again.

"Calling the police, if you must know!"

"The police are in that small place?" Astonished, he eyed the telephone receiver, which she still held in her hand.

"Yes, and they're coming to get you even as we speak."

"You lie, she-devil." He ripped the phone from her hand and tossed it aside. It clanged as it hit the floor. "You are my hostage! You talk to no one!"

"Why you!" she seethed, giving a shove to his immovable bulk. He turned aside slightly, just enough to set her off balance. She fell, landing on the unmade bed, and instantly twisted onto her back, worried that he might take advantage of the moment to physically assault her from behind.

She glanced at Alek to find him staring down at her, his legs straddling her feet, which hung over the side of the bed. A strange smoldering light glittered in his eyes as he boldly regarded her and, for the first time in her life, Marissa was truly afraid. He was not constraining his surveillance to her face, but was inspecting every curve of her figure as she lay below him.

"Don't you even think about it," she warned through gritted teeth, trying to show her usual tough facade.

"Think about what?" Alek retorted, dragging his stare back to her face. "Gagging you again, you jabbering she-devil?"

His humor stunned her. She had expected brute force, assault, lascivious caresses, even rape—but never humor. For an instant she stared at him in complete astonishment. Then she took advantage of the moment to scramble backward.

"You will go to Doctor-Wood-Ward's house with me as my hostage." Alek said. He reached down and grabbed the front of her robe, pulling her upward. "And after I am returned to my people, you can chatter all you want."

"Gee, thanks. I can't wait."

He glared at her, his face very close to hers. "Now we go."

"Gladly. But not with you."

"Do not argue with me, woman!"

"I'm not going with you because it won't do either of us any good." She pulled at the lapels of her robe to straighten them. "Dr. Woodward doesn't like me. He couldn't care less if you hurt me. So that kind of blows the hostage part of it for you."

"Blows?"

"And besides that, I can't waste any more time running around with you." She crawled off the bed, putting the mattress between them. "I have to find my sister, Leslie."

"Leslie?"

"Yes. Leslie. She's missing."

"There is a woman named Leslie at Doctor-Wood-Ward's house."

Marissa jerked to attention. "What?"

"There is a woman at Doctor-Wood-Ward's house. They call her Leslie."

"What does she look like?"

"She has blond hair and is small, like the woman called Diana."

"My God." Slowly, Marissa moved around the end of the bed. "Dr. Woodward has Leslie at his house and he didn't tell me?"

"She's in the bottom of the house. The cellar."

"Where you were?"

"Yes."

"Why?"

"I do not know."

"Have you seen her? Is she all right?"

"I have seen her only once when she was sleeping. Since then I have only heard them speak of her."

"Who speaks of her?"

"Doctor-Wood-Ward and David. They are concerned about her because of the night orchid."

"The night orchid?" Marissa rubbed the back of her neck. "What does that have to do with Leslie?"

"She has drunk of the night orchid, and she has succumbed to it."

"What do you mean, succumbed to it?"

"Your sister has not awakened since the ceremony that brought me to this world. She drank the night orchid nectar and did not wake up."

Marissa stared at him for a moment while his words sank in. Her sister was a prisoner of Dr. Woodward, trapped in his basement, and a victim of some kind of ritual. Had she willingly attended the ritual, or had she been drugged? She had probably been drugged, judging by the report of strange goings on mentioned in her letter. Either way, Dr. Woodward had no right to keep Leslie's whereabouts a secret, especially to her own sister. Yet could she believe the incredible things the warrior was telling her? She sank down upon the edge of the bed, stalling for time so she could think. "What is the night orchid? I've never heard of it."

"I have been told that it is a very rare plant. The nectar of the night orchid is used in special Druid ceremonies. Doctor-Wood-Ward must have found the secret of making the night orchid wine and gave it to Leslie."

"That bastard. I knew I couldn't trust him. I could see it in his eyes."

"Then you will go back to Doctor-Wood-Ward's house with me."

"Yes." She glanced up at him. "But not as your hostage. As your ally—of sorts."

She couldn't believe what had she just said. She was willing to become the ultimate warrior's ally? She must be crazy to go along with this man. Yet she did believe him. There was something about his unwavering gaze, his haughtiness, and his pride that solicited her trust.

"Then we will go now, she-devil."

"Wait a minute." Marissa held up her hand and surveyed him. "If you set one foot outside the apartment looking like that, you'll stick out like a sore thumb. The police will recognize you in a minute and throw you in jail for having assaulted those officers last night."

"So, what can I do?"

"First off—and don't take offense, Conan—you should take a shower."

"Shower?"

"A bath." She rose, suddenly full of energy and ideas, as if her intuition were substantiating her choice to believe in the warrior. "You need to wash that stuff out of your hair and the blood off your chest. And you'll need some different clothes."

"Where will I get clothing?"

"If I'm not mistaken, there's a men's boutique down the street." She hurried over to the window and drew back the curtain. "Yes, right over there."

"What is a boutique?" he asked, coming up behind her.

"A store that sells men's clothing. I could go down there and get you something to wear while you get cleaned up."

"No. You will run off. You will tell Doctor-Wood-Ward that I am here."

"No, I won't." Marissa let the curtain fall and turned to face him. "If Leslie's unconscious, I may need your help in rescuing her." She strode to the hallway. "Come. I'll show you the bathroom."

A half hour later, Marissa returned to the apartment with a bag of clothing. She had never purchased clothes for a man before and had felt silly asking the clerk for help, because she hadn't had the faintest idea what size Alek would take, being that he was so tall. She closed the door, locked it, and carried the bag down the hall to the bathroom, hoping Alek wouldn't refuse to wear what she had purchased. She knew how picky and conservative some men could be, and so far Alek had been the least agreeable man she had ever met.

She would have preferred buying him jeans and a cotton shirt, but the boutique carried a line of clothes comprised mostly of silks, cottons, and rayons in loose-flowing pants and shirts—clothes a self-respecting cowboy wouldn't be caught dead wearing. She had found a pair of black trousers and paired them with a deep, almost black, green silk shirt. Just to be on the safe side, she bought an off-white shirt as well, plus some underclothes and a belt, for Alek's wide leather belt would be much too large to fit through the belt loops of the trousers.

Marissa could hear water running in the bathroom and Alek singing in a strong baritone voice that was quite pleasing to the ear. For a moment she listened to the foreign words and melody, and then rapped on the bathroom door.

The singing abruptly ceased.

"I've got the clothes," she called from the other side, hoping he wouldn't open the door and expose himself to view. She had never seen a naked man and didn't know how she would react to such a sight. "I'll just leave them at the door."

"Wait, she-devil. Come here."

"What, in there?"

"Yes. This water—it will not turn off!"

Alek expected her to enter the bathroom while he was still in the shower? The only reason she'd consider his request was that she knew his nakedness would be concealed behind the shower curtain. All she would have to do would reach inside the curtain and adjust the knob. She steeled herself and opened the door.

"What in the—"

She broke off, too shocked to complete the sentence. Alek had taken down the shower curtain, which had allowed most of the water to spray onto the walls and floor. A puddle at least an inch deep surrounded the tub and pooled around his perfectly formed feet. And there, in all his masculine glory, stood Alek at the side of the tub with his back turned to her. She stared at his firm wet buttocks and long powerful legs and lost the power to speak. Though she had never seen a naked man before, she knew that the body before her was a rare specimen and quite a sight to behold.

He glanced over his shoulder at her. "I turn it one way and it is cold, the other it is hot!"

She snapped back to her senses and stumbled forward. "Push it in. Push it in toward the wall."

He did as directed and the water shut off.

"Ah!" he exclaimed in relief.

"Look at this mess!" Dismayed, she glared down at the floor to avoid catching a glimpse of his manly attributes. "Why did you take down the shower curtain?"

"I felt trapped. We do not bathe surrounded by drapery in my land."

"Oh? How do you bathe?"

"In the river."

"Well, it's like a river in here now. I'm going to have to find a mop or something. No, wait. Just throw me those towels!"

He pulled the terry cloth off the racks and gave them to her. She bent down and draped them across the puddle, trying to ignore the fact that a buck naked warrior stood above her. When she saw what she was doing, he grabbed two more towels and squatted down to help. Before she could avert her gaze, she caught sight of his manhood, and though she had nothing by which to make a comparison, she guessed that Alek was more than well endowed, by the looks of him. She wondered what it would be like to touch him there. Flustered, Marissa glanced up at his face and found him smiling.

"What is wrong, she-devil?"

"Nothing!"

With more force than necessary, she wrung out a towel and used it to sop up more water. Even from a foot away, she could feel the heat emanating from him and could smell the fresh scent of his clean hair and skin. The perfume of his male fragrance combined with the smell of soap nearly overwhelmed her, as if it were an aphrodisiac. She had the strongest desire to reach out to his gleaming wet shoulder and caress him as she often reached out for a horse. Yet this wasn't a horse to be stroked and patted. This was a man, a strange, potentially dangerous man. She couldn't believe she would even think of touching him. Marissa furiously attended to the task and refused to give her imagination further rein.

"The floor is dry now, she-devil."

She inspected the area. "So it is." She rose and kept her gaze on his face. "The next time you take a shower, keep the curtain up and closed, would you?"

"I will feel like a prisoner."

"Then you'll just have to get used to it."

He drew a towel off the shelf above the toilet and wrapped it around his hips. "You have never seen a man before, she-devil?"

"Not entirely. Not naked."

"You have not been touched by a man?"

"That's none of your business." She hung the wet towels over the side of the tub.

"Since you have not seen a man, then you must have never been with a man."

"You can think what you want, Conan." She straightened and turned around to face him, thankful that he had covered himself.

He leaned his hip on the counter of the sink and crossed his arms. The softness of the terry cloth contrasted sharply with the ridged muscles of his tanned abdomen. "You are not married?"

"No."

"Why?"

"I've got my reasons."

Before he could ask any more personal questions, she moved to the door and put her hand on the knob. "Do you need a razor for your face?"

"What is a razor?"

"It's a blade to shave your beard."

"I use my knife."

"You've got to be kidding."

"The blade is sharp. You will see."

"I'm not going to stand here and watch you hack up your face, Conan. I'm going to go have a cup of coffee."

Without waiting for a reply, Marissa opened the bathroom door and hurried back to the kitchen. She called a cab, fixed herself the last cup of coffee, and plopped down on the chair to wait for Alek. As she sat there, she remembered the way he had inspected her as she lay upon the bed thinking he was going to assault her. Yet he hadn't touched her. Why? Marissa lifted the mug to her lips. Was there something about her that had induced him to make a joke instead of a pass? She heard Jeb Vincent's voice in her head, telling her she wasn't a woman meant for breeding. Did that mean she wasn't desirable? When men looked at her did they think she was too lean? Too flat-chested?

She had no desire to be sexually assaulted, but she didn't want to be laughed at either, or overlooked for a reason she couldn't fathom. Alek's behavior puzzled her. Was there something about her that he found amusing? And if so, what was it? Did all men view her in the same way as Jeb Vincent? Did men, with their animal instincts, sense that she was androgynous and not meant to be taken? The thought that she might lack sexual allure struck at the deepest core of her, where she stashed all her fears.

Marissa squeezed the coffee mug between her palms and glared at her hands. The coffee burned in her gut as she sat there trying to force her thoughts back to the place deep inside, where they belonged. Before she had time to calm herself, however, she heard the bathroom door close in the hall behind her, and then Alek's footfalls on the wood floor.

She turned her head, and when she saw the warrior, the rest of her body twisted in the chair as if in afterthought, for her shock was so great at Alek's changed appearance that she forgot to even take a breath.

10

The white-haired ultimate warrior had vanished. In his place stood a tall man dressed in the loose-fitting white shirt and black trousers, which seemed to have been designed to make the most of his broad shoulders and slender hips while downplaying the bulk of his muscles. He stood outlined by the light of the hallway, hands in the pockets of his trousers, and his head held high in his peculiar haughty pose. He had shaved his face without injuring himself, much to Marissa's surprise, leaving a smooth tan jawline and strong chin with a circular cleft. But the most significant change was his hair. Gone was the stiff white mane and in its place was glossy brown hair, the color of rich wet earth, which fell below his shoulders.

She stared at him, awestruck. At his neck gleamed the intricately carved golden torc, and on his hips was slung his belt with the dagger hanging to his thigh, lending the clothes a foreign and undeniably masculine appeal. His appearance balanced precariously between elegance and savagery, as if she had draped a panther in silk, as if any moment the panther would leap out of its civilized trappings. The contrast of his wildness robed in finery captured her imagination as no man's appearance had ever intrigued her before.

He stared back, proud and tentative, looking slightly from the side.

"The clothes—" she managed to blurt out, rising on rubbery legs. How could she let this man affect her so strongly? "Do they fit?"

"They are loose, but not uncomfortable. However, I did not like this garment." He pulled something white out of his pocket and let it dangle in the air. The cotton briefs.

Marissa smothered a grin, not wanting him to think she was laughing at him. "You didn't like the underwear?"

"Too tight. A man must be free, she-devil, as I have told you."

Before she thought twice, she glanced at his crotch, wondering what it would be like to go around without underwear, especially for a man. Fortunately, the loose-fitting trousers concealed his lack of briefs. She decided to change the subject immediately.

"Your hair—"

He passed his left palm over the side of his head, as if smoothing away her comment.

"I thought you were blond."

"No." His chin lifted a fraction higher. "I am cursed."

"Cursed?"

"I have been touched by gods or demons—no one is certain which—who have branded me with hair that is not the hair most Gauls possess."

"Gauls?"

"A race of blond, blue-eyed people. My people."

"But you have brown eyes."

"I have changeling blood, she-devil. And no one but my father and mother has seen the true color of my hair except you. You will tell no one. Do you understand?"

"Why would I tell anyone about your hair? It doesn't matter."

"It would to my people. They are frightened of things they cannot understand. To them a Senone is blond. And to be different is unacceptable and dangerous."

"That's ridiculous!"

"Not to me. Not to my people."

She gazed at him, realizing the depth of his convictions. He must have hidden the color of his hair for years. And how many years had that been, exactly? Now that she saw him without his strange costume, she had trouble guessing his age. He had the body of a man in his early twenties, but the composure and authority of someone much older than herself.

"Okay. I won't tell anyone. Not that I ever expect to see any of your people anyway."

He nodded. "And your police—they will not know me?"

"I doubt your mother would recognize you, Alek."

"Ah." He smiled slightly, in an utterly charming lift of the corners of his full mouth. "You call me by my true name. What can this mean, she-devil?"

"Nothing." She tore her gaze off him. "I must be slipping."

She grabbed her keys off the table. "Come on. It's time to pay Dr. Woodward a visit."

They had just cleared the stairs when the door opened and Mrs. Pitts hobbled through, carrying an upright vacuum cleaner.

"Miss Quinn!" she greeted. "Good morning."

"Good morning, Mrs. Pitts."

The manager hardly spared her a glance. She was far too occupied with her inspection of Alek. In fact, she stared so long that Marissa knew she was waiting to be introduced. Now what? How was she supposed to explain Alek's presence?

"Mrs. Pitts," she began, gesturing toward Alek. "I'd like you to meet Alek, my . . . a friend of mine. Alek, this is Mrs. Pitts, the apartment manager."

"How do you do?" Mrs. Pitts beamed, extending her hand. "I'm afraid I didn't catch your last name."

"It is just Alek." He stared at her hand, as if wondering why a woman would offer hers to him.

Marissa paused. What would Mrs. Pitts think of such odd behavior? What would she think of the scabbard hanging at his hip? What if there had been a news bulletin about the strange warrior in the park and she had made the connection between him and Alek? Marissa forced a smile. "He never shakes hands, Mrs. Pitts."

"Oh?"

"Yes, he's a . . . he's a pianist. A very famous pianist, actually—from . . . Budapest—and he can't take the chance of injuring his fingers."

"From shaking the hand of a poor old woman like me?" Mrs. Pitts waved the air. "Nonsense!"

"It's true." She saw Mrs. Pitt's glance drop to the dagger again and knew she had to offer some kind of explanation for the weapon. "What do you think of Alek's costume? He likes to add a certain spice to his program by dressing up in romantic outfits."

Mrs. Pitts shot her a hard glance and then returned her attention to Alek. "He looks dangerous."

"Great! That's just the effect he wanted."

Alek nodded and smiled, crossing his arms over his chest.

"What about Leslie?" Mrs. Pitts put in. "Have you found anything out yet?"

"No, but I should soon." She took Alek's elbow. "Ah, I see our cab just arrived. We must be going, Mrs. Pitts."

"All right. Nice to have met you, Alek."

He nodded again and stepped through the open door, with Marissa at his heels. As they walked to the curb, Alek turned to her.

"What is a pee-nist?" he inquired. "I do not like the sound of it."

"I'll tell you in the taxi."

They rode to the Woodwards' house in the Wallingford district, which was just over two miles from Leslie's apartment. Alek stayed behind while Marissa went to the door, ostensibly to recover her purse and hat, which she had left behind during the melee of Alek's escape from the cellar. Their plan, however, was for Marissa to divert the Woodwards' attention while Alek went around to the back.

Diana opened the door, squinting from the bright sun of the late spring morning. She was dressed in light blue linen slacks and a long cotton tunic with a scarf looped around her shoulders.

"Marissa, what a pleasant surprise."

"Howdy." She found it difficult to retain a civil tone to her voice, knowing that Diana, David, and Kyle had lied through their teeth to her the night before. No wonder the conversation at dinner had been stilted. They probably were worried sick that one of them would make a slip. "Is the doc around?"

"No. He's speaking at a seminar today." She motioned toward the foyer. "Won't you come in?"

"Thank you kindly." Marissa stepped across the threshold.

"Are you all right?" Diana asked, quietly closing the door. "We were so worried about you."

"Alek didn't hurt me."

"Thank goodness!"

"Is he really the doc's nephew?" Marissa watched Diana's face, especially her eyes, for signs of evasiveness.

"Well—" Diana suddenly broke off and touched her arm, as if something had just occurred to her. "You know what Kyle forgot to take to you last night, Marissa? Your purse. And your hat. Let me get them for you."

So much for the truth. Marissa followed her to the coat closet under the stairs. At least Kyle Woodward was gone. That left only Diana to deal with, and Marissa was confident that she could outmaneuver the other woman.

Diana reached up to a shelf and pulled down Marissa's leather bag and her black hat, which she held out.

"Thanks." Marissa settled the hat on her head and then looked across at the slight woman before her. "You seem awfully nervous, Diana. Is something bothering you?"

"Me?" She laughed, forcing the sound into a tittering semblance of gaiety. "No. I'm afraid I'm just high strung."

"Really? You're as skittish as a heifer in a bull pen. I'd say you were nervous. Do I make you nervous?"

"Heavens no!" Diana touched the side of her light blond hair with her right hand. "Why would you think that?"

"Because I believe there's something going on here."

Diana blanched. "Oh? Like what?"

Before Marissa could answer, she heard the back door open. Diana jerked around at the sound.

"Someone's breaking in!" she gasped.

"Don't worry. It's only Alek."

"Alek?" Diana whirled to face her. "He's here?"

"Yes. Just a friendly visit by your favorite nephew."

"Nephew?"

"Why are you frightened of him, Diana?" Marissa asked, clutching the blond woman's arm to keep her from fleeing.

"Because he's a brute!" Diana tried to pull away, but her strength was nothing compared to Marissa's firm hand. "He'll kill us."

"He didn't kill me."

Just then, Alek strode into the hall. Diana gasped at the sight of him and for a moment they stared at one another. Diana's breath came fast and hard.

"Dr. Woodward is gone," Marissa informed the warrior.

"That is bad news. I wanted to see him." Alek walked forward while Diana shrank back against Marissa.

"What . . . how . . ." she broke off, too surprised at his altered appearance to string more words together.

"I don't think you've given your nephew enough credit," Marissa commented. "He's not the brute you think he is."

"He's an animal! He's—"

"Perhaps you've never been properly introduced to him."

As if on cue, Alek stepped forward. "How do you do?" He perfectly copied the tone and inflection of Mrs. Pitts as he held out his hand. Marissa fought down a grin while she watched Diana shrink from his outstretched hand.

"Don't touch me!" Diana shrieked.

"Alek may be chauvinistic, but he's got a good heart," Marissa put in, even though she still harbored serious doubts about the man. "Give him another chance."

"What do you want?" Diana breathed. "What's going on?"

"What's going on?" Marissa released her, certain she wouldn't try to run now that Alek stood guard. "I'll tell you what's going on. I'm here to get my sister."

"Your sister?"

"Don't play dumb, Diana. Leslie's downstairs, isn't she?"

Diana's hand slowly splayed over the folds of her scarf while she shot a worried glance at Alek, who stood at Marissa's elbow.

"And don't lie. I don't like it when people lie to me. Alek particularly doesn't like it when people lie."

"That is true," the warrior averred.

Diana wilted against the wall, and for a moment Marissa was worried that she would faint. Diana hung her head. "I begged Kyle not to do the experiment. But he wouldn't listen. And now look what's happened!" Then the blond woman seemed to rally her strength and swept the hair out of her eyes. She breathed in deeply, as if what she was about to say had weighed heavily on her mind. "All right. I'll tell you the truth." She pushed away from the wall and crossed her arms over her chest in a defensive gesture. "Leslie is downstairs. Kyle never meant to keep her there, though, it's just that something went wrong."

"What went wrong?"

"The dosage of the night orchid was too strong."

Marissa glanced at Alek. He had mentioned night orchid, too. Perhaps he had been telling her the truth as well. His entire concentration was upon Diana, however, and he didn't seem to notice Marissa's intense glance. She turned back to face Diana.

"I want to see Leslie right now, Diana."

"You can't." Diana continued, as if she didn't hear Marissa's command. "Kyle doesn't want anyone to discover what he's been working on. It's very secret and very important."

"So important he would jeopardize the life of my sister? Bullshit!"

"She'll be all right. I'm sure she'll be fine. Kyle said it might take a few days, but she'll snap out of it."

"Enough!" Alek exclaimed. "You will take us to Leslie. Now!"

"Not so fast," a voice called out from the end of the hallway.

Marissa whipped around to see David holding a small gun in his hand. Alek reacted immediately by lunging forward, but Marissa grabbed his arm.

"Don't Alek! He might shoot you!"

Alek halted and stood glowering at David.

"That's right, Alek. Don't take another step." David aimed the gun at Alek's chest and then motioned with his left hand. "Come here, Diana."

She ran to him and clutched his elbow as he pulled her protectively against him. "Thank God, David!" she breathed.

"I came in the back door and heard voices," he explained. "I never dreamed the brute would return in the daylight."

"The *brute* and I came to get my sister," Marissa put in. "We're not here to hurt anybody. So just put down that gun and show us where she is."

"I'm afraid I can't do that, Miss Quinn."

"Why in the hell not?"

"Because Dr. Woodward wants Leslie here. And Alek." He stepped backward. "So what say we all go down to the lab?"

"Not to that prison!" Alek retorted. "No!"

"It's either a cell or a bullet in your head," David replied. "Personally, I don't like violence, but I'm sure Dr. Woodward wouldn't care if an accident occurred that left you dead."

Marissa narrowed her eyes. Having seen David's gentle nature, she wouldn't have expected such tough talk from him. Surely he was bluffing for the benefit of the warrior. David was the type of man who could never pull a trigger and hurt someone, unless he was taken by surprise and had to act purely on instinct.

"Come on," David barked. "I haven't got all day."

Alek shot a glance at Marissa.

"That gun could kill you," she commented. "We'd better do as he says."

David and Diana took them down the hall and around to the back of the house to the cellar door. Marissa stepped down the stairs, expecting to descend into a labyrinth of dark musty rooms and old wiring, and was surprised to see a modern, well-lighted corridor flanked by smaller rooms whose doors were closed. It was more like an office suite than a cellar. At the end of the hallway was a metal door with wire-reinforced glass on either side. Marissa surmised that the laboratory lay beyond the sturdy door.

"Open that door on the left, Diana," David instructed, keeping the gun trained on the warrior.

Diana obeyed and pushed open another metal door to reveal a small chamber filled with books and file cabinets.

"Get in there," David said, pushing at Alek's back.

Reluctantly, the warrior trudged into the small room.

"You, too, Miss Quinn."

"Me?"

"Yes. To keep you from calling the police before Dr. Woodward gets back. Now get in there."

Marissa obeyed him and joined Alek in the chamber.

"David," Diana countered, "Marissa hasn't done any harm."

"She might. And we can't give her the chance."

"She was only trying to help her sister."

"You can take it up with Kyle when he gets here. Maybe he'll decide to let her go."

Marissa saw Diana frown. Obviously Diana was not totally on the side of the good doctor. Could she be persuaded to help them?

Before she could voice a request, however, the door was slammed shut in her face.

"Wait a minute!" Marissa yelled. "You can't do this! I want to see Leslie!"

She felt a hand on her shoulder. "It is useless, she-devil. They won't let you out." Alek's voice had lost its rough edge, and the baritone rumbled close behind her. The rich low tone unexpectedly soothed her, as did the warm palm on the top of her arm.

"Damn." She let out an exasperated sigh. "Now what?"

"Now I know your name." Alek smiled at her as she turned, pulling away from his touch while her eyes still flashed with anger. "Missquin."

"Missquin?" She screwed up her features and her dark brows knitted in a puzzled expression.

He liked the way her features contorted when she was upset or confused. Hers was an honest face not often found on a female. Most females practiced subtle forms of teasing and seduction, and their faces were full of the shadows of their veiled intents. He couldn't imagine the she-devil ever batting her eyes or cajoling a man to do her bidding. She was direct and forthright, more like a man than a woman, and he admired her for it.

"My name isn't Missquin." She put her hands on her hips.

"David called you Missquin."

"No, he called me Miss *Quinn*." She shook her head and gave him a begrudging smile. "Quinn is my second name. Miss is the title given to an unmarried woman."

"Quinn—your second name. What is your first?"

She tilted her head and studied him, as if judging him in some fashion. He breathed in slightly to increase the girth of his chest.

"Why should I tell you?" she questioned.

"We are prisoners together. We will come to know each other."

"Not in the biblical sense, I trust."

"Biblical?"

"Forget it, Sampson." She took off her hat, put it on the table, and passed her left hand over her glossy black hair. "The name's Marissa."

"Marissa." He let the pieces of her name roll off his tongue. "Marissa. That is a nice name. It suits you."

She shrugged indifferently.

He watched her pace the perimeter of the small room. Her boots clicked on the hard floor as she studied her prison. She had left her leather tunic at Leslie's apartment, and this time her backside was in plain view. Alek took the opportunity to survey her slim waist and hips and her long, slender legs. Suddenly the memory of Caius Sellenius slaking his lust on his mother loomed up and assailed him with visions of straining flesh and naked thighs. Against his will he felt a painful stab of longing for Marissa in his loins. He wanted to know her, wanted to feel what it was like to sink into her womanly place, wanted to cover her with his body and claim her.

But how could he do it without bringing the she-devil to her knees and making her submit to him? How could he prey upon her spirit to feed his lust as other men fed on women? He would never do it, especially to one such as Marissa.

Angry that he had let his thoughts sink to such a despicable level, he abruptly turned away. "We must try to find a way of escape, she-devil."

"How did you get out the last time?"

"When Doctor-Wood-Ward came to look in on me, I pretended to sleep so he wouldn't put the needle in my arm. When he left, he forgot to lock the door."

"I doubt we'll get that lucky again." She slid her hands into the front pockets of her jeans. "What is this place, anyway? His study?"

Alek inspected the tall metal boxes that lined one wall and the high wooden shelves filled with books that lined the opposite one. A table with a lamp stood in the space between them. "This is the place where Doctor-Wood-Ward keeps his books, what the Romans call a library."

"What do the Senones call libraries?"

"We don't have them. We do not write things down on paper. Writing is for the record keepers and law makers like the Roman dogs. We Gauls are men of action, not writing."

He pulled the handle of one of the tall metal boxes, but the drawer refused to open. The she-devil came up beside him. If she only knew what he had been thinking about her, she wouldn't get so close to him. He could smell the scent of her hair wafting upward to entice him.

"Like this," she instructed, sliding a small metal knob to the side and pulling the drawer at the same time.

Alek dragged his gaze off her hair and gave his attention to the metal box. Inside the drawer was a row of papers in yellow holders.

"Doc's records," Marissa mused, thumbing through them. "Grant proposals, insurance records, that sort of thing."

Alek crossed his arms. He could not make sense of the words on the folders. He knew some Latin words and a smattering of Greek, but not the words of this world.

"Papers will not help us get free of this room," he declared, reaching out to close the drawer. She stood to one side as he shut the file.

"For a research biologist, the Doc certainly owns a lot of history books," Marissa commented, glancing at the hundred or so bound volumes. She leaned closer and ran her finger along the bindings of the books. *"History of the Ancient World, Druids and Their Sacred Groves, The Celts, Gauls in Northern Italy, The Invasion of Rome."*

"If Doctor-Wood-Ward thinks to gain knowledge of Druids from books, he is gravely mistaken. The Druids would never pass down their secrets in a book."

"How did they pass down their knowledge?"

"Through memory. Becoming a Druid is a long journey. The instruction can last twenty years or more."

Marissa raised her eyebrows in surprise.

"I was chosen to be a priest, but my father wanted me to follow in his footsteps as a warrior."

"I can't imagine you as a priest." She shot him a lop-sided smile.

"Why?"

"Because you're every inch a warrior—so tall, so powerful, so—" She broke off as if she had just realized she was praising him. Alek felt disappointed at the interrupted appraisal of his attributes.

"Yes?" he put in, hoping she would continue.

"You just don't look like a priest, that's all I'm saying."

"And what do you do, Marissa, since you are not a wife?"

"I'm a rancher."

"What is a rancher?"

"Someone who raises livestock. In my case, it's cattle."

"Ah!" Perhaps their worlds weren't vastly different after all. The Senones tended cattle, too. In fact, they were known far and wide for the fine herds they raised on the verdant plains at the foot of the Alps. "My people are ranchers, too."

"Ranchers in Venetia."

"Yes."

She shook her head and looked upward, as if she didn't believe him. "Say," she commented, "there's a small window up there." She backed up for a better view and pointed to the wall above the bookshelves.

Alek looked up to see a rectangle of light near the ceiling.

"Maybe we can break out the window and get away from here," Marissa suggested.

"It is a small window, Marissa."

"I'll have a look at it." She stepped onto the second level of the bookshelf, obviously hoping to use it as a ladder. The bookcase tipped forward precariously, and only Alek's quick action kept it from falling. He pushed it back to the wall and held it there while Marissa jumped off.

"Sorry! I thought it could bear my weight."

"Be more careful, she-devil, or you will injure yourself and be no use for your sister." He stood back from the shelves. "I have an idea."

"What?"

"I will lift you up to see." He laced his fingers together. "Step into my hands and I will hoist you up."

She peered askance at his hands. In the intuitive way of a woman she must have picked up on his lascivious thoughts of moments before and was reluctant to trust him. Smart woman. He could barely trust himself at this point.

"Come, she-devil." He kept his tone brusque and his eyes full of casual indifference, even though he ached to feel her hands upon him.

She took a step closer. "No funny stuff, Conan."

"None. I am not a funny man."

His reply seemed to convince her. She closed the distance between them and lifted her foot. The movement caused her to lean off balance, which she countered by planting a hand on his shoulder. He fought off a shudder as the warmth of her palm sank through the fabric of his shirt. Then she placed her other hand on the opposite shoulder. Before he lost total control, he straightened and lifted her upward. Her hands left him as she gained her balance and stood up. Alek braced her knees against his chest. To add to his distraction, he found that her hips were just above eye level, tantalizingly immediate. Alek swallowed and stared at her tight trousers, trying to banish the vision of sinking his face against her woman's belly and crushing her small rear with his hands. He wanted to devour her and ravish her, and the feeling was stronger than anything he had ever experienced.

"How big is it?" he managed to choke out, feeling himself swelling with desire now that she was so near to him.

"Not big enough."

She was wrong. It was big and getting bigger with

every wave of his need for her. He had completely for-gotten about the window or escape. All he could think about was this woman of the Otherworld and her lithe body and raven-colored hair. He had lost control of himself and couldn't hide the damning result. Once she looked down, she'd see the jutting truth. What now? He couldn't let her look down, but at the same time he couldn't hold her in the air forever.

11

Alek closed his eyes and prayed to the Mother-goddess for help. He didn't want to hurt this woman and he didn't want to debase her, but so help him, he wanted to couple with her. He squeezed his arms around her calves and gritted his teeth.

"Alek?" she inquired in a tentative tone he had never heard her use before. She bent down and braced a hand on his shoulder. "Alek?"

"Woman," he whispered. "You undo me." He looked up, knowing his face was contorted with agony and self-loathing. She stared at him in surprise and then her hand trembled, betraying her. For an instant a questioning look passed through her eyes, turning them liquid, soft, and utterly vulnerable, and that vulnerable look was the last step of his undoing. He loosened his hold on her calves, allowing her to slowly slide down his torso until they were face to face and his hard length was pressed between them. Her eyes glanced downward in alarm and then back to his face.

He couldn't let her say anything. He couldn't allow her to push him away or deny him. He felt as if he would shatter into a thousand pieces if he were forced to release her now. He couldn't do it. He just couldn't do it this time. With a moan that seemed to erupt from somewhere deep in his soul, he crushed her against his body and clutched her braid, tipping her head back. She stared up at him, wide-eyed and tense, holding her hands in fists near his shoulders. Then he sank his mouth onto hers, trapping her lips to his until he tasted his fill of her soft sweetness. Her slender body, with its subtle curves and lean lines, pressed against his hard one, making him ache and pulse for her. Why were men designed to want so much from women when the females were fashioned to want to flee from their mates? Why had nature not balanced the drive and pleasure for both? In an agony of longing, Alek felt himself plunge into dangerous territory, a place he had never permitted himself to travel, as if he were in a swift river full of rapids and heading for a thundering water-fall. He kissed her cheek and her ear and could neither stop his progress toward the edge of the waterfall nor control the flood into which he had fallen.

He expected her to pummel his chest and demand to be released, but to his amazement he felt the buds of her fists slowly unfurl like flowers upon his chest as he kissed her. Then she spread her fingers wide as if to span the muscles of his chest. She wasn't pushing him away. She seemed to be hesitantly exploring him. He couldn't believe it. He felt himself plunge over another set of rapids and didn't look back.

"She-devil," he gasped against her lips. He felt her hands move up to the column of his neck, sending flash-es of chills and heat over his skin. Did she know what effect her slightest touch had on him? He closed his eyes and spread his hands over her back, running his palms down the graceful curve to her backside. Then he lifted her against him, cradling her over his rigid manhood as he imagined what it would feel like to tear off their barriers of clothing and feel her skin to skin. The trousers he wore were made of thin fabric that allowed his sensitive skin to feel the warmth emanating through the thick fabric of her jeans, and the sensation drove him wild. He kissed her, slipping his tongue into her mouth, yearning to break down the rest of the barriers between them. At the touch of her warm, wet mouth, he lost himself to an undulating rhythm of tongue and hips and breathing that became a whirlpool of desire, pulling him deeper and deeper to its dizzying center. Then *he* became the whirlpool, surrounding her tender frame in the swirls of his passion, enclosing her lips, shoulders, and hips as he turned with her in his arms and backed her against the side of the bookshelf.

Her body tensed at the sudden change in position and her fingers slipped from his neck. With a gasp she broke away from his mouth. "Alek, no—"

"I want you," he blurted, surprised at the thickness of his tongue. His voice was rough with passion and his words raw with honesty, making him sound just like the brute she supposed him to be, the kind of man he had vowed never to become. Why had he been so blunt? Why did she have to ruin everything with words of denial?

He was a man. She was only a woman. It was his right to take her if he desired her and she was no man's wife. It was his right! So why did he hesitate? Beside himself with hunger, Alek shut his eyes and pinned her to the bookcase, his hands cupping her thighs, his loins pushed against hers in a blatant show of force. He ignored her futile attempts to shove him away and kissed her throat while he ground against her, trying to block her protests from his thoughts, trying to ignore the memories of his mother beneath his father, of vanquished Roman women weeping beneath his Gallic brethren. How could he do this? How could he *not* do this? He wanted her so much he couldn't bear it.

"Alek!" she gasped. "Alek!"

Her voice cracked on his name, just as his mother's voice had shattered that day in the clearing by the river. Something inside him broke apart and made him falter, dousing the fire in his loins. Crazed with lust and shame, he sank his forehead against the cool wood of the bookcase. If he did this to Marissa, he was no better than Caius Sellenius. He was no better than a Roman dog if he took this woman by force. How could he dishonor himself? How could he stoop so low? He had to stop.

Marissa's body seemed to melt beneath his as she felt him back off. Her legs moved downward and he let them slide out of his hands. Ashamed and deflated, Alek remained leaning against the wall while Marissa slipped out of his grip and ducked away from him. Alek straightened and closed his eyes in anguish, lifting his face toward the ceiling as he once again took painful command of his senses.

He wanted to ask for her forgiveness. But no man begged the forgiveness of a woman. To do so was to admit he had done something wrong. And what had he done wrong? Nothing. If he had been any other man, he would have taken her against the bookshelf and satisfied himself once and for all. She should be grateful that he had denied himself his just due.

He glanced at her over his shoulder. She stood near the door, her back to him, clutching her arms to her chest. Had he repulsed her? Was she crying? A hundred questions and doubts shot through him, but he knew it was better to remain silent.

Then, feeling an aftershock of his arousal, he sensed an odd constriction in his chest, a frightening tightness that took away his breath. Alek panted, trying to snatch air into his lungs while he clutched the fabric near his throat.

Marissa jerked around and stared at him.

He sank back against the side of the bookshelf, gasping for breath.

"What's the matter!" she demanded, taking a single step toward him and then pausing as if suspecting a ruse.

"Nothing." He closed his eyes in an effort to concentrate on his breathing. If he became too frantic, it only made the constriction worse.

"Alek!"

"Leave me"—he panted—"alone!" Slowly he sank to a sitting position against the side of the bookshelf. Then he braced his forearms on his knees and leaned back against the wood. Beneath his half-closed lids, he saw her edge closer. Was she worried about him? He doubted it.

He turned his attention to his tight chest and forced his breathing to maintain an even rhythm. This would pass. He had survived the incident before and he would do so again, if he could just concentrate. Alek willed himself into his own world, the place he sometimes went just before battle, when his mind and heart and soul were one, fused with a single purpose and entirely separate from his body.

Was this Otherworld gradually strangling the breath of life from him? Would he one day cease to breathe altogether in this strange land? He sucked in a breath and slowly let it out, forcing himself to relax. Any moment now he would get the better of this demon. He concentrated with all his might, angry that Marissa was a witness to his weakness.

After leaving Marissa and Alek prisoners in the cellar, Diana couldn't concentrate. She had a strange feeling of unease, as if life as she knew it had taken a sudden turn and would never be the same again. Perhaps that was the price to be paid for Kyle's excursion into the occult rituals of the Druids. From the very first Diana had experienced a dark foreboding about Kyle's new venture and had begged him to cease his research. But he had only laughed at her, calling her a superstitious fool. Now it seemed as if things were getting far too complicated, especially since innocent people were involved.

Too upset to do anything but the most simple of physical tasks, Diana spent the afternoon weeding her flower beds at the side of the house, and didn't stop until David came out for a breath of air. He had kept guard in the basement the entire day.

"Still at it?" he greeted.

"Yes." She rose to her feet. "Is everything quiet downstairs?"

"Yes, oddly enough." He looked down and smiled gently. "I could have used some company, though."

"I couldn't stay in the house." She remembered the way he had held her the night before and her body ached and thrilled at the memory. Yet she also remembered her vow to stay away from him. "I'm afraid the warrior makes me too nervous."

"He didn't seem all that bad."

"Still, he frightens me." She found it hard to look into David's eyes since they had breached the emotional and physical wall that separated good friends from lovers. She knew that something special had begun between them, something more intense and infinitely more fragile than friendship. How could she look into his eyes without revealing her love and need for him? Fragile things broke easily, and she would rather die now than shatter the bond with David.

"Would you like some coffee? I'm ready to take a break."

"Sure." He looked down at her equipment. "You don't use weedkiller?"

"No. I don't like to put poison in the ground."

"Good for you, Diana." He picked up the tools while she grabbed the blue weeding pad, and together they walked to the detached garage where the yard equipment was stored.

Diana opened the door and passed into the dark building, which smelled of oil and cement. Shafts of filtered light angled through the window, highlighting the grill of her '57 T-bird, a car Kyle had purchased for her years ago and then had forbidden her to drive because it was a collector's item. Diana had never seen the sense in it, but then she didn't understand much of what Kyle did for her. On the other hand, he rarely asked what she wanted and thought she should be grateful for his gifts.

She walked to the garden supply area, and was highly conscious of David standing behind her as she drew off a dirty garden glove and placed it on a shelf.

"I hope I didn't come on too strong last night," he said, reaching around her to deposit the trowel and claw on the shelf beside her glove. His sleeve brushed her arm.

"No," Diana answered, pulling off her other glove. "I didn't mind."

He fell silent and she couldn't trust herself enough to

turn around and look at him. So she stood with her back turned, fumbling with her nails as if to clean out dirt that wasn't there.

"Since last night I've been thinking a lot about you, Diana. In fact I—I can hardly think of anything else."

"David—"

"I know I shouldn't press you, but—" He took her shoulders in his hands and pulled her against his chest while he lowered his head. The touch of his cheek upon hers made her legs grow weak. "Oh God, Diana—I can't help myself!"

The sound of his raspy voice in her ear was her undoing. She let her head fall back against his shoulder while his hands slid down her arms and wrapped around her torso. The touch of his hands was heavenly. It had been so long since a man had caressed her that she sank back, overcome with a painful longing that Kyle had never been able to ease, not even in the early days of their marriage, when they had still shared a bed.

David pressed a fervent kiss upon her cheek. "You've been in my thoughts for months, Diana. And being around you without telling you how I felt has been sheer torture."

"Please, David—" She turned in his arms as if to extricate herself from his embrace, but when she put her palms on his chest, she lost all thought of breaking away. Her hands seemed to fuse to his shirt by the heat she felt between them. In wild confusion she looked up just in time to see him bending down. And then their mouths met in a brief press of the lips.

"David, no," she gasped. "I should go!"

"Just one more kiss," he murmured. "That's all I ask."

"One," she repeated before his lips muffled her. His mouth opened over hers and she was flooded with the warmth of his tongue and his passion as he gathered her in his arms. She clutched the pocket flaps of his shirt in her fists as she put up a slight show of protest. But she couldn't fight her hunger. She hadn't the strength. It rose up like a starving child, clamoring for more, clanging on its empty bowl. Morally she knew it wasn't right to kiss David, but emotionally and physically the kiss was everything she had needed, everything she had ever wanted and more.

Feeling as if her heart was breaking, Diana kissed him back, angling her mouth against his, curving her hands around his neck to pull him near, and arching on tiptoe to stand as close to his body as she could. Her surrender only increased the strength of his embrace and fired his kiss. He was warm and strong, and there was more than just desire in his kiss. There was longing and jubilation and recognition in his kiss, the kind of kiss she had only imagined to be possible.

David was the man she should have had long ago, if she had only waited.

In the distance—what seemed like miles away—she heard the crunch of gravel in the driveway, signalling the approach of a car and the return of her husband. She pulled away, afraid they would be discovered in the garage.

"Kyle's home!" she said. "I have to go!"

Silently David stepped back and released her. "Go on. I'll come in the house later."

She rushed to the door and paused to glance back. David stood near the shelves with a wild smoldering look about him and his chest heaving. She had aroused him as much as he had aroused her. She was certain of it. The fact made her heart lurch in her chest.

"Go on," David repeated, giving her a crooked smile.

She hurried out of the garage, hoping that Kyle wouldn't detect anything out of the ordinary in her appearance. She knew her cheeks must be flaming red. How could she hide her face from Kyle?

Diana swept out of the garage just as Kyle came around the front of the car.

"You're home early," she commented, hoping the shade of the horse chestnut tree at the side of the drive would hide her blush. "Is the seminar over?"

"Not yet. But I need to attend to our Gallic friend." He snatched his briefcase out of the car and headed for the back door.

"You know he's here?"

"David paged me."

"Did he tell you he's detained Marissa Quinn, too?"

"Yes."

"What are you going to do with her?"

"I haven't decided."

"She shouldn't be here. You have no right to detain her."

Kyle turned to face her. "Diana, at this point the meddlesome Miss Quinn is the least of my worries." He stormed into the house.

Diana trailed behind him. She should have known he wouldn't detect any difference in her, because he was too wrapped up in his own problems and work to notice anyone else.

"What are we having for dinner, anyway? I'm famished." He put his briefcase on the table near the cellar door. "That banquet food is always so terrible, I can barely choke it down."

"I made chicken crepes."

"Chicken crepes?" He walked down the hall to hang up his coat. "I had chicken for lunch, Diana."

"Sorry. I had no way of knowing."

He turned to face her, pinning her with his hard blue stare. "If you used any sense, you'd realize that almost every seminar luncheon is comprised of chicken in some form."

"I don't go to seminars."

"I would have thought you'd catch on after all these years simply by the comments I've made."

He was expecting her to read his mind. That's what he really wanted her to do. The ultimate mate for Kyle would be a woman who could read his mind, see to his every physical comfort, keep herself immaculately groomed for all social appearances, and never say a word. Diana flushed with anger. For all the years of their marriage, she had tried to be a good wife. She had tried to provide Kyle with a warm, loving home. And what had she ever got for it? Criticism.

Now that her time was precious and limited, she was unwilling to fill her days with his unyielding, perfectionist demands. There had to be more to a relationship and much more to life than polished silver and shriveling disdain.

"If you don't like the menu, Kyle," she replied, straightening her shoulders, "perhaps we should order out."

"Order out?" he said in horror. "As in pizza?"

"Pizza, Chinese, whatever suits your palate."

"You must be joking! Order out? You know better than that, Diana." He strode to the stairs. "I'm going to take a shower. Tell David I'll be down soon."

She watched him ascend the stairs while anger burned in her chest. Other people ordered out once in a while. What was wrong with it? Granted, the food was sometimes less than nutritious, but as long as ordering out was the exception and not the rule, what harm could there be in it? Why, it might even be fun to have all those little white boxes of Chinese food brought to the door, sit in the family room, and watch old black-and-white movies.

But no. At the Woodward residence, there was always a gourmet dinner, a perfectly set table, a glass of carefully selected wine, and a half hour of forced conversation or intense silence, one of Kyle's many rituals. It was as if he were afraid to do anything else, as though if he even once broke the routine, he would start on a downward spiral from which he would never recover. It was as if someone had imprinted the ritual on him when he was a child and he wouldn't consider any other way of behaving.

Diana knew the time had come to break rituals, to stand up to Kyle and tell him what she thought, what she wanted. After all, what did she have to lose? Her life was finite. What could Kyle do to her that was worse than the disease already unleashed within her? The best use she could make of her remaining days was to champion the cause of Marissa Quinn and her sister and help the innocent women escape the clutches of her husband. If she was successful, at least someone would get away from Kyle, if not herself.

But how would she get Marissa and Leslie out of the house? She would have to get Kyle's keys, free Marissa and Leslie, and return the key ring without him taking notice. He kept his key ring with him at all times, so that meant she would have to steal the keys during the night while he slept. That involved slipping into his bedroom and praying he wouldn't awaken to find her. She would do her best that night, and could only hope that the seminar had tired him out enough to make his slumber deep.

Later that night, Diana lay on her bed waiting to make sure that Kyle was asleep. He and David had labored far into the night to make more of the night orchid serum, which was distilled from the nectar of the purplish-black blossoms of the plant. Diana wished the plants would die, leaving nothing to use in the rituals. She hoped her husband would use the serum to send Alek back to wherever he came from and try to rescue the missing Steven, but she had a niggling suspicion that Kyle would go ahead with his search for a Druid healer instead of wasting the precious concoction on the warrior. And what would happen to Alek once Kyle decided to dispose of him? Would her husband kill the warrior? Surely not. But what else would he do with the unwanted by-product of his experiment?

Diana hugged her pillow and thought of David, who was sleeping in the guest room down the hall. He had stayed overnight with them on other occasions when the work in the laboratory had lasted until dawn, but she had never felt such an aching need to seek him out. Now, it was all she could do to remain in her chamber and keep her wayward thoughts at bay.

How easy it would be to slip down the hall and into his room, to crawl into bed without speaking a single word and caress him the way she longed to. David wouldn't refuse her. He would draw her to his body and make love to her—with no excuses or promises for either one of them. Yet, Diana remained in her own bed, too hung up on propriety to indulge in her desires.

She also had to stay on track. Making love with David was not part of the plan for getting the key to the laboratory. She had stayed awake for hours, waiting for the men to retire. Fortunately, her medicine often kept her awake at night, which is why she usually had to nap during the day. She glanced at her watch. Four o'clock in the morning. Surely Kyle was fast asleep by now.

Diana rose and pushed her feet into her slippers. Then she stole down the hallway to Kyle's room. His door was slightly ajar, and she paused at the opening to listen to his respiration. His breath came in slow steady sighs of slumber.

Stealthily, Diana tiptoed across the floor, making sure to keep to the rugs so her slippers wouldn't make noise on the wood floor. She approached his bed and surveyed the nightstand in the darkness. Kyle had a habit of removing all jewelry from his person when he went to bed. As usual, he had placed his wedding band and watch on the nightstand alongside the key ring.

Biting her lip in concentration, Diana clutched the keys, squeezing them together so they wouldn't jangle. She glanced at the bed. Kyle hadn't moved and still slept on his side, facing away from her. Diana turned and, just as stealthily, tiptoed back out of the bedroom.

Through the dark house she hurried, too worried about waking Kyle to turn on any of the lights. She stubbed her toe on the wall at the top of the stairs, but bit back her cry as she hobbled down the steps. Once she reached the cellar stairs, she flipped on the light and descended the steps to the lab.

Diana fingered the keys as she padded down the hall. She didn't want to release the warrior, but knew she wouldn't be able to keep him imprisoned if she freed Marissa. She had no weapon to force him to remain behind, and she couldn't very well wake David and ask to use his gun.

For the first time in her life, Diana was defying her husband. She pushed the key into the lock of the storeroom and knew she would soon have to face Kyle's rage. But in her heart she knew she was doing the right thing, and the knowledge gave her strength.

Hand trembling, she turned the cold knob and pushed the door open. Light from the hallway filtered into the small room, showing a slight figure slumped against the file cabinets. Where was the warrior? Had he done something to Marissa? Diana ventured into the room.

As soon as she passed across the threshold she was yanked off her feet and a large hand was clamped over her mouth.

"Make no sound!" the warrior warned in a low but menacing voice near her ear.

Diana shook her head in agreement and tried to twist around to get a look at his face. His left arm surrounded her ribcage and held her off the floor, nearly squeezing the breath out of her. Was he going to kill her?

Then she saw Marissa scramble to her feet. Diana blinked in surprise while the realization sank in. They had tricked her into coming into the room. They must have heard her approaching and devised a plan. Alek seemed to have sensed her surprise and clutched her more tightly, which put pressure on her internal organs. A spiral of intense and gripping agony swirled through her and she gasped in pain.

"Let her down, Alek," Marissa said. "I think you're hurting her."

After a slight pause, Alek lowered her to the ground.

Diana bent over, cradling her abdomen with her arms.

"Are you all right?" Marissa asked, stepping closer.

"I'll be okay. I'm not well, that's all."

"Why are you here?" the warrior put in.

"To let Marissa go." Slowly, Diana straightened. "My husband has no right to keep her here."

"And Leslie?" Marissa inquired.

"You can take her with you. I have the keys to the lab."

Marissa smiled in relief.

"You do not speak of me," Alek crossed his arms over his chest.

Diana turned to the warrior. "I think you should remain here until Kyle decides what to do with you. But I realize that I have no way of forcing you to stay."

"No man holds my life in his hands."

"Kyle might. Without him, how will you get back to where you came from?"

"I will find a way."

"I hope you're right, for all our sakes."

"You can't hold Alek, so the point is moot," Marissa put in as she walked to the door. "Let's stop wasting time and get my sister out of here."

12

Marissa hurried to the door of the laboratory and waited impatiently for Diana to find the key that would turn the lock. Now that they had gotten this close, she couldn't bear the thought that David or Kyle would discover them in the cellar and lock them up again without her having the chance to see her sister, much less help her. Once the door was opened, she flipped on the lights and trotted through the main room. At the back was a corridor that looked as if it led to a series of smaller rooms. Marissa headed for it while Alek moved cautiously around the lab, exploring the room as he followed her.

Each door that opened onto the corridor had a small window at eye level through which Marissa peered, hoping to find her sister. In the last room at the end of the hall, where the shadows were deeper, she spied a blond figure lying on a cot.

"Here!" Marissa called out in a hoarse whisper and motioned for Diana to come running.

Diana had to try five keys before she found the one to fit the lock. Marissa nearly went crazy with the wait, and could almost hear the seconds ticking away like the timer of a bomb.

Finally Diana found the right key and pushed the door open. Marissa burst past her and fled to the cot. There lay her beautiful sister, one arm draped over her waist and the other hanging limply over the edge of the bed. Alongside Leslie was a metal stand that held an IV drip that was plugged into her wrist. She appeared thinner than usual, but her face was peaceful, as if she were simply sleeping. A slight wave of relief passed through Marissa at the sight of her, and she hoped that Leslie's condition might not be too serious after all.

However, no normal person could have slept through the noise. Just how strong was the effect of the night orchid? And how long would the effects last? Marissa reached out and brushed a strand of pale hair off her sister's forehead. The sooner she got Leslie to a doctor, the better.

Alek walked into the room and joined Marissa at the bed. "She is still in her deep sleep?"

"Yes."

"I will carry her."

"Wait. Let me wrap her in the blanket. It will be cold outside."

She slipped out the IV tube and pulled the end of the blanket from the end of the mattress while Diana hovered at her elbow. "Where will you take her?" she asked.

"Somewhere far away from your husband."

"Shall I call a cab?"

"Yes. Have them meet us a block away. You tell them where."

"All right." Diana scurried away.

"You trust the woman Diana?" Alek inquired after she had left.

"Yes. Call me stupid, but I think she has a good heart."

"So do I."

Marissa's gaze met Alek's and held for a moment, as if they understood that they had to work together regardless of what had happened in the storeroom earlier that day. Could she forget the way Alek had pinned her against the bookcase? Marissa doubted she would ever be able to put those few moments out of her mind, and wasn't certain if she wanted to banish them from her memory anyway. Never in her life had she witnessed the sort of unbridled sexual appetite Alek had shown. The rawness of it, the powerful wildness of it had nearly swept her away. She still didn't know why Alek appealed to her or why she had let him go so far. Perhaps she responded so strongly to him because he was elemental and uncomplicated—like a beast on the range living life as nature intended and taking what was natural and necessary. She understood that kind of life and wished people might learn from the examples of animals.

Yet Alek was no beast. He was a man. And if any other man had tried to take her by force, she would have fought like a she-cat to get away and would even now be planning how to make him pay for his transgression. So why wasn't she boiling mad at Alek? Why was it that she could even consider leaving the Woodward house with him? A hot flush coursed through Marissa.

The truth was she hadn't been repulsed by Alek's advances. In fact, when he had let her slip down his body, she had felt a hunger flare inside so strong and hot that she had been frightened of her own need. Her own raging hunger had made her break away. And when she had asked him to let her go he had honored her request. That's why she wasn't planning any revenge. She didn't resent Alek. She admired him. This warrior—this uncomplicated brute of a male—possessed more honor and self-control than she would have ever guessed possible in a man.

She watched him as he reached down, gathered Leslie's body in his strong arms, and hoisted her up.

"Let us leave now, she-devil, before Doctor-Wood-Ward awakens."

"Good plan," she answered.

Diana met them at the door of the lab. "A taxi can get here in five minutes," she said. "I told them to pick you up at the yellow house on the next block. You'll be able to tell which one it is. It has a flagpole in the front yard."

"Good," Marissa replied as Alek passed by her and down the hall. "Thanks for letting us go."

"It was something I had to do, for you and for me."

"I hope the doc doesn't get too upset with you when he finds out."

"Maybe he'll think Alek broke free again."

"I hope so, for your sake."

"Hurry, now, Marissa."

Marissa didn't need to be told again. She ran down the hall, popped in the storeroom to get her hat and purse, and dashed up the stairs. She held open the back door while Alek carried Leslie onto the back porch, and then looked back at the small form of Diana Woodward, who raised her hand in a subdued wave. Marissa touched the brim of her hat in salute and followed the warrior into the darkness of early morning as a flash of lightning rent the sky.

◦   ◦   ◦

Tired and worried, Diana closed the back door and retraced her steps through the house to the second floor. She slipped into Kyle's bedroom and passed silently over the floor to his nightstand, praying that he wouldn't wake up and discover what she'd done. In her nervousness, she misjudged the distance in the darkness and the keys rattled as she put them down.

Kyle rolled over at the noise. "What—who's there?" he demanded in a groggy voice.

Diana's blood seemed to freeze in her veins. His eyes opened and he peered up at her.

"It's just me. I—I was worried," Diana lied, stepping closer. "You seemed so tired at dinner. I was just checking on you."

Had he noticed her hand on the keys? Would he detect the tremor in her voice and know she was lying?

"Checking on me?" He reached out and grasped her wrist. "How thoughtful of you, my dear. I didn't think you cared."

"It was just that I was concerned—"

"You don't often come into my bedroom at night."

Diana stiffened, knowing he referred to his sarcastic comments about sharing his bed and the many times she had pretended not to understand him. She touched his forehead.

"No fever," she commented, trying to change the subject.

"I've got something else for you to feel, my dear." He smiled and drew off the covers to reveal an unmistakable shape in his pyjamas. His impotence had been one of the factors that had made them drift apart, and to see him with a full-blown erection quite surprised Diana.

"I think it's from handling the night orchid," he explained. "But whatever it is, I'm ready to go. I could go at it all night."

Diana instinctively stepped back. She thought of David in the guest room. He had also handled the night orchid. Had it produced the same effect in him? She flushed at the prospect.

"Diana," Kyle said, pulling her closer. "Let's not waste the opportunity. This might be the answer to our problem. This might be good for us."

"Kyle, it's late."

"You can sleep in tomorrow. It's Sunday."

"What about your back?"

"It will be fine."

"I don't know. It might hurt me now."

"Let's find out." He pulled her down and rolled to the side, trapping her with his right leg. She could feel the hard length of him against her thigh. The last place she wanted to be was beneath him, but she was worried that if she refused his advances he might start to think twice about what she'd been doing in his room. Better to lie back and suffer through just this once if it meant helping Marissa Quinn and her sister to escape. She closed her eyes.

Except for the one night with David, Diana's sexual experience had been limited to Kyle, who had spent the first few years of their marriage travelling on a lecture circuit. He would come home to Seattle, tired and busy, and take her to bed as if on an afterthought. Their love-making had been businesslike, brief, and infrequent. At the time Diana wasn't aware that anything was missing. She had heard the sex act should be enjoyable and had even heard of women ruining their lives to sleep with certain men. She couldn't believe such tales, because to her sex was something to be endured, not enjoyed. Now, however, she knew better. Making love with the right man was like no other experience on earth, and was not an experience she cared to share with her husband.

"I might not have found a cure for cancer," Kyle whispered near her ear, "but I may have discovered something almost as good!"

She swallowed as he pushed up her robe and nightgown. He didn't even have the decency to kiss her or hold her or do the things that lovers did in the movies, things that sometimes made her ache deep inside. Kyle was too intent on his own pleasure to waste any time on her, just as he had always been.

In moments he had disrobed himself from the waist down and situated himself between her legs. She prayed he would be as quick as usual and get it over with, and hoped that, once he spent himself, he would be unable to achieve another erection. He pushed himself into her and Diana lay there and waited.

Marissa felt the curious stare of the cab driver as she and Alek gently maneuvered Leslie into the back seat of the taxi. She didn't owe the man an explanation, but she didn't want him to suspect any wrongdoing either.

"My sister," Marissa commented, shaking her head. "The drunk. Goes out jogging around the lake and where do we find her? Out cold with nothing but her shirt and shorts on."

The taxi driver scratched the stubble on his cheek. "Yeah? I got a buddy like that."

"I get calls in the middle of the night all the time."

"I know what you mean, lady. It's a real drag."

"You're telling me." She got in the cab and shut the door, thankful to be out of the rain that had begun to pelt the sidewalk.

The cab driver took his seat. "Where to, lady?"

"The Sheraton. I can't take her home to her hubby like this. He'd have a fit."

"The Sheraton it is."

Marissa cradled Leslie's head on her lap and stroked her serene face as the cab sped through the nearly deserted city streets. The closer they got to the heart of the city, the louder the thunder cracked overhead. Rain poured out of the sky, and the sound of the persistent windshield wipers dominated the cab. The center of the storm must be located in the heart of Seattle, in the exact direction they were headed. Marissa only hoped they wouldn't get struck by lightning getting out of the cab. Alek watched the lights and buildings pass by and didn't say a single word during the trip.

They hurried from the curb into the hotel lobby, where Marissa told the night clerk that they'd been traveling by car and her sister had become too ill to continue. She was feverish, which explained the blanket. And the blanket conveniently concealed the weapon slung on Alek's hip. The young clerk didn't question them and was eager to help, sending Alek on ahead while Marissa filled out the registration form. He even offered to call for a doctor, but Marissa told him that they would take her to a clinic in the morning if she wasn't better by then. She was anxious to catch up with Alek before he got lost in the hotel or got caught on an escalator. There was no telling how much trouble the warrior could encounter in the huge hotel or how much attention he would call to himself. She wanted to keep both to a minimum.

She found Alek around the corner from the lobby, still holding Leslie in his arms as he looked at a map of the hotel on the wall.

"Make any sense?" she asked, coming up beside him.

"No. This is a very large place, she-devil."

"Yes. And if we're lucky, the good doctor won't be

able to find us here." She touched his elbow. "Come on. Let's take the elevator."

"Ell-vator?"

"You're going to like this." She smiled wickedly at him and was amused to see the puzzled expression on his handsome face.

She pushed the button and the elevator arrived immediately. At first Alek hung back, claiming the elevator room looked suspiciously small.

"Either you ride the elevator or you'll have to carry my sister up ten flights of stairs."

Alek considered his options for a moment and then reluctantly passed into the elevator. When they swept upward, he expression froze in place, and Marissa was certain that he had put on a mask to hide his alarm. Then, when the car dipped to a stop, which caused Marissa's stomach to flipflop, she saw Alek turn pale.

"We're here," she commented, hoping to offer him encouragement without mentioning how green he looked around the gills.

"You are wrong, she-devil," he said, stepping into the hall. "I do not like the ell-vator."

"You'll get used to it."

A few minutes later, they found their room, the only one available in the hotel. Marissa hadn't listened to the clerk when he explained what kind of room it was, since she had been too concerned with Alek's whereabouts to pay any attention. Now she found that she had paid for a suite, complete with parlor, two bedrooms, and a sunken tub in a very luxurious bathroom.

Alek carried Leslie to the nearest bedroom while Marissa hurried ahead to pull down the bed covers. He lowered Leslie to the sheets and made sure her legs were stretched out straight. His attention to Leslie's comfort touched Marissa. Gently, she unwrapped the blanket and drew up the sheets and comforter to cover Leslie. Then she sat down beside her and watched her sleep as Alek padded around the suite checking the windows and doors while the storm raged outside. Something about the fact that Leslie was finally out of the clutches of Dr. Woodward, that they were in a warm room protected from the thunder and lightning, and that Alek was prowling around the rooms gave her a sense of peace and security. Marissa took off her hat and set it on the dresser nearby. Perhaps everything would be all right after all.

Yet how could she be selfish enough to think everything would be all right? Had she forgotten Alek's predicament? During the time spent locked in Dr. Woodward's basement, she had read all about Alek's people in the history books she'd found in the storeroom. She knew now that everything he had told her was the truth—that he was a warrior from another time, that Dr. Woodward, by re-enacting a Druid ritual, had brought Alek into the modern world. There was indeed a people called the Senones, who had lived in northern Italy before the birth of Christ, before Julius Caesar, in fact. These people had settled north of the Po River and fought continually with the Romans.

To get her mind off Alek's unsettling behavior, she had read steadily the entire afternoon and evening while locked in the cellar room. Reading had served a dual purpose—one, to ignore Alek, and two, to find out whether or not he was all he claimed to be. She had found plenty of information in Dr. Woodward's books, and in a way wished she hadn't found out as much as she had.

She now knew the fate of Alek's people. While the Senone men were otherwise occupied, the Roman army swept into Senone territory and slaughtered nearly all the old men, women, and children. Griefstricken and outraged, the Senone warriors and their allies marched on Rome to avenge the deaths. They met the Roman forces on the lower Tiber and engaged in a fierce battle. By then, however, the Romans were wise to Gallic battle tactics and inflicted a crushing defeat upon the Senones in what is now known as the Battle of Vadimonian Lake. According to the book, the swampy banks of the reedy pool where the battle took place still yield the battle axes, lances, and bones of the men who died in 285 B.C. So devastating were the numbers killed at the massacre and during the slaughter at the river that the Senones soon ceased to exist as a people.

But what made Marissa even more worried was the mention of a certain celebrated warrior of the Senones who was captured during the battle and later sent to Rome, where he was castrated and then tortured to death in front of the cheering Roman populace. The name given in the text for the warrior was Alaric. But Marissa knew enough about translation errors and misrepresentation of historical facts to guess that the warrior who had met his doom in Rome was not Alaric, but Alek. Her Alek. Somehow, he would get back to his own time to avenge his people, only to come to a terrible end.

"Will you sleep?"

Marissa jerked to her senses and looked up to see Alek standing in the doorway.

"What?" she blurted, rising to her feet.

"Will you sleep?"

She brushed a stray strand of hair off her forehead and tried to get her mind off the painful facts she had learned in the history books. "I think I'll get cleaned up first. Will you sit with Leslie while I take a quick bath?"

"Yes." He strode into the bedroom, his scabbard belt riding seductively low on his hips. How could anyone castrate this man? She couldn't bear to think about it.

Marissa tore her glance off his belt. "Thanks. I'll only be a few minutes."

She ran a bath in the huge tub, undressed, and slipped into the steaming water, knowing the hot water would make her drowsy and allow her thoughts about the Senones to fade. At first she had considered telling Alek about what she had read in hopes that she might save him from his fate. But how could a person be saved from his fate? It wasn't possible. Fate was tied to a person like a shadow. And she didn't think it would be fair to tell him the path of his life and the manner of his death. Even more, she knew she should not alter history, for drastic changes might result from a single modified incident. So she kept silent, even though the truth ate at her.

When Marissa finished with her bath, she wrapped herself in a huge white towel and gathered up her garments, wishing she had a change of clothes for the morning. She'd just have to pretend it was roundup time and she was out on the range without benefit of a bath or clean duds.

Quietly, she walked to the bedroom, her footsteps muffled by the thick carpeting and the sound of the rain beating on the windowpanes. She could see Alek sitting at Leslie's side. As she got closer, however, she saw a hand slip around the back of Alek's neck, and she distinctly saw the hand caress him.

She froze in the doorway. What was going on? A shaft of jealousy pierced through her so swiftly that she gasped from the sheer force of it. Alek twisted to look back at her, and in doing so displayed the female hand that was passing over his chest. Leslie was caressing

Alek? Or was Alek trying to seduce her sister while she had been in the bath?

Marissa stalked forward, determined to find out what was going on.

Alek looked up, not in the least contrite, even though Leslie's hands roamed over his shoulders. "She is regaining her senses."

"Oh?" Marissa's voice was ice cold.

Before she could say anything more, she watched Leslie sit up and loop her arms around Alek's neck. For a moment Leslie's eyes fluttered open and then she reached up and kissed him on the lips.

"Hold it!" Marissa sputtered, grabbing Leslie's arm.

Alek pulled away from the kiss and caught Leslie's wrists in his hands. He was grinning, and Marissa had the greatest urge to belt him. She didn't find anything remotely amusing about the fact that her sister was acting like a wanton hussy or that Alek seemed to be enjoying her unusual attentions.

"It's the night orchid," he chuckled, trying to extricate himself from Leslie's snakelike arms. "It is an aphrodisiac."

"Oh, really?" Marissa winced at the jealousy she heard in her own voice, but she couldn't seem to help herself when she'd seen her sister's advances upon the warrior.

"Perhaps this means your sister will awaken soon." Alek got off the bed, still chuckling. For a moment Leslie reached for him as if in a trance, then sighed and lay back down on the pillow.

"I could have used the night orchid in my land, had I known its effect on women."

"Why?" Marissa crossed her arms. "Couldn't get a date? Were all the Senone women too busy washing their hair?"

Alek glanced at her and his smile faded. "You are angry. Why?"

"I'm not angry. I'm not in the least bit angry. Not at all."

He regarded her and she thought she saw a sparkle in his eyes. The last thing she wanted him to know was that she was jealous of him and her own sister. She turned her back to him and plopped down on the bed.

For a moment he said nothing, and she felt him studying her. Then she heard his footsteps as he walked away. He paused at the door.

"I will take a bath, she-devil. Then I will watch Leslie for you while you sleep."

"Oh no you won't. She'll be fine."

For the longest time, Marissa sat on the edge of the bed, fuming. She heard Alek draw a bath and heard him humming aimlessly as he washed. All the while she listened, she thought of the way his hard body had felt pinned to hers, how his strong hands had taken command of her, how his mouth had claimed hers. She didn't want any other woman feeling the same things she had felt in his arms. Not even her sister. Leslie had enjoyed her share of men, while Marissa had never known the touch of a man. It wasn't fair that Leslie should have Alek, too.

Marissa stood up and yanked her towel tight. She was jealous. She had to admit it. She was insanely jealous that Leslie had embraced Alek. And why? Because she wanted him for herself. That was the truth of the matter. She desired Alek for herself.

The realization made her heart wrench painfully. She wanted Alek as she had never wanted a man. Yet how long would he be in her world? A day? Two? A week, if she was lucky? And then, if the history books were accurate, she would lose him to the Roman army and a horrible death. She couldn't wait around for roses and Saturday night two-steps at the grange hall. She didn't have the luxury of the time it took to fall in love. If she was ever to experience what it was like to know a real man—specifically Alek—she would have to act and act soon.

Marissa glanced at the bathroom door, which Alek hadn't bothered to close all the way. She raised her chin and adjusted her towel. She was newly scrubbed. Alek was naked in the tub. If she truly wanted him, now was the time to go get him.

13

Marissa walked toward the bathroom, adamant about keeping to her goal even though she was assailed by self-doubts with every step she took. What if Alek refused her? What if he didn't like what he saw when she dropped her towel? What if he didn't want to risk the pain of being aroused to the point of madness and then asked to back off again? She wouldn't blame him for turning her away, but she prayed that he would not.

And how did a woman make advances to a man? Should she slink around the doorway and coyly display a white shoulder and a bare thigh? Should she think up a clever phrase to let him know what was on her mind without being too blatant? Or should she walk up to the tub and offer to wash his back—as she had seen actresses do in the movies?

Marissa hesitated at the door and rubbed the back of her neck, trying to decide what to do and feeling woefully unsure of herself. One thing she did know—she wasn't an actress. And this wasn't a movie. This was real life. She wasn't about to pretend to be something or somebody she was not. What in tarnation was she afraid of anyway—a little rejection? That had never stopped her before. Why had she suddenly become so damned lily-livered about a relationship with a man when she met everything else in life head-on? Had she forgotten who she was?

A rumble of thunder rolled across the sky as if to answer her. She raised her chin and glared at the door. She was Marissa Evelina Quinn, the best damn rancher in the state of Montana. If Alek didn't like what he saw, fine—he could tell her. And she could take it.

Armed with her logic and pride, she pushed open the door and barged into the bathroom.

Alek turned at the movement and looked up. He stopped lathering his chest.

Marissa came to a halt in the middle of the room and stared at him, struggling to come up with something to say on the spur of the moment—something natural, something she would normally say to a man. The trouble was, she had never approached a naked man in a posh mauve hotel bathroom—or anywhere, for that matter— and, to her chagrin, found herself at a complete loss for words.

Mute and embarrassed, she challenged herself to stay on course. If words failed her, she would resort to action. Before she lost her nerve altogether, she walked to the side of the huge tub, which was sunk like a jewel into the plush pile of the carpet and lit by one small light overhead.

"Mind if I join you?" she asked in a voice as business-like as she could muster. She placed one foot on the edge of the tub.

Alek stared at her foot and then back at her, his face bright with astonishment.

"No," he said at last, pulling his knees up. The water was so deep and sudsy she couldn't see his lower torso or the tops of his legs, which was probably for the best. She might have lost her nerve altogether if she had seen the full extent of his nakedness.

Still draped in her towel, she stepped into the tub, and found the ledge upon which to sit, but never once took her gaze off his face. To look away would be a sign that she was embarrassed, and she would not admit to him that she was anything but confident of her actions.

"You wish to bathe again?" He seemed genuinely puzzled.

"Yes."

The moment of truth had come. She had to take off the towel and expose herself to him. She could either drop it and dive for cover like a yellow-bellied coward, or she could take pride in her appearance, however flat-chested she was, and disrobe with grace and confidence. Marissa swallowed and reached for the terry cloth.

Alek watched her without moving a muscle, without so much as a single blink, waiting to see what she would do.

Marissa breathed in and unfastened the towel. Steeling her hands against the—in her—unusual inclination to tremble, she pulled the cloth away from her breasts, opening herself like a butterfly emerging from its coccoon. Cool air wafted over her naked skin, followed by the heat of Alek's gaze. His eyes traveled down her neck to her breasts and then to her belly and thighs, branding her skin with his slow regard. She forced herself to remain standing on the ledge and to endure his inspection, feeling as if she'd stood there a lifetime, when she knew that only seconds had elapsed. She saw his Adam's apple bob in his throat and a strange glint appear in his eyes when he looked back at her face.

"You look very clean to me," he said at last with a slow grin.

Marissa's heart skipped wildly. He not only seemed to have accepted her appearance, he had managed to break the tenseness of the moment with his offbeat comment. Another man might have said something provocative to lead her on, but Alek's humor set her more at ease than anything else he could have said or done.

"Yes, but I—I forgot to wash my hair."

"Ah." He motioned toward the side of the tub opposite him. "Then you must wash it, she-devil."

Marissa dropped the towel on the floor and slowly sank to a sitting position on the ledge. Thankfully, the water was quite deep and the soap suds reached all the way to the tips of her breasts, so she didn't feel completely exposed to view any longer. If she slumped just a bit, she could submerge up to her neck. But now what? She had no idea where to go from here.

"Come here and I will unbraid your hair," he said as if sensing her hesitation.

She stared at him, unsure how close she could move toward his bare chest.

"Come to the middle and turn around," he added.

"All right." She slipped through the water and slowly pivoted to present her back to him, grateful that he had made the next move. She knelt on the bottom of the large tub at his feet. The water sloshed in the tub as he shifted his left leg and straddled her. She was acutely aware of his naked knees near her elbows beneath the surface.

"Women in my village have blond hair," he commented, lifting the end of her braid. "Or very light brown."

"My dark hair must seem strange to you," she replied.

"Your hair is beautiful."

She flushed and closed her eyes, enjoying the sensation of the gentle tugs on her scalp as he unfastened her braid and combed through the twisted strands with his fingertips. The sensation was wondrously erotic, and she found herself tipping her head back for more.

"I like your hair," Alek murmured as he gathered the tumble of tresses in his hands and lowered his face into the raven cloud. "I like the way it smells, the way it feels."

"You have a nice touch," she replied, instantly wishing she had thought of something more poetic to say. "For a warrior, you are surprisingly gentle."

"My mother taught me the value of gentleness." He pulled his fingers through her hair, spreading it over the surface of the water in a black fan. When his fingertips touched her flesh, she felt a million sparks of delight burst over her skin.

Marissa sighed and felt herself melting into the hot water. She had never dreamed her entry into his bath could be this easy, this relaxing.

Alek continued to speak in a low, resonant voice that rumbled into her very soul. "There can be two sides to a man, she told me. And the gentle side makes a strong man even stronger."

"Your mother must be a wise woman."

"She is." He cupped a hand at the base of her skull. "Lean back, Marissa, and I will wash your hair."

She twisted to look at his face. "You don't have to."

"I want to."

She saw him survey her again, from the bubbles near

her neck, to the wild profusion of her hair, as if he were
trying to see her body through the suds. His magnificent
chest rose and fell three times before his perusal swept
back to her face. "Let me do this for you, Marissa."

She couldn't remember the last time someone had
washed her hair. If the experience was at all similar to
the way he had unbraided her hair, she would gladly
surrender to his request.

"All right." A faint smile hung on her lips as she
turned back around. Then she eased back to let her hair
dip into the water.

"More," he urged, lightly supporting her head.

She tipped farther, leaning into his hand, placing herself completely under his control. For a moment she
wondered if he could see her breasts in this position.
But she quickly decided to ignore the fact that he might
glimpse her nakedness and concentrate on the things he
was doing to her hair instead.

He lathered her tresses with soap, or shampoo—she
didn't care which. She was quickly losing herself to the
wonderful swirling action of his hands, the strength of
his fingertips as he massaged her scalp, and the amazing
way this powerful, wild man was pampering her.

"That feels so nice," she murmured, smiling.

"Good." He continued to work at her hair for a few
minutes. Then he told her to dip back and rinse. She
closed her eyes and sank into the water while he carefully rinsed the lather from her hairline with the backs of
his fingers. She dared not look up at him, afraid to break
the spell he had woven with his hands.

Then he touched her at the base of her neck. She
tensed, waiting to see what else he would do, and forgot
to breathe as he slid his palm down her breastbone to
her right breast. His hand was unbelievably warm and it
encompassed the entire orb of her breast, sending

waves of almost painful ecstasy through her. She gasped as her body seemed to bloom beneath his hand. It was all she could do to keep from arching upward. What was he doing to her? No man had ever touched her like this, and she didn't know what to expect.

"You feel very nice," he murmured. "You are so lean. Firm."

"Nothing to jiggle," she replied, hoping to cover her lack of experience with self-effacing humor.

"Not true, she-devil," he countered. "You jiggle in all the right places." He nudged the rounded base of her breast and it bounced pertly. When had her breasts been heavy enough to jiggle like that? Had they metamorphasized since her entry into his bath? Whatever had happened to her, she liked it, especially when Alek leaned forward and cupped both breasts, crushing them upward and kneading them in a glorious circular motion.

She reached up and grasped his knees, arching upward. She heard him sigh raggedly as if her body were affecting him in a glorious way, too. Marissa thrilled to the sound.

Effortlessly, he slid into the water behind her, and she felt the length of his shaft press against her back as he gathered her in his arms. The surprising hardness and the sheer length of him made her thrill all over again. She had seen the extended members of stallions and bulls and had watched animals mate since she had been a small child, but nothing had prepared her for the way Alek's silken engorged shaft felt against her back. What would it be like to have that hardness inside her? Would it hurt? She tensed, suddenly wondering if this was what she wanted—to make love to a virtual stranger from another world and another time. Yet, Alek's primal honesty and strength touched the very heart of her as no man had.

"You are here with me," he said near her ear, "and you are not afraid?"

"No. I trust you." The response slipped out before she could think twice, but deep in her heart she knew the words were not unfounded. She did trust Alek, more than any man she had ever met.

"You have not been touched by a man, Marissa. You don't know what a man can do to a woman."

"So far, so good, Conan."

"You are naive if you can say that." He clutched her breasts even tighter. "I am a brute, just as Diana Woodward says. I have tried not to be a brute, Marissa, but it is the nature of men to want things of women."

"I know." She tried to twist in his embrace so that she could read the expression on his face, but he held her tightly.

"I have promised never to brutalize a woman, to slake my lust on her."

"I don't believe you'll brutalize me."

"Even if I touch you here?" His hand slipped down her belly to the warm place between her legs, the place that was becoming warmer with every word he uttered.

"You are no brute, Alek. I like how you touch me." As if to prove it, she lifted herself upward and into his hand. He sucked in a breath, and his grip tightened.

"But I want to do things to you—and not with my hands."

Marissa paused. Something in his words and his peculiar hesitation struck her as odd. Didn't Alek know that making love could be enjoyable for both parties? Had no woman responded to his touch before? She found that impossible to believe, not when he was so warm and gentle. How could a woman not respond positively to such a man?

Then the realization dawned on her. Alek was a

virgin. Marissa sat up straight, shocked out of her bubble of comfort. Alek was a virgin. He was every bit as inexperienced as she was. This strong ultimate warrior had never known a woman, had never given himself to another human being. The knowledge not only flabbergasted her, it deeply moved her to think they might learn of love with each other and share their first time together, both of them novices in the ways of the flesh.

"I have seen men take women," he continued, "and I have seen the women weep."

She twisted, and this time he eased his grip, allowing her to face him. She floated slightly upward, but not before his shaft brushed her belly. Alek reached up and pulled her back down, settling her upon his upper thighs and slipping his hands around her waist. Somewhere beneath the bubbles between them rose his erect manhood, but she didn't have the guts to reach out and touch him. Instead she lightly caressed his cheek. "It doesn't have to be like that, Alek. A woman can enjoy it. I will enjoy it."

"How do you know?"

"Because of the way you touch me. You make me feel desirable." She pressed on, amazed how the words slipped out so easily. "I want you to touch me. That's why I am here."

"You want me to take you?" He stared at her, his brown eyes feverish but unwavering.

She stared back. "Yes."

He looked at her for a long moment, as if making certain he had heard her correctly. His thumbs pressed into the flesh of her waist.

"You want to couple with me?"

"Yes," she swallowed, knowing she could not turn back now, but sure this was what she wanted. "I do."

At her reply, he lifted her up by her ribcage, as easily

as if she had been a child, and brought her closer. She braced her hands on his wide shoulders as he lifted her partially out of the water.

"Am I hurting your wound?" she asked, worried about the bandaged gunshot in his shoulder.

"I do not feel pain at your touch. Only pleasure." He looked up at her. "Much pleasure."

Fervently, he pressed his face to her stomach and kissed her navel and then slowly lowered her, pressing kisses upon her torso until her breasts met his mouth. He moaned raggedly, as if a floodgate had opened, and then took her left breast into his mouth while his hands squeezed her and his teeth pulled at her aching nipple.

"Alek!" she gasped. The sensation of his teeth biting her was both shocking and arousing, and she didn't know whether to push him away or clutch him closer. He seemed to derive as much pleasure from suckling her as she did from his ravenous mouth. She had heard that a woman's breasts could be a source of pleasure, but she had never guessed it could be like this. His tongue and teeth sent her to a place she had never been before, a place full of primal need and shameless desire. She gave in to the feeling while something full and intense began to throb deep inside her.

How could she have lived for twenty-three years without knowing the ecstasy of her own body? Why had she denied herself this pleasure until now with Alek? Though a small voice whispered inside her head, trying to tell her that she had waited for the right man, Marissa turned away from the truth and let herself be swept away by pure physical pleasure.

Marissa's elbows buckled, and she melted downward with a long sigh of aching wonder as he suckled her other breast. His shaft came up against her womanly place and she flinched in surprise.

"Oh, Alek!" she breathed, "That's heavenly."

His damp hair tickled her neck and she shuddered.

"You are cold?" he asked in a husky voice.

"No, I'm hot," she replied, plunging her hands into his hair and bringing him back to her breast. "I'm on fire for you—"

"Ah, woman," he replied, kneading her free breast until the nipple grew as hard as stone. "I am on fire, too."

She found herself wanting to arch against him and rub herself against the firm planes of his chest, to feel every inch of him against her nakedness. Her nipples ached for contact with his bare flesh, and something even more persistent yearned for closeness, as if she were desperate to crush her heart against his and lock him in a bone-shattering embrace.

Either he desired the same closeness or else he read her mind, for Alek shifted his grip from her torso to her backside and lowered her to her knees. She put her palms on the hard bulges of his upper arms and leaned forward, sliding the nubs of her breasts down the expanse of his chest and throwing her head back in ecstasy. Shafts of pleasure as bright as lightning shot through her as her breasts skidded across his wet flesh. She moaned, unable to contain the sound of her pleasure.

He responded by nipping the sensitive flesh between her neck and shoulder, as a stallion nips his mate. Marissa let out a sound, half gasp and half giggle. Her chest seemed to burst with heat and joy, and she felt a crazy roiling of sensations, as if she wanted to laugh out loud and sob at the same time. What was happening to her? Surely, Alek's brand of coupling had no connection to the human heart. What they were doing was purely physical—no emotional strings attached. Yet, why was her heart exploding?

Marissa couldn't think about it. All she wanted to feel was her skin and his skin melding as one, his lips on hers, and their tongues entwining in a mating ritual as blatant as what was to come. Once again, he answered her by kissing her until she squirmed in desperation for the rest of him.

Alek kissed her throat, and she raised up to drag her nipples across him again. This time he lifted her rear and urged her closer, and when she arched downward, he spread her legs. As if choreographed, she sank upon him in a graceful dip.

With a cry of surprise, Marissa snapped out of her erotic trance and glanced down. His blunt manhood pressed against her, and she wasn't sure if she would be able to accommodate him.

"Alek!" she gasped, tensing her legs and nearly losing him.

"Don't!" he demanded, clutching her hair in his fist and bringing her back downward. "Sit down on me, she-devil. Sit down!"

She tried to relax the muscles of her thighs, but only managed to shift helplessly, which seemed to inflame him. His head sank back and he closed his eyes tightly as he pushed upward, struggling to gain entrance. For a split second Marissa feared they wouldn't find the right combination and the thought sent her into a frenzy of frustration. She undulated her pelvis and was just about to guide him into her with her hand when Alek growled and launched upward, sloshing the water over the end of the tub. She hung on to him as he pivoted and put her down on the edge of the tub, where the plush mauve carpeting met the narrow ring of tile.

Together they collapsed onto the thick carpet, half in the water and half out. Before Marissa could squirm all the way out of the water, Alek pinned her hips and, with a powerful thrust, pushed into her.

"Alek!" She felt her body stretch to accommodate him while the overwhelming need to take him in made her arch her pelvis for more. She spread her knees apart a bit farther, desperate now for his entire length. He groaned.

Then he leaned down, kissed her throat, and plunged into her, burying himself.

Marissa hung motionless, unbelievably filled with him, her hips fused to his, knowing now what people meant when they claimed lovers became one. She had thought the phrase referred purely to emotional joining, not to this glorious, heated physical union that was giving her sustenance she had never known she lacked. She felt him shudder and slipped her hands around the wonderfully muscled width of his back, thinking he was the most magnificent man she had ever seen. At that moment, she wanted to say something that would convey how he made her feel. But what could she tell him when all she could think of was the phrase, "I love you."

I love you, I love you, I love you.

What had come over her? Love had no place here. This was a physical act, and it would be idiotic to get emotionally involved.

Alek pulled back, his chest heaving and his eyes still closed while his hands framed her hip bones. He almost looked as if he were in pain, but she knew from the intensity of her own feelings that they were experiencing something far different from pain. To be linked like this had nothing to do with pain and a whole lot to do with pleasure—pure primal pleasure.

Then Marissa moved her hips, slightly up and forward. Alek moaned and his hands slid to cup her shoulders. He thrust back into her, allowing some of his weight to sink upon her. At the pressing of his weight, Marissa let out a small cry of delight and slipped her hands down his back to his buttocks, which seemed to increase a strange, urgent feeling inside her.

"Woman," he murmured in a voice that sent chills down her spine.

Alek's hands roamed up and down her back as he caught her rhythm and moved with it, and every once in a while he caressed her breasts, and moved down to kiss them. His mouth spun her into a frenzy. His hands vaulted her into rapture. Even the sound of his strident breathing made her crazy. Soon she was bucking against him, nearly out of control with hunger. The faster she went, the more intense the feeling became. Though no one had ever described orgasm to her, she knew she was a hair's breadth away from experiencing it.

Suddenly, she felt Alek swell even larger within her, and he wrapped his arms around her, pinning her to his torso. Frenetic and breathless, he found her mouth and kissed her frantically, pushing her further and further from the tub in his frenzy.

"She-devil!" he exclaimed in a constricted voice against her neck, his body straining as if he were going to shove her through the carpet into the floorboards beneath.

His tongue pushed into her mouth as his body drove into her. With each thrust he groaned deep in his throat as if he were trying to hold back but couldn't fight the demands of his desire any longer. The passionate sounds sent Marissa over the brink. She cried out and opened even wider for him, wanting him to drive into her as far as he could go. He grabbed her buttocks and plunged into her again and again.

Then he threw back his head and cried out her name while the veins in his neck bulged as if they would pop and his fingers clamped around her hips like a vice. Marissa felt something explode inside her, a great burst of ecstasy, as she was overwhelmed by a shattering climax. She clutched Alek's straining neck and felt the hot streams of his seed pouring into her, while her own body squeezed him again and again in powerful satiating waves. She clung to him, amazed at the sensation of fusing with him, of taking his seed into her, of giving and receiving so much pleasure.

And then her heart burst apart and she knew she had failed to maintain her emotional distance from this man. She didn't want just his rigid manhood locked inside her, she didn't want just his seed spilling into her womb. She wanted his heart and his love and his loyalty. Shattered, Marissa pressed her cheek to his jaw and her lips to his ear, dying to whisper the words that screamed to be said.

She held him as Alek moved against her a moment longer, still in the throes of his overwhelming climax. All the while he caressed her with incredulity and reverence and covered her face and neck with ardent kisses. After a few minutes, he touched the side of her face and looked down at her, his eyes glowing like burning topaz.

"She-devil!" he said, panting. "I did not hurt you?"

"No," she replied, as breathless as he. "That was the best thing that ever happened to me."

He grinned and squeezed her rump. "And to me."

Then he sobered and dragged his thumb across her lower lip, searching her face. Obviously, he was not the type of man to couple with a woman and roll away for a cigarette.

"I had no idea, Marissa," he began. "I never dreamed that a woman could enjoy this."

"It depends on the man she's with," Marissa replied softly. She pushed back the dark hair that fell over his forehead and heard her own words echoing in her thoughts. It did depend upon the man, and she knew that losing her virginity to anyone but Alek would have been far less than satisfactory.

"If the woman has feelings for the man," Marissa continued, "making love is something she longs to do with him."

"Making love?" he smiled and tried the phrase on his tongue. "Yes. Making love. That sounds much better than coupling."

"Making love entails more than just coupling, Alek, and that's the difference. It involves feelings and respect."

"You have feelings for me, she-devil?"

"Yes." There, she admitted it, even to herself.

For a long moment he didn't reply and quietly looked down at her face as if he were memorizing her features. She wondered if she had overstepped the bounds of the warrior with her mention of feelings. Perhaps warriors pretended not to have emotional ties with women.

Then Alek slowly relaxed, drawing her with him into the now-tepid water. He sat upon the ledge and she settled into his lap. As if tied to their lovemaking, the thunderstorm had abated, leaving in its wake a comforting patter of rain on the window nearby. In the moment of quiet contemplation in his arms, the thought of Alek's hopeless future welled up like a dark cloud. How could this beautiful, vigorous man meet with such an end? She couldn't bear to think about it, especially after he had made her feel so alive. Marissa laid her head upon his chest and embraced him with all her strength, as if to deny that bleak future.

He stroked her hair until their breathing returned to normal.

"I wanted you," he said, breaking the silence with the

low rumble of his voice. "As I have wanted no other woman."

Marissa felt a thrill course through her at his confession. Being wanted by a man like Alek was an honor.

"All the other times when the hunger came upon me, I had the power to turn away. But not with you. You must be a demon."

"I'm no demon. I'm a woman."

"Then this world must be a place the Romans have made to trap me so that I will not want to go back to my people."

"It is no trap, Alek." She closed her eyes and slipped her hands around the girth of his chest, reveling in the power of the man she held in her arms. "When the time comes, you will be free to go. I have no right to ask you to stay."

"Then why did you come to me? If not to enchant me, why did you make love with me?"

"Because I wanted to know what it was like to be with you. When this is all over, Alek, I'll go back to my old life and I'll remember making love with you. And that memory will keep me going when I'm all alone."

"You speak as if there are no men of merit in your land, no man for you, she-devil."

"There *are* no men like you, Alek. I guess that's the problem."

"There are no women like you in my land either. None that please me in the ways you do." His caressed her right breast. "And I have a thirst for you that cannot be slaked with just one drink."

She felt the sharp stirring of renewed desire in his loins and looked up at him.

"You see?" He smiled, and his white teeth flashed. He reached out and kissed her, sighing with pleasure as he sank back to the edge of the tub. She felt herself succumb to the same thrill as before when his hands began to stroke her back and arms.

"For tonight then, Marissa, we will forget our worlds and know only each other."

"Yes." She melted against his mouth. For a warrior, Alek had a poetic grasp of language which lent him a surprisingly romantic streak.

"And I will drink of you all that I want."

"Yes." She put her hands on either side of his face and gazed at his strong, sharp features and clear golden brown eyes. For one night she would let herself love this warrior as her heart called out for her to do. And God grant her the strength to let him go when the time came for farewell.

14

A faint noise outside the room awakened Alek, where he lay sprawled on the massive hotel bed. He opened his eyes and listened for a moment, but the noise was not repeated, and he supposed it was just another normal sound in this new and noisy world into which he had travelled. Satisfied there were no intruders breaking into the hotel suite, Alek turned his gaze to the woman lying beside him.

Dawn light filtered through the crack in the drapes and slanted over her naked shoulder, outlining the deceptive delicacy of her arm. Alek was not fooled by her lean arm and feminine shoulder, for he had felt the power in her embrace during the night. And what a night it had been! He drew Marissa's naked body against his, marvelling anew that her slender length fit so well against his large warrior's frame. The last few hours with her had been the most wondrous, deeply satisfying time of his life, and he knew that he would find it hard to part with this woman.

Could he convince her to return to Ballachulix with him, should he find a way to go back to his own country? Would that be too much to ask of this spirited woman from Montana? He couldn't imagine not being around her, especially now that he had shared the night with her.

Whatever happened, he'd take what he could get from the time they had in this world, and trust in the gods to decide the future. Alek caressed Marissa's small but exquisitely formed breasts, closed his eyes, and drifted off to sleep with the scent of their sweet love-making drugging his senses.

When he slept, he dreamed of the day he had discovered his mother hurrying through the forest early in the morning during a snowstorm. Normally he wouldn't have been up at that early hour, especially during the winter, but he had been given a test by his teacher, the old battle hero Alorix, who had challenged him to endure the entire night standing on a bluff with nothing to cover himself with but the light bracae worn after Beltane and a wolf pelt thrown over his shoulders.

Alek, thirteen years old and full of fire, had climbed to the top of the bluff, confident that he could withstand the buffeting wind and the knee-deep snow. Before long, however, the chill seeped through the seams of his leather boots, which were stuffed with straw, and numbed his feet. The winter night was long—and soon seemed endless—as he stood proudly upright, his lance staked in the ground beside him. When the storm hit, he withstood the flakes that coated his hair and lashes and turned the wolf pelt completely white. He withstood the pain in his fingers and toes and the burning cry in his back that called for him to sit upon the ground, if only for a moment.

But a moment would ruin him, and he refused to give in. He stood tall and determined as the hours dragged on, forcing his mind to separate from his freezing body. His pride turned in circles, keeping him steadfast. At first he endured for himself and his sense of worth. Then he stood there out of spite, to prove to his father that he was made of something just as strong, if not stronger, than Brennan. When the snow began to drift around his legs and his entire body felt stiff, Alek remained at his post out of desire, hoping to gain approval in the eyes of his teacher and mentor. At thirty-five, Alorix, the once-powerful champion of the Senones, was past his prime but still more man than Brennan would ever be. Scarred, maimed, and blind in one eye, Alorix still maintained the straight-backed stance of his youth, and his face still glowed with strength and courage. But he was wracked by a persistent cough that plagued him, especially during the night. Not many of the other men of the village knew of Alorix's illness. But Alek, who had enjoyed special treatment from the battered warrior and secretly thought of him as the father of his spirit, had spent many evening hours in the home of his teacher and was well acquainted with the man's private suffering.

Alek had been sworn to secrecy, however, for Alorix claimed the only way a warrior should die was in glory, not from a wasting disease. He wanted no one to know of his weakness, and when the time came to face the Romans, he would roar into battle and die a hero before he became a complete invalid. Alek insisted that he be treated by his mother, who would surely have an herbal remedy that would ease his suffering, if not cure the malady altogether. But, like many warriors, Alorix would never admit to pain of any kind, not even the night he returned from battle with two of his fingers cut off and a gaping wound that showed the bone in his thigh. Alorix had begrudgingly allowed Helin to sew his leg and treat his hand. But he had adamantly refused to see her about his cough and forbade Alek to mention it to her or to anyone.

Alorix was all man—proud, strong, unbending but fair. Alek prayed that one day, when he was a man, he would be just like his teacher. He breathed in and squared his aching shoulders, vowing to meet dawn on the bluff even if it killed him.

Hours later, when the bleak winter sun pushed back the black hood of night, Alek saw a familiar shape stealing down the path at the base of the bluff. There was no mistaking his mother's pace, even when she was wrapped in a brown woolen cloak against the cold. She had a graceful way of walking, very quickly but lightly, as if her feet barely touched the ground, which allowed her to proceed soundlessly through the forest. But what was his mother doing out at this time of the morning? And what was she carrying?

"Mother!" he called, but she couldn't hear him over the wind.

Reaching out with a stiff arm, Alek grabbed his lance and yanked it out of the snow. Dawn had come. The vigil was over. He could leave knowing he had met the challenge and conquered the weakness of his body. Exalting but frozen, he waded through the snow until he came to the path in the forest where the ground was sheltered by the fir boughs overhead. He brushed the snow from his wolf pelt and shook out his hair. Though he was exhausted and chilled to the bone, he was curious to discover Helin's mission. He set off after his mother, calling her name to no avail.

By the time he caught up with her, she had left the path and struggled through the snow to a grove of oak trees. Alek hung back, always reluctant to enter a grove, as if an invisible force pressed against his chest to keep him away. Was it because he had taken the path of a warrior and not a priest? Was he refused entrance by the spirits because he had denied service to them? Or was it because of his changeling blood? His mother passed into the grove as if it were a haven. He hung back at the edge of the trees, detained by the strange sense of alienation that had shadowed him all his life.

He saw Helin lift the small bundle and tenderly place it in the crotch of a great oak. What was she doing? What ritual was this?

"Mother?" he called.

This time she heard him and snatched her hands away from the bundle. She turned around swiftly and stood in front of the tree, as if to conceal the bundle behind her.

"Alek!" she replied, but the last part of his name was lost to the wind. Helin clutched her cloak around her and stood at the base of the tree, unable or unwilling to walk to him.

Hardening himself against the invisible force of the grove, Alek swept forward, one hand on his lance, the other on the hilt of his dagger. The hairs on the back of his neck stood up as he crossed through the snow to his mother. He didn't like it here and felt an urgency to leave as soon as possible.

"What are you doing here?" he asked, trying to see what she was hiding behind her.

"Attending to a womanly matter. And you, Alek?"

"I was standing on the bluff. Part of my training." He craned his neck to look around her shoulder. "I saw you walk by."

Helin's small white hands clutched the cloak at her neck. He hadn't seen his mother for weeks, and now that he was this close to her, he noticed that her eyes were full of haunted lights and dull fatigue. A bruise shadowed the flesh on her left cheekbone and another marked her right eye socket. Brennan had beaten her again. A wave of hatred washed over Alek, and his fist clenched tightly around the shaft of the lance. He knew he had to wait until he was taller and stronger to avenge the mistreatment of his mother, but when he saw her like this, his powerlessness churned in his gut until he wanted to retch.

"Alek, you look frozen to the bone! Your lips are blue."

"Never mind me," he said, brushing off her concern. "You're the one who shouldn't be out in this storm."

"I had a task to perform."

"What task?" He reached for her arm. "What was in the bundle you carried?"

"An offering." She stepped away from the tree and out of his grip. "Come, Alek. Return with me and I will make you some hot tea to drink."

When she moved away from the oak, his attention was drawn downward by a crimson drop on the snow. Even in the dim light of dawn, the red splotch was like a brand.

"Mother!" He grabbed her arm again. "Are you hurt? You are bleeding!"

She glanced behind her and saw two more spots in the snow. Then she calmly turned to him. "It is my woman's flow," she replied, giving him a faltering smile. "Do not worry, Alek."

A shadow flitted across her face, and Alek saw through the deceptive serenity of her expression. It wasn't like his mother lie to him. Yet her tired eyes were dark with sorrow, and he knew there was more to this than she wanted to admit. Was Helin like Alorix, concealing her pain out of a sense of pride? If she was suffering, why wouldn't she tell him? Over the years they had shared everything. Everything! Alek was deeply hurt that she would lie to him, for he knew a special closeness with his mother that few boys shared. She had always been more a friend than a mother to him. They were allies against Brennan's violence, and had formed a bond much stronger than love.

Allies and friends did not keep secrets from each other.

"What task brings you out in the storm?" he demanded, his voice cracking. The sudden dip in his voice reminded him that he was still half-boy, half-man, and far too young to take on the beast of his father. "What offering makes you endanger your own life?"

"A private offering."

"We have no secrets between us, Mother. Tell me!"

"No, Alek," she countered and tried to pull away.

The pelt flapped around his elbows while she turned away from him, her face hardened by cold and determination.

"Mother!" He held her fast and kept her from walking away only for an instant, only for the time it took for him to realize that he was using the same kind of force on her that his father wielded. Flushing with shame, Alek released her arm.

"Leave it be, my son!" She turned to face him. "Some things are better left to the darkness."

"You speak in riddles!"

"Life is full of riddles."

"I want to know!" He glared at her, but she refused to speak. The instant she turned to leave, he whirled around to the tree. If Helin didn't tell him what was going on, he would find out for himself. He staked the lance in the snow and reached up for the bundle.

"No!" Helin cried.

He pulled the woolen bundle from the crotch of the tree. It was just the right size to balance on his palm.

"Alek, no!" Helin stumbled through the snow, leaving a crimson trail behind her as she lunged for the offering in his hand.

He pivoted out of reach and flung away the woolen folds of cloth to reveal the offering that had compelled his mother to walk such a distance in the dead of winter.

Alek stared down at his hand and felt a new kind of chill seize him. He felt rigid fingers of frost harden his hand, his jaw, his heart, preventing him from uttering the slightest gasp of horror. Resting in his palm was a tiny dead infant.

"Why, Alek?" Helin wailed, dropping to her knees in the snow. "Why did you have to look?"

Alek stared in stunned silence at the little girl child, her ten fragile fingers slightly curled, her teeny, perfectly formed lips gently pursed, and her sweet miniature eyelids closed to the light of day.

Helin broke into wracking sobs in the snow, her pale hands covering her face.

Slowly, Alek came to his senses. Carefully, he covered the still form with the folds of the small wool blanket, wishing somehow that the fabric might warm the child, even in death. Shattered and trembling, he returned the bundle to the crotch of the tree.

Then he turned to Helin. "I'm sorry, Mother," he said, hoping she would forgive him.

Helin did not answer him. She had collapsed to her knees in the snow. For a moment Alek gazed helplessly at her, incapable of giving her solace or even knowing what to say.

"Come, let me take you back." He gathered her up in

his arms. Her small frame was much lighter than he imagined, never having picked her up before.

"Alek!" she sobbed, sinking her head upon his shoulder. She was exhausted. He could feel the strength flooding out of her. "No one must know of this. Brennan must never find out."

"That you delivered a stillborn child?"

"That I was pregnant as well." She clung to his neck. "Please, Alek, no one must know."

Alek nodded. Women were often judged by the number of pregnancies they counted during a lifetime and the successful outcome of childbirth. It was no secret that Brennan and Helin's union was unusually fruitless. Except for Alek, they had produced no other children. The fact that Helin wished to conceal a stillbirth came as no surprise to him. Brennan would accuse her of purposely ending the pregnancy and then beat her for failing to give him more children, for robbing him of the glory of siring big, strapping sons to follow in his footsteps.

"Oh, Alek," Helin's hand curled at the base of his neck as she sobbed. "I so wanted this child! How I wanted her!"

Alek strode through the snow toward the village, incapable of offering her words of solace. He couldn't reassure her with the hope of more babies. In fifteen years of marriage Helin had produced only one child, and it was quite possible that there would be no others after this one. Helin was no longer a young woman.

He could only wonder where the blame would be placed for the lack of children. Everyone pointed their finger at Helin. But what if Brennan's seed was bad? What if Brennan was the reason his wife's womb lay fallow? The only way to prove Brennan's manhood was to discover the number of children he had gotten on other women. It was no secret that Brennan had bedded many others besides Helin—when drunk he often bragged about the women he'd taken—but so far no one had come forward to name him as the father of their son or daughter.

Yet, if Brennan's seed was bad, how could he have fathered a son and daughter? Alek trudged through the snow, reluctant to examine the only other way Helin could have become pregnant, but knowing he could not ignore the possibility that she might have been taken by another man.

Instantly, Alek thought back to the summer afternoon when he had come upon the Roman raping his mother. How many moons had waxed and waned since Caius Sellenius had spilled his seed into his mother? Alek strode more quickly through the snow, mindless of the pain in his shoulders and arms, as he numbered the moons since the rape and compared them to the tiny girl child that might have been his sister.

The realization staggered him. The child might have been the result of the rape. And yet his mother had longed for the baby? Alek clenched his jaw and stumbled toward the village gate. Why would she want the child of a Roman dog? Was she mad? Had she finally lost her mind to the grief and violence of her life?

Alek carried her to the house and left as soon as she was comfortable. He turned down her offer of tea, frantic to get away from her and the dark thoughts that came at him from all sides like hornets. He ran from his mother's home and dashed out of the wooden enclosure that surrounded the village, running back to the oak grove where he had left his lance and the last vestiges of his childhood.

With each pump of his knees, he fought off the dark suspicion that nipped at his heels. But he refused to look back, afraid of what he might find out about his own life, for such an idea was too awful for a proud young warrior to contemplate.

Alek jerked awake, his dream still flaming hot. He glared at the ornate wall of the bedroom while the memory hit him with full and brutal impact. He turned and clutched Marissa to his chest as if to hold off the truth by remaining in her world, where he had no past and no future. But the nearness of her body could not protect him from his own churning thoughts.

If Brennan's seed was bad and Caius Sellenius had fathered the stillborn child, who, then, had fathered him?

Marissa turned in the big bed and felt Alek's warm palm slide off her thigh. He slept beside her, and she gloried in the fact that she shared his bed. He had spent the last few hours at her side, and his warm body gave her a sense of belonging that she had never dreamed existed. Sleeping in his arms was precious, something she was glad she had known, if only for one night.

She looked across the expanse of the pillow to the place where he lay his head upon the crook of his arm. Against the darkness of his hair, his nose was sharply defined, slightly hawked at his brow line and pointed at the tip. Even in sleep, his lips looked firm and determined, his cleft chin defiant. He was a man who knew what he wanted and said so, and she liked that about him. She remembered the way he had told her he wanted her, and the very phrase made a thrill course through her.

Alek reminded her of a wild mustang her father had once captured. For days they had tried to break the stallion and for days he had defied them—and had sent more than one bronc buster to the hospital. Marissa had watched the efforts from her perch on the corral, marvelling at the wild perfection of the horse, his undeniable spirit, and his flawless form. After a week, she had begged her father to let the horse go. The stallion was not meant to be broken and, even if they managed to get a saddle on him, he would die before he bent to the will of a man. To ruin the mustang would be to ruin a masterpiece. Though the rest of the men thought she was a softhearted fool, her father understood her and finally agreed to give up and release the horse.

How well she remembered that day. She had opened the gate and stepped back, watching the mustang study her with his haughty stare, so similar to Alek's. Then the stallion snorted, shook his head, and galloped out of the corral into the early Montana morning air. His hoof beats thundered past her, and she grinned as he broke for freedom. She knew his heart more thoroughly than the bronc busters had, perhaps because she was a woman and was more attuned to the animal, or perhaps because she valued freedom more highly than most.

Later, when she rode the range searching for injured cows or strays, she would often come upon the stallion. He would always stop and regard her from a distance, and she would send him the message of her heart, hoping that he could hear how much she loved his beauty, how much she cherished his wild spirit.

Such was the spirit of the man who lay beside her— so haughty, so perfect, so rare. To know that he would end his life in chains, to visualize his beautiful body mutilated, was more than she could bear. How could it happen? Why would anyone want to destroy this masterpiece of a man? A great wave of sorrow rose up and choked her as she gazed at his handsome face, and a small scalding tear made its way down her cheek. Who would she petition for his freedom? Her father was not here this time. And she couldn't change the course of history. Alek would die the worst death a wild heart could suffer.

Then, to her chagrin, she saw Alek's eyes blink open, as if he had heard her crying in his sleep.

Immediately, Marissa turned away, hoping he hadn't seen her tears, and started to scramble out of bed. But Alek reached for her wrist and stopped her.

"Marissa," he said. "You are crying. Why?"

"I'm not," she retorted, "I just have something in my eye."

"Do not lie, she-devil." He released her and jumped to his feet on the opposite side of the bed. "You cry just like all the others!"

"No!" She whirled to face him, pulling the sheets to her breast, never dreaming that he would think his lovemaking was the cause of her tears.

"You try to be tough. You try to be a warrior, she-devil, but you are still a woman."

"Yes. And this woman thoroughly enjoyed you last night."

"You lie to show you are brave."

"No!"

"Then explain your tears."

He raised his chin, oblivious to his nakedness, and challenged her to tell the truth.

She couldn't possibly reveal the reason for her sorrow. Better to let him think that his lovemaking had repulsed her rather than tell Alek what was in store for him.

"Come, she-devil. Tell me."

"Think what you like, Conan," she replied. "I've got to check on Leslie."

She swiped the tears from her cheeks, yanked the

top sheet off the bed, and wrapped it around herself while she headed for the door. He stood at the side of the bed like a column of marble and did not look at her as she passed by him. She had a horrible feeling that Alek would never touch her again. If he turned away from her, she knew it would break her heart.

Marissa stumbled through the parlor, walloped by the gamut of emotions she had just experienced—love, sorrow, and devastation. She didn't need this complication in her life. She didn't want to need anyone, especially Alek. She had never intended to get this involved.

Steeling herself to enter Leslie's room, she paused at the door, wiped the last of the tears from her eyes, and smoothed back her hair. She didn't want Leslie to see that she had been crying and ask questions she wasn't prepared to answer. Vowing to rise above her trouble with Alek, Marissa opened the door and stepped into the room.

Leslie was nowhere in sight.

15

Before Marissa could gather her wits, she heard the latch of the parlor door click shut behind her.

"Alek!" she cried. Marissa turned and ran across the parlor, stumbling on the sheet as it wrapped around her legs. She yanked open the door to the hall just in time to see Alek disappearing around a corner, wearing only his trousers and boots, headed for the elevator.

"Alek!" she repeated, more to herself than to his vanishing form. Dejected, her shoulders slumped. Leslie was gone and Alek would be out of the hotel within minutes. Where was he going? It would be useless to follow him. By the time she got dressed he would be long gone.

She closed the door and turned the lock. Would she ever see him again? She couldn't bear the thought that he would drop out of her life. Yet Alek was under the impression that he had hurt her, that he had defiled her by coupling with her. If Alek had the sort of honor she was certain he possessed, he would keep his distance from her, and perhaps avoid her altogether.

Even more pressing was the question regarding Leslie's whereabouts. Where had Leslie gone? Had she finally awakened during the night from her drug-induced coma? What if she had been disoriented, thought she was being kept prisoner in a strange room, and had fled?

But to where? And how long had Leslie been gone? Marissa snatched her watch off the bureau and peered at the face. Eleven o'clock? She and Alek had slept until eleven? Marissa hurried to the phone and dialed Leslie's number. After four rings, the answering machine kicked in. Marissa left a message for her sister stating that should Leslie arrive home soon to please remain at the apartment until Marissa got there, which would be within the hour.

Then the thought struck her that Leslie might not be lucid. She might very well be wandering around downtown Seattle in her stockinged feet, oblivious to traffic. She could get picked up as a transient by the police. Or she might still be under the influence of the night orchid nectar and behaving as amorously as she had with Alek. Leslie could get herself into a lot of trouble coming on to the wrong people.

Marissa hurried to the bathroom for a quick shower. She never should have slept with Alek those few precious hours. She should have spent the time keeping vigil at Leslie's bedside instead. How could she have been so selfish? And now, as a result of her selfishness, they were both gone—the two people who meant the world to her. She should have known better than to indulge her own desires when there were more important matters to attend to.

With impatient tugs, Marissa braided her hair, got

dressed, and checked the rooms of the suite for stray belongings, finding Leslie's shoes and Alek's discarded shirt. Then she took the elevator down to the lobby, paid her bill, and caught a cab to the apartment in Woodland Park.

Diana heard a knock at her bedroom door and awoke with a start, surprised to find she had slept until eleven o'clock. "Yes?" she asked as she slowly rose to her elbow.

"It's David." Her door opened slightly. "Are you decent?"

"Yes, but—" She sat up, pulling the covers to her chin as David came into the room bearing a tray.

"No buts, Diana." He smiled. "I brought you some breakfast."

She didn't know whether to be elated or alarmed.

"But David, what about Kyle?"

"He went off to church a couple of hours ago. He told me to let you sleep, said you'd had a restless night."

Diana tried to hide the frown that tugged at her mouth. Restless wasn't exactly the word she would have chosen to describe her night with Kyle.

"So I waited until now," David continued, putting the tray on the edge of the nightstand, "hoping to catch a few minutes with you before he came back. We've got to talk about the prisoners."

"What about them?" Diana bunched the covers even closer, distracted by worry and wondering if David or Kyle had discovered the prisoners were missing.

"Kyle asked me to check on them early this morning," David continued, "and when I went down to the lab, I found they'd escaped."

"Oh?" She glanced up at him. Their gazes locked and held.

"You let them go, didn't you, Diana?"

"Yes."

"When?"

"Very early this morning. About four a.m." She brushed back her tousled bangs, thankful to have someone to confess to. "Does Kyle know?"

"Not yet. But he soon will. And I don't want you to admit to what you did."

"Why not? Someone had to help those people."

"That someone should not have been you. Kyle is going to be very upset, and I'm afraid he will take his anger out on you."

"I don't care. It doesn't matter."

"It matters to me. So don't say anything. I'll handle it."

She looked up at David to find him gazing earnestly down at her. His hair was slightly mussed, but he looked wonderful to her, warm and comfortable in a way Kyle could never be. While she perused him, he sat down on the edge of the mattress, and she scooted back to allow him more room. He reached out and tucked a stray lock of her hair behind her ear, and his touch sent a delicious ripple of shivers through her.

"David," she whispered, looking down to hide the need in her eyes.

"I wanted you so much last night." He slipped his hand across her shoulder. "Knowing you were close just about drove me crazy."

She pressed her lips together, refusing to admit to having similar thoughts.

"Diana, I can't let him hurt you. You mean too much to me."

He reached out with his other hand and wrapped her in his arms, embracing her tightly. She couldn't imagine what it would be like to wake up every morning in the arms of this man. Hesitantly, she slipped her arms around his back and returned the hug, wishing her heart wouldn't twist with such agony when she was with David. He felt so right, so wonderful, and she knew they could be comfortable together, more at ease with each other than most people dreamed of being, if only she were not married to Kyle.

"I'm afraid, David," she said near his ear. "What if Kyle should return? What if he has a bug in this room to record everything that I do and say? He's like that, you know."

"So leave him."

"It isn't that simple."

David pulled away. "There you go again, making excuses. The man's an asshole, Diana. A genius in some areas, an asshole in others. You're never going to make him happy. And he's never going to attempt to please you. You know that, don't you?"

"Yes. But I can't talk about it now. I can't." She glanced at the tray.

David followed her line of sight and sighed. "Sorry," he said, lifting the tray. "We shouldn't let your breakfast get cold."

Diana wasn't hungry. Her disease and their discussion had stunted her appetite. But, for David's sake, she would feign interest in the eggs and croissant he had prepared.

"Thank you," she said, touching his cheek. "This is such a nice surprise. You're a sweet man."

"Sweet?" He gave her a crooked grin. "I'm out of my mind, Diana. It isn't natural for a man to go this long without a woman."

She paused with the coffee cup halfway to her mouth, surprised by his confession. "You haven't—"

"Not since last year. I can't. Not with anyone but you."

Carefully, she returned the cup to its saucer, concentrating to keep her hand from shaking. "You can't wait for me, David," she declared. "It wouldn't be right to expect that of you."

"No one has to expect it. I don't want any woman but you. And if I can't have you, I would rather not have anyone."

"If Kyle heard you talking like this, he'd kill you."

"Let him try, the bastard."

"If you feel so strongly about him, why do you keep working with him?" She played with the scrambled eggs.

"To be frank, I don't want to sever my connection with you, Diana. To maintain that, I'd work with Attila the Hun."

She couldn't help but smile. "I don't know who's worse, Attila or Kyle."

"I don't either." David split her croissant and chewed on a piece of the buttery roll. "But, whatever the case, I think we need to decide something between ourselves about him."

She felt a strong barb of dread, thinking he was going to bring up the subject of divorce again. "Such as?"

"How long we're going to go along with him and this night orchid scenario."

"Oh." Diana took a sip of juice, wondering how long it would be until Kyle discovered what she had done during the night.

"I don't know about you, Diana, but I don't approve of what he's done so far with the Druid ritual. And the deeper into it he gets, the more reluctant I am to follow."

"I feel the same way, David. I keep asking him what he plans to do with Leslie and the warrior, and he never answers me."

David nodded. "Something has been changing in

Kyle these past few days. I don't know what exactly, but he's lost his objectivity in this experiment. Once a scientist crosses the line, he loses some of his powers of rationalization, which is dangerous for anyone, but especially for a man of science."

"What can we do?"

"Well, I'll tell you what I've been thinking." David shifted his weight on the bed. "I'll help Kyle find the warrior. Then I'm going to convince Kyle to send Alek back to wherever he came from and leave the night orchid alone. It's far too dangerous to be dabbling in something that powerful not knowing how to handle it."

"Do you think he'll listen to reason?"

"He'd better, or I'll get the police in on it."

"That might ruin him."

"Perhaps the threat of the police will be enough. I'm hoping it will be. Kyle isn't completely crazy."

"Do you think he is crazy, though?" Diana asked, returning her empty coffee cup to the tray.

"I don't know. But he's going off the deep end with this research." David frowned and stared past her, lapsing into his own thoughts. He suddenly seemed very far away, and Diana reached out to touch his arm.

"Don't worry so much, David," she urged softly. "It will all work out somehow."

"I hope you're right. But I have to tread a very fine line here, Diana, because if I say too much, he might tell me to go to hell, and then I won't be around if you need me."

"I don't want you to put yourself in danger," she said. "Not for me. It's not worth it."

"I disagree." He laid his hand on top of hers. "You're worth the world to me, Diana."

He leaned forward and kissed her lightly, but Diana soon found the kiss turning into something far deeper, something far too serious, as he pressed her against the mound of pillows. When David kissed her, she felt as if she were falling into a chasm, spiralling into uncontrolled circles of joy and need. Her breasts reacted immediately, swelling and hardening in anticipation of his touch, and her heart slammed against her chest, begging to be heard. She pulled back, breathless, before she allowed herself to plunge into the abyss.

"Kyle will be back any minute," she said. "I should get up and get dressed."

Reluctantly, David sat up. "All right." He got to his feet and picked up the tray. "But, whatever happens, I want to keep you out of it. This is Kyle's little screwup, and you shouldn't have to suffer for it."

"Neither should you, David."

"Don't worry. I can take care of myself."

He walked to the door, opened it, and then turned. "I hear him now, Diana. I'm going to have a talk with him and get this settled."

"Wait," she replied. "I want to be in on the discussion. I'll be down in a few minutes."

Diana showered and stepped into a rayon sundress in dark blues and greens styled in the fashion of the thirties. She dispensed with any makeup, knowing nothing would hide the pinched way she felt inside, which was reflected in her pale complexion and worried eyes. In less than ten minutes she walked into the kitchen, where she heard Kyle and David talking in strident tones. Diana hurried around the corner toward the family room, shocked to see who sat on the couch near the fireplace.

Leslie Quinn.

Shaken, Diana paused in the doorway. Surely Kyle

must know now that the prisoners had been set free by someone. There was no hiding the truth, even if she'd wanted to.

Kyle looked up at her entrance. "Good morning, dear." He gave her a self-satisfied smirk. "Sleep well?"

She ignored the question and crossed the floor to stand in front of Leslie, who slumped against the back of the couch, her eyes vacant and unseeing. "Leslie?"

Leslie didn't respond and sat gazing at the wall, her eyes glassy and her mouth slightly parted. Her chest rose and fell almost imperceptibly. But at least she was breathing.

"I'm afraid she doesn't hear you, Diana," Kyle put in.

Diana waved her hand before the glassy stare.

"Or see you. She isn't fully functional," Kyle commented. "But there is hope."

"Hope?" Diana lifted Leslie's right hand and found her arm flaccid and her fingers cool to the touch. How long would it take for Leslie to fully recover from the injection of night orchid nectar? Would she ever completely recover? Diana flushed with shame and concern that her own husband had done this to another human being. "Her condition doesn't look hopeful to me. How did she get here?"

"She came back of her own accord."

"I can't believe it! Why?"

"Apparently she hasn't yet had her fill of the night orchid nectar."

"So she came back to the house? How?"

"She had a moment of lucidity, I assume, and caught a cab. I found her just getting out of the taxi when I arrived. It's a good thing I was there to help her. She had no money." He motioned toward her feet. "Why, she wasn't even wearing shoes."

"And what about Marissa? Where is she?"

"I don't know yet. But I'm going to find out."

Diana resisted the impulse to look at David to see what he thought of the situation. The last thing she wanted was for Kyle to think they had been talking behind his back.

Kyle fingered his beard. "How do you suppose she got out of the laboratory?"

Diana took a step forward, ready to confess, when David interrupted her.

"I let her go. Her sister, too. And Alek, simply because I couldn't hold him."

Shocked, Diana whirled to stare at David. She didn't need him to lie for her, to protect her. It was high time she took responsibility for her own life and her own decisions, no matter what the consequences.

"That's not true, Kyle," she put in. "I was the one who let them all go."

Kyle glanced from David to Diana, his cultured veneer cracking from the incredulity in his eyes as he stared at his wife. "You?"

"Yes. You had no right to keep them. Imprisoning people is against the law."

"You idiot, Diana! You little idiot!"

Diana blanched at the insult but refused to look away.

David came around the end of the counter and positioned himself between Kyle and Diana. "She did what was right, Kyle. You could get in serious trouble if anyone found out what you've been doing."

"No one *would* have found out."

"How could you have kept it secret? Eventually you would have had to release Leslie and her sister."

"Not necessarily."

"Oh, and how's that?"

"It doesn't matter now, does it?" Kyle retorted.

"Knowing I'll want to keep this out of the papers, that Quinn woman will probably sue me for all I've got." He narrowed his eyes. "However, I do have her sister. That's something I can use to my advantage."

"Give it up, Kyle," David said. "It will only get worse."

"It already is worse!" Kyle turned on him. "My wife betrays me, my time-traveling prisoner is still on the loose, and that ill-mannered cowgirl from Montana is probably telling her tale of woe to the nearest policeman." Nervously, he tapped his fingertips on his moustache. "And I am still as far from finding the cancer cure as I ever was, with only enough nectar for two more rituals."

"No more rituals, Kyle," Diana protested. "You don't know what you're doing!"

"I know enough to bring a man across time, Diana. That in itself is a major accomplishment, unparalleled in the history of science."

"What you're doing isn't science anymore, Kyle," David countered. "It's witchcraft!"

"Nonsense! It's a fully documented botanical experiment."

"Using human subjects, Kyle. You know the restrictions on that. Had I known what you were doing, I never would have become involved."

"Well, you are involved, David. You are involved up to your neck. So don't give me any lectures on ethics and the like."

"I'll withdraw from the research."

"Oh no you won't. You're going to see this through."

The two men glared at each other at a virtual impasse.

"Leslie should be put in bed," Diana put in.

"Yes." Kyle glanced down. "She is probably suffering

from dehydration. The fools failed to take the IV with them." He crossed his arms. "As you can see, Diana, it is better that Leslie remain with us until she is recovered."

"And when will that be?" Diana inquired cooly.

"She's already showing signs. She got herself here. I am confident that she will gradually have longer lapses of lucidity until she is fully recovered. David, carry her back to the lab."

David frowned. "I don't approve of this."

"I can always alert the authorities and tell them that this was all your idea. It would be your word against mine, and I am sure my voice would be heard over that of an unknown young botanist from a university forestry department, who has a record of being—what shall we say?—unconventional. You and I both know that one more political indiscretion on your part could mean your career."

David shifted uncomfortably and slipped his hands in his pockets. "Aren't you are discounting the unconventional Miss Quinn?"

"Our cowgirl? I think one phone call can fix her. If she goes to the authorities, she will be signing the death warrant of her sister. If she waits and agrees to sign a release regarding our little experiment, she can have her sister safe and sound. I will call her as soon as we see to Leslie's comfort."

"Make your call then, Kyle." David strode to the couch. "I'll take care of Leslie."

"Good." Kyle smiled and reached for the wall phone near the bar. "I'm pleased that we are cooperating once again." He took out a small book from his suit jacket and flipped through until he found the number to Leslie's apartment. He punched it in and glanced at Diana, who felt as if she had once again lost all control of her world.

"Don't look so glum, my dear," Kyle drawled. "Miss

Quinn will be fine. Once I bring a healer out of the past, I'm sure we'll find out what to do about the negative effects of the night orchid nectar."

Diana blanched anew. "You must not repeat the experiment!"

"Oh, but I must. And I can't understand why you're fighting me, Diana. After all, I'm doing it for you."

"For me?"

"To cure you. To make you well, so that our life can be as it once was."

"And how was that?"

"Happy. Loving."

"You were never loving, Kyle." She watched David lift Leslie and carry her down the hall toward the cellar door. "You were—"

He held up his hand to stop her and calmly stated his demands into Leslie's answering machine. Diana stared at him, enraged that he would cut her off in mid-sentence and incredulous that he could behave with such dispassion when people's lives hung in the balance.

Marissa opened the door to Leslie's apartment.

"Les?" she called. Complete silence hung in the room, along with the scent of soap Alek had used in the shower. The smell brought back the memory of the way his skin tasted, the way his muscles rippled. Marissa shut the door, wishing she could shut off her thoughts as well.

"Leslie?" She walked briskly through the apartment, searching for clues that would prove Leslie had returned home. Unfortunately, no sign of her was in evidence. Marissa stood in the center of the kitchen and glanced around, wondering what her next step should be. Then she saw the series of blinking lights on the answering machine at the end table near the couch. She knew her call had been recorded earlier that morning, but there were two others as well, perhaps one from her missing sister. Marissa walked over to the answering machine and pressed the play button.

16

Leslie Quinn, this is your mother. Where in the world are you and your sister? I've been calling for two days now and nobody is ever home. If somebody doesn't call me back soon, I'm going to send Corky out there to see what's happening. So please call me, would you? Today is Sunday and it's . . . oh, I just hate talking into these machines . . . well, it's nine o'clock in the morning. And tell Marissa that the power company is trying to round up the mustangs to get them off the open range. Thought she might like to know, since she always had a special place in her heart for that one stallion. Well, anyway, give me a call when you get home. Bye now.

Marissa frowned. Damned power company. Just wait until she got back to Rosebud County. She wouldn't let them get within a mile of that stallion, even if she had to hold off the bastards with a rifle.

The answering machine beeped and she heard the message she had left for Leslie before leaving the hotel. Impatiently, she waited for her voice to quit droning on the tape and then leaned closer for the final message.

The familiar clipped tones of Kyle Woodward popped on the tape.

> This is Doctor Woodward. Leslie has returned to us of her own accord. I advise you to allow her to remain at the laboratory until she is fully recovered, and I assure you that my colleague and I will take every precaution to ensure her safety. You must not attempt another foolish rescue mission. Leslie's health will suffer if she is denied the proper medical attention. I also insist that you make no attempts to contact the authorities. If I see a single sign of the police, I will make certain that you never see your sister alive again. Do I make myself clear, Miss Quinn? Cooperate and Leslie will be returned to you in a few days. Interfere and she will suffer an unfortunate medical relapse from which she will not recover. Make no attempt to contact me. I will notify you when Leslie is ready to be discharged from my care.

"Like hell you will!" Marissa shouted at the answering machine, as if Woodward could hear her. "You don't know who you're dealing with, you stuffy, condescending bastard!"

Marissa whirled around. She was going to get Leslie away from Doctor Woodward and take her to a hospital immediately. But first she had to get a weapon, because without Alek to back her up she needed firepower if she were to break into the Woodward house. Marissa knew that Leslie had a Colt .45 somewhere in the apartment.

Why hadn't she thought of it before? Her mother had insisted that Leslie take one of their father's guns to protect herself in the big city. The question was, where had she put it?

Boiling mad at Kyle Woodward, Marissa stomped down the hallway. She'd begin her search in the bedroom and keep going until she found the revolver. And as soon as she had Leslie out of the clutches of Doctor Woodward, she'd call her mother and allay her fears. The last thing she needed right now was to have Corky show up on the doorstep.

Diana sat on the couch in the sitting room, still dazed by Kyle's behavior, and wondered what she should do. David was right. Something was happening to her husband, something that frightened her as much as the untimely death of the grad student. In the message he had left on the answering machine, Kyle had threatened to end Leslie's life in a similar manner. Was Kyle so confident of his power and sure of her subordination that he was unconcerned she might make a connection between the two? Or was he becoming so unbalanced that he was growing careless and not thinking rationally?

While she was still sitting there, David appeared in the doorway.

Diana looked up. "How is she?"

"Well, we've got her hooked up to the IV again. And Kyle checked her vital signs. Everything seems normal."

"David, should we just call the police and face the music?"

"I'd almost say yes." David leaned his left shoulder on the oak woodwork of the doorway. "But if the lab is closed down, that means the warrior will be trapped in our world. And God knows where Steven is. I still think we ought to try to get both men back to where they belong before we do anything rash."

"But wouldn't that mean repeating the ritual?"

David frowned. "It might be the only way."

Diana sighed and closed her eyes as a shooting pain passed through her abdomen.

"Are you all right?" David asked, striding forward.

She nodded, unable to speak. David sank to the couch beside her and leaned close to try to get a look at her face. He slipped a hand over hers.

"Diana—"

As if on cue, Kyle breezed into the sitting room. Startled, Diana managed to look up and found Kyle had paused in the doorway, holding a tray, his expression dark and suspicious. Instantly, however, he slipped on his mask of superficial congeniality and ambled into the room. "Well, well, it looks as if we could all use a brandy."

She wasn't fooled by his graciousness. He had seen David sitting near her, touching her, and had jumped to his own jealous conclusions. Nothing she could say would change the way Kyle thought once he had made up his mind. Apparently David realized an explanation would be useless as well, for he made no excuses, and slowly pulled away from her to lean back against the couch. She was glad David said nothing, for excuses would cheapen the way they felt about each other.

Kyle reached for a small snifter on the tray and handed it to Diana. "You're as pale as a ghost, my dear," he said.

"I'm not feeling well."

"A sip of this will help."

Diana doubted it, but took the snifter anyway. "Thank you."

"David?" Kyle lifted another glass.

"All right. Thanks."

Diana watched as the glass exchanged hands and was struck by the glittering expression in Kyle's blue eyes. He looked like a statue with eyes made of faceted sapphires, and the expression alarmed her. What was in Kyle's mind right now? Why the brandy on Sunday morning? She was just about to reach for David and keep him from drinking the brandy when Kyle raised his snifter.

"A toast," he proclaimed. "To the end of my cancer research."

Diana froze in utter disbelief. "The end?"

"Yes. I've seen the error of my ways." He smiled slightly, just enough to raise the tips of his moustache, and nodded toward his glass.

"I'll drink to that," David put in. He tipped the snifter to his lips while Diana watched, still distrustful of Kyle's sudden change of heart.

"Diana, my dear, you aren't going to toast the end of the research? I was under the impression that you wanted it to cease."

Diana dragged her stare off David's face. "I do. It's just that—"

"Then drink!"

Reluctantly, she placed the rim of the snifter on her lips, careful to let the brandy come up to her mouth but no farther. Kyle seemed satisfied and took a sip of his drink.

"So you've decided to listen to reason, Kyle?" David swirled the brandy and leaned back again.

"Yes. I've been bullheaded and irresponsible. I can see that now."

Diana stared at her husband, amazed at the words coming out of his mouth.

Kyle sat down in the chair opposite the couch, seemingly unconcerned that another man sat so close to his wife. "You see, I had convinced myself that if I could find the cure for cancer, I could save thousands of lives and I believed the sacrifice of one or two lives during the research would be worth the results. I realize that every human life is precious, but just imagine—no cancer on earth. Cancer going the way of smallpox. That's what has driven me all these years, the eradication of the greatest plague mankind has ever known. But most of all I've done this all for you, Diana, so that you would be free to live a full and happy life."

David's head whipped around. "You have cancer, Diana?"

She glanced at him and then found she could not look away, no matter what Kyle suspected was going on between them. David's eyes were dark with shock and hurt. Should she have told him months ago? What was worse—his pity, or this awful look of betrayal? How she longed to sink into his arms and hold him, to tell him that she had learned to accept her impending death, that everyone had to die sometime, that dying was just part of a grand adventure—all the things she had learned to tell herself. How she yearned to lose herself in his kiss and chase away her own dark shadows. But the few inches of upholstery that separated them seemed like miles.

"Diana, is it true?" David's voice cracked. "You have cancer?"

"Yes."

"Why didn't you tell me!" He jumped to his feet. "God, Diana, why didn't you ever say anything!"

"I didn't want anyone to know."

"But I'm your friend!" He gulped his brandy, as if he

couldn't figure out what else to do with himself. "I had a right to know!"

Diana watched him pace the floor and felt Kyle's heartless stare as he surveyed the peculiar drama unfolding before him. No one could witness David's reaction without questioning the depth of feeling he harbored for Diana. Yet she didn't care. She was too tired to worry about it any more. It would almost be a relief to say to Kyle's face that she loved David and wanted to spend the rest of her days with him. But then she remembered Kyle's jealous streak and his cruelty. She could never admit to her feelings for David, as they would only serve to put him in danger.

"I didn't want anyone to worry about me," Diana said at last, putting her brandy on the coffee table. "Or to pity me."

"Is it terminal?" David asked in a constricted tone.

"It has metastasized," Kyle put in. "The doctors give her four months."

"Jesus!" David plunged his left hand into his hair and stared at Diana. For a horrible minute she thought he was going to break into tears. She gazed at him and felt her heart slowly cracking in two at the sight of the grief that had already galvanized his face.

"So you see, David, why I have persevered with the experiment knowing I was violating certain ethics."

Distracted, David glanced at Kyle and then turned his back, as if he couldn't face either of them any longer.

Kyle fingered his snifter. "Wouldn't you do the same if you were in love with Diana?"

The question hung in the air like a thunderclap.

David did not turn around. Diana stared at his back, wondering how in the world he could reply. To spare him, she decided to intervene.

"I don't want to be the reason for someone else's

misfortune," she stated, rising to her feet. "How do you think that makes me feel, Kyle? Did you ever once consider that?"

"Now I do, yes." He glanced up at her. "I didn't know how important it would be to you. But you've made me see what I'm doing is wrong. That's why I'm going to investigate other avenues of research and put this one aside."

Diana felt an immense amount of relief. "I'm so glad to hear you say that."

David turned. "What about Leslie Quinn? And Alek?"

Kyle crossed his legs at the knee and thoughtfully took another sip of brandy. "I hope to locate the warrior. In fact, I expect him to return and demand that I help him. Then we'll do the ritual one last time and send him back."

"What about the threat you made to Leslie's sister?"

"Oh, that?" Kyle waved her off. "That was just to keep our meddling cowgirl in line. I have no intention of hurting Leslie. None whatsoever."

David exchanged a quick look with Diana. She couldn't believe Kyle had changed his mind, but she was wildly hoping he was serious.

"Well," David said at last. "I'm glad you've had a change of heart, Kyle."

"Thanks to you and Diana," Kyle replied. "Would you like any more brandy?"

"No thanks." David took off his glasses and massaged his eyes. "As a matter of fact, I'm feeling bushed. I think I'll go home and catch a few winks if you can handle it here for a few hours."

"Why don't you stay?" Kyle suggested, rising. "In case the warrior comes back. That way I can get you to help me."

"All right. If Diana doesn't mind me crashing in the spare bedroom again."

"I don't mind," she said, wishing she could talk to him privately. His eyes were still full of the pain of betrayal because of the way he had found out about her illness. She longed to tell him that she hadn't meant to hurt him by withholding the truth.

David replaced his glasses and headed for the door. "Wake me first thing if Alek shows up."

"Don't worry," Kyle replied. "I will."

A half hour later Diana stole up the stairs to the guest room, leaving Kyle resting in his chair in the study. None of them had got much sleep during the last three days, but she was beyond tired at this point. Even more, she felt a pressing urgency to talk to David and settle the cancer issue between them, if it could be settled.

The guest room door was slightly ajar. She pushed it open and tiptoed across the floor to the side of the bed, where David slept face down on top of the comforter. His glasses lay folded on top of the nightstand and one arm hung over the side of the bed.

She looked at the side of his face and the waves of his dark hair and longed to lie down beside him as she had once done so long ago, when they had shared their one night together. Not long afterward, she had been diagnosed with ovarian cancer. Was the cancer a punishment for her sin? She had asked herself that a thousand times. And though she knew it was a preposterous notion, she wondered if she might be paying a high price for her precious affair with David. Yet she knew if the decision were to be made again, she'd choose David just as she had a year ago.

How she loved him! How she wished they had not

met under such restrictive circumstances. How she wished she were whole and healthy and could present their love to the light of day.

Carefully, she sank to the side of the bed, wincing.

"David?" Lovingly, she touched the side of his face.

He didn't open his eyes.

"David?" She stroked his hair and leaned down to kiss the pink ridge of his ear. "David, wake up."

He didn't move a muscle.

Could he be so tired that he didn't know she was there? Diana straightened and stared at him. It wasn't like David to sleep so soundly.

She shook his shoulder. "David!"

His torso jiggled with the force of her shake and the headboard rattled against the wall, but David did not awaken.

A jolt of panic coursed through Diana. She shook him harder. "David!"

"David!" a falsetto voice mocked her from the doorway.

Diana whirled around to spy Kyle standing on the threshold holding a gun.

She froze. Suddenly everything made sense. The brandy on Sunday morning, Kyle's glittering expression as he gave the drink to David, and even his unusual admission of error. It had all been a ruse. Kyle wasn't contrite about his experiment. And he obviously wasn't unaware of Diana's feelings for David, either.

"You drugged him!" she exclaimed.

"Yes. I intended to drug you, too, but you didn't drink your brandy."

Slowly, she got to her feet. "Why, Kyle? Why are you doing this?"

"Why? To protect my project. You and David were about to jump ship. I could tell."

Diana took a shaky step forward. What did Kyle plan to do now? Kill them both?

"I don't want your cure for cancer," she said. "I don't want you to do this for me."

"I'm not doing it for you, you little slut," Kyle sneered. "Not anymore. Why should I? So you can jump into bed with him? What do you think I am—a moron?"

"But you said—"

"I began the research because of you, Diana. But I'm completing it for me. People will remember Doctor Kyle Woodward one day, not for being a cuckold with a cheating wife, but for finding the cure for cancer. I'll be more famous than Jenner or Salk."

"Not if you kill anyone. They'll put you away."

"Do you really think I'd harm anyone, Diana?"

She ignored the question. "Are you going to kill David?"

"No. I need him."

"And me?"

"No." Kyle gazed down at her and almost smiled. "We'll let you go the hard way, so you can think about your life and how you've made a mess of our marriage."

She'd made a mess of their marriage? What a joke. Diana raised her chin, refusing to listen to his abuse any longer. The important thing was that David would be safe, at least for a while.

Kyle motioned toward the door with his gun. "As for now, my dear, I'm going to have to put you where you can't undermine my progress."

"And where is that?"

"Downstairs. Leslie needs a nurse. And you seem to have a good bedside manner—at least with some people."

Diana walked past Kyle. She had never hated him more than at that moment. And if there was any way to thwart him, she vowed she would find it.

o   o   o

To make her approach to the Woodward house less obvious, Marissa slipped out of the taxi a few blocks away and walked the short distance to the old mansion with her father's Colt .45 hidden in her big leather purse. Just as she came around the corner, she saw a taxi cab in front of the Woodward house and the driver wildly gesticulating to a tall man with long dark hair. Marissa caught a glimpse of a sharply defined profile and recognized the warrior's unmistakable face. She couldn't believe it. Alek had taken a cab to the house? How had he known the address? And what was he using for money?

Marissa hurried forward, anxious to quell the quickly escalating argument. If the Woodwards heard the men shouting, she would lose the element of surprise in her plan of attack.

She ran down the walk, her heavy bag swinging in her hand. At her approach, Alek glanced aside and she was gratified to see a look of relief in his face when he recognized her.

"Alek," she puffed. "What's going on?"

"Explain to this fool—"

The driver turned on her, his bleary eyes bulging from beneath the bill of a soiled tweed cap. "You know this nut?"

"I know him, yes."

"What is he—retarded or something?"

Marissa narrowed her eyes at the cruel question. "No, why?"

"He takes me all around the damn city, trying to find this house, and then thinks he can pay me with a crummy piece of costume jewelry."

"Crummy? What does he mean, crummy?" Alek crossed his arms and glared at the taxi driver and then Marissa.

"What jewelry?" Marissa asked, hoping to defuse both men.

"This!" The driver held up one of Alek's armbands, intricately carved with vines interlaced with the bodies of dragons. Marissa regarded it, careful to hide her surprise. The armband was probably fashioned of solid gold, which could pay the cab fare thousands of times over. She wasn't about to let the driver know what he held in his hand, for if he knew the value of the piece, he might refuse to give it up.

"That?" Marissa forced a laugh. "Sorry. Where my friend comes from, they still use the bartering system."

"Some damn foreigner—shoulda known."

"Give the band back," she said, "and I'll pay the fare. How much?"

"Forty."

"Forty?"

"Hey, lady, we've been driving for over an hour. Your friend doesn't even know his numbers."

"Numbers are for Romans!" Alek interjected heatedly. He would have lunged for the driver's throat but for Marissa's quick reflexes.

She grabbed Alek's elbow to detain him. Alek scowled at her, but acquiesced and stood near the large elm tree by the sidewalk. Marissa hoped the tree might shield them from view. "My friend hasn't been in the country very long."

"Oh yeah?" Brave now that the threat of attack had subsided, the driver leaned against the side of his cab and glanced at Alek, raking him up and down. "I heard on the news the other day that a big guy beat up two cops at Greenlake. They said he was some kind of weirdo, a really tall guy that looked like a Viking. The guy's still on the loose."

"Really? What does that have to do with anything?"

Marissa pulled two twenties and a five out of her wallet, careful to conceal the fact that she was hauling around a weapon. Thank goodness Alek had the sense to remain closemouthed.

"I'd say your friend here fits the bill."

"Alek?" Marissa forced another laugh. "He wouldn't hurt a fly."

"Only worms and snakes," Alek put in acidly.

The driver glanced at him and straightened, on guard again because of the comment. "Then why's he carrying that knife?"

"Alek's into costumes. He's an actor, touring with a Polish group."

"You don't say." The driver curled his lip and glanced at Alek again, studying him while he played with a toothpick lodged in the corner of his mouth.

Marissa held out the money, praying that Kyle Woodward hadn't seen them by now. "Here you go. We'll take that armband now."

Slowly, the driver took the money and held out the golden ornament, never once taking his eyes off the warrior. Marissa watched him, afraid the driver wasn't swallowing her story.

Alek snatched his armband away from the driver and stood glaring at him, his eyes glittering. It wouldn't take much for Alek to completely lose his temper, and she was well aware of the violence that could result.

"Come on, Alek." Marissa took his arm, pulling him away before the two men started to argue all over again.

Reluctantly, Alek left the curb. Marissa clutched his elbow until they reached the bushes at the end of the driveway. She edged behind the shielding foliage in an effort to conceal them in case Woodward hadn't seen them already.

"Alek, you shouldn't start trouble like that. You'll draw attention to yourself."

"The fool would not honor my payment."

"Lucky for you." She glanced at the torc that gleamed around the base of his powerful neck. "The jewelry you're wearing is probably worth a fortune. Why waste it on him?"

"Still, he was a fool!" Alek pulled out of her grip.

"Just be thankful I arrived when I did."

"And what are you doing here, she-devil?"

"I've come to get Leslie. They've got her again."

"How?"

"Apparently she came back by herself when we were—when we were—"

"Ah."

Marissa was amazed to see him blush and duck away, as if embarrassed. He strode up the driveway. Marissa scampered after him and grabbed his arm again.

"Alek, Woodward might see us!"

He stopped and glanced down at her. "He is not here."

"How do you know?"

"I saw him leave in his wagon."

"You did? When?"

"As we were coming up the road, that fool and I."

"That makes it easier, then." She smiled up at him, but her smile faded when she saw the look on his face.

"Maybe for you it is better, but not for me. I need Doctor-Wood-Ward to send me back to my people."

"So what do you plan to do?"

"Wait for him to return."

Marissa glanced at the house. "Is David Hodge here?"

"I do not know. I did not see him in the wagon with Doctor-Wood-Ward."

"How about Diana?"

He shrugged.

"Well, the only way to find out is to go in." She pulled the gun from her purse. "Will you help me get my sister?"

"Yes." He watched her spin the chamber. "But this time you will take her far away from this city, she-devil, where Doctor-Wood-Ward cannot find her and she cannot find him."

"I'm planning to, Conan. I'm going to take her back to Montana first thing—where I should have taken her yesterday."

"This Montana place. It is far from here?"

"Yes." Marissa slung her purse strap over her shoulder. "Very far."

"How many days?"

Why was he asking? Was he considering traveling to Montana if the ritual didn't work? The prospect of seeing Alek again, especially at the ranch, pleased her considerably.

"On horseback, the ranch is probably twenty to thirty days away."

"Ah." A shadow passed through his eyes. "That is very far, she-devil."

"Montana's a big place. But by wagon, as you call it, it's much faster. Just two days."

He nodded. Her gaze met his, and for a moment they regarded each other. His golden brown eyes flickered in the midday sun, appearing much lighter than they had in the dimly-lit bathroom the night before. Marissa wished he would stoop down and kiss her. She wished he would take her in his strong arms the way he had last night. But their time together was over. Alek would not dishonor her again, not unless she explained her reaction to his lovemaking, and that was something she couldn't do. She knew it was better this way. They'd met each other as equals, enjoyed each other's bodies, and parted without floundering in complicating emotions. They'd experienced a neat and tidy interlude with no strings attached, the best kind for a woman like her and a man like Alek. What she had to do now was convince her heart that no strings attached was what she really wanted.

"Come to the back of the house, she-devil," he said at last, taking her elbow this time. "And I will break down the door for you."

"That's one way of finding out who's home."

He nodded and smiled, and the sun seemed to burst upon all his features, dazzling her. She gripped the Colt tighter, trying to hold on to her resolve not to give her heart to the warrior. But, little by little, she knew she was losing the battle, and it wouldn't be long until she was unable to deny her love for him. The sooner they got this rescue mission over with and she went back to Montana, the better.

17

Marissa stepped aside as Alek bashed the door with his foot and sent it flying back on its hinges. For a moment they both stood poised in the doorway, waiting for someone to come running. When no one did, Alek advanced into the back porch with Marissa close at his heels, gun raised and ready.

"Let's just go downstairs," Marissa said lowly. "And hurry, in case they have a burglar alarm system we can't hear."

Alek hurried down the stairs and loped along the corridor that led to the laboratory.

"The door is locked," he called over his shoulder.

"Then stand back." Marissa waited until Alek retreated a few paces and raised the revolver with both hands. With expert aim she shot the knob, which mutilated the tumblers enough to unlock the door.

"That gun," Alek said, pushing into the lab. "I will take one back to my people."

"Oh, no you won't." She trotted past the work tables

and computers. "Come on. If anyone's here, they would've heard the blast."

She ran to the back rooms where they had found Leslie the last time. Marissa looked in the window of the chamber at the end. Sure enough, a blond woman sat on the bed, but when the woman looked up, Marissa was surprised to see Diana's pale face. Woodward must have discovered Diana's part in their escape the previous night and was now keeping her prisoner. What a worm.

"Stay back!" she called out. Once again she blasted away the lock. Alek kicked the door and stood aside as Diana rushed toward them. Her hair was disheveled and her face drawn with worry, a far cry from the beautifully poised creature Marissa had met three short days ago.

"What's going on?" Marissa demanded. "Where's my sister?"

"Kyle took her," Diana replied. "I think he's going to do the ritual again."

Marissa's heart fell. She had counted on finding Leslie and taking her home. She had expected some trouble, maybe a confrontation with the good doctor, but she hadn't even considered the possibility that Woodward might transfer Leslie to another location.

"Where has he taken her?"

"To the grove, most likely."

"Where is that?" Alek put in.

"A remote area on the Olympic Peninsula." Diana rubbed the backs of her arms as if the mention of the place gave her the chills. "You'd never find it."

Marissa frowned. "Do you know how to get there?"

"Yes."

"Then will you take us there?"

"I'd like to help you, but I have to see to David first."

"What happened to David?"

"Kyle drugged him this morning. He may need medical attention."

"Damn." Marissa took off her hat and rubbed her forehead with the back of her hand as she quickly thought things through. "All right. We help David get to a hospital and then you take us to the grove. How about that?"

"Okay." Diana led the way up the stairs, one hand on the railing and one hand on her slender abdomen. She was puffing by the time she reached the top.

"Are you all right?" Marissa asked.

Diana nodded and pressed on toward the front of the house and the grand staircase that led to the second floor. Marissa kept a wary eye trained on the doorways and halls and a sharp ear tuned for the slightest unusual sound. Apparently Diana was the only one in the house, however, for they passed unmolested to the second floor.

Diana pushed open the door to the guest bedroom and paused.

"David's gone!" she exclaimed, her voice quavering with fear. Then she turned. "Kyle's got a gun, Marissa, and I'm so afraid he's going to hurt David."

Marissa put a reassuring hand on Diana's shoulder. "So you think Kyle has David with him?"

"Probably. Kyle said he needed him. Maybe he's going to use David in the ritual with Leslie."

"What is this ritual he does, anyway?"

"It has to do with harnessing the energy given off during the physical union of a man and a woman."

Marissa stared at her. "You mean when they're having sex?"

Diana flushed and nodded, glancing briefly at Alek, who turned away.

"It is called sex-magic," he said gruffly. "We can talk of it on the journey to the grove."

Leslie had been subjected to a strange sex ritual? With whom? Just the thought of it made Marissa's stomach turn. More than ever she knew it was imperative that she get Leslie away from Doctor Woodward.

Marissa let Diana pass by to follow Alek back down the stairs and back through the rest of the house. "We'll have to rent a vehicle. We came in a taxi and Kyle took your car."

"Not to worry," Diana replied, taking a ring of keys from a rack near the back door. "I have a car of my own."

Marissa looked at her face and was surprised to see Diana smile.

Curious, she followed Diana to the garage. In minutes, they were backing down the drive in a mint condition '57 T-bird, turquoise with white interior, with Alek taking up a great deal of the space in the front seat. After a few close calls as Diana got accustomed to driving the car, they wound their way down to the Seattle waterfront, took a ferry across the sound, and drove down the peninsula.

Darkness had fallen by the time Diana pulled off a narrow lane deep in a cedar forest of the peninsula. After leaving the highway at about seven-thirty, they had driven for nearly an hour on a wet gravel road, winding deeper and higher into the forest. The trees were so high and dense that what little light was left got hung up in the boughs overhead. Festoons of gray-green Spanish moss hung from the lower limbs, and the ground was carpeted with a lush covering of deer moss and ferns.

Marissa got out of the T-bird and switched on her flashlight. Not a sound broke the eerie hush of the forest, and the oppressive stillness sent a chill racing down her back.

Alek stood up and took a deep breath. "Ah, this is the scent of my homeland," he said. "Just smell it, Marissa. So fresh and sweet!"

"You have cedar trees in your land?"

"Some, but not as many as here."

Marissa glanced around. "I am amazed that oaks would grow among all this cedar."

"The grove is in a clearing about a mile up the road," Diana explained, drawing on a sweater. "But I didn't want Kyle to hear the car, so I stopped here."

"So what's our plan?" Marissa asked, buttoning her suede jacket.

"We can probably sneak up on Kyle while he is in the middle of the ritual. Alek can easily overpower him."

"If he does not have that small weapon with the needle." Alek scowled. "It seems my strength is nothing against that needle."

"Oh? Well, I'll bet my aim against Woodward's hypo any day," Marissa put in.

"All right." Diana switched on her flashlight. "We can use our flashlights for most of the way, but when we come to the top of the rise, we'll have to turn them off so Kyle won't see us."

Marissa nodded.

They locked the car and set off down the road without speaking another word. Marissa had been in plenty of forests before, but never one so shrouded and dank. She was accustomed to the open range and the dry floors of the ponderosa pine groves of Montana. This forest felt enchanted—haunted was a better word—as if it were inhabited by the fantastic and often grotesque creatures she had seen carved on coastal Indian totem poles. A bear she could deal with. A moose or a cougar she could handle. But a thunderbird or mythical sea creature was another matter altogether. She could just imagine a weird animal slithering through the lichens, stalking them. If anyone had asked, Marissa would have denied that the dark and foreign forest frightened her. But she was glad that Alek walked beside her.

Marissa was physically unaffected by the walk up the slight rise in the road, but by the time they reached the crest and turned off their flashlights Diana was breathing heavily and the pace had slowed.

"Are you all right?" Marissa whispered.

"Yes. Just a bit winded." Diana reached out for Marissa's arm. "Can you see that trail over there?"

Marissa allowed her eyes to adjust to the sudden gloom, and gradually her vision cleared. A path led off to the left, through two giant cedars that served as natural gateposts.

"Yes, I see it."

"The grove is at the end of the trail."

"I will go first," Alek declared. "Then Marissa, then you, Diana."

Marissa nodded, and they followed Alek's powerful silhouette toward the path.

Without flashlights to guide them, they stumbled and tripped, smothering their gasps of surprise and pain. Though the trail was fairly level, there were many tree roots that crossed the path and patches of mud which had probably been there for thousands of years. What kinds of life forms lived in such ooze? Marissa didn't even want to think about it.

Alek, on the other hand, never once lost his footing. He seemed to have an uncanny ability for feeling the forest floor with his feet—or with a sixth sense the modern person no longer possessed. Soundlessly, he passed through the grove of trees as if he were part of the forest, and for the first time Marissa saw him in his natural element. He was no longer a confused and frustrated giant crashing around in a world he knew nothing about; he was a sleek, silent panther, slipping through the night as if born to it.

Once again, she was reminded of Alek's wildness and his closeness to the earth, a closeness that she had lost to technical progress and modern conveniences. Sometimes on the range, when she was alone with just her horse and the scrub grass, she had felt the strange primal connection to the earth, a beguiling sensation that made her question the very thought of returning to the ranch. Why not stay out on the prairie by the river and simply live as nature intended? Why struggle so hard to support a lifestyle that was full of stress and worry?

Eventually, Marissa had always turned her horse around, back toward the ranch, where her family and her responsibilities awaited her. But the song of the wild was never far from her consciousness, and now Alek had become part of that haunting primitive call.

Suddenly Alek stopped.

"He is there," the warrior said lowly.

Marissa peered around Alek's shoulder and saw a clearing ahead of them. In the center of the clearing was a huge stone, flattened on top—an altar? All around the stone were candles glowing in the darkness, their flames strong and bold in the still night air. Kyle moved from candle to candle, putting a match to the wicks of the ones still unlighted. He was dressed in a long white robe and had a garland of leaves in his hair which concealed his identity. The costume didn't conceal his silver hair and beard, however, or the short, precise movements peculiar to the doctor.

Kyle was there. But where were the others?

Marissa scanned the area, squinting to see through the grove. Beyond the clearing was a small cabin and the dull gleam of a vehicle parked nearby. Perhaps David and Leslie were in the cabin or the car.

Alek crouched and the women followed his lead.

"We will separate," he advised. "Marissa, you will stay on this side of the clearing. Conceal yourself and wait. If I am not successful in surprising Doctor-Wood-Ward, you must use the gun on him."

"Right."

"What about me?" Diana inquired.

"You and I will go to the small house over there." He pointed across the clearing to the cabin. "See it?"

"Yes."

"I will lie in wait for Doctor-Wood-Ward and try to surprise him. You shall see what is in the house. Perhaps David and Leslie are there and you can free them."

"Okay."

"We must make every effort to go without a sound. Go carefully and slowly."

Marissa nodded and felt Alek's warm hand on her shoulder.

"Do not take chances, she-devil," he said. "The man is dangerous, and the forces he calls upon are dangerous as well."

"I'll be careful."

For a moment Alek said nothing, and she looked up to find him staring at her, his eyes boring through the gloom as if to see her face. If something terrible happened, they might not see each other alive again. Marissa had to face the fact that Kyle might kill any one of them. This was not the time to repress her emotions. She reached up and placed her palm along the line of

Alek's jaw, her thumb beside the corner of his chiseled mouth.

She ached to kiss him. But she was highly aware that Diana crouched close by and would be shocked to see a modern woman display romantic interest in the Gallic warrior. Marissa frowned at her own thoughts. So what if Diana might be shocked? When had she ever worried about what people thought of her actions?

Marissa rose up and pressed her mouth to Alek's and gave him a quick kiss. Alek stiffened in surprise, but just as his lips were softening to deepen the kiss, Marissa pulled away. "You be careful, too," she murmured.

"She-devil—"

The gravelly scrape of raw emotion in his voice nearly overwhelmed her. To resist the temptation of sinking into his arms and kissing him in earnest, Marissa scrambled to her feet. "Let's go."

She didn't glance at Diana to check her reaction to the kiss. What went on between her and Alek was nobody's concern but their own.

She waited until Alek and Diana disappeared into the darkness and then crept through the ferns and salal bushes, making her way to the trees nearest the altar.

Diana kept pace behind Alek, careful with each footstep not to tread on a stick that might crack and betray their presence in the grove. She had a terrible suspicion that Kyle could sense things normal people were unaware of and that, no matter what she did, he would somehow find out about it or know what she was thinking. She only hoped that she would find David unharmed in the cabin.

Diana's gaze returned to the warrior's back. What was going on with Alek and Marissa? She had kissed him! At first Diana had thought the kiss was simply a gesture of good luck, something less inhibited women could bestow on others with ease. She herself had never possessed the emotional spontaneity required for such gestures and admired people who did. But the kiss had been much more than a gesture. No one could mistake Alek's reaction for anything but anguish. What had passed between the warrior and Marissa? Didn't they know that a relationship between them was doomed from the very start? Diana recognized the symptoms of doomed relationships immediately, for she was an expert in the subject.

They walked toward the cabin which Kyle had purchased the previous summer for an outlandish price. He had insisted that the site was perfect, since the cabin bordered Quinault Indian land. Apparently the land had been considered sacred at one time, even though no one ever visited the place any longer. Kyle had spent a lot of time at the cabin, and at first Diana suspected he had taken a lover, but she had recently discovered that he used the cabin as a base for his ritual experiments. Alek had appeared at this grove nearly a week ago, and had been drugged and spirited away to the laboratory in Seattle. She wished she had never seen the grove, that Kyle had never found it.

Five minutes later, Alek took them around to the back of the cabin. He motioned for Diana to go in through the back, and then he crept alongside the house, heading for the front, where a large deck was elevated on wooden pilings.

Diana tested the back door and found it unlocked. Quietly, she slipped into the cabin, tiptoed down the small hall between the two bedrooms, and poked her head around the corner to check out the main room with the adjoining kitchen. David lay on the small couch, his legs draped over the end. Was he dead or drugged?

Before Diana could move closer to find out, she saw the front door open and Kyle stride toward the couch. Diana pulled back into the shadows of the hall and pressed against the wall. From her position she could see David, but could only hear Kyle.

"Show time, David," Kyle declared.

Diana heard a rustling sound and then saw Kyle's hands reach out and poke a hypodermic needle into David's shoulder. Almost at once, David stirred and opened his eyes. He struggled to raise his head, but Kyle put a hand on his forehead.

"Take it easy, David," he advised.

"What happened?" David rose to his elbows. "Where are my glasses?"

"You had quite a nasty blow on the head," Kyle replied. "Don't try to get up."

David squinted and looked around. Diana shrank back even farther, afraid to let David see her when his thoughts were so muddled. He might reveal her presence without thinking. "Where are we—the cabin?"

"Yes. Take it easy now, David."

"What happened?"

"The warrior hit you."

"He did? I don't remember."

"As I said, David, you had a nasty blow. I wouldn't be surprised if you'd suffered a concussion."

David squinted again and ran a hand through his tousled hair. "I feel as if I was run over by a truck or something."

"I'm not surprised."

Diana clenched her teeth against the urge to shout out loud that Kyle was a liar—a crazed liar who had lost his grip on reality and would do anything to achieve his goal. Regardless of who he hurt or deceived, Kyle was determined to bring a healer out of the past and force that healer to reveal the secrets of Druid medical practice, hoping to gain fame and immortality by exploiting another culture's knowledge. How she wanted to scream at David to get out before Kyle did him further harm.

But Diana couldn't shout yet. She had no weapon against her husband. She certainly couldn't outrun him, either. It wouldn't do her or David any good to be captured by Kyle. Better to wait and hope that Alek would ambush Kyle on his way to or from the cabin.

"So you're going to do the ritual then?"

"Yes."

"Is Diana here?"

"I'm afraid Diana isn't feeling well. These past few days have drained her."

"Understandable in her condition."

"We've work to do, David. Do you think you can function?"

"I don't know." He struggled to sit up and held his temples as if the movement caused him great pain.

"Listen, David. I could give you an analgesic to alleviate your discomfort, but we simply don't have the time to wait for it to take effect."

David rubbed his temples. "What are you saying, Kyle?"

"I could give you an injection that would have immediate results."

David sighed.

"The sooner we get this over with, the more relieved Diana will be," Kyle put in. "I think it will do her a lot of good to have the warrior out of our lives and the experiment laid to rest."

"Yes. You're right." David pushed up the sleeve of his sweater. "Go ahead and give me whatever."

No, David! Diana bit her lip against the cry that threatened to break from her mouth. What drug was Kyle going to administer this time? Surely he wouldn't give him a lethal injection. He needed David to help him. He'd said as much. In fact, David would have to be the male used in the ritual. There was no one else to perform the sex-magic. Surely Kyle couldn't conduct the ritual and participate at the same time.

Diana stared at David as he bunched his fist and found a vein for Kyle to use. The needle punctured his flesh, and Kyle patiently pressed the serum into his bloodstream.

Diana was amazed to hear David chuckle as Kyle straightened and removed the needle.

"Hey, Kyle. That feels great, whatever it was."

"Feeling no pain, are you, David?"

"None." He rose and pulled down his sleeve. "What was it, morphine?"

"No. Something infinitely better."

Without looking at Kyle, Diana could tell he was wearing the smug smile that she had grown to detest over the years. Kyle was never more full of himself than when he smiled in that way.

David passed a hand over his torso and smiled to himself, as if he had just eaten a satisfying meal. "God, I'm—" He broke off and sighed.

Diana couldn't believe the sexually frustrated depth of the sigh. Her body instantly responded with an intense throbbing feeling.

"You're what?" Kyle asked.

David strode out of sight and sighed again. "I'm hornier than hell, that's what!"

Kyle had given him the night orchid nectar.

"Whoa!" David exclaimed. "That's some feeling!"

Diana heard more rustling.

"Take off your clothes and put this on," Kyle said.

"I've never felt like this!" David chuckled. Then he breathed a heavy sigh, full of longing.

"Patience," Kyle admonished while David's clothes dropped to the floor. After a moment he spoke again. "Too bad Diana is feeling ill, isn't it?"

"Diana?" David's voice trailed off. She prayed he wouldn't betray his feelings for her any more than he had already.

"Wouldn't you love to have Diana, David? Just think of it—her creamy white legs wrapped around you. She has incredible legs, you know."

A long silence stretched and Diana craned her neck to peek around the corner. David stood in front of Kyle, dressed in the same kind of white robe in which Kyle was was attired. Diana held her breath, wondering what David would say in his drugged state.

Somehow he managed to control himself while under the influence. He swore and turned away.

"Come on, David. I can see you're ready for the altar—so to speak."

He took David's elbow and led him out of the door. Diana could still hear David and Kyle talking after the door closed behind them.

Diana straightened. Kyle had his man. Now all he needed was a woman. That meant Leslie Quinn was in the cabin somewhere. If by some chance Kyle were to complete the ritual, one of the participants would be flung into the past. Who would it be—David or Leslie? She didn't want either one to suffer such a fate. But Leslie was the innocent victim in all this, much more innocent than David. She didn't deserve to have her life robbed from her.

Diana turned in the hall and headed for the bedroom on the right. There was only one thing to do. Before Kyle returned to the cabin, Diana had to find Leslie and exchange places with her. It really didn't matter whether she spent her life in the present or the past, because her life was nearly over. Perhaps she could make up for her part in this terrible experiment by sacrificing herself for the sake of Leslie Quinn. And what better way to meet her fate than in the arms of the man she loved?

18

Poised for action, Marissa crouched behind a huge oak at the edge of the clearing and waited for Dr. Woodward to approach the altar, which was glowing in the darkness. She could see Alek creeping toward the corner of the cabin on the other side of the grove, waiting in the shadows of the elevated deck to ambush the doctor. His torc and armbands glinted in the moonlight every so often, reassuring her that he was still there. Impatiently, Marissa focused her attention on the cabin windows, where she could see the silhouette of Dr. Woodward. Who was he talking with and when was he ever coming back out? Was he readying David and Leslie for the upcoming ritutal?

Just as she settled back on her heels for a long wait, she glimpsed a flash where she had last seen Alek and heard a cracking noise in the underbrush, as if someone had broken a large stick. Marissa rose to her feet, straining to see Alek in the darkness, and failed to discern the outline of his bare, broad shoulders or the soft glint of the golden necklace that hugged the base of his neck. What had happened to him?

Keeping low, she scurried along the perimeter of the clearing, wondering all the while if Alek had been shot. Surely the cracking noise couldn't have been a gunshot. Had someone come up behind Alek and hit him over the head? And if Alek had merely fallen, had Woodward heard the cracking noise? So far, he hadn't come out of the cabin, but he very well might be looking out of one of the windows, since she could no longer locate the black shape of his silhouette. She would have to be doubly careful not to be seen. Marissa crept forward, her eyes boring holes in the darkness, her muscles tensed behind the gun she carried.

She ducked under the low branches of an alder and was surprised to see Alek sprawled on the ground. Her first thought was that he *had* been shot, and a terrible, wrenching shock passed through her. She dropped to her knees beside him and touched his firm, warm shoulder, all the while inspecting his body for a sign of injury or wound.

"Air," he gasped.

She peered at his exposed back, thinking he might have been hit in the chest or throat, but could find no bullet hole. However, his breathing was uneven and labored, just as it had been in the store room of the Woodward house. Was Alek having one of his spells again? She thought back to the way he had sunk to floor of the storeroom, heaving for breath until he managed to put himself in some sort of trance, as if to gain control over his body's inner rhythms. Gradually, he had regained his normal respiration pattern. But this time his condition appeared much worse. He didn't seem strong enough to get off the ground. Did his attacks have something to do with being aroused or threatened?

Such a situation usually increased a normal person's heart rate, but not enough to incapacitate them. Apparently, however, Alek's heart raced out of control for some inexplicable reason.

"Alek, what happened?" she whispered.

"Air," he wheezed.

Marissa struggled to push him onto his back, worried by his strident gasps. Above her, on the deck, Woodward opened the cabin door. If he were to look to the right and down, he'd surely see Alek's booted feet sticking out at the corner of the cabin's deck. She'd have to move the warrior and move him quickly.

She laid the gun on the ground and grabbed Alek under his arms. The door shut, and Marissa heard a man sigh overhead. She strained with all her strength, trying to drag the warrior out of sight. Footsteps above clumped across the deck toward the steps. In seconds, whoever was on the deck would see Alek's feet. Desperate, Marissa lurched backward, using her weight as a counterbalance and praying all the while that the darkness would hide them. Slowly Alek slid across the damp ground—only a few inches, but just enough to hide him.

Marissa sank into the moss behind Alek, with his head in her lap, trying to silence her own respirations, while she watched David and Dr. Woodward, both dressed in white robes, walk toward the altar. Apparently they hadn't seen anything and hadn't heard Alek's breathing. A huge wave of relief swept over her, enough to allow her the chance to really look at Alek.

Even in the darkness, she could tell his face was a strange ashen color, and could feel the weight of his heavy, lifeless limbs. His eyes were closed, his hands limp at his sides. The only part of him that was moving was his ribcage as he fought to catch his breath.

The activities of Dr. Woodward and David shrank in

significance as she centered her entire concentration on the warrior in her arms. What could she do to help him? Should she sneak into the cabin and see if there was a phone she could use to call for help? Alek seemed in serious need of medical assistance, perhaps oxygen or some kind of drug to relax his air passages. But how long would it take an ambulance to get to the cabin? It might be hours. And she would not only have Dr. Woodward to deal with, she would practically be relinquishing Alek to the authorities.

Perhaps he would come out of the attack on his own as he had done in the storeroom. But if he managed to overcome the breathless spell, how long would it take him to get back to his normal self?

"Hold on, Conan," she whispered, caressing his clammy cheek with a trembling hand. She had to remain calm, had to think. It could mean life or death for the man she loved.

Then, to her horror, she saw Dr. Woodward coming back toward the cabin.

Slowly, so as not to make a sudden move, Marissa slipped out from behind Alek and carefully lowered his head to the damp earth. His chest and golden ornaments might show in the darkness, but her dark brown suede jacket and dark hair would not. As lightly as she could, she draped herself over Alek, trying not to exert any pressure on his heaving abdomen and chest. The position might have been provocative, had she not been worried sick about the warrior and too concerned about him to acknowledge the way her body reacted to his prone figure. She only hoped the folds of her jacket would muffle his gasps.

"Hold on, Alek," she said near his ear. "Just hold on."

She couldn't leave Alek's side when he was suffering like this. Doctor Woodward's ritual would have to go on as planned without her interference. She prayed Leslie would be all right and that she would survive the ritual and stay in the modern world. Torn between her sister and the warrior, Marissa made a difficult choice, based on the known possibilities. Until she knew that Alek was all right, she couldn't desert him.

Diana lay on the bed which had supported the sleeping form of Leslie Quinn only seconds before. Leslie was now in the closet, propped against the wall, stripped of the white robe in which she had been attired, deep in slumber and seemingly indifferent to the change in her surrounds.

With a steadiness of hand that surprised even herself, Diana adjusted the hood to cover most of her face and waited for Kyle to return. For the first time in her life, she felt dead certain of her actions, as if this masquerade was meant to be, and she was ready for whatever fate tossed her way. She prayed that Leslie would recover and that David would not succumb to the aftereffects of the night orchid, and if anyone were to be flung into the past, she hoped it would be her. But most of all she prayed for Alek to jump out of the shadows and put an end to her husband's insanity.

Diana heard a step in the hall, and in moments the door swung open. She dared not move her head to look for fear the cowl would fall away and reveal her identity. Crazed with apprehension, she forced her eyes to remain shut and her breathing to flow steady and low while she felt the intense surveillance of her husband. Did he notice something different? What about her shoes? In the rush to change places with Leslie, she'd forgotten to change her shoes!

Damning her error, Diana resigned herself to the

fact that she had been discovered and would have to face Kyle's fury. Why wasn't he pulling her to her feet and yelling? The moments she waited for the inevitable burst of outrage seemed like hours, and beneath the woolen robe a sheen of perspiration beaded up on her skin. Yet Kyle said nothing, and remained standing above her as if considering something. Then he reached for her wrist and raised her right arm, pushing back the long sleeve of the robe until her elbow was exposed. Tightly, he clutched the top of her arm and, before Diana could figure out why, she felt the sharp poke of a hypodermic needle in the inside of her elbow.

An immediate rush of well-being washed over her, a sensation she hadn't experienced since learning of her cancer diagnosis. She collapsed into the sensation as if swept away by a warm ocean current, and she let herself go, marvelling at the way her body responded with an intense throb of sexual desire. She sighed and melted into the bedspread, languishing in the strange and won-derful sensation. Would Kyle hear the sigh and know she wasn't Leslie? She hardly cared. All she could focus upon was the image of David in the white robe, waiting for her at the altar, aching to claim her as intensely as she ached to claim him.

Vaguely, Diana sensed Kyle bending lower and felt him slipping his hands beneath her body. He picked her up, still surprisingly strong for his age, and carried her out of the cabin.

Kyle took her across the clearing. Diana could smell the dank, damp earth and the sharp scent of cedar and could feel the mist-laden air on her chin and hands, cooling her beneath the robe. As Kyle strode with her toward the altar, he began to chant in the strange tongue that he had used in the previous ritual. The ancient words sent a chill rippling down her spine, as if she instinctively knew the nefarious meaning of the chant. The words mixed with the heat of her primal lust and whirled her into a dizzyingly primitive state that tore away her modern defenses.

In a haze, she wondered what had happened to Alek. Why hadn't he burst from the underbrush to stop Kyle and rescue her? Then the thought slipped away as easily as it had come, and she forgot all about the plan to stop the ritual. Under the influence of the night orchid, she ached for the ritual to continue and longed to be joined with David more than anything she had ever desired.

Kyle laid her upon the stone altar, which he had draped with a white fur. Fortunately, the heavy fabric of the cowl remained in place and didn't slide back to reveal her face. She felt Kyle straighten her legs. She moaned and nearly reached out for David.

"Ah," David mumured close by. "I just about can't stand it any longer."

"Yes," Kyle replied. "And this time, the experiment will be a success. I feel it. It's right this time."

Kyle stepped back and began to chant again. Diana could smell the acrid smoke of something he passed over her body. The cadence of his voice mesmerized her, hypnotized her, as she flowed with the tide far away from the Diana she had been and moved toward the uninhibited Diana she had never allowed herself to explore. She could feel her pulse in her throat, in her wrists, and in the warm womanly place between her legs. The thrum was like a drum beat that surged in time with Kyle's voice, sending her farther and farther into the very roots of her being. She couldn't fight the trance even if she had wanted to. But she had no intention of fighting anything. She wanted David to come into her, join with her, and spill himself in her. She would have wanted it even without the administration of the night orchid serum.

"It is time," said Kyle.

Diana felt David's hands on her hips as he pulled her to the edge of the stone, leaving her legs to dangle in space. He pushed up the robe with desperate hands and she realized that he was as driven as she was to complete the coupling. This was not going to be a gentle act of love. This was to be a raw and savage intercourse that would unleash a maelstrom of psychic energy, enough to transfer two human beings through time.

He shoved his hands up the robe and planted them on her naked breasts. She arched upward, helplessly awash in desire as he kneaded her flesh. She could feel her nipples hardening, her womb aching in preparation for the moment to come. And as she arched her back, tilting her hips toward him, he groaned and plunged into her.

"David," she gasped, astonished by his rough invasion.

He paused.

In the shadow of the hood, she opened her eyes and looked up to find David staring down at her with an expression of total astonishment on his face.

He sank upon her, his chest crushing her breasts, his mouth just below her right ear, while his hands slid down to imprison her hips.

"Diana?" he whispered hoarsely into her ear.

In answer, she kissed the line of his jaw just under his ear, and then clung to him, not too far gone from the night orchid to recognize the anguish in his voice. He clutched her tightly.

"I want this," she whispered.

"Ah, God, no!"

"Yes."

And suddenly she, too, was certain the night orchid would weave its potent magic this time, because the ritual had to be at its most powerful when the couple on the altar truly loved each other—just as sex became wonderful lovemaking when deep emotions were involved. Because of her love for David and David's love for her, Kyle would get his healer. His experiment would be a success. And she would have David one last time. But if the experiment was successful, it would send one of them into the past. Which one of them would go? She couldn't think about that now. It would ruin this one last time with David.

She clung to him as he thrust into her again, too preoccupied to care that Kyle might find out who she was beneath the robe. Her awareness of Kyle, the grove, Alek, and Marissa dissipated into nothingness as she wrapped her legs around David's hips and surrendered everything to their joining—her body, her heart, and her sense of the here and now. With incredible ease, she slipped into a world that encompassed only the two of them, a world of pleasure and need that sent her spirit spiraling, spiraling, spiraling into the night sky above.

Marissa glanced over her shoulder at the undulating figures on the altar, well aware that her face flushed at the sight of the two people having sex out in the open. She had watched animals mating numerous times, but to watch humans in the act seemed a rude violation of everyone's privacy—theirs as well as hers. Quickly, she averted her gaze.

Until witnessing the sex-magic ritual, Marissa had been convinced that Alek had been a virgin when they had made love in the bath at the hotel. But now she was not so sure. How else could he have broken through the

time barrier? Had he taken a woman upon an altar, too?
Had the woman been someone he cared about, perhaps
even loved? The thought that he might love someone in
his own time made her heart constrict with pain.
Though she knew Alek couldn't stay in her world, she
harbored the secret hope that she might have a special
hold on his heart, and that he might have never relinquished his heart to anyone before.

She turned back to Alek and looked down to find him
gazing up at her.

"What happened?" he gasped.

"You had one of your spells."

"I fell?"

"Yes." She studied him, still worried. "Are you all
right now?"

He nodded and coughed softly behind his fist.

"Teutates!" He struggled upward, leaning upon his
elbows on the damp moss, and at the same time catching a glimpse of the activity at the altar.

Marissa followed his line of sight. "Looks like it's too
late to stop the ritual now," she said.

"Yes. David is like a bull and cannot control himself
because of the night orchid."

"And my sister—what is it like for her?"

"The same. The night orchid has taken them to a savage place—a place where the barrier between man and
beast breaks down."

His eyes glittered as he returned his gaze to her,
and for a moment they stared at one another, both
deeply affected by the sight of the mating ritual.
Marissa felt the tips of her ears burning and was suddenly aware of the way she spanned his midriff, her
hips on one side and her weight resting on the hand
which she had braced on the other side of him. His
tightly muscled abdomen was mere inches from her

breasts. Though they were in the midst of danger, Marissa could barely force her thoughts away from the image of sinking down upon Alek and seeking the savage place of which he had just spoken. She wasn't afraid to go there, especially if the journey included the warrior.

Slowly, she straightened, knowing that if she didn't remove herself from such close proximity to Alek she would surely succumb to her hunger for him. As if he, too, recognized the danger of the position, Alek scooted back and rose to a sitting position.

"What about Diana?" Marissa sat back on her heels.

"She went into the cabin and did not come out."

"The doc probably locked her up again, just our luck."

Alek ran a hand through his dark hair. "Get your weapon, Marissa, and we will stop Doctor-Wood-Ward from taking any more prisoners."

He lumbered to his feet, swaying just a little as he took a step forward.

"Alek?" Marissa questioned, scrambling to stand up before he fell again.

"I will be all right, she-devil."

"Are you certain?"

"My strength returns." He glanced at the altar and then back again. "Stay along the edge of the grove, she-devil, and guard my approach. I will try to stop Doctor-Wood-Ward, but if he has a weapon, you must fire your gun at him. Do you understand?"

She nodded. "Be very careful, Alek." Still worried and unwilling to part with him, she peered up at his face. In that moment, standing there in the dark forest with him, she felt a connection to him that went far beyond friendship or love. The connection was a knowing, a familiarity, a tie that defied limits or description.

Stunned by the sheer depth of the sensation, she stared at him.

Without speaking, he reached for her shoulders, clasping them in his big hands, and bent to her lips. She closed her eyes as his mouth came down upon hers in a kiss both warm and strong. He pulled her against his chest and she melted against him, slipping her hands beneath his arms and embracing the powerful width of his back. The kiss was like a brand, marking the unique bond that had risen between them, giving a symbol to their unusual rapport, which flowed deeper than words. How could she let the connection be severed? How could she let him return to a world where he would meet his death, without warning him and begging him to stay with her? Yet how could she ask a man to turn his back on his own people? Such a request would demand that he sacrifice his honor, and she would never ask such a thing of him.

His tongue swept into her mouth, and she opened her jaw in welcome, sighing as his clasp grew tighter, his lips more insistent, as if he were telling her with his body all the things he couldn't relay in words, as if he were making a promise to her, or assuring her of a great truth. Did he love her? Surely he could tell that she was falling in love with him. She hugged him fiercely, as if to press her heart upon him to create an impervious armor that would keep him safe in all ways, in all worlds, whatever happened.

After a long moment he pulled away from her mouth and placed his forehead on hers, and with his hungry hand he stroked the back of her head, where her French braid began. The puffs of his breath mingled with hers while she slid her palms down the tops of his shoulders to rest upon his smooth, hairless chest. She opened her mind, longing to receive his thoughts and the message of his heart as he rested his forehead against hers. She ached to know if he loved her. Did he? Was that what he was trying to say?

Finally, he sighed and lifted his head. For a moment he held her in a strong embrace. Then his hands slid down the backs of her arms and he reluctantly stepped away. "Go now, she-devil," he whispered.

Alek waited until she slipped into the shadows of the tree trunks and then he took off, loping across the clearing toward the altar.

As if waking from a long dream, Diana stretched and opened her eyes, surprised to find herself lying on an altar in an oak grove. But something was different. She sniffed. The air was scented with a rare perfume, something that smelled fresh and green and, well . . . luxuriously rich with a clean earthiness she had never smelled before. The fragrance went far beyond the refreshing cedar-laced air of the Olympic Peninsula. She sucked in a deep breath and sat up, feeling unusually invigorated. Where was she—in Alek's time, or some other world altogether? As she looked around in the darkness, she adjusted the robe to cover her nakedness, and still felt the glow of David's lovemaking. For a moment she was overwhelmed by the thought that she would never see David again, that they were separated for all time, and knew that she would have to endure her own private hell. Perhaps this was her ultimate challenge, her purgatory—to live without David for the rest of her life in a land full of strangers. At least she had spared Leslie Quinn from such a fate, and in the end perhaps she would be judged by her sacrifice instead of her sin. She hoped so.

Just as Diana slipped off the altar stone, she saw a

slight figure appear at the edge of the clearing and hurry toward her.

"Linna?" a woman called.

The words sounded strange, but Diana realized that she could comprehend perfectly what was being said. She brushed out the wrinkles of the white robe and looked up to see a small woman wrapped in a brown woolen cloak standing there gaping at her.

"You are not Linna," the woman said.

"No. I'm Diana Woodward."

"Who?"

"Diana. Diana Woodward—from Seattle."

"Seattle? I have not heard of such a place. Are you Roman?"

"No. American."

"American?" The older woman tilted her head, inspecting Diana from her blond hair to the hem of the robe. Then her glance raised to Diana's eyes. The woman's face was full of kindness and intelligence, and Diana had the strangest feeling that she could trust this woman. "I have never heard of an American."

"I'm from a place far, far away."

"Oh." The woman studied her again, as if trying to make sense of her words. "I heard a cry," the woman continued. "I thought Linna was up here."

"No. She is—well, she's far away too, I think."

A tense silence fell between them as both women tried to decide what to do next. The older woman kept studying her, and Diana just stood there, unsure of where she was or what to expect.

"You shouldn't be up here alone," the older woman said after a moment. "There are still Roman soldiers about."

"I have no place to go," Diana replied.

"Where are your people?"

"Far away. And I don't know how to get back to them."

"You are lost?"

Diana nodded. "Yes."

The small woman touched Diana's arm. "Then you must come back with me to our camp. No one should be out tonight, not when there are Romans about."

"Thank you." Diana smiled, feeling an odd sense of calm when the woman's fingers lay upon her arm, almost as if she were being comforted by her mother. Suddenly, she didn't feel alone. In fact, a blast of warmth radiated through her, as if she had come home to a place she recognized through every sense but sight. Shaken to her very core, Diana glanced again at the woman's face, wondering who she was.

"Pardon me," she said, "But who are you?"

"I am called Helin." The woman smiled with infinite tenderness and gently squeezed her arm. "Now please, let us leave this place before the Romans come back. It is not safe here."

Diana took a step forward and felt as if she were entering a life she had intuitively sought ever since she was a child. And walking just ahead of her was a small, graceful woman with a careworn face—the mother she had never known. Diana breathed in another draught of the wonderful air and followed Helin without a moment's hesitation.

Just as Alek came up behind Doctor Woodward, he was stopped in his tracks by a strange blinding light that shimmered upon the altar, a light much brighter than the candles now sputtering in their holders. He squinted, shielding his eyes with his forearm, as he watched David and the woman lying prone on the altar become completely engulfed in the light. Was this what had happened when he had made the crossing?

Then he heard a strange noise, like the clear tinkling of small bells, and the light ebbed and glimmered until it faded completely, leaving an odd, silvery tumescence on the altar and the figures who lay there. For an instant, everyone remained frozen in place. Then David leaned over the woman and stared into the shadows of the cowl. Time seemed to hang unmoving. Even the forest was silent, as if waiting. Then David staggered back, holding his hands to the sides of his head.

"No-o-o!" he wailed, and the plaintive sound destroyed the magic that had kept them all in a trance. David sank to his knees at the base of the altar, his face to the stars, his expression broken with anquish. "No-o-o!" he cried again. "Di—ana!"

"What do you mean—Diana!" Doctor Woodward stepped forward.

David turned to face the doctor. Alek was stunned by the haunted look of grief he saw in the man's face. "Diana's gone!" David croaked. "*I* didn't go—*she* did."

"But what about Leslie Quinn?"

"Diana took her place."

"Then who—"

Before Doctor Woodward could yank aside the hood to see what kind of person had been exchanged for Diana, Alek grabbed him.

"No more prisoners for you!" Alek exclaimed, yanking the doctor back and nearly off his feet. Out of the corner of his eyes he saw Marissa break from the shrubbery and dart across the damp grass.

Doctor Woodward twisted in Alek's grip to look up at him. "What are you doing here?"

"Diana brought us here to stop you."

"Why, that little—"

"What you are doing is wrong, Doctor-Wood-Ward. You play with a power of which you know nothing about."

"So far, so good for a novice, I'd say."

"You think you can learn in months what takes a Druid to learn in half a lifetime? You fool yourself."

Doctor Woodward sniffed and tried to wrench his arm away, but Alek held fast. When the doctor realized that sheer brute force could overcome his intellectual prowess, he glared at Alek. Alek grinned slowly and squeezed harder to make the position uncomfortable for the doctor and force the man to listen to reason.

Before he could make his demands known, however, the hooded figure, which had been lying unmoving on the altar, suddenly stirred.

"If that isn't Diana, who is it?" Doctor Woodward asked.

The figure struggled to sit up, moving as if in pain. Then she slowly raised her hand, which Alek noticed was covered with blood, and pushed back the white woolen hood.

Moonlight streamed across flaxen, braided hair and a head that looked vaguely familiar to Alek. But the woman's face was smeared with blood and prematurely aged by the cruel hand of violence. Alek let his grip on Doctor Woodward's arm go slack and felt as much as saw Marissa come up behind him.

"Linna?" he gasped.

Slowly, as if stunned, the woman turned her head to look at him.

19

"*Alek?*" *the woman answered,* coughing and holding herself with both arms linked around her abdomen. "Is that you?"

"You know this woman?" Doctor Woodward demanded.

David stepped closer. "Where's Diana?"

Alek ignored the doctor and David. He could see a red blotch seeping through the front of the white robe which was draped over Linna's ample shape. Was she wounded?

"Linna, what has happened to you?"

"The Romans," she replied, coughing again. "They attacked Ballachulix without warning. It was a massacre, Alek! Men, women and children fell to the sword—even the old ones."

"No!"

"We were taken completely by surprise."

"My mother?"

"I think she was spared."

"Brennan?"

"He lives. As does Alorix." Linna hugged her chest again and coughed. "But Rowan does not."

"Ah, no!" Alek swore. It felt as if a huge hand had just reached into his chest and ripped out his heart. "I should have been there! I could have—"

"Not even you could have stopped the Romans," Linna interrupted him. "We were outnumbered, Alek. Woefully outnumbered. They caught us during the night in the midst of a terrible storm." Linna broke off, coughing harder this time.

"Let the woman rest," David put in, stepping closer to the altar. "She's hurt. She needs medical attention."

"She'll get it as soon as she answers a few of my questions," Doctor Woodward said.

"No!" Shattered by the news of the massacre, Alek lost his head and shoved the doctor, sending him sprawling. Doctor Woodward toppled to the ground, landing on his backside in an ignoble position that silenced the man with the sheer shock and embarrassment of it. Alek glared at him. "No questions from you!"

He tore his glare off Doctor Woodward and gestured for Marissa to point her weapon at him.

"Guard Doctor Woodward," he ordered, "while I see to Linna."

"My pleasure. Get up, Doc," Marissa ordered, pointing the barrel of the Colt at him. "And no tricks."

"I can't believe it," Woodward protested, rising. "The ritual is a success and you people won't even let me question her!"

David turned on him. "Shut up, Kyle. Can't you see the woman's in trouble?"

"But she could tell us the secret."

"What about Diana? Aren't you even concerned about her?"

"It's the cure for cancer we've done this for, David! We can't let it slip away!"

No one paid Woodward any attention. Alek turned away in disgust and stepped up to the altar. "Where are you hurt, Linna?"

"My belly. I was run through."

Alek glanced at the red blotch of blood and knew the spot had grown larger in the space of time they had been talking. He motioned toward David, who stood near his shoulder. "This man, David, can help you, Linna. I will carry you to the house, where he can attend you."

"No one can help me, Alek," she replied, her eyes dull above the dark shadows that ringed her eye sockets. "The wound will fester inside of me. I know this kind of wound."

"Do not give up hope, Linna. This world has magic of its own. You will see."

Alek gently gathered Linna into his arms, making sure he showed no sign that the woman's bulk strained his strength. She wrapped her arms around his neck and sank her head against him, as if the weight of her skull was too heavy to support any longer. Though this was the woman responsible for sending him on his strange journey, he could not be angry with her, not when she was so seriously wounded. Besides, without Linna's ritual, he would never have met Marissa, which was an experience he would treasure always.

"Alek, where are we?" Linna whispered.

"In the U.S. Ovay. A very strange place."

"And Alek—what happened to your hair? It's so dark."

"I will explain later. Quiet now."

He was glad when she settled against him and fell silent. He concentrated on carrying her to the cabin as the others talked behind him.

"You have medical supplies in the cabin?" David asked Doctor Woodward as they hurried across the wet grass of the clearing.

"Yes, but I insist on asking her about the cancer cure."

"No way, Kyle. She's too hurt."

"Fool!" Doctor Woodward shot back. "You'll be wasting valuable time if you try to treat the woman when what we really should be doing is tapping her knowledge before she expires."

"We don't even know if she's a healer or not, Kyle."

"Oh, don't we? Didn't you see that strange scar on her forearm?"

"No."

"That's the mark of one of them. We've summoned a Druid healer this time, David. Don't you understand?"

"We've got ourselves a seriously wounded woman, Kyle. That's what I understand. I'm not going to drill her with questions while she suffers."

"You never could see the big picture, David. That's the trouble with you. You'll never amount to anything if you don't stop getting hung up on the details."

"When details involve human life and suffering, I won't be anything but concerned. And that's final, Kyle. If you want to argue about the way things are being done, take it up with Marissa."

Marissa poked the gun into the doctor's back. "Too bad, Doc, but I don't see the big picture either. I just want to know where my sister is."

"Idiots," Woodward fumed. "You don't understand what I have accomplished, what can be reaped from this!"

"Just tell me where Leslie is," Marissa retorted.

"Your precious sister is most likely in the cabin," Woodward responded tersely. "That's where I left her."

"Then get up there." Marissa indicated the steps of the cabin with the gun.

David held open the door. Alek passed by him and strode to the couch, where he carefully laid Linna on the cushions. She moaned as he set her down.

David hovered over her. "We're going to have to cut away the robe and have a look at you," he said kindly. "And then we'll take you to the nearest hospital, where you can be cared for by a doctor."

"Hospital?" Linna repeated, turning to glance up at Alek.

"Rest, Linna." Alek dropped to one knee and reached for her hand. Though he had never been particularly close to Linna, he felt a strong sense of kinship with her now simply because she was a Senone in this world of strangers. He hadn't expected to see any of his countrymen or women ever again. Gently, he stroked her hand. "Rest. They will help you."

David turned to Kyle. "Do you have scissors in your supply kit?"

Kyle reluctantly nodded yes.

David fished around in the leather satchel until he located the instrument and then he began to snip through the wool, starting at the hem of the garment.

Once again, Alek saw Linna turn her gaze to him. "Alek, the remaining Senone men are joining forces with the Boii and Etruscans to march on Rome to seek revenge for the slaughter. I fear for our people. For without you, the Senones have lost their champion and their spirit. They think you have deserted them."

"No! Never!"

"I tried to tell them about the ritual and how you disappeared, but they blamed me for sending you away to keep you safe."

"It is a lie!"

Kyle edged closer. "You were with Alek when he disappeared?"

Linna's glance flickered over to land on the doctor. "Yes."

Marissa studied the raw-boned, coarsely featured woman, wondering if by some wild chance Linna was the object of Alek's affection. Surely not. Yet, who knew what kind of woman attracted the attention of the warrior? A ripple of jealousy niggled at her even though she fought against it.

Kyle stepped even closer, until he stood at David's elbow. "And did a strange man appear in his place?"

"Yes. A man who is called Stee-Ven."

"What happened to him?"

Linna sighed as David snipped all the way to her throat. For a long moment she closed her eyes, and Marissa thought she had lost consciousness. Finally, however, she blinked back awake as if she had gathered enough strength to continue, and spoke. "He was afraid. He ran. I think he is living in the forest to the west of the grove."

"So there *was* a complete transfer!" Kyle crossed his arms over his chest as if pleased with himself and the world, and appeared completely oblivious to the pain of the woman in front of him. Marissa had never met a more callous human being.

Gingerly, David drew back the wool fabric, exposing a crimson slash that stretched from Linna's navel to just under her right breast. Marissa stared at the gaping red wound only for an instant and then turned away, overcome by the sight of Linna's entrails bulging out of the wound. Even Kyle averted his face.

"You see," Linna spoke quietly, as if separated from her wounded body and looking down at herself. "It is a grievous wound."

David nodded. "I'm going to clean it up as best I can, bandage it closed, and then we'll get you out of here." He left to get a basin of water and some soap and towels while Linna once again looked up at Alek.

"Save your strength, Linna," Alek urged softly. "Don't speak."

"I must." She swallowed.

Marissa noticed Linna's lips had become parched and dry. "Are you thirsty?" Marissa asked. "Would you like some water?"

"Yes."

Marissa motioned toward the corner of the kitchen where David was banging around in the cupboards. "Get her a drink, Doc."

She kept her eyes on the doctor as he walked across the room and her ears on Linna as she continued to speak.

"The soldiers came when I was in the grove, praying for the Goddess to return you to the Senones. They violated my body, Alek. Seven of them. Then they ran me through and left me for dead."

"The bastards!" Alek swore.

Marissa felt her own blood heating at the tale, and her hand tightened around the wooden pistol grip of the Colt. She reached for the glass that the doctor held out and gave it to Alek.

The warrior, with amazing gentleness and compassion, slipped his arm around Linna's shoulders and tipped the glass to her lips. She seemed much relieved when he laid her back against the pillows. For a moment she was quiet, lying with her eyes closed, but then her lids fluttered open and she sought Alek's face again.

"You must go back, Alek. You must avenge our people."

"When you are able to travel we will both go. I will take you back with me, Linna."

"No. My time is almost upon me. I can feel it. But our people need you, Alek. You must go as soon as you can."

Alek glanced up at Marissa, and their gazes locked and held for a heartrending moment. She knew he would leave her then; it was inevitable. Alek would return to his own time and people, where he would meet his fate and be lost to her forever. The special bond she had felt, the familiarity of spirit which she had experienced with no other human being until meeting Alek, would be torn to shreds just as her heart was tearing even now at the thought of his departure.

He broke off the glance and looked back at Linna. "I can't leave you here," he said. "Not all alone like this."

"It doesn't matter. I will be of no use to our people if I go back. But you, Alek—you could save them." With great effort, she reached out and clutched his arm. "The ritual must be repeated. Now."

"Just one minute," Kyle put in. "No one's going to be doing the ritual again, not—"

"No?" Marissa held the gun to his head. "I bet I can change your mind, Doc."

"But that means using the last of the night orchid serum. It could take months to harvest enough for another ritual."

"All we need is enough to send Alek back."

"It's a waste to use it on him!" Doctor Woodward glared at her. "What if this one dies without telling us anything?"

Marissa didn't give his heartless question the dignity of an answer. Instead she turned her attention to David, who sat down next to Linna and began cleaning her wound.

Kyle wouldn't let his protestations rest. He leaned closer to Marissa. "And just who is going to perform the ritual with the big brute here?"

Marissa turned and glared at the doctor. "I will." Never once did she let her stare waver, even though the prospect of making love in front of Kyle Woodward didn't suit her in the least.

"You?" Woodward sneered in derision. "What happens if you get sent back in time?"

"I'm willing to take the chance."

"You're insane."

"Oh yeah?" Marissa narrowed her eyes. "Look who's calling the kettle black, *Doctor* Woodward." She waved the barrel of the gun at the leather bag near the couch. "Now grab some of your magic potion and get on with it."

"But the candles need replacing, the moon—"

"Then replace the damn things!" She felt her temper slipping as her emotions roiled to the boiling point. In all her years on the ranch, she had kept a cool head and rarely lost her self-control. But her tenuous hold on her temper seemed tied to her fragile emotional state. If she thought about Alek's impending departure she would burst into tears, and she could never allow that to happen. Her dread of that moment of farewell came out in anger which she could barely contain. "Do what you have to do, or so help me, I'll blow your fricking brains out!"

Her glare seemed to convince Kyle. Swearing under his breath, he strode to the kitchen and gathered a supply of candles.

"I don't have an extra robe for you," he declared, coming back to the couch.

"Forget the robe. Just tell me one thing before we start all this. Where in the hell is my sister?"

"The last I saw Leslie, she was in the back bedroom. But since my wife intervened on her behalf, your sister may not be there."

"Why don't we find out." She nodded toward the back of the cabin.

With head held high, Kyle fumed down the hall. At the doorway, he stuck out his hand, pointing toward the open door.

"See? She's not there."

Marissa craned her neck to see through the doorway. The double bed bore the imprint of a body, but the rest of the room was empty, except for the bedside table and a clock.

"Check the closet," Marissa ordered.

Kyle obeyed, throwing back the narrow door with an angry whipping motion, making sure that Marissa knew he didn't like being bossed around.

There in the closet sat Leslie, naked except for a T-shirt, panties, and tennis shoes, slumped in the corner and oblivious to the world.

Marissa's heart leaped and then plummeted. She had found her sister, but Leslie was still in a frightening, catatonic state. Would she ever recover from the night orchid? And if by some chance the ritual sent Marissa into the past, who would take care of Leslie? Could she trust any of them to see to Leslie's welfare?

For a long moment she agonized over the choice to be made. Yet what else could she do? She had to help Alek return to his own time. She had to take the chance even though it gambled with the safety of her own sister. Marissa squeezed her hand around the gun, trying not to think of the moment to come, when one way or the other she would have to bid her warrior farewell.

"Pick her up, Doc, and put her on the bed."

He glared at her, hate a palpable wave that streamed from his eyes. Doctor Woodward couldn't abide a woman who stood up to him, who wouldn't accept his manipulative power games, and who issued orders as if expecting to be obeyed. Marissa forced a grin, knowing it would make him all the more angry.

"Pick her up, Doc."

He sniffed and turned to the closet. With a lurch, he raised Leslie off the ground and grunted as he straightened.

"Gently, now, Doc."

She kept the gun trained on him as he deposited Leslie upon the chenille bedspread.

"Make her comfortable."

"She is comfortable. She's in a fantasy world."

"I said, make her comfortable!"

Woodward straightened Leslie's legs and adjusted the pillow beneath her head. Leslie murmured and shifted on the comforter. Marissa edged closer, calling Leslie's name—praying for a response—and tapping her lightly on the cheek. But Leslie didn't wake up. Marissa watched her, hoping for further signs of life. For a moment, even Woodward seemed interested in her progress. But Leslie didn't make any more sounds or movements.

Then Woodward turned to Marissa and dusted his hands, all the while glaring at her, his eyes like shards of ice.

"Cover her."

Woodward sighed and turned back to the closet. He grabbed a blanket from the shelf and draped it over Leslie's sleeping form.

"Is there a sheet up there? Get a sheet."

Woodward obeyed with sharp movements that conveyed his annoyance.

"Good. I'll take that."

The doctor shoved the sheet into her hands.

Marissa tucked the folded linen beneath her arm.

"All right. Come on, Doctor Do-Damn-Little. We have a ritual to perform."

Back in the main room of the cabin, Alek gazed at Linna, knowing he was seeing her for the last time. Though he had never held any strong feelings for her, it was hard to leave her. She was the only link to his other life, and her death would leave him utterly adrift again should the ritual be ineffective.

He had no wish to desert her, especially when she was dying, but he knew he had to leave. Doctor Woodward and Marissa had already left the cabin to prepare for the second ritual and soon they would be waiting for him. The gods knew he was as anxious as anyone to see the ritual to successful completion.

"Linna—" He broke off, not knowing what to say and choked by the lump in his throat.

She managed to touch him again, offering him the comfort he should have been providing to her. But that was Linna's way, always giving of herself to others.

"Go, Alek," she whispered. "I salute you." She wet her parched lips. "I salute you as a free man."

Alek fought the unfamiliar urge to weep, which was something a warrior simply didn't do. What would Linna think of him if he were to collapse into a blubbering mass? He had to remain strong—clearheaded and dry-eyed.

He clasped her forearm in the gesture usually reserved for a man, since he had no doubt that Linna deserved that gesture of respect. She smiled and grasped his forearm with her clammy fingers. Her grip was weak but heartfelt. "And you, Linna, my friend. Go a free woman."

She smiled at him, her blue eyes dancing with tears.

And then Alek leaned over their clasped forearms and tenderly kissed her, knowing intuitively that a kiss would please her as nothing else would.

"Farewell," he said, raising his mouth from her lips.

"Alek—" She broke off with a sigh and gazed at him with her strangely glittering eyes. "I have always loved you. I always will."

He stared at her. He had suspected she cared for him more than she cared for other men. But what woman came out and admitted to having feelings for a man? Didn't Linna know what a man could do to her?

"I—"

She touched his cheek with her other hand and smiled. "Don't speak, warrior. Let me go on thinking that I might have been yours."

"Linna—"

"Go now, Alek. I need to rest."

He nodded and stood up. For a moment he gazed down at her and then glanced at David.

"Take good care of her," he said.

"I will." David extended his hand. "Good luck, Alek. And if you find Diana, tell her that I love her. Keep her safe."

"I will."

Alek shook David's hand. Then he glanced one more time at Linna, turned, and strode out of the cabin.

Marissa disrobed from the waist down on the far side of the altar while Kyle replaced each candle with a new one. His every movement was fraught with anger and frustration, but she didn't care. He deserved each maddening moment. This was a man who had sent his associate into another world, who had imprisoned a young woman in a comatose state, who had displaced a great warrior and prevented him from protecting his tribe, and who had pulled a mortally wounded woman through time, forcing her to die among complete strangers. Even his own wife had fallen victim to his schemes, and yet he hadn't exhibited a shred of remorse for his actions. Marissa had no pity or tolerance for the man.

She wrapped her nakedness in the sheet taken from the cabin.

"Injection?" Kyle drawled, pulling the hypodermic out of his bag.

"No thanks."

"But you'll need it to reach the proper state."

"I'll get there on my own." She hoisted herself backward onto the fur-covered altar. She hoped to tip the balance of the ritual by not partaking of the night orchid nectar, thus making it less likely that she would be the one to travel back in time. Alek needed all the help he could get in returning to his homeland, and she would do everything in her power to aid his cause. She needed no foreign substance to heighten her desire for Alek; her own hormones were doing more than an adequate job. Besides that, if she landed in pre-Christian Gaul, what would happen to Leslie?

"Don't forget, Miss Quinn, you'll be having relations with the brute."

"I happen to love the brute."

"You've got to be joking." Woodward stared at her as if she had admitted to loving the man in the moon.

So what? She didn't care what Woodward thought of her personal affiliations. In fact, she rather enjoyed the look of utter amazement on the good doctor's face.

"He's more man than you'll ever be, Doctor Kill-Joy."

"Really?" Woodward's lip twitched. "What makes you think you can prevent me from taking that gun of yours during the ritual and killing both of you?"

"What makes you think you're faster than me?" she countered. "Besides, you want to get rid of Alek, don't you? It would make your life a lot more simple. I'm doing you a favor here."

"I don't give a damn about the brute. And I don't want to waste the serum on him."

"Well, you're going to have to, Doc. That's all there is to it." She glanced over the doctor's head. "Here he comes now."

She felt a surge of sexual desire as Alek stormed toward them, his torc glinting and his dark hair wafting around his shoulders in the soft breeze that had come up since the last ritual. In moments he would be joined with her and would become part of her for the very last time. She vowed to honor their union with all her heart and soul and with no regrets whatsoever.

Alek gained the altar. "Are you ready?" he asked the doctor, avoiding eye contact with Marissa.

"You need an injection." Kyle held up the needle.

"Give that to me," Alek replied, snatching the hypodermic away. He fumbled with the apparatus for a moment and then pressed out some of the serum onto his palm. He sniffed the small pool of liquid.

"It smells like the night orchid."

"It is the night orchid," Kyle growled. "Don't waste it."

Alek held out his arm. "Put it in me then. I am ready."

Woodward told him to ball his fist and then applied enough pressure to the warrior's upper arm to bring out a vein. With practiced aim, Woodward punctured Alek's skin and delivered the serum directly into the warrior's bloodstream.

Alek closed his eyes and sucked in a deep breath. When he let it out, he half opened his eyes and let his gaze slide to Marissa. She could see his eyes literally glowing with lust beneath his lids.

Marissa fought back a wild thrill and trained the pistol on the doctor, concentrating to keep her hand steady. "Okay, Doc. Do your thing."

Frowning, Woodward began his chant. At first Marissa tried to focus on the sound of his voice. But then she let her gaze wander to the warrior standing before her. Alek was so tall, so intense, so proud. She felt her heart flip over at the physical presence of the man. The way he stood looking down at her and the deep rise and fall of his muscular chest made her heart race with anticipation. He had been gentle at the hotel, but what would he be like under the influence of the plant? Yet she was not afraid. Marissa knew she would want Alek in all ways, in whatever fashion he took her, because she trusted the core of the man inside that warrior shell. She knew his heart as well as her own. This man would never hurt her. Only by leaving her would he make her suffer. But his departure was not something he could command, so she would never blame him for the wound to her heart she was about to receive.

Her anticipation was dulled slightly by the bleak future which stretched beyond the grove, for Marissa was well aware that she would never share this special bond with a man again. This was it for her. The final hurrah. The last rodeo.

Marissa swallowed the huge lump of sorrow in her throat. How could she live without Alek? How could she face a day without his company? Wasn't there some way she could go with him to the past? She didn't care if she never saw Montana again as long as she was with Alek. Couldn't she stay with him forever? If she convinced him that to go was foolish, that to stay was logical—

She breathed in, panting, trying to control her

heaving emotions. And then Alek stepped closer, placing his hand on her shoulder.

"Do not be afraid, she-devil," he said beneath the chanting.

"I'm not." She placed her hand over the back of his. "Alek, there is something I have to tell you—"

She broke off, ashamed that she would use her knowledge of the future to bind him to her world. She shouldn't do it. She couldn't do it. And yet, how else could she explain the futility of his sacrifice and the loss it would cause to two lives.

He caressed her arm and slid his hand up to her neck, his breath coming more quickly with each stanza of the chant. Languidly, sensually, he passed a blunt fingertip across her lips. "Don't talk, woman. Feel."

"I—" She gaped at him, unable to broach the subject of his impending death, and equally unable to encompass with mere words the way he had affected her life. "I want you to know that—"

He cut her off by reaching out with his other hand and slipping it around her neck, stepping even closer at the same time, so that his hips came in contact with hers. The touch of his body was like a jolt from an electric fence. She closed her eyes, feeling as close as she had ever come to swooning.

"Marissa," he said, his voice thick with desire. "You do not have to say anything."

"But I want to." She reached up and caressed his jaw. He leaned over her, urging her backward. His magnificent torso loomed above her. He smelled musky—all male, all heat. And his manhood swelled as hard as stone against her. She answered with a rush of longing from deep inside.

"Alek!"

He kissed her, pressing her back against the soft,

white fur. He had never kissed her with such insistence, such driving need. His tongue thrust into her, a precursor of the moments to come, and he ground his hips over hers. They both knew the mechanics of lovemaking now and were free to indulge in the pure pleasure of it. Even without the night orchid, she was rapidly losing herself to his touch. Alek seemed to have learned his lesson in the bath exceedingly well by the way he was rubbing against her, using his hard maleness to fire her womanly softness. With a cry, she arched into him, hungry for more as the blaze between them flared into an all-out brushfire.

"Marissa, I want you," Alek growled. "From the very first I have wanted you, as if we were meant for this."

"Yes!" she answered breathlessly. She wondered if he had felt the same strange connection she had known with him. Her head lolled back, and she revelled in the sensation of his mouth upon her throat as he kissed her. She felt a giddy sense of freedom as his touch released all her inhibitions.

"You are mine as no other," he declared in his raw and haughty manner.

She looked into his eyes and knew hers were burning as brightly as his. "Yes," she answered with equal bluntness.

Then Alek embraced her, settling his weight on top of her so as not to crush the breath from her. With her free hand, she stroked his bare back in long, trembling passes while he moved against her, seduced by the potent, silent intensity of his desire. The sheet and his trousers still provided a barrier between them, but even the two layers of fabric could not shield her from her hunger for this man.

"Ah, Alek!" she moaned, lost to the thunder of his breathing and the fire in her blood.

"I may not see you again," he rasped near her ear. "I cannot bear the thought."

"I can't either!" She squeezed her eyes shut, damning her lack of poetic ability at a time like this. She needed a poignant phrase to say to him, something that would convey all she felt without seeming too common or too flowery, for there was nothing common in the way she felt about her warrior. Yet what could she say that would speak the language of her heart?

"I want you, she-devil," he growled, "but I don't want to hurt you."

"Oh, Alek!" She hugged his neck with both arms. "You won't hurt me! Your lovemaking is the most glorious thing I've ever known."

"Truly?"

"Truly."

"Then why did you cry at the hotel?"

"Because I knew this moment would come someday. I knew you would have to leave me."

"Marissa." He squeezed her tightly. "Forgive me."

"There is nothing to forgive."

She smelled an acrid odor of smoke as Kyle passed something over them, all the while droning his chant. In her emotional state, she had forgotten all about the doctor. She gripped the pistol all the more tightly.

"Come back with me," Alek breathed against her jaw as he struggled to undo his trousers. "Come back."

"How?"

"I do not know. But I cannot leave you!"

"You have to. You have to fight the Romans."

"I would give anything to change fate," he said. "Anything!"

"Not your honor," she replied. Then she kissed him, and in her kiss she said good-bye to him and honored him.

Alek returned the kiss in kind and didn't stop until Woodward told them it was time.

The warrior ripped off the sheet that covered her and pulled her hips to the edge of the altar. He bent down and kissed her belly in heated reverence. Then he rose up and guided himself into her. With a long moan of satisfaction, he sheathed himself into her moist depths.

"Marissa!" he gasped.

He sank his head into the small of her shoulder and plunged into her again. She opened to him fully, giving herself without thought to Kyle, or to the gun in her right hand. All she could think about was Alek, her warrior, who was thrusting himself into her soul, but out of her life.

"I love you," she whispered into his ear. He made no response. Had he heard her over his labored breathing? Or had her admission been lost to the four winds? She closed her eyes. It didn't matter. Love would soon be a thing of the past, something she would never know again, for she would never, ever meet a man like this one.

My warrior. My warrior. My warrior. Her private chant thrummed in her ears, blotting out every sound until she could hear nothing but her inner voice screaming in anguish.

$\overline{20}$

In a state of shock and devastation, Marissa saw the undulating silver cloud envelop her and Alek. She could no longer feel him inside her. As a matter of fact, when he had climaxed she had lost consciousness for a few moments, and woke to the sound of tinkling bells. Now, from her position in the glimmering cloud, Alek looked unusually distant even though he was not more than a few feet away. All she could make out was the line of his brow, the sharp angle of his nose and the curve of one shoulder, but she had the strongest sense that he was looking at her. The rest of him was lost in the glimmering fog. She longed to reach out for him, to call to him to come back, that he was headed for his death if he went into the past, but her entire body seemed paralyzed, as if the silver cloud were depleting her energy. She didn't like the feeling one bit and vainly struggled to command her arms and legs to move, but her limbs wouldn't budge. What if Dr. Woodward noticed her paralysis and tried to take the gun away?

Could he even see her clearly through the glittering cloud? She hoped not.

The next thing Marissa knew, Alek's misty form had disappeared, replaced by the silhouette of a much slighter, smaller man.

Alek was gone. In a burst of energy and light he had been wrenched from her life, just like that.

Marissa closed her eyes, overcome by sorrow and pain, wondering if she would ever grow accustomed again to the emptiness of her world. Alek had made her want more out of life, had made her see that a man could exist who was her equal in all ways. But that man was gone. And now she was worse off than when she had started. The longing and emptiness she had felt on the ranch would be multiplied tenfold now that she had tasted the sweetness of Alek's lovemaking and enjoyed the gentle strength of his personality.

And Alek—her beautiful, haughty Alek—would soon be in Roman chains, headed to his death.

She would have chosen to die right there, right on the altar, and cut her life short, but for the thought of her sister Leslie lying helpless on the bed in the cabin. She couldn't end her life just because Alek had vanished. She had to help Leslie and the others. She didn't have the luxury of wallowing in misery and self-pity. There was work to be done, just like the ever-present work she would face on the ranch when she returned to Montana, work that would keep her from going stark, raving mad with loneliness.

Marissa felt the cloud lifting and gradually her physical power returned. As soon as she was able to move, she sat up, covered herself with the sheet, and twisted around to see what Woodward was doing. He stood in the white robe while the wind fluttered the ends of the wide sleeves, and peered intently at the strange figure near the end of the altar.

"Steven?" he called out.

The man turned at the name. "Doctor Woodward?"

Marissa stared at him. Steven? Wasn't that the name of Leslie's supposed boyfriend, the man with whom her sister had run off, according to Dr. Woodward. It was clear now that the doctor had lied to her—repeatedly. All this time, Steven had been trapped in the past after having performed the ritual with Leslie. Marissa grimaced, thinking of the way it must feel to perform the sex-magic with a complete stranger. There was no way Leslie would have consented to giving her body for the ritual, not unless she had been doped up by the night orchid serum. The question was, how many times had Leslie undergone the ritual until Dr. Woodward got it right? In her letter, Leslie had mentioned losing track of time, of feeling odd. Had the experiments been performed over a period of days? Or weeks? How many injections had Leslie been given? How many times had she been sexually assaulted?

Marissa slid off the altar. The figure cringed at the movement and glanced at her. He was a fairly short man with strawberry blond hair and sloping shoulders, not the type of man to fit in well with a warrior society. His clothes were in tatters, his face and arms filthy, and his thatch of hair was tangled with twigs and leaves, as if he'd been sleeping on the ground. Linna had said he'd been afraid and had fled into the forest. It was no wonder, seeing his slight frame and the fearful expression in his pale blue eyes. Her anger at Steven quickly dissipated as she realized he was just another member of Dr. Woodward's long line of victims. Steven might have been as innocent as Leslie.

Then, as if he realized he was back in his own time, a place he knew well, the man straightened to his full height.

"You son of a bitch!" Steven cried, lunging for the doctor.

Woodward reeled backward to avoid him. "Stay back!" he ordered.

"Stay back?" Steven shouted, his voice cracking. "Stay back? I've been in a living hell, Woodward, something you failed to mention would happen when you roped me into your research."

While they talked, Marissa hurriedly slipped on her clothing.

"You're delirious, Steven."

"Delirious? Yes, I'm delirious! I thought I was a dead man! They tried to kill me, Woodward! No one would help me! I've been living like an animal—starving, cold, with nowhere to go! You didn't tell me it would be like that!"

"You must be hallucinating, Steven, an aftereffect of the night orchid serum."

"What are you talking about?" Steven held out his dirty hands. "You call this hallucinating? I've been living like a savage, thousands of years back, in Roman times."

Woodward shifted his weight and sighed, as if trying to communicate with a child who wouldn't listen to him. "Steven, the experiment was a failure. You didn't go anywhere."

Marissa stared at the doctor. Another lie. She had half a notion to butt in, but then thought better of it and decided to let the scene play out.

Steven stared at the doctor, too, his eyebrows angled in disbelief. "What?" he gasped.

"You didn't go anywhere, I tell you. You had a bad reaction and ran off into the woods. We tried to stop you, but you outran us. We've been searching for you for days. Thank God we found you."

"No." Steven studied the doctor, his chest heaving with rage and uncertainty. "No, it wasn't like that at all."

"I'm afraid it was, Steven."

"I didn't hallucinate what I just went through. I was there—every bloody awful minute of it! There was this huge battle, with people being slaughtered all over the place! No one believed me when I tried to tell them who I was! I was afraid both sides would kill me! I didn't dream that up! I don't know enough about that era to dream of it in such detail!"

"Steven, settle down. You're safe and sound. That's all that matters." Woodward reached for him, but Steven yanked away.

"You're lying to me, you son of a bitch! You're lying!"

"Why would I lie to you, Steven?" Woodward smiled reassuringly. "What good would it do?"

"It would keep this whole thing secret, that's what! And that's what you want, isn't it, Woodward?" Steven glowered, betraying a more forceful character than his outside appearance suggested. "You're a good one for secrets—I've found that out."

Woodward stiffened. "The drug has made you paranoid, Steven."

"Paranoid? You'd like to make everyone think I was paranoid. Then you wouldn't have to explain what you did to me and Leslie. You lied to me, Woodward. Just a simple injection, you said. Stabilizing my electrolytes, you said. What a bunch of crap! That injection made me do things I never would have done to a woman. And I was trapped in a nightmare world for weeks. But you know what kept me going, Woodward? Do you?"

"I haven't the faintest idea."

"I lived for the moment when I'd make you pay for the suffering you caused me, for the lies you told!"

"Really?" Woodward slipped his right hand into the side pocket of his robe, a stealthy movement that did not escape Marissa's practiced eye. She raised the pistol while the doctor continued to speak. "And how will you do that, Steven?"

"I'm going to go to the press and tell them everything about you, Woodward. Everything!"

"I wouldn't do that if I were you."

"Why?"

"The world isn't ready to hear about my research yet."

"You call what you did to me research?" Steven balled his fists. "You're crazy, Woodward! And soon everyone's going to know it!"

Woodward grabbed Steven's upper left arm and yanked him closer while at the same time he whipped his right hand out of his pocket. Marissa saw the metallic flash of a hypodermic needle. What was Woodward going to do to Steven—inject him with a tranquilizer?

"Potassium," Woodward said. "No one will ever suspect a thing."

He raised the hypo as Marissa took aim. Just as Woodward lowered the needle toward Steven's bare forearm, Marissa followed the line of movement and squeezed the trigger. The shot shattered the hypo and the tips of several of Woodward's fingers. He staggered back in surprise and pain.

"No more injections, Doc," Marissa stated, stepping forward as both men stared at her in amazement.

At that point Woodward seemed to realize he had lost the battle. There was nothing left for him but to surrender to Marissa or make a run for it. He pressed the bleeding fingers in his hand and backed up.

"No funny stuff, Woodward," Marissa warned.

"No, of course not," he replied, still moving backward, toward the edge of the clearing. "But you wouldn't shoot an unarmed man, Miss Quinn."

"You don't think so?"

"No." He sneered at her and turned suddenly, dashing into the shrubbery.

Marissa raised her gun in both hands. "Stop!" she cried.

Woodward kept running, his white robe bobbing through the underbrush.

"Stop or I'll shoot!" she exclaimed. She shot into the darkness, hoping to wing him.

Woodward didn't pay any attention, and in a matter of seconds he had vanished into the cedar forest.

"Damn!" Marissa swore, lowering the gun. "Damn!"

"He meant to kill me." Steven said, coming up behind her. "The bastard was going to kill me with an injection of potassium."

"Yes."

"You saved my life."

Marissa swept a stray hair from her forehead and smiled wanly in reply, worn out by the stampede of emotions she'd ridden through in the last hour or so and nearly broken by her grief for Alek.

"Thanks," Steven added.

"No problem. But do me a favor, Steven. Don't talk with the media about this. If someone starts investigating, we might have some explaining to do about our part in this." She sighed and surveyed the spot where Woodward had crashed through the shrubbery. Letting the doctor get loose was a mistake—a big mistake.

"Damn!" she said again.

Someone opened the cabin door. "What's going on?" David called.

Marissa turned. "It's all right. Nobody's hurt."

"So what do we do?" Steven edged closer.

"We get out of here before Woodward comes back. Come on." Marissa set off at a quick clip toward the cabin. Steven jogged to catch up with her.

"Not to be rude or anything, but who are you anyway?"

"I'm Marissa Quinn, Leslie's sister."

"Oh!" Steven grimaced. "About Leslie—I—"

"Don't worry about it, Steven. I know now that what happened to you and Leslie wasn't your fault."

Ten minutes later, they left the grove in Woodward's large sedan, leaving the T-bird parked down the road where Diana had left it. David knew the way back to the main highway, so he drove, with Marissa in the back seat holding Linna on one side and propping up Leslie on the other. Steven rode in the front with David and chattered the entire way about his trip to the past. David nodded but barely said anything. Marissa could tell by the closed expression on his face that David was thinking of the past in an entirely different way and wondering how Diana was faring in the strange land. She sympathized with David's stony expression and distracted conversation because her thoughts centered on someone in the past, too, and she was glad that no one was chattering away to her. Leslie moaned a few times and mumbled in her sleep, but never reached consciousness.

They decided to go to Leslie's apartment, where Linna could be made as comfortable as possible. She begged them not to take her to a hospital, where her appearance would raise too many questions and her passing would not be peaceful. Marissa agreed, sympathetic to a person's desire to die in the place of her choosing. She could smell death on Linna, as she had smelled death on animals. It was only a matter of time before the healer succumbed to her wounds.

David carried Linna up the stairs to the apartment and was winded by the time he laid her on the bed. Then he returned to the parked sedan with Steven to help Leslie out of the car. Marissa held the doors, hoping and praying that Mrs. Pitts wouldn't see their comings and goings. The last thing she needed right now was a visit from the nosy manager.

They made the transfer unnoticed and Marissa closed the apartment door with a grateful sigh. Then she took over in her accustomed fashion, sending Steven off to the shower, seeing that Leslie was comfortable on the couch and that David had everything he needed for Linna. Then she banged around in the kitchen trying to make something for them to eat. Everyone was ravenous. She even found some beef broth for Linna, hoping the healer could take some food. When he was showered, Steven dressed in the extra shirt Marissa had purchased for Alek, rolling up the sleeves to take up the loose fabric that his short frame could not fill. Marissa could not look at him without grieving for her warrior.

They took their soup and sandwiches into the bedroom and sat around Linna's bed as if keeping a vigil with the healer. Marissa studied Linna's round face, wondering if Alek had loved that countenance. She couldn't be jealous of the woman, though, for there was something about Linna that shone in her eyes. Linna was special, a keeper of a strong spirit. Of that, Marissa was certain.

Marissa noticed that David hardly touched his food. His hand shook as he lifted his coffee mug.

Linna, waking from a fitful rest, looked over at

David, studying him with feverish eyes. Finally, she spoke. "Something troubles you, David," she murmured. "What is it?"

"I'm worried about Diana."

"The woman who crossed over with me?"

"Yes."

Linna nodded and slowly closed her eyes. She breathed in. "I saw her as we passed through each other."

"You did?"

"Yes. I could see into her, through the web of the wasting disease."

David leaned closer. "You could see that in her?"

"Yes. She is very ill, this Diana."

"Can your people help her? Is it too late for her?"

Linna opened her eyes. Light seemed to stream out of them. "They can help, yes. Alek's mother, Helin, will help her. And the air will help her."

"The air?"

"Yes." Linna licked her dry lips. "The air is thin here, not as sweet as in my land. In my land the air is thick with goodness. It comes from the trees, you know. The sweet air will help heal Diana."

"Thank God!" David smiled for the first time that night. "Thank God!"

"If—" Linna held up her forefinger in a weak gesture. "If the Romans don't kill the healers who know the cure for the wasting disease."

The smile vanished from David's face. "Is that possible?"

"It is very possible."

"Oh." David ran his hand through his hair. "I feel so helpless! What will happen to her?"

"We can only hope for the best, David. And pray to the gods that Alek will be victorious."

Marissa sipped her coffee and watched them over the rim of her cup, her heart heavy with anguish for David. But Linna's mention of the air made her wonder if Alek's breathing problems were linked to the thin air of the modern world. Had pollution and worldwide clear-cutting done even more damage than scientists thought? Had pollution robbed the air of its healing properties? What other effects had the altered air produced in modern man?

She sat on the edge of her chair. "What about the difference in languages, Linna? How can you and Alek speak English so well?"

"I do not know. Perhaps when the transfer is made, the knowledge of language is exchanged between the two people. Stee-Ven could understand our tongue as well as speak it when he was there."

"That's right. I could." Steven bit into his sandwich and spoke with his mouth full. "I didn't even notice I was doing it!"

"It is an amazing process," Marissa put in. "Truly amazing."

"Now I must rest," Linna declared softly. "I am tired."

Steven and Marissa both stood up, but David remained seated by the healer's side. "I'll stay and keep an eye on Linna," he said, glancing at Marissa.

"All right. If you get tired, I'll spell you."

"Thanks."

Marissa took his dirty dishes and followed Steven out the door. She still had to call her mother and assure her that everything was okay. She only hoped she could mask the desolation that filled her heart, because she wasn't ready yet to tell her mother about Alek. But before she called her mother, she planned to drive Steven to his house and exact a vow from him that he would never tell a soul about the ritual and what had transpired in the oak grove deep in a forest of the Olympic Peninsula.

Near dawn Marissa was awakened by a light touch on her shoulder. She jerked awake and looked up to see David standing between the couch where Leslie slept and the overstuffed chair where Marissa had fallen asleep.

"Is Linna worse?" she asked, rubbing the sleep from her eyes.

"She is fading. I can tell by the way she's breathing. And she has a fever now, which is a bad sign."

"Want me to stay with her for a while, David?"

"Not exactly." He glanced at Leslie's slumbering figure and then back at Marissa. "Would you come into the kitchen for a minute so we can talk?"

Sleepy but curious, she rose from the chair and stretched her arms high above her head to relieve the crick in her back. Then she yawned and ambled after David as he led the way to the kitchen. He pulled out a chair and indicated that she sit in it. Then he lowered himself into one. He looked terrible. His eyes were bloodshot, his face was grizzled with two days' growth of beard, and his features were stamped with the haggard expression of someone who was overwhelmed by emotional trauma or grief. David looked like Marissa felt inside.

He opened his mouth to speak, stopped, and bent forward with his forearms crossed over his thighs. He sighed.

Marissa squinted, trying to wake up after so few hours of sleep. "What's going on?" she croaked.

He glanced up and grimaced. "I want to ask something of you, but I don't quite know to begin."

"How about at the beginning?"

David looked down at the floor. "I know you don't owe me anything, Marissa. And I wouldn't blame you for refusing my request, seeing how I was Kyle's partner in all of this." He glanced up again, his red-rimmed eyes full of sincerity. "But believe me, once I found out what Kyle was up to, I wasn't going to let him repeat the experiment. All I was trying to do was get Alek back to his own time and do the best for Leslie."

"But what about—" Marissa caught her voice growing louder in indignation and instantly lowered it. "What about Leslie? How could you let Woodward subject her to such treatment?"

"When it happened, I couldn't bring myself to prevent it. I'm sorry."

"But what about the second time?"

"Second time? There was no second time."

Marissa narrowed her eyes, wondering if he were being truthful with her. "Leslie wrote to me before Woodward kidnapped her. She thought she was being drugged and assaulted."

"Not to my knowledge."

"Could Woodward have done it? Did he work alone?"

"Often."

Marissa clenched her teeth. Had Woodward touched Leslie? She couldn't bear the thought. She wished she'd have shot him in the balls instead of the hand.

"But, as I said," David continued. "I've been thinking. Because of my relationship with Diana, Kyle could make life very difficult for me."

"You have a point, David."

"But that isn't my biggest worry, Marissa. Living a life without Diana is. Without her, life will be a prison sentence for me. Although you probably don't understand—"

"I believe I do understand." She averted her gaze and concentrated on the rack that held Leslie's keys, afraid that David might see the tears welling in her eyes. She swallowed hard, twice, forcing the lump back down to a manageable size.

"I can't stop worrying about her, wondering if she's all right. What if the Romans get a hold of her and rape her the way they raped poor Linna? I couldn't bear to think that Diana is struggling out there and I can't reach her or help her."

"So what are you saying, David?"

Slowly, he sat up, leaned on the back of the chair, and leveled his gaze upon her. "I want to go to her."

"You can't. Kyle isn't here to perform the ceremony. And there isn't any night orchid serum left."

"Yes there is. Part of a vial was left in Kyle's bag."

"There was?"

"Yes. What if Linna could perform the ritual? What if she could do it without leaving the bed?"

"David, she's probably too weak."

"But she might be able to!"

Marissa gazed at David. Had he reached the end of his emotional endurance? Poor man, was he losing it? She reached out and slipped her hand over his. "David, you're driving yourself crazy. There are some things you simply have to accept. Diana's in a better place now. Isn't that enough?"

"No!" He hung his head. His shoulders shook. Marissa leaned forward and touched the top of his arm, trying to comfort a man she realized was far beyond consoling. "God, I miss her. I can't go on without her!"

"David, you're tired. You're distraught. You need some sleep."

"No!" he jumped to his feet. "I need Diana. She needs me! I know it! I can feel it. I never should have gone on with the ritual, but she begged me to, and I wanted her so much. So much!" He passed a trembling hand down the lines on either side of his mouth. "Linna can do it. I know she can."

"What about a ritual partner? You must have a woman to help you through the transfer process."

"That's what I wanted to talk to you about. I know it's a lot to ask, Marissa, but would you be willing to subject yourself to the ritual one more time—with me?"

21

Marissa scrambled to her feet. "What?" she gasped, amazed at the words David had just uttered.

"I need you to serve as a ritual partner. And either way, it will work."

"What are you talking about?"

He swallowed and placed his open hand over his chest. "If I go back to the past, the ritual will be successful." He gestured toward her with the same hand. "If you go back, it still will be successful. You'll be with Alek."

"How do you know I want to be with Alek?"

"I saw the way you looked at him in the cabin. You feel the same way about him as I do about Diana, don't you?"

"I don't think that's any of your business." She pushed the chair into place against the table. "Besides. You're forgetting one thing, David."

"What is that?"

"If we perform the ritual again, and one of us goes

back?" She turned to him and looked him in the eye. "Just who do you think is going to transfer into our world?"

He stared at her and she could see the realization dawn on him that his plan had a hole—a big hole. David's expression sagged, as did his shoulders.

"Whoever comes into the present will be stuck here, David. We can't do that to someone, no matter how much you're worried about Diana."

"I hadn't thought of that."

"I didn't think so." She walked up to him and patted his arm. "Sorry, David, but I can't be party to another person's displacement in history, not unless they want to be displaced."

He nodded grimly. "I just hoped. I just thought—"

"Get some sleep, David. I'll watch over Linna for a few hours. Okay?"

"All right."

"Take the chair. It's fairly comfortable."

He dragged his dull gaze across the room until it landed on the overstuffed chair.

"I'm sorry, David," she added, wishing there was some miracle that would solve both their heartaches.

"Wake me if there's any change in Linna."

"I will."

She watched him trudge to the chair and sink into the cushion, his every movement dragged down by grief. Marissa turned away. She wouldn't let herself succumb to sorrow. She would be strong. For all of them.

Alek woke up in the sacred grove, as if he had been asleep on his feet. He zipped his trousers and shook his head, trying to shake out the sluggishness of his thoughts and the aftereffects of coupling with Marissa.

At the thought of her, a sharp pain jagged through his heart, but he forced himself to turn his attention to the grove. No one was about, not even stray Roman soldiers. They had probably retreated to Roman territory beyond the Po River after the brutal attack on Ballachulix. Frowning, Alek loped across the clearing, glad to leave it behind him, and headed down the hill to the trail that led to the village. Before he made his way home, however, he sidetracked to the base of the tree where he had buried the sword of Caius Sellenius eight years ago. Now was the time to unearth the blade and renew the hostility between him and the Roman commander. This time he would use the sword to avenge his mother and his people. What better way than to run the blade into the body of the Roman dog?

Without the slightest trouble, Alek located the pine tree and used a stick to unearth the sword. After he had dug a hole as deep as his forearm, he was rewarded by the sight of the woolen-wrapped weapon. His memory had served him well. With a grunt of satisfaction, Alek pulled the sword from the earth and raised it above his head.

"Caius Sellenius," he declared to the dawn sky. "I come for you!"

Then he rose to his feet and walked into the village as the cocks crowed, heralding the new day. But the sound that usually brought him joy didn't even reach his heart. He turned the corner into the clearing and stopped short. The upright wall of timbers that surrounded the main compound of Ballachulix had been knocked down like so much kindling and every house had been burned to the ground. Pigs rooted through the charred debris and hounds wandered aimlessly, noses to the ground as if searching for their missing masters. Where were all the people? Alek slowly lowered his sword arm, taking in the sight of the devastation, shattered by the heartbreaking scene. Ballachulix had been his only home. No matter how often he had felt an outsider here, this village had been his sanctuary, one of the few places the Romans had never intruded upon. But they had managed to destroy even this small symbol of security at a time when he was unable to defend it.

Like a wild animal howling his pain, Alek tipped back his head and bellowed his outrage, yelling until his cry had silenced every living creature in the forest.

Then he stomped forward, determined more than ever to hunt down the Romans and make them pay for this, no matter if he had to fight them alone, hand to hand, with nothing but the Roman blade.

He tramped through the ashes until he came to the river and remembered the camp his people sometimes made during the hot summer days, where they were close to the water and could care more easily for their animals. Perhaps the remaining Senones were there. He hurried down the trail that followed the riverbank. Sure enough, there, on an easily defended knoll, he found a straggle of people lying on blankets and furs stretched upon the grass. Most of them were wounded and had various cloths wrapped around their injured limbs. A few horses and cows grazed on the slope that angled up from the river, probably the only livestock left to the Senones. A small lone figure walked slowly among them, lugging a bucket of water from the river. He recognized the slight form of his mother.

She looked up as he came abreast of the clearing. At the sight of him, she dropped the bucket and rushed toward him, and he ran to her, arms oustretched to sweep her off her feet. She squeezed him tightly around his neck and he was reminded of Marissa's heartfelt embrace. The wrenching feeling struck him again, and he wondered if he would feel the tug of the she-devil's memory for the rest of his life. He couldn't imagine ever forgetting her.

"Alek!" Helin exclaimed, her face contorted with joyous incredulity.

"Mother!" He hugged her tightly and then stepped back to inspect her. Her linen shift was smudged with dirt and stained with blood, and Alek prayed the blood was not hers. "Are you all right? Are you hurt?"

"I am not hurt, my son." She looked in wonder at the black trousers he wore, the bandage upon his shoulder, and his unlimed hair. "But how about you? Where have you been?"

"In another world, Mother. You would not believe where I have been. But I am unhurt."

"Thank the gods!" She touched his face. "So much has happened since you disappeared, Alek. The Romans attacked us."

"I heard."

"And two strangers have appeared in the grove—a man and a woman, harbingers of trouble, both of them."

"Is the woman here?" Alek inquired, glancing at the sleeping figures.

"Yes. She is ill with the wasting disease. I knew it the moment I saw her."

"I know the woman."

"And she claimed to know you, but we could not see how that was possible."

"Where is she?"

"Come, I will take you to her. She's resting."

Helin took him across the clearing to a pile of rushes over which was thrown a brightly dyed wool blanket in reds and greens. Upon the blanket lay Diana, her hands daintily slipped beneath her cheek and a bear pelt pulled over her for warmth. Her face looked peaceful in slumber, less tense than he had ever seen her.

Alek knelt down beside her. "Diana," he said softly.

She stirred and gradually opened her eyes. Instantly, she jerked backward, first in fear and then in recognition. "Alek?"

"Yes. I have come back. And I have a message from David."

"You do?" Her eyes softened with love. Alek had seen that look on Marissa's face, and he felt the sharp pain of separation from her. Diana touched Alek's arm. "What did he say?"

"That he loves you and is thinking of you. Always."

"Thanks." She smiled tremulously and pushed back her blond hair, tucking it behind her ear. Then she raised herself up on one elbow. "I never thought I'd say this, but I'm glad to see you, Alek."

He had to smile, remembering how afraid of him she'd been the first few days, until she'd allowed herself to see the man and not the brute.

"Are you all right?" he asked. "No one has mistreated you?"

"No, your mother has been very kind to me. And in the few days that I've been here, I've actually felt better—even without my pain medication."

"Few days?" Alek questioned. "You have been here only since last evening, when you and David did the ritual."

"No, I've been here three days. Hasn't it been three days, Helin?" She glanced up at the older woman, who nodded.

"Three days? How can this be?" Alek frowned at the discrepancy in time. Then he turned to his mother. "How long have I been gone from Ballachulix, Mother?"

"Oh, a full cycle of the moon, I believe. At least."

That long? He had been in Marissa's world not more than seven days. Of that he was certain. Did time spin more quickly here in his homeland than it did in the world of U.S. Ovay? He was still trying to make sense of it when he felt the thunder of horses approaching from upriver, heard the muffled hoofbeats in the morning mist and the clanking of weapons as a large group of riders came around the bend in the river.

Alek jumped to his feet while Brennan and his warriors poured into the clearing, their horses lathered with foam and blowing with fatigue. Brennan, at the lead, pulled his mount to a halt with a rough jerk that yanked back his horse's head.

For a moment Brennan stared just past Alek's left shoulder as his horse danced to the side, white-eyed and nervous. Beneath his pointed helmet, the older warrior's face creased in disdain, pulling up one side of his huge blond moustache and revealing the red arc of his lower lip. An illness he'd suffered years ago prevented the muscles on the left side of his face from moving and made his eyelid droop, which increased the ugliness of his thick features and the dull cruelty in his expression, reflecting the violent and ugly spirit inside the man. His coarse blond hair, shot with gray, lay in two thick braids upon his chest, similar in line and color to the huge, yellowed bull horns that curved out of the sides of his helmet.

Without a word to his son, Brennan turned to his right and barked an order that Diana should be brought to him at once.

Brennan hadn't even acknowledged Alek with a single word or gesture, but the other men stared openly at Alek's dark hair, never having seen him without his whitish limed coif. Alek refused to be ashamed of his true coloring and was relieved to be standing honestly before his fellow warriors at last. But Alek did feel the shame of his father's silence. He remained standing tall in spite of the pointed slight, however, while his father slid from his horse and dropped heavily to the ground.

Oswall, one of his father's generals, yanked Diana out of her bed and pushed her toward Brennan. She stumbled and fell at his feet, crying out as the impact shifted her abdomen.

"Have mercy!" Helin exclaimed, reaching out in protest. "She's ill."

"She needs no mercy!" Brennan bellowed. "She's to be sacrificed to Teutates."

"What?" Helin gasped in horror.

"We burn this demon as a sacrifice. Today!"

"No!"

"The gods must be appeased before we ride on Rome!"

"She's not a demon!" Helin stooped to help Diana to her feet, but Brennan shoved her out of the way. Alek lunged forward and caught his mother to save her from falling to the ground. He glared at Brennan, his blood boiling from a lifetime of such treatment at the hand of his father. Without breaking eye contact with Brennan, he motioned his mother to step aside.

"You've hit my mother for the last time, you pig!"

The warriors behind Brennan stirred uncomfortably at the horrible insult Alek had dared hurl at his father. Men had died for less. Very few men had ever stood up to Brennan, even though Alek was aware that most of the Senone warriors disliked his father. They followed him out of fear and a grudging respect for Brennan's strength, not because they admired his leadership abilities.

Brennan seemed to take notice of Alek for the first time. He cupped his hand to his helmet in mockery.

"Do I hear the weak voice of a woman whining in my ear?"

Alek straightened his shoulders, aching to show Brennan what he was made of. "I am no woman."

Brennan dropped his arm. "You are no man either. You ran from the Romans. You knew they were coming. And how did you know?" Brennan pointed at the Roman sword that hung at his hips. "You even carry a Roman blade."

Alek stared at him. Was his father accusing him of disloyalty? Of siding with the Romans? The mere thought made him want to retch in anger.

"Coward!" Brennan spat on the ground. "Woman!"

"I am no woman!" Alek retorted, stepping toward his father even though he was armed with only the short sword. "And you will find me harder to push around than my mother!"

Alek lunged for Brennan's throat. The impact of his weight sent Brennan back a pace. His horse shied away, and a youth grabbed the reins and pulled it out of the way as Alek and his father rolled on the ground. Though Brennan had the strength and cunning of a seasoned warrior, Alek was backed by twenty years of anger, which until this moment he had been forced to swallow. Alek scrambled to his feet as Brennan rose up, swinging. Alek struck out in revenge. Each crushing blow of his fist was an answer to a bruise on his mother's face or a swelled lip, or the way she held her abdomen and wept. Years of anger came out in a flood of blows, the likes of which astounded the other soldiers and Brennan as well. Mercilessly, Brennan pounded his son, but Alek was immune to the pain. With rage serving as his armor, Alek hit his father again and again, matching Brennan blow for blow, until Brennan began to tire.

A man of dignity might have surrendered gracefully

then and retained his honor with a heartfelt apology and good-humored recognition of a strength more powerful than his own. But Brennan was a cruel man and a bully, and he had known nothing but victory over lesser men. To fail in a fight with his own son was unimaginable and unacceptable. So, long after he should have given up, he stood like a huge tree with his feet planted far apart, withstanding hit after hit and swinging as wildly as a drunken man whenever Alek got within range.

Then Alek struck him in the underside of the jaw, snapping his head back. Brennan staggered backward. For a moment he swayed on his feet, his fingers scratching frantically at his chest armor as if he couldn't breathe, and then his huge legs bent at the knee. Like a giant oak toppling in a storm, Brennan tipped backward and crashed to the ground.

Alek stood above him, winded and exhausted, ready to keep fighting whenever Brennan decided to get up. But Brennan didn't get up. In fact, he didn't move. Oswall ventured forward and peered down at the fallen warrior as complete silence hung over the crowd.

"Brennan," Oswall said, nudging him in the shoulder. "Brennan!"

Alek wiped the sweat from his brow with a swipe of his forearm and looked down at his father. Though his own body thrummed with pain, he barely took notice of it, for the satisfaction he felt in thrashing this bully far exceeded his physical discomfort.

Still Brennan did not stir. Oswall shook him once more. "Brennan!"

Alek stood above him, panting and sweating, trying to catch his breath.

Oswall dropped to one knee and slid off Brennan's horned helmet. A trickle of blood oozed from Brennan's nose, and his eyes were already swelling shut, two huge red puffs of flesh. Alek noticed a second trickle of blood in Brennan's right ear and knew from experience that Brennan was not going to get up ever again.

"He's dead," Oswall declared, glancing up at Alek, his countenance both startled and dark.

"Dead?" Helin repeated in disbelief.

Alek forced his expression to remain unchanged. He could not rejoice in another man's death, but he would never mourn this man's passing.

"He must have hit his head," Oswall continued, placing the helmet on Brennan's chest. "He must have cracked his head, falling like that."

Helin came up behind Alek and stood beside him to stare down at the husband she had feared for thirty years. One by one the other warriors dismounted and joined them, forming a ring around their fallen leader in a solemn gathering of the pitifully small Senone army. Never once did Alek look any of them in the eye, but kept his gaze cast down upon his dead father. He wondered what the reaction of the other warriors would be. Like Brennan, did they all believe he was a traitor? And what would they think of a man who was responsible for the death of his own father? He had always felt like an outsider, and this act of violence would probably call for banishment altogether if he were lucky, or death if he were not.

Suddenly, Alorix broke from the ranks, unsheathed his sword with a metallic swish, and raised the weapon above his head. "Hail, Alek!" he shouted. "Champion of the Senones!"

Alek jerked his head up in surprise and stared at the old battle hero, his teacher. Alorix was crazy to support his cause. The others would probably fall on him and beat him to death.

But then, much to his utter amazement, the rest of

the warriors saluted him in a similar fashion. In a clanking of metal, they drew their swords and honored him,
cheering and hooting and whistling until Alek flushed
and gestured for them to quiet down.

Helin linked her arm around his and squeezed him,
relaying her heartfelt thanks for the deliverance from
her tormentor, and her pride in his strength.

"There will be no sacrifice," Alek declared, using the
moment of victory to spare Diana's life. "We will prepare Brennan's funeral pyre instead. We will take the
women and children to the Boii stronghold. And then
we march on Rome."

The warriors cheered and whooped. Someone produced a plank, and together Oswall and Alorix carried
Brennan's body toward the sacred grove.

Linna spoke something under her breath, and Marissa
turned her head to see if the wounded healer was
becoming delirious or simply having a dream. She
reached out and touched Linna's forehead, and found
she was burning with fever. She had tried giving the
healer a pain reliever which would reduce her fever, but
Linna was adamantly opposed to taking medicine of
which she knew nothing about.

Tirelessly, Marissa took the cloth from Linna's head,
refreshed it in the basin of cool water on the nightstand,
and then draped it over her forehead.

"Alek!" Linna mumbled. Her eyes rolled from side to
side and her fingers jerked upon the blanket. "Alek—
no!"

Linna's voice cracked with anguish. Marissa touched
her shoulder, hoping to bring her out of her terrible
dream.

"Linna," she called. "Linna, wake up!"

"Alek!"

Marissa stared at the healer, wondering what awful vision she saw in her dream. Whatever it was, Alek was either suffering or in trouble.

She patted Linna's cheek. "Linna, Linna, you must wake up!"

Suddenly Linna's eyelids popped open. Her once-turquoise blue eyes were the color of quicksilver now, a product of her raging fever. She blinked and seemed to have difficulty focusing on the woman who stood above her.

"Linna, are you all right?"

The healer passed her tongue over her dry upper lip and peered at Marissa with fear and terror streaming from her eyes. "Alek!"

"What about him?"

"I saw him! He has been captured by the Romans. He and two others have been taken to Caius Sellenius. All the others—killed!"

"It's just a dream, Linna." Gently, she stroked the top of her head. "You're delirious."

"No! I saw it! The Tiber River runs with blood! Senone blood!"

Marissa's hand stopped in mid-stroke. She remembered the line in Woodward's reference book which had described the famous battle of Vadimonian Lake by saying the lower Tiber River had run red with Gallic blood. So many Senones had perished in the battle that day, they ceased to exist as a people. Could Linna have been given a vision of the actual event? It really didn't make any sense that Alek could go into the past and march nearly to Rome, all in the space of one night. Yet, perhaps the passage of time was skewed between then and now. Perhaps Alek had been in the past for a few days and Linna's vision was accurate. If so, Alek was now in the hands of his hated enemy and soon would be on his fateful trip to Rome.

Marissa felt her heart constrict with fear and longing. There was nothing she could do to help him now. Nothing. She closed her eyes and remembered the last thing he had said to her, that he would give anything to change fate—anything. How she wished she had forced him to stay in her world! She should have held him at gunpoint and forced him to—

Marissa broke off and slumped in her chair. She never could have kept Alek with her by force. She might have kept him here with the bond of love. But neither alternative would have been acceptable to a man of honor. And Alek's sense of honor was what she had loved most about him.

She felt a warm hand clutch her around the wrist and glanced over to see Linna staring at her.

"What I see is true, Marissa," she said. "I walk the world between this one and my own as my spirit seeks a place for death. What I see is real."

"I believe you, Linna. I do."

The healer sighed and seemed to relax. Her fingers loosened and slipped away as she closed her eyes. "Alek—" she murmured.

Marissa watched her, thinking of Alek's future. He would be taken to Rome, imprisoned for two years in a wretched cell, and then tortured to death for the entertainment of the Roman citizens. How could she let it happen to him? And if the days flew by so quickly in the past in comparison to her own time, how soon would Alek be facing his death in a coliseum full of strangers?

I would give anything to change fate—anything!

Marissa bit her thumbnail as Alek's voice boomed in her thoughts, and a vision of him crying out in pain twisted in her heart. She had to do something. Alek had done his part for his people. He had gone to battle with them and fought his hardest. Dying for an annihilated tribe would prove nothing, accomplish nothing, and mean nothing. And that was the worst thought of all—that her proud warrior would die a tortured, meaningless death.

She rose to her feet as a new resolve burned through her helplessness. Unknowingly, Alek had given her permission to act, to change history for him. And she would do it. Or at least give it her best Montana try.

"Linna," she said, bending closer. "Listen to me for a minute. I have an idea."

22

Marissa took Linna's hand in hers and squeezed it gently. "I know you are in great pain, Linna. But I also believe that you want to help Alek as much as I do."

"Yes. I love the warrior."

"So do I."

Linna's eyes glittered up at her in surprise. "You do?"

"Yes. And I believe Alek could be happy in my world, at least in the part I come from. It is an open place, full of grass and trees—not like this city. I raise cattle, just like your people do, and I could use a man like Alek to help me with my ranch." She blinked and looked down. "Plus I believe that Alek cares for me, too, and might consider sharing a life with me."

"Alek doesn't care for me in that way, Marissa. You are lucky if he loves you, for he is a good man. A kind man."

"Yes, I know." Marissa squeezed her hand again. "And that's why we have to help him."

"How?"

"By performing the ritual one more time, if you have the strength, and if you can transfer Alek and only Alek."

"I will summon the strength," Linna answered firmly. "And I can call Alek's spirit to the grove. But what about the nectar and—"

"We have a few drops left, enough for one person. We could give it to David to ensure that he is the one to travel into the past."

"David would go to the past?"

"Yes. He longs to be with Diana—the woman who is ill."

"But if he went there, he would never be able to return."

Marissa nodded and sat down in her chair. "He knows that."

"Diana may not even be alive by now."

"I believe David is willing to take the chance that she is. He loves Diana very much."

Linna nodded and closed her eyes. "There will be much love in this ritual act. You for Alek. Alek for you. David and Diana. The forces will be very strong. This will help me."

"Good." Marissa scooted eagerly to the edge of her chair.

"But for you to join with David will not be good."

Marissa's eagerness fizzled. "Oh."

"This is a rare case, Marissa." Linna tapped her fingers on the blanket and appeared much more alert. She seemed to be drawing energy from the possibility of helping Alek. "I believe I could use a different method and try the ritual with David alone."

"With just one person?"

"It has been done. And with the forces of love helping me, it might very well work."

Marissa stood up again. "Tell me what you need, then. And let's get started."

Linna listed the items she required and Marissa strode to the bedroom door. She stopped on the threshold at the sound of Linna's voice.

"Marissa?"

Marissa turned. "Yes?"

"The man who summoned me—" Linna coughed. "Where is he?"

"Dr. Woodward? I don't really know. I hope he's still out at the cabin."

"The man is evil. You must be wary of him."

"I know. I'd like to hightail it out of town where he'd never find us, but you are in no shape to travel just yet."

"You should go anyway."

"And leave you? Never, Linna. End of story."

Marissa glanced at Linna's troubled face and then ducked out of the room.

As dawn came, Alek grunted and raised himself onto his elbow. He was lying on the stone floor of a small room and was shackled to the wall behind him by two lengths of heavy, rusted chain which were attached to wide metal bands clamped around his wrists. To hobble him, a link of chain also stretched between his ankles. The room had a wooden door hung on crude iron hinges, no windows, and a pile of moldering straw thrown in the corner. Near him sat Alorix, his back to the wall, his head hanging down as he snored and coughed. On his right lay Oswall who had died of his wounds during the night.

Sighing, Alek averted his gaze and stared dully at the floor, trying to block out the images of the massacre in the river two days ago. Though the Senones and their allies had fought bravely, they had failed to vanquish the Romans. Caius Sellenius had lived long enough near the border of Gaul, and had fought enough skirmishes with Brennan and the other bands to learn Gallic battle tactics. Once the roaring, naked hoards of northern warriors could make a Roman legion freeze in horror. Not so any more. Sellenius had grown wise to the ways of the Gauls and saw through the trick of the mind the Gauls played upon their enemies.

Alek frowned again. If only Brennan had adopted some of the structure and discipline of the Roman legionnaires, the Gauls might have had a better chance of success in battle. But the obstinate, fearless nature of the Gauls—a nature that clung to old ways and celebrated the power of the individual—had been their downfall against the highly organized Romans. While crossing the lower Tiber in a wild rampaging charge against the Romans, the Senones had been cut down by the score and had paid a heavy toll for their independent nature.

Alek was brought out of his thoughts by the *tramp tramp tramp* of soldiers approaching his prison cell, their sandals slapping the hot, packed soil. There were four of them, Alek guessed.

The door was flung open, and Alorix jerked awake. Two soldiers entered the room, glancing in disgust at Oswall's body, while the other two remained guarding the door. One reached out and unlocked Alorix's manacles and then roughly pulled him to his feet, leaving his ankles chained.

Alorix wrenched his arm back. Prisoner or not, he would maintain his dignity, as all Gallic warriors would. He looked back at Alek, neither sure of seeing the other again. Alek nodded slightly in response, and Alorix turned back to face his captors. With a shout at the men at the door, the soldier with the key shoved Alorix out of the prison. The door slammed shut behind them and the soldiers marched away, leaving Alek in even deeper silence than before. He sank against the wall, wondering what was happening to Alorix and if the Romans were mistreating him. He turned his thoughts away, for the image was too painful to entertain. Instead, he closed his eyes and thought of beautiful Marissa—Marissa of the raven hair and flashing eyes, Marissa of the full, red lips and shapely breasts. Alek took a deep breath and let it out in a long, desolate sigh as he thought of running his hands down her naked torso. It was painful to think of Marissa, too, but he couldn't help himself. How he missed the she-devil!

Much later, the soldiers approached again and burst into the cell just as they had when they had come for Alorix.

The soldier in charge unlocked Alek's wrist manacles and barked a string of Latin at him, most of which Alek didn't comprehend. Then he was shoved and prodded out of the prison and across a yard through the warm morning sunshine to a small villa which was surrounded by the striped tents of the Roman army. The leaders of the Roman army were most likely housed in the villa ahead of him. Why would he be taken there? Was he to be given one last insult before they put him to death? He had heard of Gauls being castrated in front of the Roman legions and then being used as human targets for javelins. Is this what was planned for him and Alorix, if Alorix wasn't dead already?

Dirty and hungry, Alek staggered up the marble stairs to the portico of the villa, doing his best to cope with the chain at his feet so he wouldn't fall to his knees in front of the Roman pigs. That would hurt his pride almost as much as being captured by them. His body ached from every blow taken in battle and from sleeping on stone. Every few seconds the squad leader would shove him in the shoulder or poke him in the back with the handle of his lance, just to infuriate him. Alek was seething by the time they passed through the shady atrium and stopped in front of a door on the right.

The leader rapped on the door and a voice told them to come in.

Alek was thrust into the chamber and was momentarily blinded by the darkness of the room. After a moment he managed to make out a man standing near a table covered with scrolls and the figure of a slight woman hovering behind him. She stood in silhouette in front of a set of windows on the far end of the room, and something about the curve of her body looked familiar.

"Leave us," the man at the desk ordered in a crisp, restrained voice.

The soldiers tramped out, shutting the door quietly, in a vastly different way than they had shut the door of the prison.

"Come closer," the Roman said, speaking in the Senone tongue and motioning with his hand. He wore no luxurious toga and cloak, but was dressed in leather and bronze, the uniform of a true soldier. His only concession to his rank was a scarlet tunic beneath the leather cuirass he wore around his trim abdomen. He wasn't a young man, either, probably in his fifties, with gray sprinkled in the dark brown of his closely-cropped hair. But he was in excellent physical condition, and a gleam of intelligence and guarded respect flashed in his light brown eyes when he surveyed the Gaul before him. He seemed vaguely familiar, but Alek couldn't recall where he had seen the man before.

Alek stared down his nose at him, suddenly aware that he was in the presence of an equal. Sometimes he had felt this strange awareness, regardless of the race or rank of a man, and he had definitely felt it with Marissa Quinn—the feeling that the mind of the other person was something known and familiar and, well, equal. That he could consider a Roman his equal shocked him. He wanted nothing to do with a Roman pig. Alek shifted his feet, and the chain clanked.

"So you are Alek of the Senones," the Roman said, walking around from behind the table. His legs were long and well muscled, with powerful calves above the straps of his leather boots. Alek imagined this commander could still hold his own in hand-to-hand combat, an impossiblity for most of the other Roman leaders, who were soft with rich food and debauchery.

Alek refused to speak. He raised his chin and kept his eyes on the Roman. The commander strode to another table, picked up something with a metallic clanking noise, and turned. Alek immediately recognized the scabbard of Caius Sellenius' sword.

"Where did you get this?" the Roman demanded.

"From a Roman pig. He gave it to me."

"Gave it to you? This is a valuable weapon, with much history behind it."

"You accuse me of theft?" Alek glowered. His head throbbed whenever he shouted. "A Senone does not steal. Only Romans steal."

"Some Romans don't. And some Senones do."

Alek snorted in disgust and disbelief and crossed his arms over his chest.

The commander stepped closer. "This sword belongs to Caius Sellenius."

"Yes. And I intend to give it back to him—in his entrails! Then I will take his head back and hang it above my mother's door!"

The woman turned sharply at Alek's outburst, but she still didn't come out of the shadows. Alek shifted his attention back to the Roman officer. The officer was studying him, his eyes dark with concern.

"Why your mother's door?"

Alek snorted again. "Because the Roman pig violated my mother. I saw it."

"Some things that are seen are not what they seem," the officer said.

"Speak plainly, Roman," Alek retorted. "We are men, not oracles."

A wry smile flitted across the officer's firm mouth. He laid the sheathed sword on the table with the scrolls and turned back to Alek.

"I have it on good authority that Caius Sellenius never violated a woman in his life. In fact—"

"Your authority must be blind and deaf."

"In *fact*," the officer continued, undaunted by Alek's harsh interruption, "he has loved one woman and one woman only for most of his adult life."

"I am not interested in the Roman pig's love affairs," Alek replied acidly.

"You should be. Humor me for a moment."

Alek fell silent while a cold trickle of unease began to creep over his scalp and slide down his spine.

"This woman he loved also loved him. But she would never—" The officer sighed sharply and glanced at the window and back again, as if marshalling his thoughts. "But she was married, you see, and she would never leave her husband. No matter what cruelties she suffered, no matter what unhappiness she endured, she would not leave her people for a Roman."

Alek's mouth went dry. He shot a glance at the cloaked figure by the window while the feeling of unease turned into a burning sensation in the pit of his stomach.

"This woman bore a son to Caius Sellenius, but she

never told him there was a child between them. Caius would have taken that child and raised him as his own. You see, he has no sons or daughters."

"I care nothing for his lack of family," Alek declared.

"The only reason the woman has come forward is to plead for the life of her son. She knows the Roman would not wish to kill his own son."

"The Roman deserves what he gets! It is just like a Roman to want another man's wife!"

"You and I both know that Brennan was no man. He was an animal."

Alek felt the color drain from his face, as every doubt, every suspicion, every question about his past, his mother, and Brennan was substantiated. His mother was the woman of whom this officer spoke. His mother was the one who had lain with a Roman and loved him as she should have loved her Gallic husband. His mother was the one who had spawned a bastard child, half-Gaul and half-Roman, and raised him in a lie. Deep down, he had known it all along, but had never allowed himself to examine the possibility and all its damning ramifications.

Alek had felt like an outsider all his life, had been called a changeling, had gone to great lengths to conceal his unusual coloring, always trying, but never fitting in. Nothing would have helped, because nothing could change the seed from which he had sprung. He wasn't a Gaul. He wasn't Brennan's son. He was the son of a Roman. He was the son of Caius Sellenius—the man responsible for the death of his mother's people.

"Alek!" the woman cried from the darkness.

Alek recognized the voice of his mother. He stared at the cloaked figure and then back at the officer standing before him, tall and straight and handsome. He knew suddenly, as he had intuitively known from the very first moment he stepped into the room, that the sword he had unearthed, the sword he had carried to inflict a bloody revenge, belonged to this man. Only the graying hair and leaner physique of the man had kept Alek from immediately recognizing the Roman officer he had fought on the river bank.

"You," he gasped, barely able to contain his outrage. "You—"

"Yes. I am your father."

"No!" Alek bellowed. He couldn't help himself. His heart—his soul—the very stuff that made him what he was—was breaking in pieces with the truth. Everything he had built his life upon was a lie. He belonged nowhere, to no one. His bloodline was forked, damning him to eternal limbo, for he could never straddle the line between Gaul and Rome. It was too bloody a wall, too violent a bridge. He was a man with no true father, no true people, and now no true past.

"No!" he shouted again. He lunged for the officer, but his shackled feet tripped him and he fell to his knees. For a moment he hestitated on all fours, nearly overwhelmed by hopelessness and shock. His mother fled to his side and put her hands on his shoulders to comfort him during this awful revelation of truth. He wanted to blame her. How he wanted to blame her!—to lash out at her, to accuse her of bringing him to this. But he knew too well the life his mother had suffered. He couldn't fault her for desiring the love of a decent man, for having one small flicker of happiness in her life. But why had she chosen a Roman to love? *This* Roman! Why?

"Alek," Helin cried. "Please, my son. Please try to understand."

He couldn't look at her. He struggled to his feet.

"Caius, can he not be unchained?"

"Yes." Caius broke for the door and barked a command to the soldier waiting outside. In moments, a guard was removing the manacles while Alek kept his back turned to everyone. He couldn't control his expression. He didn't know what to think. He was afraid that if he looked at Caius and Helin he would either attack them or burst into tears. Chest heaving and eyes burning, Alek stared at the wall, too full of confusion and pain to speak or move.

"Had I known, Alek," Caius said quietly behind him. "I would have sent for you years ago."

Alek clenched his teeth. Would he have traded his violent upbringing in Brennan's house for the life of a privileged Roman? Would he have fit in any better as a Roman? He could make no answer. He *had* no answer. He would never *know* the answer.

"Whatever you think of me," Caius spoke again, "you are a son to make a man proud."

Alek had never received a single word of praise from Brennan, but such words could not penetrate a heart hardened by his upbringing, especially when the praise came from a Roman.

"I was to send you to the capital," Caius continued, "so that Caesar could see the champion of the Senones."

"And make sport of him," Alek growled.

"Yes, unfortunately. Those were my orders."

"You will not follow orders now, Roman?" Alek's heart and voice were quickly filling with bitterness. "What kind of soldier are you?"

"An honorable one. I want to take you to Rome, Alek, but not as a prisoner. As my son."

"You bastard!" Alek whirled, his heart cracking in two. "I am not your son. I am no one's son!"

Helin sank against the table, weeping. Alek glanced at her, feeling like the bastard he was, but unable to control himself.

"Take me to Rome, cut off my balls!" Alek said curtly. "I don't care what happens to me! I have no people! Do you understand that, Roman dog? No people!"

"Alek! Don't!" Helin exclaimed. "It can be all right. You just have to—"

"No!" Alek shouted. "It will never be right! You are a woman. You have never been able to see the lines between people. But I am a warrior, Mother. A warrior! And this man is my enemy."

"He is your father!"

Alek glared at Caius, seeing the reflection of his own eyes, his own nose, and his own mouth. But the reflection wasn't enough. Too many bloody years had passed between Senone and Roman to ever call this man his father.

Alek crossed his arms over his chest.

"Send me to Rome," he declared.

Caius shook his head. "No. I am sending someone else instead."

"Who?"

"Caesar wants a champion. I am sending a champion. The old one."

"Alorix?"

"Yes. It was his idea. And the names are similar enough to confuse the recordkeepers."

Alek blinked in surprise and glanced at his mother.

"He wants to go," Helin put in. "He wants to die for you and our people, Alek."

"No!"

"It is an honor for him, Alek. You know this to be true."

Alek fell quiet again. Alorix had wanted to die in battle, cutting his coughing disease short with the glory of the sword. He hadn't fallen in battle, so the next best thing would be to die in the place of a great champion, thus playing a trick on Rome. Alorix would revel in that, no question about it.

"What of me, then?" he inquired after a deep silence.

"You are free to go." Caius picked up the sword again and turned to face Alek.

"Free to go where?" Alek retorted, the bitterness tart on his tongue.

"Anywhere you like."

Alek flashed on the image of Ballachulix, burned beyond recognition. He saw the straggling remains of the Senone women limping into the Boii stronghold, and then he recalled the scene of the slaughter of his fellow warriors on the banks of the Tiber. Free to go? What a cruel jest.

Then, from deep within him, came the vision of the she-devil's face as she lay beneath him on the altar. *I love you,* she had whispered. She had held him, and in those few moments he had known a sense of belonging so great it had nearly burst his heart. He had never felt anything like it, because he had never truly belonged anywhere, to anyone, but Marissa.

That was where he wanted to go. That was where he belonged—with Marissa Quinn of Montana in the land of U.S. Ovay. But the land of U.S. Ovay was out of his reach now and he knew it.

"I can supply you with anything you wish," Caius Sellenius commented. "You have but to ask."

Alek stared at the door, his emotions, his heart, and his soul turned to stone. "A horse. My sword. And a flask of wine."

"Surely there must be more that I can—"

"No." Alek turned away. "That is all I ask, Roman. I want nothing else from you."

He would ride. He would ride as far north as he could go, far from the Romans and the Senones and any memory of what his life had been.

23

Marissa headed for the kitchen hoping Leslie would have a stock of candles on hand and the herbs Linna would need for the ritual. Marissa recognized most of the herb names even though she hadn't spent much time in the kitchen. With any luck Leslie was enough of a cook to keep them on hand.

Just as she turned the corner from the hall to the dining area, she was shocked to see Leslie standing near the table, her blond hair as wild as the vacant look in her eyes.

"Leslie?" Marissa called softly.

At her name, Leslie turned and stared at her as if completely disoriented.

"Leslie?" Marissa repeated, walking forward, careful to keep from rushing toward her sister and alarming her. There was no telling what was going through Leslie's mind, or how much she comprehended.

Leslie stared, her blue-gray eyes wide with uncertainty and one hand draped at the base of her throat, as if she had begun to make a gesture and had been distracted in the process. "S-S-Sis?"

"Yes! It's me—Marissa." Marissa's heart leapt for joy as she heard the first words her sister had said to her since her arrival in Seattle five days ago. She took both of Leslie's delicate shoulders in her hands. "Are you all right? How are you feeling?"

"Shaky." Leslie smiled tremulously, an expression that nearly broke Marissa's heart with sheer happiness. She hadn't expected Leslie to ever make a voluntary movement again.

"Well here, sit down." Marissa dragged out a chair and patted the seat. "Let me get you something to eat. You must be starving."

"I am."

Marissa stood rooted to the floor for a moment, unable to move out of sheer disbelief.

Leslie sank onto the chair and slumped as if she had no reserves of energy. She slid her forearms onto the table and gazed at the backs of her hands. She was so silent that Marissa reached out and touched her shoulder again, worried that Leslie was about to lapse into her zombie-like state once more.

"Les?" she asked. "Are you still okay?"

"W—what are these little plastic things on my hands?"

"Hep locks for an IV. Dr. Woodward had you hooked up to an IV because you couldn't eat."

"I couldn't?" Leslie turned and glanced up at her sister.

"No. You've been in a trance for days, Leslie, in something like a coma."

"I have?"

"Yes. They gave you too much night orchid nectar— or so they tell me."

Leslie blinked and looked back at her hands. "Night orchid?" she mused in a vague voice. "I can't remember—"

"Don't try, at least not now. The important thing is to get your energy back to normal." She squeezed Leslie's left shoulder. "Why don't I make you a sandwich or something. How about some soup?"

"Soup sounds good." Leslie sighed. "My hands are shaky though."

"I can help you." Marissa bent down and hugged Leslie, something she hadn't done in years. "Oh, Les, it's so good to have you back! I'm as happy as all get-out!"

"Mariss," Leslie smiled back at her. "You're in Seattle now. Over here we say 'as happy as a clam.'"

Marissa grinned. She knew that Leslie was going to be all right.

The ritual had to be performed at dusk, which meant spending an entire day waiting for the evening hours. The first thing Marissa did was call her mother to reassure her that everything was all right and that Corky didn't have to come all the way to Seattle to check on them. Then Marissa stepped out to buy candles and herbs for the ceremony and some groceries to replenish Leslie's diminished larder. When she returned, she took a nap while David sat with Linna, who drifted in and out of consciousness and was very near death. The healer's dreams seemed to be filled with disturbing visions of Alek, for she often called out his name in anguish. Marissa didn't know who the dreams affected more, Linna or her, because each time Linna cried out, Marissa ached for and worried about the warrior, wondering what was happening to him and if he were hurting. She could barely endure the image of Alek suffering and alone, and prayed the ritual would bring him out of his pain.

Marissa knew better than to expect the ritual to be a success or that Linna would even live long enough to perform it. Even if the ritual went well, they might have waited too long to rescue Alek, and he might arrive mutilated and half dead. Could she live with that? Every time hope flickered inside her when she thought of Alek coming back to her world as a whole man, she doused the tiny flame immediately, knowing the likelihood that he would appear was extremely remote—and that he would appear unscathed even more so.

After a huge breakfast, Leslie languished in the bath and then slept most of the afternoon. Marissa checked in on her periodically, concerned that Leslie had slipped back into her comatose state. But late in the afternoon, Leslie woke up and actually helped her make dinner, even though she merely sat at the table and methodically ripped lettuce for a salad. She had yet to recover her full strength, and the slightest physical effort exhausted her. But simply having Leslie walking and talking was enough for Marissa.

At long last the shadows of evening lengthened in the apartment. Marissa and David took all pictures off the bedroom wall and moved the furniture out of the chamber except for the bed on which Linna dozed. They carefully arranged a circle of candles around the bed and prepared the herbal packets as Linna had instructed. David left to wrap himself in the robe he had worn at the cabin. Then, when he returned, Marissa quietly woke Linna, who struggled back to consciousness. Her breath came in labored gasps as Marissa lit the candles one by one, and then Linna began to whisper incantations. The bedroom took on an eerie glow as the ring of candles flickered in the encroaching gloom and flashed shadows on the bare walls. Leslie sat in the far corner, watching the ritual with a faraway expression on her face, entranced by the light and the musical whisper of the Druid's soft voice. Marissa prayed that the ritual wouldn't trigger a relapse in her sister. Linna waited until the moon appeared in the window and then she raised one finger in a weak gesture.

"Drink of the night orchid," she murmured.

David picked up the wine glass in which they had poured the precious drops of nectar along with a drought of wine according to Linna's instructions.

At that moment they heard a crash in the living room, sounding very much like the door bursting in. Marissa glanced in alarm at David, but before anyone could speak or move, they heard the sound of running footsteps in the hall pounding toward the bedroom.

"Drink!" Linna urged. "Hurry!"

David raised the glass to his lips and was just about to sip from it when the bedroom door burst open.

"Stop!" a familiar voice called out.

Marissa was astounded to see Dr. Woodward in the doorway, a gun in his hand.

"Kyle?" David gasped, still holding the goblet near his mouth.

"Give me that glass," Woodward demanded. "Now!"

"No!" Marissa cried. In that instant she could see her dreams dying, could envision Alek perishing, and knew that Woodward was going to have his way—after all they'd been through.

"I've had enough of you, Miss Quinn," Woodward said, pointing the gun at her. "Quite enough. So just be quiet." He thrust out his bandaged right hand toward David. "Give me that glass!"

"No," Linna said in a voice weakened with pain.

David could do nothing but obey the doctor. He held out the glass and Woodward snatched the night orchid nectar out of his hand.

"This nectar belongs to me," he exclaimed. "Not you, David. Or you, Miss Quinn. Me!"

David took a step toward his former colleague. "Kyle, don't use the night orchid again. You don't know what you're doing!"

"Don't I?" Kyle lifted the goblet to his lips. "I have transferred four people through time, which makes me believe that I *do* know what I'm doing. And you people simply are afraid of my power."

"You know nothing of power," Linna put in, wheezing. "Or you would respect it more. And fear it."

"What is there to be afraid of?" Woodward held the glass up in a toast to the dying healer and downed the contents. "I know how to perform the ritual. All I have to do is go back, find Diana, learn the cure for cancer, and get one of your Druid friends to return me to my own time. I should have thought of this sooner."

"You think it will be that easy?" Linna asked.

"Certainly. I know the ritual. I'll just get more orchids."

"In my world," Linna put in with a heavy sigh, "night orchids are very rare. You will find it a lifelong task to gather enough for a ritual."

"Nonsense! You are merely trying to scare me." Woodward ran his bandaged hand down the front of his chest and glanced at Leslie as the night orchid took effect. Marissa followed his line of sight and wondered if Woodward had plans to use her sister in the ritual again. Outrage burned through her. Woodward would never touch Leslie again, even if she had to sacrifice herself to stop him.

"So, witch, let's get on with it," Woodward quipped. "Keep up your chant while I choose a partner."

Marissa stepped in front of him. "It's not going to be Leslie, Doc."

"Oh?" He gave her a quick but scathing perusal. "You then?"

"You couldn't handle me, Doc."

"Oh?" His eyes glinted at her in a look full of hatred laced with sexual curiosity. Marissa stared back, amazed at the expression in the doctor's eyes, as if she were looking into the face of something less than human.

"You don't need a partner," Linna declared. "You have powers, Doctor Woodward, strong enough to make a partner unnecessary."

"Really?" He turned toward the healer. That's too bad. I was looking forward to doing the sex magic with Miss Quinn."

Linna ignored his sarcasm. "And as long as you have taken the night orchid, you might as well take your journey." Linna ran her tongue across her lips and glanced at Marissa. Her eyes were once again the strange silver-blue color, like the surface of a mirror.

Marissa leaned closer and clutched Linna's hand. "But what about Alek?" she protested. "And David?"

"Trust me, this is all for the better, Marissa." Linna squeezed Marissa's fingers in a nearly imperceptible nuance of meaning. For a moment the two women glanced at each other, communicating on a level made possible by their mutal love for Alek. In that moment, Marissa knew that Linna had something in mind, some secret plan she was about to execute. Then Linna closed her eyes, as if tiring. "And since the night orchid is gone—"

"That's enough chatter." Woodward interrupted. "Let's get on with it!"

Linna opened her eyes. "Then you must come closer, Doctor Woodward, and join hands with me."

Woodward stepped up to the side of the bed and tentatively held out his bandaged right hand while he remained holding the gun with his left. Instinctively, Marissa backed away and joined David at the foot of the bed. Woodward glanced at David and Marissa to make certain they were keeping their distance and then turned back to Linna.

"You know the prayer, Doctor Woodward," she urged. "Say it and I will join my voice to yours. Your energy will flow into me and give me the strength to help you travel to the other side."

"God, I can't believe this!" David cried. "He'll go back and find Diana and—"

"Quiet, David!" Woodward retorted. "Or I'll shoot you where you stand."

David broke off, glowering, and crossed his arms over his chest. Marissa slipped her hands through the crook of his elbow to warn him with an insistent clench of her fingers. He glanced down at her in surprise and she tried to relay to him with her eyes that he should stop protesting. Both their dreams of joining the ones they loved were being crushed into oblivion by Dr. Woodward, but if by some chance Linna could outwit Woodward, at least there would be no violence from the gun. Right now the best thing they could do was bide their time and see what happened.

David sighed and Marissa felt the stiffness bleed out of him. They both turned their attention to the opening incantation of the ritual.

In a low sing-song voice, Woodward began to chant. His dry tone was joined by the raspy, quavering voice of the dying healer. At a certain phrase which Linna had coached Marissa to recognize, she reached for the smoldering pile of herbs on a dish and passed it between the healer and the doctor. Soon afterward the silver light descended upon the bed and a breeze pushed through the screened window, fluttering the curtains which hung on either side. Marissa stepped back and held her breath as the silver light enveloped both figures, glittering and twinkling and undulating. She waited for the tinkling bell sound which would signal the transfer of people, wondering who would come through the veil in place of Dr. Woodward. By some miracle, could Linna bring Alek out of the past? Or Diana? Would the night orchid nectar not be lost on the doctor after all? For David's sake and Diana's safety, she hoped the person to be transferred would be Diana. But for her heart and her own selfish need, she longed for Alek to appear.

Instead of the twinkling sound there came a low hum, so deep and vibrant that the window rattled in its frame. The sound increased, both in amplitude and vibration, as if a giant boulder were thundering toward them. The sound grew so loud that Marissa had to cover her ears. The noise mushroomed and transformed until it sounded as if the room were filled with millions of bees. This ominous sound was nothing like the beautiful tinkling of bells in the previous rituals. What was going on?

Then, over the thrumming, she heard a man's piercing scream, as if he were falling into a well or a deep chasm. Marissa felt the hairs on the backs of her arms and neck stand straight up, for she recognized pure terror in the cry. As the wail faded, so did the silver light, until nothing remained but the sputtering candles, the bed, and Linna lying on the rumpled sheets. Her hair had turned completely white.

Woodward had vanished, and no one had transferred to take his place.

For a tense moment, no one moved. All they could do was stare and try to recover from the blast of noise and the horrible wail of human terror that had shaken the bedroom. Then Marissa stepped forward.

"Linna!" she gasped. Was she dead? What had turned her hair white?

Marissa dashed to the side of the bed while Leslie rose up from her chair and David edged closer.

"Linna!" she repeated, slipping her fingers over the healer's limp hand. "Are you all right?"

"Hurry," Linna panted. "You must find more nectar. You must get it now!"

"But what happened? Where is Dr. Woodward?"

"Where he belongs. Where he can learn the true meaning of power."

"Not in the past with Diana?"

"No." Linna clutched Marissa's wrist. "He is suspended in an underword where I can drain his power to help us. But I will not last long. If we are to try to help Alek, we must do so at once."

"But there is no more night orchid nectar."

Leslie came up behind Marissa. "My orchids are blooming, Sis. How about them?"

"That's right!" David said. "You do have some plants, don't you?"

"And what about your manager, Mrs. Pitts," Marissa put in, with a sudden and exquisite shaft of hope coursing through her. "Doesn't she have some night orchids?"

"Yes. And if mine are blooming, hers probably are, too."

Marissa turned to David. "How long will it take you to get nectar from the plants?"

"Enough for a dose? I don't know. An hour?"

"Do we have an hour, Linna?" Marissa asked, looking down at the exhausted healer.

"I am not certain. I am very weak. Get the nectar and I will rest." She sighed and closed her eyes. "But we race the moon, you understand. You must hurry. Before the moon fades, we must do the ritual once more."

Leslie raced downstairs to Mrs. Pitt's apartment, hoping to convince the old woman that she had come up with a pest treatment for the orchids that needed to be applied while they were in bloom. And more, she had to do it upstairs in her own apartment, a treatment that could take a few hours but wouldn't harm the orchid. In this way she hoped to get her hands on the orchids without having nosy Mrs. Pitt's tagging along. She knew the manager rarely stayed up after ten-thirty and wouldn't be interested in a lesson in biology in the middle of the night.

While Leslie was gone, Marissa helped David extract the nectar from the orchids in the living room, using an eyedropper and a needle. The blossoms had tiny bowls full of the syrup, protected by convoluted petals and an intricate reproductive system design. If any particles of pollen were to drop in the nectar, it would seriously affect the potency of the plant, which was why the process was so time-consuming. Harvesting the nectar required a steady hand, a wealth of patience, and extreme concentration. David was the perfect man for the job.

While David attended the plants, Marissa made sure both he and Leslie had everything they needed while making countless trips to the bedroom to encourage Linna. She replenished the candles and the herbs, and then simply had to wait for the others to finish their task. She felt desperate to succeed this time, fairly certain that Linna would not survive the night. But she couldn't hurry the process, which made her all the more anxious.

"Quit pacing!" Leslie exclaimed as eleven o'clock chimed on the grandmother clock near the couch.

"I can't help it. Aren't you just about finished?"

"A few more blossoms," David replied, without looking up. "Just hang on."

By the time midnight arrived, David and Leslie had managed to glean a quarter of a teaspoon of nectar from all the plants they had found. David looked at the goblet in his hand, his gaze skeptical.

"Will it be enough?" Marissa asked, trying to keep the edge of desperation out of her voice.

"I hope so," he answered. "I think we had more before. About twice as much."

"Here," Marissa offered him a measuring cup partially filled with white wine. "Add this to it."

David poured the wine into the goblet and swirled it around. "Okay, let's try it again."

They hurried to the bedroom and David stepped up to Linna. Then he paused and looked back at Marissa. "Wait a minute. If Woodward somehow returns, we can't let him ruin this. We've got to be ready for him."

"This time I am." Marissa reached behind her and pulled the Colt .45 from the back waistband of her jeans. "If he shows up, I'll be waiting."

"Good." David hiked up the robe and reached into his back pocket. "And if Alek makes it over"—he pulled out his wallet and held it up—"let him assume my identity. His looks and coloring are enough like mine to pull it off."

Marissa nodded, unsure of the legal ramifications of someone entering the U.S. from another country, let alone from another time.

David tossed his wallet on the nightstand. "Everything's there, if you need it."

"Thanks."

Marissa strode to Linna's side and looked down. "Linna," she called softly. "We're ready. Think you can try again?"

For a moment Linna didn't respond, and Marissa felt a sickening twist in her gut. No matter what she tried to tell herself—that this might never work, that Alek might not appear, that Linna would fail, that she had to be prepared for the worst—she couldn't help but want the best. Now that Leslie was going to be okay, she wanted the ritual to work. She wanted David to go to Diana. She wanted Alek to come into her world. She wanted it more than anything she had ever wanted in her entire life. She wanted it with every ounce of her soul, as if the wanting were a fire deep inside her that would consume her if the experiment failed.

"Oh, Linna!" she exclaimed, kneeling by the bed and slipping her hand around the healer's hand. "Please try! Please try once more!"

Linna stirred slightly, as if bringing herself back from a great distance. Gradually, she opened her eyes.

"I am here, Marissa." She fumbled to lace her fingers with Marissa's. "But I can no longer see anything."

"Oh, God!"

"David, come closer. Touch my other hand."

David followed her instructions.

"Drink the nectar."

He downed the contents of the wine glass.

"You know what to—" Linna gasped with pain, then gathered her strength and pressed on. "You know what to do, Marissa. I will do the prayer. You must do the rest."

"Okay. I'm ready."

"Keep holding my hand. Your strength sustains me."

"Linna, I—"

"For Alek," Linna whispered. Then she closed her eyes and began to chant.

Marissa entered a strange world then. The sing-song voice of the healer swept her away into a trance-like state where she was conscious only of the chant, the smell of the candles, and the cool curl of Linna's fingers through hers. When the time came to pass the smoldering herbs between David and Linna, she stood up without breaking the handclasp with the healer. And when the silver cloud came down, Marissa felt herself losing all sense of time and place. Was this how it felt to be hypnotized? To faint? She hovered in an eerie limbo, drifting around the spiral of Linna's faint voice, and vaguely wondered if she would be swept from the present into another world where Linna or no one else would ever be able to reach her.

She blacked out and woke up to the sound of tinkling bells to find herself draped over the edge of the bed. She raised her head and peered into the silver mist above the bed. The tinkling noise indicated a normal transfer. There was no guarantee that Alek would cross over, but she grinned anyway simply to fight off the tears which lay just behind her flimsy facade of hope.

Then, suddenly, she was aware that her hand clasped the air and that Linna's fingers no longer entwined hers. Marissa glanced down in surprise and couldn't see Linna's arm, either. Where was she? Had Linna disappeared altogether, just as Woodward had done? She couldn't tell for sure because of the silver cloud that was still in the process of fading. Had the ritual worked? Or had only Linna been transported? With her heart pounding like a stampede in her ears, Marissa slowly rose to her feet.

"Mariss!" Leslie whispered in awe behind her. "Mariss, look!"

Marissa swallowed and raised her glance upward, unsure of whether she wanted to know what the ritual had brought forth. This could mean ecstasy or devastation for her. This could mean joy or heart-crushing madness. But she could not *not* look.

Leslie grabbed her elbow and squeezed so hard that Marissa gasped.

"Who *is* that?" Leslie exclaimed.

Marissa looked up, past a pair of lean legs wrapped in brown trousers crossed with leather thongs and a sword belt and scabbard, past a naked, powerful torso gleaming in the candlelight, past the straight, full line of a pair of wide shoulders brushed by locks of dark brown hair. And then she looked all the way up—into the man's face, into the haughty, sharp-featured face she knew so well.

"Alek!" she cried. And though she had known no greater happiness in her entire life than at that instant, she burst into tears.

24

"She-devil!"

Marissa launched herself toward the warrior, and he caught her up in his arms to sweep her off the floor in a bone-crushing embrace.

"Oh, Alek!" she cried again, flinging her arms around his neck. "Alek! You made it! You're here!"

"Yes!" He swung her around, still holding her tightly, his happiness too great to contain by standing still. He grinned and then hugged her and laughed outright. She had never heard him laugh like that and the sound filled her heart. Marissa wanted to shout out loud, wanted to toe-tap a Texas two-step all around the room. Instead, she reached up and kissed him fervently. His kiss was all she had remembered and more, because this time their kiss was not haunted by the specter of Alek's departure. This time she didn't have to worry about holding back, because the man she loved wouldn't be gone forever. Now that Alek had come back to her world, she could love him freely and without remorse, and the notion heightened the glory of the reunion. After a long, long kiss of homecoming, she finally broke from his mouth, and he let her slowly slide down his torso until her feet touched the floor again.

"Alek!" She drove her fingers into his glossy hair and looked him in the face while she fought a strange compulsion to cry again. "Oh, God, Alek! I never thought I'd see you again!" Her hands slipped down to the full curve of his shoulders as if to gauge his condition in a single touch. "And you're all right, aren't you?"

"I am good now. With you. Yes." His glance sobered while the grin hovered on his lips for an instant and then disappeared as something serious and wonderful transformed his eyes to melting topaz. Marissa felt her heart burst at that look.

"The Romans didn't hurt you."

"No. Not my body." He flashed a quick but sad smile and then caressed her cheek with his big hand. "How I have missed you, she-devil!" His voice was rough-edged with emotion.

"And I've missed you, Alek. So much." She kissed his thumb as he passed it across her lips. "So much!"

"Did Doctor-Wood-Ward do the ritual again?"

"No. Linna did it."

"Linna?" He looked at the bed. "Where is she?"

"I'm not sure. During the ritual she and the doc simply disappeared."

"They vanished?"

"Yes. Maybe they went to worlds we know nothing about. Or maybe they just transformed into pure energy."

Alek raised his eyebrows in doubt. "Wherever Linna is, I hope she is no longer in pain."

"I have a feeling she is in a better place."

Alek smoothed the hair at her left temple, and she studied his face.

"I saw David pass through when I was coming to you. He is to be with Diana?"

"Yes. He wanted to go."

"Is that why you and Linna brought me here?"

"No. We didn't do it just for David. I didn't want you to die. I couldn't bear it!"

"You knew about the battle?"

"Yes. I read about your people in a book when we were locked in the basement of Dr. Woodward's house—remember?"

"Ah, yes."

"I suspected that you were going to be sent to Rome and killed. And when Linna lay dying, she had visions that you were in trouble. We just couldn't let you suffer. So we decided to bring you back here."

"I am glad."

She pulled away, just enough to really look at him. "You are?"

He nodded. "There ceased to be a place for me in my own world, Marissa."

"What do you mean?"

"I will tell you all soon, for there is much to tell. But now is not the time for that, she-devil." He reached down and cupped her derriere in his hands, pulling her roughly against him. "Now is the time for making love."

He dipped to kiss her again, but Marissa flushed scarlet and planted her palms on his chest. "I'd love to, Conan, but my sister is here—"

Alek raised up in surprise and got his first glimpse of Leslie, who was standing off to the side near the window. His grip loosened enough to allow Marissa to turn slightly. She caught sight of Leslie's knowing smirk and wanted to belt her. She could just imagine what was going on in Leslie's thoughts about her little sister, who had never dated a man in her life.

"Leslie is awake?" He asked, incredulous.

"Yes. She is recovering quite well as a matter of fact." Somewhat flustered, she decided to introduce the two of them. She motioned Leslie forward, and her sister ambled toward them.

"Leslie, this is Alek, a friend of Linna's."

"And a friend of yours, too, it appears," Leslie replied, extending her hand. "Nice to meet you, Alek."

Alek shook her hand thoroughly, until Leslie pulled back with a laugh. Marissa decided to continue with the formalities.

"And Alek, as you know, this is my older sister, Leslie."

He inclined his head toward her. "I am glad to see that you are better, Leslie."

"Thanks. But I'm curious—why do you call my sister she-devil?"

"She is a warrior woman. A she-devil."

"She-devil, eh?" Leslie wiggled her eyebrows at Marissa, who was still trying to fight a blush.

"She gives me nicknames, so I give her nicknames."

"I see." Leslie broke into a wide grin.

"She is a good woman."

"Yes, she is. And you must have something the Montana boys don't have," Leslie commented, trying to suppress a wicked grin, "to get my sister to carry on with you like that."

Alek glanced at Marissa and smiled. Then he tucked her close, as if pulling her under his wing. The gesture made Marissa's heart swell with love for him. She wrapped her arms around Alek's torso, reveling in the feel of him and the rumble of his voice as he spoke, and was grateful for the opportunity to stand beside him once again.

"I am not certain how I am different from the men in

Montana," he replied. "I only know that the she-devil and I are special to each other."

Special. That was a good way to describe the feeling she had for Alek. He was very special to her. And he always would be.

"So." Leslie crossed her arms. "What's the plan? Do we hang around here to see if anyone shows up? Or what?"

"I say we go to the police in the morning and try to explain what happened." Marissa thrilled to the feeling of Alek's hand slowly moving up and down her side. "Someone's bound to report Woodward and Diana missing, as well as David."

"I say you take advantage of David's offer and let Alek become David Hodge. It will be a whole lot easier to explain his presence that way than convincing someone he's a time-travelling Gaul. They'll think you're both crazy."

Marissa shrugged. "I don't know, Les. I'll decide later."

"Meanwhile, it's way after midnight and I'm tired. We can talk to the police in the morning."

"All right." Marissa brushed back a strand of hair that had come loose from her braid. "And then I have to get back to Montana, Leslie. There's a few things I have to straighten out."

"I'll come with you, if you don't mind," Leslie added. "I think it would be a good time to take a vacation from work, especially since Woodward won't be there."

Marissa nodded.

Leslie glanced up at the warrior. "What about you, Alek? Do you want to go to Montana, too?"

"Yes. I go with Marissa."

Marissa hugged him tightly. She couldn't wait to share Montana with Alek—to take him on a tour of the spread, ride with him up to the mountains, camp with him beneath the big Montana sky, and show him the herd of mustangs that roamed the periphery of her ranch. He would love everything about her country, she was sure of it.

"Well," Leslie glanced around the room. "The sooner we get this place back in order, the sooner we can get to bed."

An hour later, Marissa padded down the hallway from the bathroom to the living room and peeked at her sister to make sure she was all right. Leslie had graciously offered Alek and Marissa the use of her bed while she took the couch for the night. She was already fast asleep there, worn out by the day and her weakened condition, when Marissa leaned over the back of the couch and listened to her sister's breathing. Satisfied that Leslie was sleeping soundly, Marissa straightened and headed back to the bedroom with anticipation mounting at every step.

Wearing nothing but a light summer robe, Marissa slipped into the room, closed the door behind her, and glanced across the room. Alek was lying on the bed with his hands behind his head, which made his chest appear wider than ever. He had taken a shower earlier and reclined upon the comforter with the dark green towel still wrapped around his hips. He looked tanned and supple and totally tempting, which produced an odd effect in her legs. Her knees buckled beneath her and Marissa sank against the door, overwhelmed by the thought that this magnificent man was waiting for her to come to bed with him. He looked down his sharply-ridged nose at her.

"You are clean now, she-devil?"

"Yes."

"Did you not need me to wash your hair?"

"Not this time, Alek."

"Why do you wait over there?"

"I was—well, before I turn in, is there anything you want? Are you hungry? Thirsty?"

"Yes." He turned and propped his head on his hand. His eyes sparkled with a warmth she had never seen in a man before. "Come here and I will tell you want I want."

She flushed but pushed away from the door, unconsciously pulling the belt of her robe more tightly about her waist. When she came close to the bed, Alek reached up and grabbed the ends of the belt, dragging her toward him until she had to put a knee on the edge of the mattress to keep from falling, which forced open the front of the robe and revealed her slender thigh.

"Closer, woman." Alek transferred the belt to his left hand while his right hand caressed the smooth curve of her thigh, and he slid his palm all the way to her naked hip.

Marissa sucked in a deep breath and felt herself melt at his touch like an icicle held to a hot branding iron.

Alek smiled. "Ah, that is better." He gave a small yank on the belt and she tumbled onto his incredibly firm body. He surrounded her with his arms and rolled her onto her back, trapping her with a thigh thrown across her legs.

"You ask if I hunger?" He kissed her ear, sending flashes of delight through her. "I am hungry for you, she-devil. Very hungry." He nuzzled her until she squealed with pleasure.

Then Alek untied the belt and opened the robe to reveal her naked body. For a moment he simply gazed at her, his cheeks flushed. Marissa stared at him, fascinated and unwilling to move, lest she break the spell.

"You ask if I thirst?" He bent down and kissed her right breast while the other one ached for him. "Yes, I am thirsty for you."

"How thirsty?" she gasped.

"As if I had not drunk for a thousand years."

"Oh, Alek!" She held his head to her breast, sighing at the way his soft hair brushed her tender skin. She stroked his glossy brown locks while his tongue flicked over her hard nipple. "It seems like a hundred years since I've held you. I thought I'd never see you again."

"No more worrying, she-devil." He kissed her left breast and ran his hand with tantalizing slowness down her abdomen and over the slight mound of her belly. "I am back."

But for how long? Would he stay with her in Montana? What would happen if he decided she wasn't the woman he thought she was? After all, they had known each other only a week. Either one of them could change their minds—although she was certain she would love Alek until her dying day. She was ready to take him into her life right now, as surely as she was about to take him into the intimate recesses of her body. Did he feel as strongly as she did? He said they were special to each other. But what did special mean to him, exactly? Did he love her?

Marissa clutched Alek all the more tightly and wished she could ask the questions that burned in her heart. But somehow she sensed the importance of waiting to see what the future held. For now, it was enough to know that Alek was alive, that he was here with her in her bed, ready to make love with her. She should be satisfied to have this much. The future could be left to . . . well . . . to the future.

"You like this?" he asked, rising slightly from her breast.

"Yes!" She arched upward and sighed while he suckled her again and pressed kisses between her breasts and on her neck and mouth. Then she twisted at the shoulders to pull her arm out of the sleeve of the robe, desperate to throw off her clothing. She wanted to be naked against him, to feel every warm inch of him against her bare flesh. There was nothing in the world as wonderful as the feeling of Alek's naked body against hers. While he kissed her, Marissa reached for the knot of his towel, which was flattened against her hip.

"I'm hungry, too, Alek," she said, pulling apart the ends of the terry cloth. "Ravenous. Starving."

"Then show me, woman." He rolled onto his back, leaving the towel to fall on either side of his hips. Alek lay displayed in all his glory, his manhood jutting up like a fence post.

Marissa stared at him, never having seen his arousal in plain sight before, and was amazed that a man's body could transform in such a way. Without taking her gaze off him, she shrugged her other arm out of the robe and let it fall where it may. Too fascinated to be shy, she reached out and stroked Alek with two fingers and her thumb and was shocked by the smooth rigidity of him.

"You are a beautiful man, Alek," she murmured.

"Beautiful?"

"Far beyond handsome. Everywhere." She continued to stroke him while she explored the unfamiliar flesh of his maleness. Every once in a while he let out a short burst of air, as if he were trying to hold his breath but couldn't keep it in.

"Marissa—"

"Your eyes, your nose, your mouth, your—"

"Marissa, you—you must stop!" He grabbed her wrist

in mid-stroke and held her hand away from him while his body stiffened and he squeezed his eyelids shut. For a moment he seemed to hang in limbo, and then his eyes opened slightly. His glance was heavy with the smoldering lights of desire.

"Woman—what you do to me," he declared, "by touching me like that!"

She leaned closer, until her breasts grazed the warm planes of his chest. "I like to touch you."

"You do it well."

He lay back again, and she ran her hands over the mounds of his chest, memorizing the landscape of his body with her fingertips. His nipples, though smaller than hers, had hardened with desire just as hers had. Gradually, her hands moved lower as she stroked his abdomen and thighs, marvelling at the way his coarse hair titillated her palms. When she once again circled his shaft, Alek sighed and closed his eyes. She glanced at his face and grinned when she saw a beatific expression glowing there. He had to be feeling the same thing she felt when he suckled her—that peculiar sensation of intense yet painful pleasure. What would it be like to put her lips to him, as he had put his mouth on her breasts? Would it feel good to him?

Marissa leaned down and kissed him, first just the tip of him and then all the way down the length of him. Alek was unusually silent. Even his breathing grew shallow, and his hands dropped to his sides as if what she was doing had immobilized him. To know that she could silence him with pleasure immensely gratified her.

Spurred on by his reaction, she took him into her mouth, loving the salty taste of him and the silken texture of his skin.

Alek groaned, and the sound went straight to the throbbing place between her legs. He gently clutched a fistful of hair at the back of her head and urged her downward, until she had taken a good deal of him into her mouth. She could tell that she was driving him to distraction with her tongue and lips, just as he had driven her crazy moments before. Alek writhed beneath her, murmuring her name over and over again as she suckled him.

Then, with a growl, he clamped her shoulders in his hands and pulled her up on his thigh, sitting up at the same time against the pile of pillows behind him. Roughly, almost savagely, he kissed her while he urged her to straddle his leg. She moved over the hard sheaths of muscle and couldn't help but let out a short gasp of rapture.

He clutched her buttocks and pressed her against his leg again, urging her to slide up and down on him. Marissa felt shafts of heat shooting through her.

"Alek!" she cried. "That's—"

She lost her train of thought as she moved against his thigh again and again, surrendering to the wonderful driving sensation that climbed in heat and intensity within her.

"You will know what it is to hunger as you have made me hunger!"

Instinctively, Alek moved her over him, seeming to know without words how much pressure he should apply and what tempo aroused her. With every moan she uttered, his shaft grew more swollen until it was like a marble column between them. Marissa put a hand on him and he made a strangled sound deep in his throat. And then, in a desperate writhing of hands and legs, Alek rolled her onto her back until she was the one pressed into the pillows. Then, with both hands planted on her rear to hold her still, he nudged into her.

Marissa thought she would scream if he didn't bury

himself all the way. She arched upward, trying to guide him to completion, but he sank down upon her, covering her with his muscular abdomen and lean hips, his warrior body dominating her slender frame. Forced backward, Marissa acquiesced and closed her eyes, longing to be dominated in this way, by this man.

Alek slipped his hands around her ankles and drew up her knees, forcing her legs up and back, allowing complete and utter closeness. Then he pushed into her bit by bit, driving her crazy with his measured, controlled strokes.

"Alek, don't tease me like this!" she gasped.

"Does it not feel good to you?" he asked.

"Yes, but, Alek—"

"You enjoy it, yes?"

"Yes, but, oh—"

She broke off. Waves of ecstasy washed over her, taking with them her power of speech. She could no longer see, or hear either. Her single focus centered upon the sense of touch and all the places where Alek was stroking her, kissing her, and pressing down upon her. Marissa felt herself rushing headlong into sheer sensation, swept away like a leaf in a flash flood. She held onto his rock-hard shoulders as he took her in an intense crescendo of need, both of them prisoners of a frantic, compelling rhythm that never once let up until he had burst inside her.

Alek collapsed upon her, panting and sweating and breathing like a bull.

She held him, hardly able to take a breath because of the weight of his body, but sated beyond belief by the love they had just shared. Her legs and arms trembled and she could feel his forearms shuddering.

Without speaking, he nuzzled the small of her shoulder and pressed quiet, intense kisses below her ear and on her jaw as their passion slowly ebbed into luxurious fatigue. She held him close and hoped he wouldn't move away, for to feel him upon her was an exquisite pressure she would gladly endure—now and forever. Her warrior had come back to her, and she would never let him go.

Still, she couldn't help but worry. What would happen when Alek became acquainted with her world? Would he be able to cope with modern society? Would he be satisfied with her after a few weeks, or a couple of months? What would she do if he decided to move on or found that he could not be happy in the twentieth century?

Marissa forced the troublesome thoughts from her mind. She could do little about the future. Alek was a free man and he always would be. Why did she think she had to rein him in? She, of all people, knew the value of a wild heart.

If only he would say the three words she longed to hear: *I love you.* If he would tell her how he felt about her, the moments they had just shared would be not be just a painting of passion between two people—they would be a masterpiece. Yet, it was too soon to tell what might grow between them. She hugged him and sighed. Perhaps he was wise to remain silent.

She thought back to what he *had* said—that they were special to each other. She would hold those words in her heart until the time came when he could tell her more.

25

Outside the Boii stronghold, 285 B.C.

Feeling as if she were being watched, Diana dipped her water jug in the stream. The sensation unnerved her, but she decided to ignore it. After all, what danger would lurk so close to the Boii walls? No one would dare challenge the guards in broad daylight.

She shook off the feeling and glanced downriver to the shallows, where five Boii children were splashing off the heat of an Indian summer. No one around here referred to the season as Indian summer, but Diana still clung to some of her old expressions even though she had lived among the Boii for five months. For October the weather was uncommonly warm and dry, just what the struggling Boii women needed to fatten the herds for winter and have enough time to harvest their crops. Many of their men had perished in the same battle that had devastated the Senones and robbed them of their champion, Alek, leaving the women responsible for the survival of their people.

Diana lifted the jug to her shoulder and straightened as she thought of Marissa Quinn. The outspoken cowgirl from Montana would probably never know that Alek had been taken to Rome as a captive, there to be castrated and tortured to death. People still talked of it, shaking their heads in despair at how the glorious young champion had fallen into Roman hands. Perhaps it was better that Marissa knew nothing of Alek's fate.

Diana knew nothing of David's fate either. What had happened to him? What was he doing? Did he miss her? Was he well? She pressed her lips together to hold back tears that threatened to fall and concentrated on the narrow footpath up the riverbank. Now that her cancer symtoms were no longer present, she was ready to lead a full and happy life. And, oddly enough, she felt as if she belonged to this ancient world of the Gauls, as if she had found her true home at last. Only one thing remained to make her life complete, and that was David's companionship.

She had tried to forget him. The Boii had been more than accommodating and had treated her well, even going so far as to make her an honorary member of the clan. A few men had made it clear that they desired her as a wife, if she would only agree to share the marriage goblet with them. But Diana could neither agree to their offers nor forget the lover in her past. She knew it wasn't healthy to grieve for David, but she just couldn't help herself.

At the top of the bank, she paused and looked back at the children, wondering what it would be like to count one of them as her own. She would probably never bear any children, and the prospect saddened her. Children were treasured here and were considered a woman's crowning glory, a facet of Gallic life which she found admirable. She longed to have a son or daughter of her own, but first she would have to take a husband, and she simply couldn't enter into marriage with a man whom she did not love. She'd tasted that type of life with Kyle, and the experience had left a bitterness that she would not soon forget.

She turned to continue her trek back to the village and was startled to see a man's silhouette in the grove of firs at the top of the bank. The branches of the trees formed a dense thicket which blocked the early autumn sun and shrouded the man's features. Diana paused, while the hairs on the back of her neck prickled.

"Who's there?" she inquired, ready to throw down her jug and dash back to the river.

"Diana?"

Diana's heart skipped a beat. The voice sounded familiar to her. Could her ears be playing tricks on her?

"Diana?" The figure broke from the trees and ventured forward.

Diana took a step back, lowering the jug. Though she lacked a weapon to defend herself, she could hurl the jug at the man if he had harmful intentions. Yet, if he were a stranger, how did he know her name?

"Who are you?" she demanded.

The man strode down the path toward her. His walk was familiar to her. She choked back her galloping heart, not daring to believe her eyes, and retreated a few more steps.

"Diana, wait," the figure called out. "It's me!"

She stared at the man, trying to make out a discernible feature in the shadows. Then she saw him raise his hand to his face, as if pushing up a pair of glasses. No one in Gaul wore glasses. There was only one man she knew who might be in Boii territory wearing glasses. And that man was David.

"David?" she exclaimed, her voice cracking.

"Diana!" The man broke from the grove and, the moment the light hit his face, Diana dropped the jug. Water poured over her sandals, but she barely took notice. All she could do was stare in joyful incredulity. David was here? How could this be?

He ran up to her, dressed in Gallic bracae bound with leather thongs and a flowing shirt. The clothes suited him well, lending him a romantic quality she had never imagined he could possess. Before she could recover her voice or her senses at the sight of him, he gathered her into his arms.

"Oh, Diana, it is you!"

"David!" She pulled back and stared at him as if seeing a ghost. "How did you get here?"

"Linna performed the ceremony. Alek and I switched places."

"You and Alek?"

"Yes!" He grinned and inspected her briefly while he held both of her hands. She wondered if her Gallic ankle-length dress lent her an equally romantic appeal. "Just look at you, Diana!"

"Do I look different?"

"You've put on some weight!"

"Not too much, I hope!" She grinned back.

"You look fabulous! Wonderful! Ah, Diana!" He hugged her gently, as if embracing her would injure her body.

"You don't have to be so careful," she said, wrapping her arms around his neck. "I'm not ill anymore."

"You're not?"

"No. Alek's mother has been treating my symtoms and they're gone! There's also something in the air here. You've probably noticed it already."

"More oxygen." He embraced her, drawing her against the taut lines of his body. "It makes me feel good—all over. As you do."

She smiled in reply and touched his face, caressing his lean cheek as she gazed into his eyes, still not believing he was actually here with her. "This is a dream come true for me, David, having you here!"

"In the flesh." He kissed her soundly and thoroughly, the way she had longed to be kissed by him for years. David knew how to make her feel cherished, desired, and loved, and she never wanted the kiss to end. She began to cry out of pure happiness, and David held her to his chest, stroking her back and hair as he comforted her with words of endearment.

"I've been here for months, Diana, looking for you."

"You have?"

"Yes. I landed in the grove of the Senones to the east, but no one was there. The village nearby was burned to the ground."

"Alek's village. We fled from there to here."

"As I found out, after having spent weeks wondering from village to village."

"But now you're here. And that's all that matters!" She hugged him with all her strength and was pleased when he embraced her in kind.

"I do have some disappointing news, though," David added after a long, quiet caress.

"What?"

"We're stuck here. We can never go back."

"Why?"

"No one is left who knows how to perform the ritual."

"What about Kyle?"

Briefly, David recounted what had transpired since Diana had passed from the modern world. Diana sighed and lay her head upon David's chest.

"So the Druid healer put Kyle somewhere?"

"Perhaps in another world—not here and not where we came from. But, whatever the case, he's gone."

"And the healer died?"

"I expect so. She was mortally wounded, Diana."

Diana traced the line of his shoulder and up the side of his neck. "So we'll have to live out our lives here in Gaul?"

"Yes."

She smiled against the embroidered placket of his linen shirt. There was no place she would rather be, and no other person with whom she would rather spend the rest of her days. She had found her niche in the world at last.

Crazy Q Ranch, Montana, August

From the chair at her desk, Marissa heard an unfamiliar motor running as a truck pulled up outside the house. She put her pen down and swiveled in the massive leather chair to look out the window of her office. Three men got out of the four-wheel drive Suburban and ambled toward the house. One of them she recognized immediately—Bob Hales, from the power company, the man with the sissy boots and expensive suit. He was wearing the same boots. She could tell by the way the late afternoon sun glared off his toes and heels. The other two men she had never seen before, but she could guess by their burly arms and swaggering walks that they were here to back up whatever demands Hales was going to make. The power company had gone from polite offers to out-and-out threats, anxious to acquire the ranch for strip mining. Well, she'd had enough of the power company and Bob Hales. There was no way she was going to sell the Crazy Q now. She had no intention of ever leaving it, or Montana, either.

Montana was one of the few places in which Alek could feel at home in the twentieth century. She wasn't about to uproot him, although she had to admit that he had put down far less roots than she had hoped. Over the past two and a half months she had scarcely seen the man, which had devastated her at first. Then she had come to realize that Alek was a man of pride and honor, who had much learning to do about the world. The last person to whom he would come for help was Marissa because he would not want to appear lacking in her eyes.

In fact, Alek rarely came to her at all these days, and lived in the back pasture in a tent he had erected far away from the ranch. He put in long hours with Corky working the spread, and the herd had never been in better shape than after the two months under Alek's careful supervision. After dinner each night, Alek spent the evening hours at Shorty's with the crusty rancher's oldest daughter. At first Marissa had been hurt and jealous that Alek passed so much time with a woman, and she had withdrawn into her world of work in an effort to get her mind off the warrior.

Just yesterday, however, Shorty had let it slip that Alek was learning to read and write under the tutelage of his daughter, who was a teacher at the local junior high school. Marissa had flushed with shame for not figuring that out for herself and for being suspicious of the warrior. She promised herself not to be so defensive, not to doubt Alek's every move. After all, what he did with his time was his affair and not hers. He had never promised her anything—not even his companionship. Perhaps she had misread the connection she had felt with him during their days in Seattle. Perhaps she had mistaken his depth of feeling for her, because ever since their trip to Montana, Alek had drifted further and further away from her.

Marissa stood up as she heard the men clomping their way through the house toward her office. What had come over her? She had never worried about a man before. Yet she had never loved a man before and hadn't realized how closely she would yearn to align herself with Alek. She constantly had to remind herself that he was a free man with a life of his own. If he chose to share it with her, fine. If he chose not to, she would have to accept that, too. But never in a million years would she have dreamed how difficult such an acceptance might be for her.

It wouldn't have been so hard to endure if Alek had come to her at night to share her bed, or if he had ever once mentioned how he felt about her. They worked side by side sometimes and shared meals in the evening, but, aside from being pleasant, he never once approached her in a personal way. Why? Had she done something to turn him away? His silent haughtiness, the stance that had once fired her fantasies, now made her question his state of mind. Why did he stand apart from her? Why would he never once take her in his arms and kiss her the way she longed to be kissed?

Then and there she made a vow. She would confront him this evening and put all the cards on the table and insist that he do the same. She'd take no more silence and dark suspicions. No more jealousy and hurt. She would ask him very bluntly what was on his mind and then get on with her life.

The door opened and her mother stuck her head in the office. "The power company people are here again," she said.

"All right, Mom. Send them in."

Bob Hales came first, holding his hat, followed by the larger, stouter men.

"Afternoon, Marissa," Hales greeted with feigned friendliness.

"Mr. Hales. Gentlemen." She nodded to them and motioned them to take a seat, standing until they had all found chairs.

Finally, she lowered herself into her chair. "What can I do for you today, Mr. Hales?"

"Bob to you, Marissa Quinn."

She leaned over the desk. "If I want to get friendly with you, buster, you'll be the first to know."

Hales smirked at her and suddenly reminded her of Dr. Woodward and his cruel little smiles. Her dislike of Hales deepened.

Hales leaned back in his chair and crossed his lean legs, pulling up his trousers at the knee to protect the fine crease. "Well, now, Marissa, I think you should reconsider our relationship. If my boys here don't think we're getting along, they might get feisty."

"Is that a problem?" Marissa retorted, glancing at the men who flanked Hales on either side. They were dressed in jeans topped by sports coats with wide lapels which were comically outdated. But Marissa wasn't fooled by the laughable wardrobe. These men were brutes who wouldn't find anything amusing about her or her ranch.

"That depends. If you sign the sales agreement I've brought along, we'll get along just fine." Hales reached into his jacket for a packet of folded papers. "But if you give me the same old song and dance, Marissa, I'm afraid that Buck and Willy here might have to break a few things."

"You're threatening me!" She reached for the phone. "I'm calling the sheriff."

"Go ahead," Hales gazed at her, not in the least perturbed. "Sheriff Dunn is a personal friend of mine."

Marissa paused with the receiver in her hand as a feeling of unease slowly took hold of her.

"And"—Hales straightened the sales papers on the surface of the desk—"he appreciates the work I'm doing for the county."

"I'll just bet he does." Marissa slammed the phone down, frustrated at her position. Was she the last person in this corner of Rosebud County to hold out against the power company? Didn't anyone value ranching any more?

"So, will you sign or not?" Hales said with a beaming and utterly false smile.

"You have to ask?" Marissa pushed up from her chair. "Get out, Hales."

"Not this time." Hales narrowed his eyes. "I have my instructions."

"Then you can just stuff your instructions where the sun don't shine!"

Hales shook his head as if he were dealing with an errant child. "If you're going to get on your high horse again, Marissa, I guess I'll have to show you we're serious. Boys?"

Buck and Willy lumbered to their feet.

"Torch the barn."

"What?" Marissa gasped, indignant.

Hales ignored her. "Make it look like an accident. I'll stay in here and entertain the little lady."

"Like hell you will!" She reached into her desk for the pistol she kept locked in the lower drawer. Before she could get her hands on it, however, Hales had moved around the desk, surprising her with his speed, and grabbed her arm. He wrenched her arm behind her back, using more force than necessary just to hurt her, and hauled her up against him, his nose near her ear. She struggled, but he held her in a vice-like grip. To her disgust, she felt his left hand crawl up her shirt to cup her breast.

"Cooperate with me," he drawled. "And I can make it worth your while. In all ways." He squeezed her breast.

"I'd rather wrassle a skunk!"

"Boss—" One of the burly men pointed to the window behind them.

Hales ignored him, too intent on subduing Marissa's writhing body to pay attention to Buck.

"Boss!"

Suddenly, the large window behind them imploded, spraying glass over Hale's back and littering the floor. He staggered around, dragging Marissa with him, just in time to see Alek, who was standing on the porch outside, take aim at him with a double-barreled shotgun.

Hales wilted. Marissa could feel his backbone slip away at the sight of the huge warrior standing with the shotgun outside the window.

"Let the woman go," Alek demanded, his face dark, every muscle of his body in silhouette from the sun behind him. Even Marissa, who knew the warrior well, was taken aback by his larger-than-life appearance. Her heart thrilled at the sight of him coming to her rescue, just as he had in Seattle. With Alek beside her, there was nothing to fear from anyone.

Hales released his grip on Marissa, and she lunged out of his hold, rubbing her shoulder as she put the length of the desk between her and the men from the power company.

In a fluid motion, Alek ducked and stepped through the window. He was dressed in jeans, boots, and a light blue shirt. But he had never cut his hair, and wore it tied with a leather thong at the nape of his neck. Though he was a natural rancher, he would always look half-wild and half-foreign to her. She would never cease to be amazed at how his wildness could make her heart sing. In fact, her heart was singing so loudly at this particular moment, she thought it might burst clear out of her chest.

"Take your hat and get out," Alek said.

Hales snatched his papers off the desk and never once looked at Marissa. The two henchmen stood silently by, obviously realizing that to challenge Alek would be a big mistake. Helping their boss with his little power trips was one thing. Tangling with this grizzly was quite another. Hales grabbed his Stetson and turned.

"Just you—"

"Silence!" Alek roared. "You will not come here again. Do you understand, *Bob?*"

Hale's name on Alek's lips dripped like an insult. Marissa grinned.

"You can't—"

"Do your ears need cleaning?" Alek raised the gun and hooked his finger more firmly around the trigger.

"All right, I heard you," Hales answered, holding up his hands. The papers fluttered in the breeze coming through the broken window. "I'm going."

"You're gone, bucko," Marissa ordered.

"And do not come back," Alek added.

Marissa stepped across the few feet between her and Alek to stand beside the warrior, adding her strength to his. Hales took a look at the both of them and plopped his hat on his head in frustration and anger.

Without another word, he signalled for his men to follow him and they left the house. Neither Alek nor Marissa moved until they saw the Suburban peel out of the lot and tear down the drive. She had a feeling that was the last she'd ever see of the power company.

After the truck disappeared around the bend, Alek put the shotgun on the desk. "I am sorry about the window," he said.

"Don't be, Conan. You did good." She touched his shoulder and smiled at him, all the while longing to wrap her arms around him and give him a big bear hug.

He turned and looked down his sharp nose at her. "Are you all right, she-devil?"

"I'm fine."

"Then will you come with me for a ride?"

She blinked in surprise. "You mean right now?"

"Yes. I have something to show you."

Ten minutes later they were loping across the western stretch of the ranch toward the blue hills in the distance. Marissa was astride her roan, Scarlet, and Alek was riding Big John, the huge buckskin stallion to which he had taken an immediate fancy upon his arrival at the Crazy Q. And, by all appearances, Big John had taken a fancy to Alek. Marissa's heart swelled as she looked over at the two of them—man and horse—hair and manes flying out behind them. She remembered the way Alek had outridden her at Greenlake in Seattle. He still looked like a Viking, and he still made her heart do crazy flip-flops every time she glanced at him.

Alek refused to tell her where they were going, so she simply enjoyed the ride and the cool breeze drifting over the prairie. By the time they reached the foothills, the sun was melting in the big Montana sky, pouring a golden glow over the trees and rocks and Alek's hair. Distracted, she followed him up a ridge, where the pines were more sparse. After less than a mile, he reined in and let her come up alongside him.

"Look," he pointed westward, where the mountains opened up into a huge valley, in the center of which was a beautiful turquoise lake. In a meadow along the eastern side was a herd of animals, too far away to distinguish from mere dots.

"Strays?" Marissa asked, leaning forward over the pommel. The leather creaked as she moved in the saddle.

"No. The mustangs."

She peered at the animals and then glanced back at Alek. He smiled.

"How did they get there?" she asked, incredulous. The valley was far from the coal mine, far from a road, far enough to give the mustangs the protection they needed.

"I guided them to the valley."

"How?" She stared at him. "No one's ever been able to control them."

"The gods gave some of us Senones a special gift, Marissa. I was one to receive their offering."

"What kind of gift are you talking about?" She could think of a few things that Alek was blessed with, but they had nothing to do with mustangs.

"I can whisper."

Marissa tipped back her hat, confused by his choice of words. "Whisper?"

"I can talk to horses. I can hear what they say and they can understand what I want of them."

"You talked them into going to the valley?"

He nodded and smiled.

"Alek, that's wonderful!"

He had saved her mustangs. He had listened to her worries about the mustangs and had cared enough to take them far away from contact with people. He had done what no other human could do. She stared at him, too overcome by his amazing gesture to trust herself to speak. The wind wafted through his hair, fluttering the dark locks around his bronzed neck. He had never seemed more beautiful to her than at that moment. How she loved him! She thought her heart would explode with the love she felt for this man.

In one of his graceful movements, Alek slid from his horse and looked up. "Come here, she-devil. I want to show you something more."

What could be better than the mustangs? And what lay behind that warm smile he made no effort to repress? What had transpired to change his haughty, aloof manner into the smiling man who stood before her now? Whatever it was, she liked the change and hoped he would remain in this good mood. Marissa dismounted and let the reins drag. The horses were too well trained to run off, and both lowered their heads to graze on the sweet grass of the ridge. Alek held out his hand as she came around Big John, and she clasped it in her own, surprised by the sudden initiation of physical contact. His touch was as warm and wonderful as she had remembered.

He led her to the north edge of the ridge and stopped. She stood near his right shoulder, wishing he would put his arm around her as they gazed over the plain below. In the distance, as small as a speck of dirt, were the buildings of the Crazy Q.

"Do you see your ranch?" he asked.

"Yes."

"I have learned that land is valued in your world," he said, still holding her hand. "And to own it makes it yours forever."

"Well, as long as you can make the payments." She smiled and squeezed his hand.

"Some people have enough money to buy their land outright."

"If they're lucky," Marissa mused. "If they're rich."

"I was rich for a few days," he put in with a chuckle. "But now I am rich in happiness."

"What do you mean?"

"I sold my torc and armbands to a man who considered them very valuable."

"You did?" She turned to stare at him in alarm. What sheister had tricked Alek out of his most valuable possessions? "What did he give you for them?"

"Enough to buy the land next to your ranch."

"What?" She took a step backward in utter shock. Her hand slipped out of his. She continued to gawk at him until he laughed outright.

"This is my land now. One hundred thousand acres." He spread his arms out in a grand gesture. "Next to yours, she-devil. This is the view I will have. From here I can see the Crazy Q whenever I want look to the east."

She heard his voice, but the meaning of what he was saying seemed to lag behind his words. Alek had purchased land? She couldn't believe it.

"I have learned to read and write, too!" he put in eagerly. "Look." He knelt down and wrote his name in the dirt with his fingertip. Then he continued to form letters. Marissa cocked her head enough to make them out, and her heart twisted in her chest. There in the dirt were the three words she had longed to hear for months. *Alek loves Marissa.* Still kneeling, he braced his forearm on his knee and looked up at her, his eyes shining. "It is true, Marissa."

"You love me?"

"Yes."

She bit her lip and stared at him while hot tears flooded her eyes. She couldn't move. The past two months of doubt and denial swelled up and choked her. Why had she doubted him? Why had he assumed she would not accept him for what he was? Her silence apparently worried Alek, for he scrambled to his feet.

"I have been working very hard to catch up, Marissa, to learn everything I need to learn."

"You've done amazingly well, Alek."

"I wanted to learn everything as quickly as possible."

"Why?"

"So you would see me as a worthy man, a man you could respect."

"Oh, Alek!" She put both hands to her mouth as if to hold back the rush of joy and tears his words welled up inside of her. "Don't you know what a worthy man you are?"

"I want to be worthy in your world. I want the men in your world to know why a she-devil like you would give her love to me."

"You would be worthy in *any* world!" She reached up and lay her hand on his cheek. "I have loved you from the very first, don't you realize that?"

"But I could not ask you to join with me when I had no possessions, nothing to offer you."

"It wouldn't have mattered to me!"

"It mattered to me. I am no beggar, Marissa, no lazy man whose woman will do all the work for him, own all their possessions."

She slipped her hands around his neck. "You never will be lazy or a beggar."

"I was a warrior. And I was a Senone, son of a free people. Now I will be something new."

"Yes." She gazed at him, letting the tears trickle

down her face. "And you are the most wonderful man I've ever known."

He gazed down at her, his face full of earnest concern. "Truly?"

"Truly."

"Then your tears are for happiness?"

"Yes. The most happiness I have felt in a long time!" She hugged him fiercely. "Alek, why did you wait so long? I've been in agony!"

"I will make it up on you, she-devil."

She smiled at the fractured idiom and all that it innocently implied. "Promise?" she replied.

"I promise." He caressed her, sliding both hands down her back to her jeans. In a single movement he nestled her against him, bringing her to the place she belonged, with her she-devil body pressed to his warrior frame.

"When will you make it up to me?" she said against his lips.

"Now. I cannot wait."

"You big brute."

Chuckling, he bent toward her mouth. Soon the amusement flared into a serious, driving passion that neither one of them wished to control. He kissed her long and hard, using his strength to show her how much he loved and wanted her, stroking her with sure and insistent hands. Within moments she was on fire for him, aching to give herself to him.

"I want to share the marriage cup with you," he murmured into her ear. "I want to share my life with you, Marissa. I want to be with you always."

She closed her eyes as a new and even greater joy blossomed within her.

"Always," he repeated.

"Alek," she answered, kissing his mouth before she

spoke again. "Always isn't nearly long enough for me."

He laughed and swept her off her feet, sinking with her to the grass. "Women!" he said, his eyes sparkling, "They are never satisfied!"

"Not true, my warrior," Marissa answered, reaching up for his shoulders. "Just try me."

STARLIGHT by Patricia Hagan

Another spellbinding historical romance from bestselling author Patricia Hagan. Desperate to escape her miserable life in Paris, Samara Labonte agreed to switch places with a friend and marry an American soldier. During the train journey to her intended, however, Sam was abducted by Cheyenne Indians. Though at first she was terrified, her heart was soon captured by one particular blue-eyed warrior.

THE NIGHT ORCHID by Patricia Simpson

A stunning new time travel story from an author who *Romantic Times* says is "fast becoming one of the premier writers of supernatural romance." When Marissa Quinn goes to Seattle to find her missing sister who was working for a scientist, what she finds instead is a race across centuries with a powerfully handsome Celtic warrior from 285 B.C. He is the key to her missing sister and the man who steals her heart.

ALL THINGS BEAUTIFUL by Cathy Maxwell

Set in the ballrooms and country estates of Regency England, a stirring love story of a dark, mysterious tradesman and his exquisite aristocratic wife looking to find all things beautiful. "*All Things Beautiful* is a wonderful 'Beauty and the Beast' story with a twist. Cathy Maxwell is a bright new talent."—*Romantic Times*

THE COMING HOME PLACE by Mary Spencer

Knowing that her new husband, James, loved another, Elizabeth left him and made a new life for herself. Soon she emerged from her plain cocoon to become an astonishingly lovely woman. Only when James's best friend ardently pursued her did James realize the mistake he had made by letting Elizabeth go.

DEADLY DESIRES by Christina Dair

When photographer Jessica Martinson begins to uncover the hidden history of the exclusive Santa Lucia Inn, she is targeted as the next victim of a murderer who will stop at nothing to prevent the truth from coming out. Now she must find out who is behind the murders, as all the evidence is pointing to the one man she has finally given her heart to.

MIRAGE by Donna Valentino

To escape her domineering father, Eleanor McKittrick ran away to the Kansas frontier where she and her friend Lauretta had purchased land to homestead. Her father, a prison warden, sent Tremayne Hawthorne, an Englishman imprisoned for a murder he didn't commit, after her in exchange for his freedom. Yet Hawthorne soon realized that this was a woman he couldn't bear to give up.

Harper Monogram By Mail

Looking For Love?
Try HarperMonogram's Bestselling Romances

TAPESTRY
by Maura Seger
An aristocratic Saxon woman loses her heart to
the Norman man who rules her conquered people.

DREAM TIME
by Parris Afton Bonds
In the distant outback of Australia, a mother
and daughter are ready to sacrifice everything
for their dreams of love.

RAIN LILY
by Candace Camp
In the aftermath of the Civil War in Arkansas, a
farmer's wife struggles between duty and passion.

COMING UP ROSES
by Catherine Anderson
Only buried secrets could stop the love
of a young widow and her new beau
from bloomimg.

ONE GOOD MAN
by Terri Herrington
When faced with a lucrative offer to seduce
a billionaire industrialist, a young woman
discovers her true desires.

LORD OF THE NIGHT
by Susan Wiggs
A Venetian lord dedicated to justice suspects a lucious beauty of being involved in a scandalous plot.

ORCHIDS IN MOONLIGHT
by Patricia Hagan
Caught in a web of intrigue in the dangerous West, a man and a woman fight to regain their overpowering dream of love.

A SEASON OF ANGELS
by Debbie Macomber
Three willing but wacky angels must teach their charges a lesson before granting a Christmas wish.
National Bestseller